DEAD By MORNING

DEAD By MORNING

BEVERLY BARTON

ZEBRA BOOKS
KENSINGTON PUBLISHING CORP.

ZEBRA BOOKS are published by

Kensington Publishing Corp.
119 West 40th Street
New York, NY 10018

ISBN-13: 978-1-61129-472-9

To Beth Bange Bynon,
in memory of her husband Colby

"I love thee with the breath, smiles, tears of all my life."
—Elizabeth Barrett Browning

Prologue

With the patience and precision of a surgeon, he sliced into his victim's upper arm and carefully lifted the triangular piece of flesh. After placing the small chunk in a cubbyhole of the sectioned plastic cooler he had brought with him, he returned to the job at hand. One by one, he cut out more triangles from the dead man's arms and legs and then carefully stored them in the container.

"I always used a new scalpel and then tossed it afterward."

He had purchased disposable scalpels online. They came ten to a pack, with plastic handles and individually wrapped and sterilized high carbon steel blades. Cost didn't matter. He always spent whatever necessary to accomplish the job. But the scalpels were one of the least expensive tools he had ever used—less than a dollar each. And the little blades did double duty, first to slit the neck and then to make the intricate carvings.

He hummed as he worked, a mundane little ditty that he had heard somewhere years ago.

He took pride in his kills. He never did less than his best.

"I wanted the kill to be clean, quick, and relatively painless. The sweetest pleasure is in those few seconds of initial horror they experience. I prefer psychological torture to physical torture."

Whether or not the death was quick and painless didn't matter to him one way or the other. He was not opposed to making a victim suffer and had on occasion used both physical and psychological torture, but not with these particular people.

"It's such a quiet way to kill a person. With their trachea severed, they can't scream."

His preference was not the up-close-and-personal. He preferred killing from a distance. A quick, clean shot to the head, if death was the only agenda. However, he always did whatever was necessary to accomplish his goals. That's why this kill, like the three before it and the ones that would come after it, required him to get his hands dirty.

With his task completed and the four triangles carved from each arm and each leg now stored neatly in the cooler, he lifted the old man by his broad shoulders and dragged him along the bank of the river.

"I never left them where I killed them. I would move the body, usually near a river or lake or stream. I even dragged a woman from her bedroom outside to her pool. There is something peaceful about water, don't you think?"

He had been forced to leave the first body in her apartment, but he had taken her into the bathroom and filled the tub. Not exactly a river or even a pool, but under the circumstances, it had been as close as he could get her to water. As luck would have it, he had been able to drag the second victim from the back porch, where he had slit her throat, to the river nearby. He had dumped the third victim in a shallow streambed located on the man's property.

"I always struck after midnight. Never before. I wanted the body to be found in the morning. There is something beautiful about the morning sunlight caressing a corpse."

In his opinion, there was nothing beautiful about a corpse, neither in the dark nor in the full light of day. As a general rule, the time of day—or night—was inconsequential, unless there was a reason for specific timing. But he was following a sequence of events with these murders, somewhat like following a road map to reach a specific destination. Each step in the procedure was a necessity. The exact time of death was not important—as long as the person was dead by morning.

"I had a special upright freezer where I kept my carvings."

He never kept trophies. He didn't want or need any.

The souvenirs from these kills were not for him. They were for someone else. Someone who would appreciate their significance.

Chapter 1

Maleah hated weddings and wedding receptions.

So why am I here?

She was at the Dunmore Country Club out of a sense of obligation. After all, the bride, Lorie Hammonds, was her sister-in-law's best friend and the groom, Mike Birkett, was her brother's best friend. Lorie and Mike had gone through hell to earn their second chance at love. Their reunion was like something out of a fairy tale, albeit an adult fairy tale. Against all odds, they had fallen in love again, nearly twenty years after their teenage love affair had left them both broken hearted. Maleah certainly would have bet against their ever making it to the altar.

Okay, so maybe happy endings were possible. For other people. Not for her.

"Come on." Her sister-in-law Cathy motioned to her. "They're leaving. Did you get your little bag of birdseed?"

Groaning inside, Maleah forced a smile and held up the tiny net bag tied with a narrow yellow ribbon. Following the other wedding guests, she went outside and took her place in the crowd awaiting the bride and groom's departure. The groomsmen had attached tin cans to long streamers that they had tied to the bumper of the groom's restored antique Mustang. A hand-painted sign announcing JUST MARRIED hung precariously from the same streamers.

A roar of excitement heralded the couple's exit through the double doors that opened to the front lawn of the country club. Lorie wore a pale peach tailored suit with matching heels. Mike had changed from his tux into a sport coat and dress slacks. Arm-in-arm, huge smiles lighting their faces, they hurried along the pathway. They laughed as handfuls of birdseed sailed through the air and rained down on them.

Maleah glanced across the brick sidewalk at her brother Jackson, who stood behind his wife, his arm draped around her and one big hand resting possessively over her belly. Cathy was three and half months pregnant.

When the bride and groom drove away, the crowd dispersed, many returning to the ballroom where the band still played. Maleah felt someone beside her and knew exactly who it was, even before she saw his face.

Derek Lawrence!

She turned, glanced at him, and did her best to maintain a pleasant expression. Despite his devastating good looks and undeniable charm, Derek Lawrence was pure poison as far as Maleah was concerned. From the moment they met several years ago, she had intensely disliked him. But she had to admit that after working with him on the Midnight Killer case for the Powell Agency earlier this year, she now disliked him less. And much to her dismay, she couldn't deny that she found him attractive.

What woman wouldn't?

He was tall, dark and dangerously handsome. And he possessed the kind of striking looks attributed to matinee idols of her grandmother's generation. If Derek had one flaw, it was his physical perfection. He was too damn good looking.

Being attracted to Derek—the last man on earth she should be attracted to—was why she thought of him as pure poison.

"Nice wedding," he said.

"Yes, it was a very nice wedding," Maleah replied. "Lorie and Mike seem happy, don't they?"

"They say that marriage agrees with some people."

"I've heard that."

"But you don't believe it?"

She shrugged.

"Jack and Cathy seem blissfully happy," Derek said.

"Okay, I concede that a small percentage of couples somehow manage to get their happily-ever-after, but most don't."

"Not willing to risk it yourself, are you?"

She looked at him, slightly puzzled by his question. "It's a moot point. I'm not even dating anyone right now."

"I wasn't aware that you ever dated. I've known you for quite a while and—"

"I date," she told him emphatically. Too emphatically. "I'm simply selective about whom I date." She gave him a condescending glance. "Unlike you, my tastes are more discriminating."

His oh-so-perfect lips lifted at the corners in an amused smile. "Are you implying that I'm some sort of Romeo who romances every woman I meet?"

"Oh, I'm not *implying* anything. I simply stated a fact."

Before Derek could respond, Jack and Cathy joined

them. He still wore his best man tux and she wore her matron of honor gown, a floor-length creation in light aqua silk.

"You two aren't arguing again, are you?" Cathy looked pleadingly from Maleah to Derek.

"No, of course not," Maleah assured her sister-in-law. "We were just discussing dating."

Lifting his brow inquisitively, Jack grinned. "So, who finally asked who?"

"Huh?" Maleah said.

"What?" Derek asked.

Cathy draped her arm around Jack's. "I don't think they were discussing dating each other."

"God, no!" Maleah said.

Derek chuckled. "You thought I asked Maleah for a date or that she asked me? Where would you have gotten such a far-fetched idea?"

"Oh, I don't know," Jack said. "Maybe the fact that—"

When Cathy gently punched him in the ribs, Jack grunted and instantly shut up.

"We're heading out," Cathy said. "I'm exhausted. It's been a wonderful day, but a very long one."

"I'll see y'all at home in a little while," Maleah said.

"Stay as long as you'd like," Cathy told her. "The band will be here until midnight and there's still a ton of food."

Maleah felt Derek's body heat as he moved in closer. When he slipped his arm around her waist, she tried not to gasp at the unexpectedness of his touch.

"Come on, Ms. Perdue, let's dance the night away." Derek's black eyes sparkled with a definite challenge. "Since neither of us brought a date tonight . . ."

"You two have fun," Jack told them as he led Cathy away and herded her toward their car.

As soon as Jack and Cathy were out of earshot, Maleah jerked away from Derek. "It's late. I'm tired. I have to get up early and drive back to Knoxville in the morning."

"Excuses, excuses." His grin widened. "What are you afraid of, Maleah?"

He's goading you. Don't let him get to you.

"I'm certainly not afraid of you, if that's what you're implying. You should know by now that I'm immune to your charm."

He held out his hand. "I don't doubt that you are. So . . . ?"

From the first moment they met several years ago, Derek had seen Maleah Perdue as a challenge. She had disliked him on sight, a reaction he was unaccustomed to getting from women. In the beginning, he had tried to charm her, and when that hadn't worked, he had ignored her. They had managed to steer clear of each other for the most part, more or less ships passing in the night, although they were both employed by the Powell Private Security and Investigation Agency. Maleah was a Powell agent. He was a consultant. His background as a former FBI profiler had proved to be a valuable asset to the agency. Three months ago when they had been assigned to work together on the Midnight Killer case, they had entered into the partnership reluctantly. Oddly enough, they had made a great team.

When she slid her small, soft hand into his large hand, he felt as if he had won a prize. The lady was not an easy conquest and because of that fact, he found her all the more appealing. Common sense cautioned him to keep their relationship strictly professional and not dip a toe into personal waters. But Derek had never been able to walk away from a challenge—or from a beautiful woman.

As he led her into the country club and straight into the ballroom where dozens of wedding guests remained, he subtly scanned her, out of the corner of his eye, from blond head to pale pink toes. Maleah had the type of wholesome blond beauty that once would have won her the title of All-American Girl. Five-four. Trim, nicely rounded figure. Peaches and cream complexion that tanned to a golden hue. Sun-streaked, shoulder-length blond hair. And topaz brown eyes that changed color depending on the color she wore and on her mood, alternating from a smoky yellowish hazel to a fine, golden bourbon.

When he put his arm around her waist and pulled her toward him, he felt her stiffen. "It's just a dance," he reminded her. "You're not committing yourself to spend the night with me."

"God forbid." Her gaze lifted and clashed with his.

He drew her closer, allowing their bodies to touch intimately. "Relax, honey. You're stiff as a poker."

"Don't hold me so tight." She wiggled her shoulders. "And do not call me honey."

He loosened his hold, giving her a little breathing room. "Better, Blondie?"

"Yes, thank you." She frowned. "Blondie?"

He grinned. "It suits you."

She huffed. "I suppose it's better than honey. Not quite as generic. But you could just call me Maleah, you know."

"I could." His grin widened. "Would it help to know that I've never called another woman Blondie?"

"You're determined to aggravate the crap out of me, aren't you?"

He laughed. "It's what I live for . . . Blondie."

As they danced to the smooth, romantic jazz tune, Derek tried to think of some innocent subject, something that wouldn't lead them into another verbal confrontation.

"Lorie was a beautiful bride," he finally said.

"Yes, she was."

Silence.

"It's great about Cathy being pregnant," he said. "Jack's over the moon about it."

"Yes, he is. He's really excited about being with her through the entire nine months since he missed out on doing that the first time around."

"Some men are cut out to be fathers. Jack's one of them. So is Mike."

Maleah nodded. "Cathy's a great mom. And I think Lorie will be, too. She's great with Mike's two kids."

"Do you ever think about having children?"

She paused mid-step. "I wouldn't bring a child into this world without having a husband first and since I don't intend to ever marry—"

"You're really an old fashioned girl, aren't you?"

"Only about some things."

"I agree, you know, about not ever getting married and having kids."

"Why am I not surprised? Why settle down with one woman when you can have your choice of women to sample, a different flavor every week?"

"Why indeed." Yeah, he could pretty much have his pick, had seldom been turned down, and had successfully avoided committed relationships. He had never allowed himself to care enough about any woman who could tempt him to willingly give up his freedom. He had learned, at his mother's knee, how a woman could use love to manipulate a man, turn him inside out and eventually destroy him.

Just as one tune ended and another began, Maleah pulled away, but Derek grabbed her hand and refused to relinquish his hold.

"One more dance," he said.

While she debated his request, his cell phone vibrated in the inside pocket of his tuxedo jacket. Reluctantly, he released her hand, reached inside his jacket, and removed his phone. Derek noted the caller ID. Griffin Powell, his employer.

"Yeah, Griff, what's up?" Derek's gaze connected with Maleah's, both of them aware that it was highly unlikely that Griff would be calling if it wasn't important business.

Maleah waited until he had answered the call and then walked with him off the dance floor.

"He's struck again," Griff told Derek. "I don't have all the details, but we're relatively sure it's the same person who killed Kristi and Shelley and Holt's brother."

Absolute dread tightly coiled Derek's stomach muscles as he asked, "Who's the victim?" Was it another Powell employee, as the first two kills had been, or was it a Powell employee family member, as the third murder victim had been?

"Ben Corbett's seventy-year-old father," Griff said. "Ben's the one who called me. A couple of fishermen found the body this morning, but there was no ID on the guy. Apparently he didn't have his wallet on him. They ran his fingerprints and didn't get a hit."

"How did they finally ID him?"

"It seems Mr. Corbett has a breakfast date with a lady friend every Saturday morning and when he didn't show up, she went to his home. When she couldn't find him, she started searching for him. One thing led to another and she finally went to the police earlier this evening."

"Ben's on assignment, isn't he?"

"He was in California. He chartered a plane and is flying into Birmingham and renting a car. His dad lived outside Cullman, which is about an hour drive from Dunmore. I want you and Maleah to head down that way as soon as possible. You two can get there before Ben can. When he arrives, he doesn't need to handle this alone."

"We're leaving now," Derek said. "I'll pick up my laptop at the hotel. You can send me any other info that we'll need."

As soon as Derek slipped the phone back into his jacket pocket, he faced Maleah. "The boss wants us to drive to Cullman tonight. Ben Corbett's father has been murdered."

"Damn. Griff thinks that it's the same person who murdered Kristi and Shelley and Holt's brother, doesn't he?"

"Yeah, he does."

"Why didn't you tell Derek everything that we know and about what we've decided?" Nicole Powell asked her husband moments after he ended his conversation.

"We'll explain it to him and Maleah together," Griff said. "I'll have Barbara Jean compile all the information the agency has accumulated. Maleah and Derek can read over everything and digest it all before I tell them that I expect them to take over as lead investigators on the case."

"We might be closer to solving this mystery, if it hadn't taken us more than two months to connect the dots."

Griff draped his arm around Nic's shoulders as they

stood on the patio overlooking Douglas Lake. "When Kristi was murdered, there was no way we could have known that her killer would target another agent. Until he killed Kristi and then Shelley, their murders identical in almost every way, we couldn't have known he had a specific MO. And even after Holt's brother was murdered and Barbara Jean discovered there had been three killers in the past with a similar MO—the Savannah Slasher, the Carver, and the Triangle Man—it took time to study each killer and figure out if our guy was copying one of them."

"After what we just found out, do you think Maleah is the key to everything that's happening?" Nic asked.

Griff squeezed her shoulders. "Possibly. But we can't rule out any of our other scenarios, especially since we don't know why anyone would be out to punish Maleah by killing people connected to the agency."

"Unlike you and me. We both have enemies from the past who could be targeting us."

He nodded. "Yeah, unlike you and me. The logical assumption is that whoever is behind these murders is doing it either to punish me or to get my attention."

"But it's possible that the rumors floating around Europe about Malcolm York being alive have nothing whatsoever to do with these murders. You can't assume you're the target simply because someone, thousands of miles away, may be pretending to be the man who kidnapped you twenty years ago. It could just as easily be someone from my past, someone connected to one of my cases when I worked for the Bureau."

"You're right, of course, " Griff agreed. "That's why we cannot rule out any possibility."

"You don't think there's even the slightest chance that the real Malcolm York is alive, do you?"

Griff's square jaw tightened. "York is dead. I have no doubts. Yvette, Sanders, and I killed him sixteen years ago. Unless he's found a way to rise from the dead, whoever the hell is calling himself Malcolm York is an imposter."

"This man is in Europe somewhere, not here in the U.S. To date, all the murders related to the Powell Agency have occurred here in America. We have no evidence to indicate a connection between him and these murders."

"Yes, I know. And the only apparent connection between the agency and the murders is Maleah."

"She is going to freak out when we tell her that our research shows the three previous murders almost identically mimic the murders committed by the Carver and that one of his first victims was Noah Laborde."

"It's no coincidence that the original Carver murdered Maleah's college boyfriend. What it means, we can't be sure, not at this point. But sooner or later—"

"Maleah has become my best friend." Nic rested her head on Griff's shoulder. "What better way to get to me than by using my dearest friend?"

"And what better way to send me a warning than to use my wife and her best friend to send that message?"

"Maleah will want to follow through and see this out to the end. You know she will. She'll feel that it's personal because the original Carver killed Noah Laborde."

"Yes, I know, she will. I also know that we need Derek's expertise. We need a professional profile of our killer. And Derek has a keen sixth sense about these things. I can't give him and Maleah the choice of not working together, despite their personal animosity," Griff said. "I'm putting the entire staff—office employees and agents in the field—on high alert. This case takes precedence over every other case. Until we find and stop this killer, no one connected to the Powell Agency is safe."

Nic turned into Griff's arms. He cocooned her within his embrace.

She might have doubts about why this was happening and about who was responsible, but Griff didn't. Not really. She knew her husband. No matter what she said to him or how many scenarios she presented to him, he laid the blame squarely on his own shoulders. He truly believed that innocent people were now paying for his past sins.

Chapter 2

Maleah and Derek arrived in Cullman shortly after midnight, checked into the Holiday Inn Express, dumped their bags, and drove straight to the sheriff's office. As they had expected, someone from the Powell Agency had called ahead so the sheriff himself was there to meet them. Griffin Powell and his agency had become legendary, their success rate far exceeding that of regular law enforcement. Only occasionally did the agency come up against police chiefs or sheriffs who resented Powell involvement. Thankfully, Sheriff Devin Gray welcomed them with a cautious smile and a firm handshake. Looking the man in the eye, Maleah instantly felt at ease.

Gray was about five-ten, slender and young, probably not a day over thirty-five. Clean shaven, his sandy hair styled short and neat, he projected a squeaky-clean appearance.

"Come on into my office." Sheriff Gray backed up his verbal invitation by opening the door and waiting for Maleah and Derek to enter.

The moment she crossed the threshold, she saw the

heavyset, middle-aged man sitting in the corner, his gaze directed on her. He rose to his feet and waited until the sheriff closed the door, affectively isolating the four of them from the activity outside the office.

"This is Freddy Rose, the Cullman County coroner," Sheriff Gray said. "Freddy, these are the Powell agents we've been expecting."

Freddy's round face, rosy cheeks, and pot belly made her think of Santa Claus, but his bald head and smooth face brought up an image of a short, rotund Mr. Clean.

Offering his meaty hand to Maleah, Freddy said, "Ma'am." And once they shook hands, he turned to Derek.

"Derek Lawrence." He exchanged handshakes with the coroner, and then nodded toward Maleah. "And this is Ms. Perdue."

"Ordinarily, we wouldn't share any of this information with outsiders," Sheriff Gray explained. "But when the governor calls me personally . . . Well, that's a horse of a different color, if you know what I mean."

Maleah knew exactly what he meant. Griffin Powell's sphere of influence reached far and wide, not only to the office of state governors, but to the powers that be in Washington, D.C. Griff's connections were strictly behind the scenes, of course, but she suspected he wielded far more power than anyone knew.

"We appreciate your both being here this late," Derek said. "Mr. Corbett's son Ben is one of our people. Ben is on his way here now and Ms. Perdue and I would like to get the preliminaries out of the way before he arrives. He will have enough on his plate as it is coming to terms with his father's murder."

"Absolutely," the sheriff agreed. "That's why Freddy's here. He hasn't performed an autopsy, of course, since the state boys will be here in the morning to claim the body, but he's certain about the cause of death."

"Sure am," Freddy said. "No doubt about it. Mr. Corbett's throat was slit, pretty much from ear to ear. Sliced through the carotid arteries on both sides and the trachea as well. Death occurred within a couple of minutes."

"Any idea about the blade the killer used?" Derek asked.

"The cut was smooth and straight," Freddy said. "No jagged edges. I swear it looked so damn precise, I'd swear a surgeon did it using a scalpel."

Maleah's gut reacted instantly to that bit of information. The medical examiners in each of the previous cases believed that Kristi, Shelley, and Norris Keinan had been killed with a scalpel, their necks cut with the expertise of a surgeon.

"Does that fit other murders?" the sheriff asked. "I was told you'd want to compare this case to some previous murders."

"Yes, so far, it does fit," Derek said, and then turned to Freddy. "What else can you tell us about the body?"

Freddy's gray eyes widened. "Damnedest thing I've ever seen. The killer cut out these little triangle-shaped pieces from Mr. Corbett's upper arms and thighs." Freddy shook his bald head. "Did it postmortem, thank the Good Lord."

"Does that match what was done to the other victims?" Sheriff Gray looked at Maleah. "Are we dealing with a serial killer? Is that what's going on?"

"Yes, the other victims also had triangular pieces of flesh removed from their limbs," Maleah replied. "And yes, with three murders, now four, it appears to be the work of a serial killer, but—"

"But that's all we know at this point," Derek finished for her. "We're working under the assumption that a serial killer has murdered four people now. Unfortunately the latest victim was the father of one of our agents."

Why had Derek cut her off mid-sentence like that? What had he thought she was going to say? My God, did he actually think she'd been about to reveal the fact that all four victims were in some way related to the Powell Agency? Did he think she was that stupid? Up to this point, the press had made a connection only between Kristi Arians and Shelley Gilbert. But since no "guilty knowledge" details of either murder were ever released, it was assumed that Shelley died in the line of duty on assignment in Alabama and that Kristi's murder in her Knoxville, Tennessee, apartment had been the work of another killer. The fact that they were both Powell Agency employees was believed to be simply a coincidence. Norris Keinan, a corporate lawyer, had lived in Denver, Colorado, and the fact that his younger brother was a Powell agent had not been an issue, either with the Denver PD or the local Denver media.

"I didn't know Mr. Corbett personally," the sheriff said. "But he and the mayor's dad played golf together. I understand he was a fine man, well thought of in the community. We're sure sorry something like this happened in Cullman."

"Would it be possible for us to get copies of the reports, once they're filed, and also copies of the photos taken at the scene?" Maleah asked.

"Yes, ma'am, I can see to it that you get copies of whatever you need."

"Then I can't think of any reason we should keep y'all up any later than we already have." Maleah glanced from the handsome young sheriff to the fifty-something coroner. "Mr. Lawrence and I are at the Holiday Inn Express." She pulled a business card from her pocket and handed it to Devin Gray. "We'd like to stay here and wait on Ben Corbett, if that's all right with you?"

"Certainly," Sheriff Gray said. "Feel free to use my office."

When Sheriff Gray and Freddy said their good-byes and started to leave, Derek called to them. "By any chance, was Mr. Corbett found in or near a body of water?"

Both men froze to the spot. Freddy cleared his throat before glancing over his shoulder and saying, "He was found on the riverbank, face down, his feet in the river."

"Were the others found in water?" Sheriff Gray asked, his gaze sliding slowly from Maleah to Derek.

"Yes, they were," Derek replied quickly.

"Just another similarity, huh?" Freddy said. "Guess it's looking more and more like the same person who killed those other people killed Mr. Corbett."

"Apparently so." Derek glanced at Maleah.

She knew what he was thinking.

Four innocent victims, their only connection the Powell Agency. But who had killed them? And why?

Maleah and Derek waited for Ben Corbett. When he arrived at the sheriff's office at a little after three that Sunday morning, they shared with him all the information the sheriff and coroner had given them.

Ben had been with the agency for several years, coming straight from the army after his retirement. Three-fourths of the Powell agents had either law enforcement or military backgrounds. A few, such as Maleah, had been chosen because of their high IQs and willingness to learn on the job.

Although Ben had managed to control his emotions, Maleah hadn't missed the subtle signs of anger and hurt. While they had explained what had happened and how they suspected his father's death was related to the other three murders, his gaze wandered aimlessly, often focusing on the wall. Once or twice he had mumbled incoherently under his breath, then quieted suddenly and clenched his jaw, as if it was all he could to maintain his composure.

"Dad was a ladies' man," Ben told them. "He loved to flirt. Never bothered Mom. She'd just laugh about it. He never cheated on her, loved her to the day she died." He swallowed hard. "I suspect he loved her till the day he died."

"We've been authorized to help you in any way you need us," Maleah said. "If you'd like us to make the arrangements or help you make them—"

"Thanks. That won't be necessary. Dad made all the arrangements right after Mom died. Paid for everything. Chose his casket, picked out the suit he wanted to be buried in. Made his will. Told the minister what songs he wanted at the funeral. He said he didn't want me to have to worry with any of it when the time came."

For several minutes, the three of them remained silent. Then Ben asked the inevitable question. "Who the hell is doing this and why?"

"We don't know," Derek said. "The only thing the victims have in common is their connection to the Powell Agency. The killer's MO is identical in all four cases, so we're relatively certain we are dealing with one killer. But we have no idea what motivates him or how he chooses his victims."

"At random, maybe," Ben said. "Anybody associated with the agency is a target, right? And for whatever reason, the killer picked my dad." Ben's dark eyes misted. He turned his head.

Derek clamped his hand down on Ben's shoulder. "We're going to catch him and stop him."

Ben nodded.

"Is there anything, anything at all, we can do for you?" Maleah asked.

Ben cleared his throat a couple of times. "No, thanks. I can't think of anything. I'm going over to Dad's place and try to get a few hours of sleep. When are y'all heading up to Griffin's Rest?"

"If you don't need us here, we probably won't stay longer than mid-day tomorrow," Derek told him. "Copies of the reports and the crime scene photos can be sent directly to the office as soon as they're available. I expect Nic and Griff will be moving forward with their plans to form their own task force and since I'm the agency's profiler—"

"Count me in on the task force," Ben said. "After Dad's funeral."

Neither Derek nor Maleah responded, knowing it would be up to Griff and Nic to choose the agents who would lead the investigation and those who would assist. If Ben had been a police officer, he wouldn't have been allowed near the case because his dad had been one of the victims. But Griff's rules and regulations differed from regular law enforcement. On occasion, the Powell Agency came damn close to doling out vigilante justice, a fact that often created tension between Griff and Nic.

*   *   *

He could go days without sleep and could easily get by with four hours per night on a regular basis. He was no ordinary human being. Years of training, self-sacrifice, and stern discipline had honed both his mind and body into a superior being. He had no weaknesses, wasn't vulnerable in any way, and therefore was practically invincible.

The espresso at the airport coffee bar was barely acceptable, but it served the purpose of giving him a caffeine boost. To pass the time while he waited for his flight to Miami, he flipped open his laptop and scanned the information about Errol Patterson.

Patterson was a former member of the Atlanta PD SWAT team, a crack shot and a decorated officer. He had loved his job, but when his fiancée had insisted he find a less dangerous profession, he had chosen love over duty and signed on with the Powell Agency.

He smiled.

You made a life-altering decision. Too bad for you that it was a deadly mistake.

How could he or his fiancée have known that choosing to work for the Powell Agency would cost him his life?

Patterson had been chosen for two reasons—he was associated with the Powell Agency and he was male.

I chose two women and then two men for the first four kills . . . But after that, I altered my choices, just to throw them off. I kept them guessing. That's how I stayed one step ahead of them.

He did more than stay one step ahead of the authorities. He outsmarted them, never leaving behind even the vaguest clue to his identity. Over the years, he had gone by many names, so many that it was easy to forget who he really was. His true identity was a guarded secret, known by only a handful of individuals. In certain circles, he was known as the Phantom. Nameless. Faceless. An illusion. Unseen. Unheard. A dark angel of death.

Maleah woke to the sound of incessant pounding. Inside her head? No, outside her hotel room. Some idiot was knocking on her door and calling her name.

Go away. Leave me alone.

She shot straight up in bed where she lay atop the wrinkled floral spread. Groggy and only semi-alert, she slid off the side of the bed and stood unsteadily on her bare feet for a few seconds.

"Maleah," Derek called to her through the closed door.

Damn it! What time was it? She glanced at the digital bedside clock. 8:30 A.M.

She groaned. Three and a half hours was not nearly enough sleep.

"I'm coming," she told him as she padded across the carpet. When she reached the door, she cracked it open, glared at Derek, who looked fresh as a daisy, and asked him, "Where's the fire?"

He shoved open the door and breezed past her. She closed the door and turned to face him. Obviously he had shaved, showered, and pressed his slacks and shirt. His stylish, neck-length hair glistened with blue-black highlights. His deep brown eyes focused on her with amusement.

"I forgot how grumpy you are in the morning," he said.

"You'd better have a good reason for beating down my door."

"Duty calls."

"What?"

He looked her over, taking in her sleep-tousled hair,

her wrinkled clothes and her makeup-free face. "Griff called. He wants us at Griffin's Rest ASAP."

Maleah groaned, and then when Derek's smile vanished, she asked, "What's happened?"

"What makes you think—?"

"Damn it, Derek, it's too early in the morning to play games, so let's not do twenty questions."

He clasped her shoulders, turned her around and urged her toward the bathroom. "Toss your clothes out to me and I'll press them while you grab a quick shower. We'll pick up coffee and biscuits on the way to Griffin's Rest."

She curled her toes into the carpet and dug in her heels. "I'm not moving another inch until you tell me what's going on."

"Why do you have to be so stubborn?"

"Why do you have to be such a macho jerk?"

Derek frowned. "Griff and Nic are organizing the task force today." He paused, studied her expression and then said, "I'm pretty sure they plan to put the two of us in charge."

She groaned. "Why us? Why not you and Shaughnessy or you and Angie or you and Michelle or you and Luke or—?"

"I get it. You don't want us to be partners on another case. But I don't think it really matters what we want. It's what Griff and Nic want."

"I can't believe Nic would pair us up again, not when she knows . . . well, she knows that we mix like oil and water."

"I thought we made a pretty good team on the Midnight Killer case."

Maleah huffed, hating to admit that he was right. "Yeah, yeah, I suppose we did."

"Besides, Shaughnessy is more muscle than strategist. His expertise lends itself to the physical. And now that she's pregnant, Angie isn't working in the field. Michelle is on a much-needed vacation after that last two-month case in South America. As for Luke, you know Griff reserves him for special duty."

Accepting his explanation, she nodded her acquiescence and said, "Give me five minutes." She turned and went into the bathroom.

She closed the door, stripped hurriedly, and then eased the door open enough to toss her clothes toward Derek. Smiling at the thought of him ironing her slacks and blouse, she adjusted the hot and cold faucets on the shower and stepped under the spray of warm water.

The FedEx truck had been stopped at the front gate by the guards on duty. Shaughnessy Hood had been dispatched from the main house to drive down and pick up the package addressed to Maleah Perdue in care of the Powell Private Security and Investigation Agency at Griffin's Rest.

Barbara Jean Hughes, Griff's right-hand man Sanders's assistant, best friend and lover, took the sealed, insulated shipping box from Shaughnessy, placed it in her lap and carried it with her down the hall to Griff's private study. The door stood open so that she could see Griff behind his desk, a cup of coffee in his hand. Sanders stood nearby, his gaze fixed on the box she held.

She cleared her throat.

Griff glanced up, saw her, and motioned for her to enter.

Without hesitation, Barbara Jean maneuvered her

wheelchair into the study. Sanders reached down, took the box from her and placed it on the desk directly in front of Griff.

He studied the insulated container for several silent minutes. "Did you notice the sender's name and address?"

"Yes," Sanders replied. "Winston Corbett, Cullman, Alabama."

Griff scrutinized the shipping label. "What time frame did the Cullman County coroner give for Winston Corbett's death?"

"Between midnight and five A.M., yesterday," Barbara Jean replied.

"Then I'm curious as to how Ben's father managed to send Maleah a package after he died."

Chapter 3

Cyrene Patterson stretched languidly on the beach towel, her bikini-clad, five-eight body soaking in the morning sunshine by their pool directly outside the bedroom's French doors. The deluxe honeymoon package at the Grand Resort there in the Bahamas included not only a luxury villa suite, but butler service. She and Errol had enjoyed breakfast in bed, and then made love as if they hadn't already spent half the night screwing like crazy. She had left him asleep, slipped into her bathing suit and taken a dip in the pool. Life was good. Just couldn't get much better. She had waited a lifetime for Mr. Right—thirty years. But he had been well worth the wait.

Neither she nor Errol had been naïve youngsters, with stars in their eyes, when they said their I-dos. Both had been married before when they were too young and too stupid to know what they were doing. She had married the first time to get away from home, an alcoholic mother, a father who showed up once in a blue moon, and younger siblings who were more than her grandmother could handle. Her two-year marriage to

Polo had proven the old adage about jumping out of the frying pan and into the fire. Thank God she'd been smart enough to leave the abusive son of a bitch before she got pregnant. Errol, on the other hand, had married at nineteen the first time because his girlfriend told him she was pregnant. She had lied to him, but by the time he had found out the truth, she actually was pregnant. He had lived in hell for three years. But before little Tasha's second birthday, Errol had known he needed to end the marriage and had sued his wife for full custody. Two weeks before their divorce was finalized, Errol's wife, who had been granted visitation privileges, had taken their child for a joy ride and both had been killed in a head-on collision with an eighteen wheeler. Witnesses had said that it appeared she had deliberately caused the "accident."

Cyrene lathered SPF 15 sunblock on her arms and legs to protect her golden skin from UV damage. The popular belief that darker skin didn't need protection from the harmful rays was false. Even the darkest skin could burn.

She intended to do everything possible to take care of her skin and her overall health. That's why she'd never taken drugs. Sometimes, Errol accused her of being a health nut. If following an exercise routine, being a vegetarian, not smoking, doing drugs or drinking to excess made her a health nut, she would gladly don the label and wear it proudly.

"Any place you can't reach?" Errol asked her, his voice husky with innuendo.

The moment Cyrene heard his voice, she smiled, but she didn't look at him. Instead, she held the sunblock bottle up over her head. Once he grasped the bottle in his hand, she untied her bikini top and dropped it to the patio floor. With her breasts bare, she tilted her head and gave him an enticing come-here-big-boy glance.

"Start wherever you'd like." She loved to tease him. "But don't miss a spot."

He came around the back of the lounge chair, knelt beside her, upended the open sunblock bottle and squirted a large dollop of the scented cream into the center of his open palm. After setting aside the bottle, he started at the base of her neck, lathering the lotion onto her skin. He moved steadily from shoulder to shoulder in downward swipes until his big hands hovered over her naked breasts. Her nipples tightened in anticipation. The moment his fingers caressed the hard tips, she moaned with pleasure.

Errol slid his hands beneath her, lifted her into his arms and carried her off the patio and through the open French doors. She laughed with pure delight as he tossed her into the center of the unmade bed, stripped off his bathing suit and came down over her.

Cyrene reached for him, her arms and her heart open wide for the man she loved.

Maleah and Derek arrived at Griffin's Rest that evening well before sunset. They would have arrived sooner, but they had backtracked to Dunmore to pick up Maleah's vehicle, a new Chevy Equinox. Although they had lost sight of each other during the trip from Alabama to northeastern Tennessee, he caught a glimpse of her in his rearview mirror just before the I-40 Bridge crossing Douglas Lake. The moment he saw her, he couldn't help wondering if she was pissed because he was ahead of her in the home stretch. Not that he had consciously been trying to arrive at Griffin's Rest before she did or that he saw everything in life as a competition. But during their working partnership on the Midnight Killer case, he had come to realize several things about Maleah. She hated to come in second to anyone, but especially to any man. The fact he had reached the gates outside the Powells' Douglas Lake retreat moments before she had seemed completely insignificant to him, but probably not to Maleah. Sometimes her competitive spirit drove him nuts.

"You've never had to struggle for anything in your entire spoiled rotten rich life," she had once accused him. "You're an arrogant son of a bitch because you have an inflated ego. You overestimate your self-worth."

"And I believe you underestimate yours," he'd told her.

His comment had ended that conversation once and for all. Didn't she realize that he could see past all the pseudo-confidence she tried so hard to project? He suspected that deep inside Maleah Perdue a small, helpless, vulnerable child warned her not to give up a single ounce of the hard-won control she had over her life.

Derek stopped his silver Corvette at the enormous iron gates flanked by two massive stone arches decorated with large bronze griffins. After he used the voice-activated entry code, the gates opened and he drove onto the long, tree-lined lane leading to the house overlooking the lake. Maleah followed at least twenty feet behind him. He parked in front of the house, got out, and waited for her as she pulled in behind him.

The Powell home was large, approximately ten thousand square feet, but actually rather modest for a man worth billions. Despite the mansion's size, there was nothing ostentatious about either the house itself or the décor. It had been built and decorated to accommodate the man who owned the property. Since his marriage to Nicole Baxter a few years ago, Griff had allowed his wife to make any changes she wanted. But almost as if she didn't quite think of Griffin's Rest as her home, Nic had made few alterations.

Derek snorted. Good God, why did he always do that? Why did his brain instantly delve into other people's psyche and try to figure out what made them tick? Instinct, pure and simple. His instinct dictated that he profile everyone.

Maleah emerged from her white SUV, slung the straps of her small leather bag over her shoulder and approached him. If she took more time with her appearance, she could be strikingly beautiful. She had all the ingredients, from pretty face to shapely body. Shapely? *Get real, Lawrence. The woman is built like a brick shithouse and you know it.*

"Waiting on me?" she asked.

"Yeah. What took you so long?"

She glared at him, giving him an eat-dirt-and-die look. "I'm tired, I'm hungry and I'm totally pissed at you."

"What did I do now?"

"You drove like a bat out of hell, that's what you did."

He stared at her, totally puzzled by her comment. "You lost me somewhere there, Blondie. I have no idea—"

"I got a speeding ticket, thanks to you."

He grinned. "How is it my fault that you got a ticket?"

Glowering angrily at him, she clenched her jaw and huffed. "Never mind. Forget I mentioned it. Let's go inside and—"

Before she could finish her sentence, the front door opened. Sanders glanced from Maleah to Derek. "Please, come in. Griffin and Nicole are waiting for you."

Sanders had been Griffin Powell's right-hand man

for as long as Derek had known either of them. Griff
and Sanders's association went back a good twenty
years. Rumor had it that they had met during the ten
missing years of Griff's life, when he had disappeared
off the face of the earth shortly after graduating from
the University of Tennessee nearly two decades ago.

A couple of inches short of six feet, the bald, dark-
eyed, brown-skinned Sanders possessed the bearing of a
much larger man. His stance, his attitude, and his appearance practically screamed military background.
His slightly accented English suggested a foreign birth
and upbringing.

Ever the gentleman his mother had raised him to be,
Derek waited for Maleah to enter first. Sanders led
them past the large living room with the floor-to-ceiling
rock fireplace and down the hall to Griffin Powell's private study. The door stood open and inside Griff sat behind his antique desk placed in the corner by the
windows overlooking the lake. The moment he saw
them, he lifted his two hundred and forty pound muscular body from his desk and stood at his impressive six-
four height. Griff was a big man, his mere physical
presence intimidating. Include his wealth and power
and that added up to a man only a fool would ever
cross.

But out there somewhere was a fool who was killing
people connected to the Powell Agency.

Nicole Powell stood with her back to them in front of
the massive rock fireplace, one of several in the house.
When Griff rose from his desk, she instantly turned to
face them, her soft tan eyes focusing on her friend
Maleah. Physically, the two women were opposites. Nic
was a tall brunette; Maleah a petite blond. Whenever he
saw Nic, the first thought that came to mind was Ama-

zon Warrior. Standing five-ten in her bare feet, with an hourglass figure reminiscent of Hollywood sex symbols of the 1950s, the lady's size was every bit as impressive as her husband's. Derek genuinely liked both Mr. and Mrs. Powell, but it had been easier to like Nic immediately because of her outgoing personality. Griff was more reserved, a man who made others earn his approval.

"Please, come in," Griff said, then he looked at Sanders and told him, "Close the door."

Once the five of them were closeted in Griff's private study, everyone except Sanders seated, Griff spread his big hands out over the folders lying atop his desk.

"These contain all the information we have on the four murders. The info on Winston Corbett came in mid-afternoon, so we've had a chance to go over it."

"As you already know, Ben's dad's murder fit the same pattern as the previous three," Nic said. "We don't need to wait on the autopsy report to know that."

"Our killer, for whatever reason, has targeted Powell employees and members of their families." Griff reiterated an undisputable fact.

Studying the big man's somber expression, Derek noted suppressed anger combined with grief and frustration.

Sanders said, "Protecting the Powell Agency employees and their families is of paramount importance." He stood, as he so often did, at Griff's side, his body stationed slightly behind his boss.

"Everyone is vulnerable because there is no way to predict who will be chosen as the next to die."

"I've given orders for the security here at Griffin's Rest to be expanded. As of tomorrow morning, we're doubling the guards and bringing in more agents to the estate," Griff explained. "There will be guards here at our home, twenty-four/seven, as well as at Yvette's retreat."

Most people would not have noticed the slight tensing in Nic's body, but being an observer of human nature, Derek noticed. Whenever Griff mentioned Dr. Yvette Meng, Nic reacted in a subtle, barely discernable way. He suspected Nic's friendship with Yvette hinged precariously on Nic believing that her husband had never shared a sexual relationship with the exotic Eurasian beauty. Derek also suspected that there was far more to Griff's apparent symbiotic relationship with both Sanders and Dr. Meng than anyone, including Nic, knew.

"Obviously, the problem is that we have no idea who the killer has chosen as his next victim," Nic said. "We've read and re-read the reports." She glanced at Griff's desktop. "The only thing the four victims had in common was their link to the Powell Agency. They were different ages, different sexes, were murdered in different states. One was a Powell secretary, one an agent, one a lawyer who was the brother of an agent. And now, Ben's father, a retired businessman, has been killed."

"If we could figure out how he chooses his victims—" Nic said.

Derek cut her off. "To date, he's chosen two women and then two men. If he follows this pattern then the next two victims will be female."

Griffin grunted, the growling sound coming from deep in his chest. "If that's the case, then every female Powell agent as well as every agent's wife, mother, sister, daughter, and niece could be at risk. How the hell can we narrow down the choices when we have no idea what criteria he's using to make his decisions?"

"We can't," Derek said. "My educated guess is that he

is following a specific plan and that he probably won't deviate from it. He's too methodical, too precise, as if he has a blueprint that leads him step by step."

"The way a copycat killer would mimic the original killer's MO," Griff said.

Derek's gaze met Griff's and he understood that Griff and the others knew something that he and Maleah did not.

"Are you saying you think we're dealing with a copycat killer?" Maleah asked.

"I believe it is a good possibility." Griff picked up two file folders and handed them to Sanders. "Later, I want you both to read over this information." He motioned to Sanders to distribute the folders, which he quickly did.

Derek glanced at the typed heading on the folder. *Jerome Browning.*

The name sounded vaguely familiar.

"Who's Jerome Browning?" Maleah asked.

"He is a convicted serial killer serving half a dozen consecutive life terms at the Georgia State Prison." Griff made direct eye contact with Maleah before he continued. "Browning became known as the Carver when he viciously murdered nine people by slitting their throats and carving triangular pieces of flesh from their upper arms and thighs. His first kill was twelve years ago and his killing spree lasted less than three years before he was caught, tried and convicted."

The way everyone else in the room seemed focused on Maleah piqued Derek's curiosity. He sensed that Griff was on the verge of revealing information that would in some way personally affect her. His protective instincts kicked in automatically, urging him to place himself between Maleah and whatever might harm her.

"I'm getting the distinct impression that I'm not

going to like whatever else you have to say." Maleah glanced around the room, taking note of how everyone was staring directly at her.

"Maleah, I'm so sorry . . ." Nic's voice trailed off.

"Jerome Browning's third victim was a young man living and working in the Atlanta area," Griff said. "His name was Noah Laborde."

Maleah gasped, the sound sharp and highly exaggerated in the hushed stillness. "He killed Noah?" She spoke the man's name softly . . . sadly.

"Who was Noah Laborde?" Derek asked.

Nic walked over to Maleah and draped a comforting arm around her shoulders. Maleah looked at Derek. "Noah was my college boyfriend. We . . . we were almost engaged. We broke up right after graduation. His sister called me a year later to tell me that Noah had been killed, but I . . . Oh, God, I never knew the details. I never asked."

Of all the killers this person could have chosen to imitate, why had he picked the man who had murdered Maleah's former boyfriend?

The answer was obvious, of course—because of the Powell Agency connection.

"So what do you think, Derek?" Griff asked.

"I don't think it's a coincidence." Derek knew exactly what Griff was asking. "Our killer chose this man Browning because he had killed Noah Laborde, Maleah's former boyfriend. Maleah is a Powell agent and therefore connected to the agency. He handpicked the Carver as the killer he would imitate for the same reason he has chosen his victims."

"Because they are all, in one way or another, connected to the Powell Agency." Griff pummeled the desktop with his huge fist. "God damn son of a bitch."

"I can only surmise that his real target is the Powell

Agency." When Derek's gaze met Griff's, he saw the pain in his employer's eyes. "I would assume that means his target is either you, Griff, or you, Nicole." He glanced at Nic. "Or possibly both of you."

"It's not Nic. I'm his real target," Griff said. "He's striking out at me through my people."

"That's one possible scenario," Derek agreed.

"I could be his target," Nic said. "He could be someone from my past, someone connected to one of my cases when I was a federal agent. After all, he has chosen to copy a killer who has a direct connection to my best friend."

"We can debate this all day and still won't know for sure," Maleah told them. "Once we find out who the killer is, we'll have the answers to all the whys, won't we? That has to be our first order of business—identifying our killer."

"Maleah's right," Derek said. "Since it seems obvious that the new Carver murders are copycat killings, that means we need to start with some basic questions. Is our guy someone who has been in contact with Jerome Browning, maybe visited him in prison? Is he an admirer? A student of the Carver's methods? Is he perhaps even a protégé of Browning's?"

"There is one person, other than the killer himself, who may be able to answer those questions," Maleah said.

"Jerome Browning." Derek's voice filled the quiet room. All eyes turned to him.

"Browning is the reason y'all decided to pair me with Derek on this case." Maleah stared right at Nic.

Nic simply stared back at Maleah.

"I think it's obvious that our killer wants you involved," Griff said.

Maleah gave Griff her undivided attention. "You

think because of my connection to Noah, Browning's third victim, the copycat is sending me an invitation to become personally involved."

Griff nodded. "Don't you agree, Derek?"

Reluctantly, Derek replied, "Yes, I agree. And it could be that by singling out Maleah this way, it's the copycat killer's way of getting as close to Nic as he possibly can without actually involving her. At least not yet."

"See, I told you that this could be all about me and not you." Nic glared at her husband.

Griff frowned, but didn't verbally acknowledge Nic's comment. Instead he spoke directly to Maleah. "Someone will have to interview Browning. Since the killer chose a specific connection between you and the killer he is imitating, it would seem logical that you should be the agent I send to Georgia to talk to Browning."

"I'll accompany her, of course." No way in hell was Derek going to let Maleah confront Browning alone. She might project a tough as nails image, but he knew just how vulnerable she really was.

"Of course," Griff agreed. "We'll want you to study Browning while Maleah interviews him."

"She needs to know the rest." Nic glared at her husband. "No secrets. If Maleah is going into this, she needs to go into it armed with all the facts."

Derek's gut tightened.

Griff nodded. He stood, reached down behind his desk and lifted a small thermal cooler from the floor.

"We received a package sent via FedEx this morning," Griff said. "There was a small plastic case inside an Arctic foil insulated package, the type used to ship perishables such as food and medical supplies."

Griff flipped back the lid on the cooler, reached down inside and lifted out the plastic case. "The package was addressed to you, Maleah, in care of the Powell

Agency. The sender was, supposedly, Winston Corbett."

Derek sensed that Maleah was holding her breath as Griff removed the top from the plastic case. He inched in closer, placing himself directly behind her. Looking over her shoulder, he had a perfect view of the sectioned interior of the case and the first layer of its contents.

"Are those . . . ?" Maleah swallowed hard. "Are those what I think they are?"

"We've had our lab verify that those small triangular objects are human flesh," Griff said. "I think we can be relatively certain that the pieces in the top section were cut from Winston Corbett's body and those in the other three sections belong to the other victims."

"And he sent them to me." Maleah balled her hands into fists and pressed her fists against her upper thighs.

Derek reached out and clamped his hand over Maleah's tense shoulder, conveying his support. "We're in this together, Blondie. You and me. From here to the bitter end."

Chapter 4

Despite her earlier claims to Derek about being hungry, Maleah skipped dinner that evening. The information that Nic and Griff had shared with her had not only taken her appetite, but it had given her the mother of all headaches. *Why me?* was the one question that replayed itself over and over again in her mind. Could it really be he had chosen her only because she and Nic were close friends? Or was it possible that she was simply the only Powell agent with a connection to a serial killer? She'd have to remember in the morning to ask Nic.

Lying there staring up at the ceiling, she positioned her index fingers on either side of her head and rubbed her temples in a circular motion. She had been prone to having tension headaches all her life. Usually a couple of aspirin or Aleve gave her relief within an hour or less. But this headache was hanging on.

"Maleah?" Nic asked after rapping on the bedroom door.

"Yes, what is it?"

"May I come in?"

Maleah sighed heavily, lifted herself into a sitting position and replied, "Sure, come on in." After all, she was a guest in her friend's home. And Nic was probably worried about her.

No sooner had Maleah's bare feet hit the floor than Nic entered, a serving tray balanced in one hand. "I brought you something to eat."

Maleah rushed toward her friend and took the tray from her. "Thanks, but you didn't have to do that. I don't think I can eat a bite."

"It's Barbara Jean's mac and cheese, with her Mexican cornbread. If that doesn't tempt you, nothing will." Nic closed the door and then followed Maleah into the small sitting area of the bedroom. A couple of sky blue upholstered arm chairs flanked a small, low mahogany table set between the chairs and love seat covered with yellow and blue floral material. Maleah lowered the tray to the table, removed the cloth covering and eyed the plate of food. Her stomach growled.

Maleah and Nic smiled at each other.

"See," Nic said. "Your stomach knows you're hungry, even if you think you're not."

Realizing it was useless to argue with Nic, especially when she was right, Maleah sat down on the loveseat and picked up a fork from the tray. "I've read through the folder Griff gave me, but I'm afraid I didn't retain much of the info. I have a splitting headache. I'll read the files again later."

"Did you take something for your headache?"

Maleah lifted the plate from the tray. "A couple of aspirin. They helped a little."

"Eat something. It could be a hunger headache." She scanned Maleah from head to toe. "You look like you've lost weight."

Maleah groaned. "Don't I wish."

They both laughed.

"Why don't you wait until in the morning to re-read the files on the Carver," Nic said. "It could be days before you can interview him. Griff is still working on pulling some strings to get you and Derek permission to visit him. There is a lot of red tape involved in being granted visitation privileges. If we were a government agency, it would be a lot easier. Under normal circumstances, since we're an independent firm, it would be highly unlikely one of our agents would be allowed to see Browning. Unless of course, he asked to see one of us."

Maleah lifted a forkful of macaroni and cheese to her mouth, ate the delicious casserole and dived back into the plate for more. "This is delicious." She ate several more bites before asking, "I don't suppose y'all have checked to see if any of the other agents have any connection to a serial killer, have you?"

Nic's eyes widened as her expression changed from puzzlement to understanding. "No, we haven't. Narrowing down the copycat killer's MO to perfectly match a former serial killer took some time, so we only recently came to the conclusion that our Powell Agency killer was mimicking the Carver. But I see what you're getting at. Did he choose the Carver because he's the only serial killer with any connection to one of our agents?"

Maleah munched on the Mexican cornbread and washed it down with iced tea. "I realize that with nearly two hundred people now employed by the agency, it could take forever to make any kind of connection. So, how did our killer unearth the connection between Jerome Browning and me when I didn't even know about it myself?" Maleah tightened her hold on the cool, damp glass. "God, I should have asked more questions about Noah's murder when his sister Jacque called me. But I hadn't seen him or spoken to him in over a year when it happened." Quick jabs of pain shot through Maleah's right temple. She pressed the side of the iced tea glass against the throbbing pain.

"Are you okay?" Nic studied Maleah closely. "Maybe you need something stronger than aspirin."

"No, I'll be fine. I'm just feeling a little guilty remembering how unaffected I was by Noah's death." She set the glass on the tray. "He was such a nice guy. Any woman in her right mind would have snapped him up in a New York minute. But not me. I think I broke his heart when I turned down his proposal."

"Why did you turn him down?"

"I didn't want to get married." Maleah slid her left hand beneath her hair at the nape of her neck and massaged her scalp. "I feel as if my entire head is being squeezed in a vise. I know it's just tension, but . . ."

"You don't need to tell me tonight. Maybe you should lie down and rest."

"I want you to know, to understand why I rejected him. At the time, I told myself that I didn't marry Noah because I didn't want to get married, that I intended to never marry anybody. But looking back, I realize that was only half of the reason."

"And the other half was because . . . ?"

"I don't think I was in love with Noah. I loved him, yes. But something was missing. I wanted to be in love, told myself that I was, needed to be, at least in my own mind, enough to justify the fact that he was my first."

Nic smiled. "No one ever forgets their first, do they? But we all know that most of the time, the first one is not The One, not for a lot of woman and certainly not for most men. Of course, there are exceptions, especially for our parents' generation."

"It breaks my heart to think about the way Noah died. He deserved to live a full life, with a wife and kids and . . ." Maleah exhaled a huffing breath. "Dear God, how am I going to face the man who killed Noah? How am I going to interview him without wanting to strangle him with my bare hands for what he did?"

"You'll be able to do it because you're a professional. If Griff or I had any doubts about your ability or your competence, we would never pair you with Derek again and put the two of you in charge of a case that is highly personal for us."

"Griff really does believe that these murders are somehow connected to his past, doesn't he?" Maleah looked squarely at Nic.

"Yes. And he could be right. But it's also possible that the killer wants us to believe that. He may want us to think that Griff is the ultimate target, when actually it may be me."

"Have you ever considered the possibility that neither of you are?"

"No, not really," Nic said. "The killer has murdered agents and members of their families, which means he's targeting the agency. Griff and I own the agency. It stands to reason that this killer wants to harm the agency, wants to hurt Griff and me."

"Then why involve me?" Maleah asked. "Both you and Griff have been personally involved with serial killer cases in the past. Why not copy one of them? Why go back into my past and choose someone who had killed my college boyfriend?"

"I don't have a conclusive answer for you because I simply don't know. It could be what we said earlier, that he's getting to me through you, my best friend."

"Maybe. If you're the one he wants to hurt. But if his

real target is Griff, then maybe I'm simply phase one in his plan."

"Which would make me phase two, right?"

Maleah shook her head and waved her hand in the air. "It's all conjecture at this point. I'm probably talking nonsense. I shouldn't come up with conspiracy theories when I'm tired and sleepy and can't shake a bad headache."

"Look, I'm going to leave you alone so you can finish eating, grab a shower, and then go to bed." Nic rose to her feet. "We'll both have clearer heads in the morning and be able to get a fresh perspective on things."

Maleah stood and walked Nic to the door. They exchanged hugs and pecks on their cheeks. Once Nic walked down the hall, Maleah closed the door, leaned back against it, and closed her eyes.

"I'm so sorry, Noah. Sorry that you were so brutally murdered. Sorry that I didn't ask for details about your death when your sister called me. Sorry that I didn't love you enough to marry you."

Griff poured Macallan single malt Scotch whisky into two glasses, handed one to Derek and lifted the other to his lips. After taking a sip, he motioned for Derek to take the left of two leather chairs flanking the seven-foot-high rock fireplace in his private study. As Griff sat in the opposite chair, Derek studied the man briefly, noting the weariness in his expression. The four recent Powell Agency–related deaths had begun to take a toll on the seemingly invincible billionaire.

"I had Sanders put a call in to the Georgia governor," Griff said. "I saw no point in wasting my time going through the normal channels to acquire visitation privileges for you and Maleah at the Georgia State Prison."

Derek nodded. Why indeed? There would be no point in Griff calling the prison's warden when he was on a first name basis with the governor.

Born into a wealthy, old Southern family, Derek had taken for granted all the things most people struggle for on a daily basis. His mother hobnobbed with other society matrons, his sister married a suitable young man from a proper family, and Derek's grandparents had left him a trust fund worth more millions than he'd ever spend in one lifetime. Griffin Powell had been born dirt poor, but was now one of the wealthiest men in the world. No one knew how the former UT football hero had earned his billions during the ten years after he had mysteriously disappeared.

"I'd rather not send Maleah to do the initial interview even if she is one of our best agents. But under the circumstances, I feel she's the only choice. The killer didn't choose to copy the Carver's murders without a reason."

"You're assuming Maleah is the reason, right?"

"In a roundabout way," Griff said. "He wanted a connection between the killer he copied and one of our agents. It could be a coincidence that Maleah is that agent. Or it is possible that Maleah's friendship with my wife is the reason. What hurts Maleah hurts Nic and what hurts Nic hurts me."

"That's the way love and friendship works."

Griff took a hefty swallow of the aged whisky. Holding the drink in one hand, he absently stroked the side of the glass with his other hand, tapping his fingers rhythmically on the smooth surface.

"Do you think Browning personally knows our killer?" Derek asked. His gut instincts told him that the Powell Agency killer and Browning were at the very least acquainted. Possibly friends. Or more likely, student and teacher.

"Probably. What do you think?"

"Probably."

"Browning could well be the key to unlocking our killer's identity."

Derek took his first sip of the premium Scotch whisky. He wasn't a drinking man himself, but he did enjoy an occasional sip of the good stuff. Not that he was a teetotaler by any means. But seeing what alcohol addiction had done to his father and older brother made Derek conscientious about his drinking habits. After the smooth liquor made its way down his throat and warmed his belly, he glanced at Griff, who was staring into the cold fireplace.

"We both know that Browning isn't going to willingly offer us any information," Derek said.

"No, he'll sense from the get-go that he has the upper hand. And he'll use it to his advantage. He'll want something in return for anything he gives us."

"For anything he gives Maleah."

Griff nodded. "She's strong and smart and I'd trust her with even the most difficult assignment. But this is different. From what I've read about Jerome Browning, he's going to play hardball and I don't know if Maleah is a tough enough opponent."

"She's not going into this alone," Derek reminded his boss.

"That's true." Griff stared at Derek, as if he was judging his worth as a warrior. "She's going to need you. She won't like it and may even resist your advice and assistance. You know what a stubborn little mule she can be."

Derek chuckled. "That's an understatement. She is

without a doubt the most stubborn woman I've ever known."

"Nic is worried about her. She understands why Maleah is the one who should interview Browning, but they're close, almost like sisters, and know each other's weaknesses. Nic's concerned that Browning may use any weakness he senses in Maleah against her."

"If Browning picks up on any weakness in her, I have no doubt that he'll use it. But I'll be there to advise her." Derek took a second sip of whisky and then set the glass down on the floor beside his chair. "Before we leave for Georgia, I'll go over all the files we have on Browning and do an in-depth study on the guy. After we meet him, I'll work up my own profile and compare it to the old FBI profile the agency put together."

Griff nodded. "I want the copycat killer found and stopped before anyone else dies." He downed another gulp of the Macallan, huffed out a deep breath, and took another swig.

It was Derek's opinion that recently Griff had been drinking too much. The man had a high tolerance for alcohol, was able to drink enough to knock another man on his ass, and usually knew his limit. But for the past couple of months, Derek had noticed a distinct change in his boss, and not only in his drinking habits.

"You do know that these murders are not your fault," Derek said.

Griff's grumbling growl came from his chest, a combination of anger and pain. "He is sending me a message. No matter what anyone thinks, I know that I'm the ultimate target. He wants me to suffer, to know that he's killing these people because they are in some way associated with me."

"I know that's what you believe, but there is no way you can be sure."

"I'm sure."

"Look, Griff, I've never asked for specific details about your past, about those missing ten years," Derek said. "I figured everything that happened to you and how you earned your billions was nobody's business. Certainly not mine. What I know, you've told me yourself, and I appreciate your trusting me with the information. But if there's something specific that I need to know, something that could help me—"

"Go with Maleah to see Browning. Size up the guy. Get all the info you can out of him and then we'll talk." Griff finished off his glass of whisky.

Derek didn't need to say more. He understood that Griff had dismissed him. He stood, said good night and closed the door behind him when he left.

As if he were standing guard, Sanders waited across the hall from Griff's study, his muscular arms crossed over his broad chest. With a stocky, fireplug build, every muscle toned, a sharp mind always in observation mode, the man appeared to be battle ready at all times.

"He's drinking too much." Derek paused long enough to make direct eye contact with his boss's right-hand man.

Sanders nodded.

"He thinks the murders are his fault."

"Griffin carries the weight of the world on his shoulders," Sanders said.

"Someone who knows him far better than I do needs to convince him that he's not to blame, no matter what the killer's motives might be."

"Griffin is a man who accepts responsibility."

Derek stared at Sanders, not quite understanding his comment. Did he believe that Griff was in some way responsible for the actions of a psychopath?

"No one person can right all the wrongs in the world, no matter how rich and powerful they might be," Derek said.

"One person can try."

"My God, what grievous sin did he commit that he feels compelled to atone for by wearing a hair shirt the rest of his life?"

"I advise you not to profile Griffin Powell with that analytical mind of yours, Mr. Lawrence."

Derek nodded. He now knew that he had hit too close to home to suit Sanders. Griff lived with his past sins haunting him and they were no doubt the driving force behind his need to rid the world of evil. He had founded the Powell Private Security and Investigation Agency as a means to bring to justice those whom regular law enforcement had difficulty apprehending and punishing. His clients paid according to their ability to do so and many cases were worked pro bono.

Without replying to Sanders, Derek walked away, his thoughts centered on Griffin Powell's mysterious past. Why was Griff so certain that the copycat killer was sending him a message?

Errol watched Cyrene while she slept. He had never thought it possible to love a woman the way he loved her. He couldn't look at her enough, couldn't touch her enough, couldn't make love to her enough. After his disastrous first marriage and the death of his little girl, he had thought he was destined to be miserable the rest of his life.

And then he had met Cyrene. In a coffee shop of all places. He'd stopped by to meet his sister for breakfast on his way to work and had accidentally bumped into the most gorgeous woman in the world while waiting in line. The moment she smiled at him, the whole world lit up, bright and warm and joyous. Yeah, sure, he hadn't missed the fact that she had a great body. And yeah, right after her thousand-watt smile, her big boobs had been the first thing he'd noticed. But her body was icing on the cake. The woman inside was as beautiful as the sexy wrapping.

They had dated for six months before they slept together. She was a cautious lady, determined that no man would ever take advantage of her. By the time they made love for the first time, he was already in love. And so was she.

When he asked her to marry him a few weeks later, she had only one request—that he change jobs.

"I want a husband who doesn't put his life in danger every day the way you do being an Atlanta police officer. I don't want to have to worry if the father of my children may not come home one night because he got killed on the job."

Errol reached down from where he lay beside her, his body propped up on his folded arm, and tenderly caressed her cheek. As much as he had loved being a police officer, he loved Cyrene more. Then and now.

He'd been lucky to find another job that he truly liked, one that actually paid better and afforded him and his new bride a more affluent lifestyle. He'd been with the Powell Agency for four months, having hired on a few weeks after his engagement. They had just bought a new house in Farragut a month before their wedding. And his new boss—Griffin Powell—had given them an all-expenses-paid two-week honeymoon at the Grand Resort in the Bahamas.

He laid his head on his pillow, stretched out his

naked body beneath the cool, slightly wrinkled sheet, and closed his eyes.

Life was good. At long last.

Errol knew he was one damn lucky SOB.

Wearing tan cargo shorts and a hideous floral shirt, he sat at the end of the bar nursing some elaborate rum concoction, doing his best to look like a typical tourist. Most of the visitors at the resort were couples, many newlyweds or second honeymooners. In order to fit in, he had made a point of flirting with several single ladies who were obviously there man-hunting. He had already decided that tomorrow night he'd take one of those ladies to his room and ease some of the pre-kill tension he always experienced. A night of rough sex would do wonders for him.

He was in no rush. The most important thing was timing. Errol and Cyrene Patterson were on their honeymoon and spent a great deal of time in their room. The couple had been inseparable since their arrival at the resort last week. He didn't want to kill both of them, but if necessary, he would. But only one was his target, only one was destined to become the Copycat Carver's fifth victim.

Just as he took another sip of the syrupy sweet rum drink, his mobile phone vibrated in his shirt pocket. He lifted the phone from the pocket and glanced at the caller ID.

No information. Unknown number and name.

He tapped the answer key and put the phone to his ear. "I'm enjoying my vacation in the Bahamas. I've met some lovely ladies. Unfortunately some of the prettiest women are married and here on their honeymoon. There's one woman . . ."

"I don't need to know the details tonight. I prefer to allow my imagination to paint a mental picture of all the gruesome details."

"Whatever you want."

"Did you send Ms. Perdue her gift?"

"She should have received it today."

"You sent it in care of her employer?"

"I did."

"Then it's only a matter of time before he arranges for her to visit the Georgia State Prison."

Chapter 5

Maleah wasn't surprised that Griff had managed to arrange for visitation privileges for Derek and her at the prison in Reidsville so quickly. He had placed a call to the governor over the weekend and by noon Monday, she and Derek were packing their bags. Barbara Jean, who handled a lot of the mundane details for the agency, booked them two rooms at the Hampton Inn in Vidalia, a twenty-minute drive from Reidsville. They had checked into the hotel before six and then had driven over to the county seat of Tattnall County where the state prison was located. Before they had left Griffin's Rest yesterday, Sanders, who had confiscated their laptops earlier that morning, had informed them that all pertinent files on Jerome Browning had been loaded into a file folder. One file contained info on the penitentiary, the oldest state prison in Georgia. Constructed of marble in 1937 and opened in that same year, it remained the largest contributor to the city's economy.

Numerous buildings containing four two-tiered cell blocks with single cells, the newer buildings spanning from the original structure, housed the convicts. The

cell blocks were divided by population into two cate-
gories: general population units and one special man-
agement unit. As a convicted serial killer serving
multi-life sentences, Jerome Browning was housed in a
maximum security area.

Maleah hadn't slept worth a damn. She would never
admit it to Derek, but she was more than just a little
nervous about meeting Browning. In all honesty, she
was borderline terrified—terrified by the thought of
how she might react when she actually came face-to-
face with Noah's killer. While she had tossed and
turned for hours, longing for sleep that wouldn't come,
her mind had wandered back more than a dozen years,
to the day she had met Noah Laborde, sophomore class
president. It hadn't been love at first sight. She didn't
believe in such a thing, not then and certainly not now.
But it had been interest at first sight. They had dated
for nearly a year before she had finally agreed to have
sex with him.

Remembering the past in such vivid detail, recalling
moments with Noah that she had thought long forgotten didn't help Maleah's already frayed nerves that
morning. After grabbing a quick shower and brushing
her hair up into a loose bun, she dressed in her professional garb—navy slacks, white shirt, lightweight tan
jacket, and a pair of sensible low-heel navy shoes. After
applying a minimum of makeup, she put on her wristwatch and small gold hoop earrings. She took all of half
a minute to inspect herself in the mirror before slipping her small leather bag over her shoulder and leaving the room.

She didn't bother stopping to knock on Derek's
door as she headed for the elevator. During the entire
time they had worked together on the Midnight Killer
case, she couldn't recall a single morning that he had-

n't gotten up early, always before she did. The Hampton Inn provided a full breakfast, which meant they wouldn't have to search for a place to eat this morning. Just as she had figured, he was waiting for her in the dining area adjacent to the lobby. Sitting alone at a table for two, a cup of coffee in front of him, a folded newspaper in one hand, and a soft-grip mechanical pencil in the other, he glanced up from the crossword puzzle and motioned for her to join him. As she approached, he laid down the paper and pencil and rose to greet her with a smile.

"Morning, sunshine."

God, she hated that he could be so chipper at six-thirty in the morning. And she hated even more that she had noticed how damn good he looked. Derek was nothing more to her than her partner on this case, just as he had been on the Midnight Killer case. Their personal relationship went no farther than that. They certainly weren't friends, not by any stretch of the imagination. On good days, they worked well together. On bad days, they tolerated each other.

"Have you eaten?" she asked.

"Nope." He glanced at the half empty cup on the table. "However, this is my second cup of coffee."

"Coffee sounds good. I think I'll grab some cereal and a cup of yogurt."

"You do know that breakfast is the most important meal of the day," he told her. "You should fill up on protein—bacon and eggs. And of course, a couple of biscuits smothered in butter and jelly."

"If I ate like that every morning, I'd soon be waddling when I walk."

When she headed toward the self-serve breakfast setup, she felt Derek's gaze on her and knew he was looking at her butt. Okay, so she had a bit of a hang-up about her wide hips and ample rear-end. Nic had told her guys didn't like flat asses, that her JLo butt was a definite asset. If that was true, then why was it that Derek seemed to prefer the long, lean, borderline skinny model types?

Damn it, why do you care what type of woman Derek prefers?

Maleah hurried through the line, grabbed a carton of non-fat strawberry yogurt and, deciding against eating cereal, headed toward the coffeemaker. Not fully concentrating on what she was doing, she bumped into Derek and quickly apologized before she even looked at him.

Their gazes met and locked for a full thirty seconds before Maleah broke eye contact.

"It's okay to be nervous about meeting Browning," he told her.

Ignoring his comment, she grabbed a cup, filled it with hot coffee, and picked up a packet of Splenda and a stir stick.

By the time Derek joined her at their table, she had drunk half her coffee. As he set down a plate filled with bacon, eggs, and biscuits, he glanced at her unopened yogurt carton. After he sat across from her, they ate in relative silence for several minutes.

"You aren't nervous, are you?" Maleah asked.

"Unsettled would be a better word to describe how I feel about meeting Jerome Browning this morning," Derek told her. "Unsettled, curious, and wary. You need to be wary of him, too. He's cunning. If he senses any weakness in you, he'll use it against you."

"And you and Griff think I'm weak, don't you? You think I'll fall apart just because Browning murdered my college boyfriend."

"Neither Griff nor I think you're weak. But you will

be vulnerable because of your connection to Noah Laborde."

She heaved a heavy, labored huff. Derek was right. There was no use denying the obvious.

He reached over and laid his open palm across her tightly fisted hand. The moment he touched her, she jerked her hand away and lifted it off the table.

Ignoring her reaction, he said, "The way I see this interview with Browning is you and I act as a tag team, both of us questioning him. If at any time you become uncomfortable and want to terminate the interview, then don't hesitate to let me know."

"And you'll whisk me up in your big strong arms and carry me off on your gallant white charger." The moment the silly comment left her lips, Maleah regretted it. She had a problem about speaking before thinking things through, and this was especially true with Derek.

He didn't respond.

She groaned. "Sorry."

He laughed. "I didn't know you thought of me as a knight in shining armor."

She rolled her eyes, but couldn't help smiling. "Most of the time, I think of you as a royal pain in the butt."

"Likewise, Blondie." He lifted his coffee cup and saluted her with it.

Barbara Jean had lived at Griffin's Rest for several years, ever since Griff had placed her under the agency's protection during the hunt for her younger sister's killer. Within a few days, he had put her to work, there in his home, under Damar Sanders's guidance. Her attraction to Sanders had not been love at first sight, but rather a recognition of two lonely, wounded souls in need. Despite the fact that they were lovers and sometimes in their intimate moments she called him Damar, she thought of her friend and lover as Sanders. No one used his first name, not even Griff and Yvette, his closest friends.

She admired and respected Griffin Powell as she did Sanders and shared a deep affection with Nicole. She considered Yvette Meng a friend, but they were not close, not the way she and Nic were. The beautiful Eurasian psychiatrist possessed a quiet, gentle personality. Almost shy. Her unique empathic abilities that allowed her to gain insight into a person's thoughts and feelings by a mere touch separated her from others. Until recently, Yvette had lived in London, half a world away. But then, three years ago, Griff had begun construction at Griffin's Rest on a retreat for Yvette and a small group of her protégés, young men and women with special psychic talents.

Barbara Jean knew less about the missing years of her employer's life, from age twenty-two to thirty-two, than Nic knew. And even though Sanders had told her that he and Yvette had shared those years with Griff, he had not divulged very many details. Sanders had been married long ago and had lost his wife and child. He had never told her the specifics and she had never asked. He, Yvette, and Griff had been held captive on an uncharted Pacific island by an insane billionaire named Malcolm York. They had eventually escaped, after they killed York. The horrors they had endured together had united them as comrades and bound them to one another forever.

Nic and Yvette shared a precarious friendship, somewhat one-sided since Nic couldn't quite manage to overcome her concerns about Griff's love for the other woman. Where Nic needed to know more about her husband's past and allowed the secrets he couldn't share with her to come between them, Barbara Jean accepted Sanders for who and what he was. His past was just that—his past. It had made him the man he was today, but other than that, it had nothing to do with her.

If only Nic could see things as she did.

Barbara Jean maneuvered her wheelchair out onto the patio where Nic sat in a chaise lounge, her computer resting in her lap.

"I've put on the kettle for tea," Barbara Jean said. "Would you care for a cup?"

"No, thanks." Nic glanced over her shoulder and smiled. "I've been going over the information on Jerome Browning again and some things don't add up."

"Such as?" Barbara Jean asked as she wheeled herself out into the morning sunshine.

"The original Carver didn't mail the pieces of flesh he removed from his victims to anyone. Those triangular pieces were never found." Nic paused for a moment, closed the lid on her laptop and faced Barbara Jean.

"So, the copycat killer is not following every detail of the Carver's MO, is he?" Barbara Jean said.

"No, which makes me ask why he isn't. And if he's differing in one aspect, then he's possibly going to differ in other areas."

"I haven't actually studied copycat cases in general, but it stands to reason that there might be differences between the original and the copy."

"In most cases, the copycat closely mimics the original, but often deviates in small details," Nic said as she closed her laptop and set it on the glass and metal side table to her right. "Our killer sending Maleah the triangles of flesh from the first four victims, coupled with the fact that he's copying the killer who murdered Maleah's college sweetheart, tells me that he wants her involved."

"Does that mean that neither you nor Griff is his ultimate target?"

"I don't know. My gut tells me that it's one of us, but what if this new Carver has been killing Powell Agency people in order to set things up to lure Maleah into some sort of vicious game he's playing?"

"Have you talked to Griff about your theory?" Barbara Jean asked.

"I'm afraid Griff is concentrating so much on a possible connection between the Powell Agency murders and the rumor in Europe about Malcolm York being alive that he isn't giving consideration to any other possibility."

"Sanders says there is no way York can still be alive." She lowered her voice. "When they left the island, York was dead. They were certain of it." Barbara Jean preferred not to think about the fact that Sanders was more than capable of cold-blooded murder, as were Griff and Yvette. She understood why they had killed York and knew in her heart that under the same circumstances, she would have done what they did. They had destroyed the monster who had tortured them with such great pleasure.

"Griff says the same thing." Nic stood to her full five-ten height, her feet bare, her long, tan legs clad in white walking shorts. An oversized orange and white UT T-shirt hung loosely to her hips. "He's convinced that someone in Europe is using York's name, but he has no idea who or why."

"I know very little about the years Sanders spent on Amara, only that he blames York for the death of his wife and child, and that York forced him to do some terrible things."

"I've grown to hate Malcolm York with every fiber of my being." Nic walked to the edge of the patio and gazed out over Douglas Lake. "Even after all these years, he still haunts Griff."

"As he does Sanders and Yvette."

At the mention of Yvette's name, Nic glanced over her shoulder at Barbara Jean. "They both love her, you know. My Griffin and your Sanders."

"Yes, I know. And she loves them. But . . ." Barbara Jean paused, hoping to find the right words. "Griff worships the ground you walk on. You are the love of his life. Never doubt that for a moment."

Nic offered Barbara Jean a forced smile, then looked back out over the lake. "I don't doubt his love for me. But as long as he doesn't trust me with the complete truth about his past, that past will stand between us."

Maleah was in the driver's seat. Derek had learned early on during their partnership on the Midnight Killer case that she preferred being the driver. Since he couldn't care less, he hadn't put up a fuss about it. No doubt it had something to do with her personal control issues. The lady most definitely had a problem with any man—but him in particular—being in charge of her.

He kicked back and relaxed as she headed her Chevy Equinox southeast on GA-30 E/US-280 E. If they weren't delayed by roadwork or accidents blocking the highway, they should be at the prison in about twenty minutes. Even though their scheduled visitation with Browning was at ten, Maleah had insisted on leaving the hotel at nine.

"I'd rather get there early and have to wait than run the risk of our being late," she'd told him.

He had learned the hard way not to argue with her over insignificant matters. He chose his battles. Otherwise, they would be at each other's throats all the time.

In the beginning of their professional association, they had disagreed on everything. If he said the sky was blue, she'd say it was gray. If he said the sun was shining, she'd say it was partly cloudy. If he voiced an opinion she didn't like, she'd call him an arrogant jerk.

"Do you want to go over anything again before we get there?" he asked.

"No. I think we've talked the subject of Jerome Browning to death, don't you?"

"Probably. Just remember—don't underestimate him. And don't expect him to give us anything without wanting something in return."

"I'm not an idiot, you know." She kept her gaze fixed on the road ahead.

He wanted to reply that no one had said she was an idiot or even thought it. A prickly pear, yes. High-strung and confrontational, yes. But instead, he asked, "Mind if I find some music on the radio?"

"Be my guest. But please make it something soothing."

He found a "lite sounds" station, the first tune, a relaxing piano concerto. "Does that meet with your approval?" he asked.

"It's fine." When she glanced his way, he smiled and winked at her. She frowned and hurriedly looked away, returning her gaze to the view through the windshield.

Ignoring her completely, he closed his eyes. His mind immediately focused on Jerome Browning.

Derek hated the deals law enforcement made with criminals, plea-agreements that allowed lesser sentences in exchange for information. The DA who had prosecuted Jerome Browning had been forced into one of those god-awful deals. Browning, who should be on death row, was instead locked away in the maximum security division of the penitentiary. He had brutally murdered nine people, five women and four men. But not long after his arrest the authorities learned that he had killed before, when he had been a teenager. Twenty years before Browning had been arrested and charged with the Carver murders, a series of six missing teen girls in Browning's old neighborhood had been presumed murdered. Their bodies had never been found. And all six cases had remained unsolved. Browning had bargained for his life—and won! He had agreed to confess to the murders of the six teen girls and tell the police where they could find the bodies. In exchange for the information that could bring closure to six families, Browning had been granted life imprisonment instead of the death penalty he deserved.

Browning would spend the rest of his life behind bars, but he was alive. Like the families of the people he had murdered, Derek believed that Browning should have been executed.

Everything Derek knew about Browning forewarned him that Maleah would be facing a deviously clever psychopath, one who would not hesitate to use her for his own amusement.

But Maleah was no featherweight in any battle of wills. She was strong, tough, and smart; and God help her, she never gave up on anything or anyone she believed in with her whole heart. He didn't know what demons she had fought and won in her past, but he saw beyond the exterior beauty to the deep scars inside her. Maleah Perdue was a survivor.

Derek suspected she just might be a worthy opponent for Browning.

But at what cost to her?

Griffin Powell had entrusted Maleah to Derek, expecting him to keep her safe and protect her from emotional trauma. Griff had a protective attitude toward all of his employees, but Maleah was special to him because she was his wife's best friend. And the big man possessed an exaggerated sense of responsibility when it came to the people in his life, especially the women. Apparently, on a subconscious level, Griff thought of women as the weaker sex. He was, in so many ways, an old-fashioned gentleman. A good old Southern boy, raised the right way by his mama.

Derek might have been born with a silver spoon in his mouth and Griff a poor boy, but Griff was far more of a gentleman than Derek ever had been or would be. Derek had spent most of his life rebelling against his mother, his family, and the inherent snobbery and self-indulgent lifestyle that inherited wealth so often imposed on the heirs to multi-million-dollar fortunes. From his early teens, he had deliberately done the unexpected, anything and everything to piss off his mother and grandparents, and to snub his nose at the society in which they existed. Military boarding school had been their solution. His response had been to skip college after high school graduation and bum around the world like a penniless vagrant. He had certainly seen the world through the eyes of a man who had to earn his keep wherever he went.

At twenty, flat broke and determined not to touch his trust fund, he had joined a group of unsavory characters, a sort of ragtag group of wannabe mercenaries, bluffing his way into their fold. He had learned later on that he hadn't fooled them and they hadn't expected him to survive his first mission. He'd been nothing more to them than an expendable foot solider.

At twenty-four, he had returned to the States, world-weary and old beyond his years. Then he had taken just enough money from his trust fund to attend Vanderbilt and had graduated summa cum laude. He came from a long line of highly intelligent savvy businessmen and his family had expected the prodigal son to take his place in the business world alongside his uncles and cousins. He had shocked them all when he had joined the FBI.

"Are you asleep?" Maleah asked Derek.

"Nope."

"We're almost there."

He opened his eyes and sat up straight. "Have you ever been inside a maximum security prison before today?"

"No, I haven't." She paused just long enough to inhale and exhale. "I suppose you have."

"Yes, I have."

"I don't need another lecture, so whatever you were going to say, keep it to yourself."

"I wasn't going to give you a lecture," he told her.

"Good. Just remember that I will be conducting the interview, okay?"

"Sure thing. As long as you understand that I may want to occasionally make a comment or ask a question."

"Keep your comments and questions to a minimum, will you? You're here as an observer. That is your area of expertise, isn't it, observing and forming an opinion?"

"Yes, ma'am, it is."

He had to bite his tongue to keep from telling her that he had been observing her for quite some time and had formed a definite opinion. She was, without a doubt, the most irritating, aggravating, combative woman he'd ever known.

They followed normal procedure, up to a point. They had parked in the facility's designated visitor parking lot. They had presented positive ID prior to their admission and then undergone a preliminary search by electronic surveillance instruments. But after that, they were escorted to the warden's office. Slender, gray-haired Claude Holland greeted them with quiet reserve, his facial expression giving away nothing and his handshake firm and quick. He scanned Maleah, his gaze simply sizing her up. She suspected that her appearance surprised him as it did so many people who expected a female private security agent to be big and burly, not blond and petite.

"I've arranged for you to meet with Mr. Browning in our visitation area, but there should be no physical contact with the prisoner at any time," Warden Holland said. "I mention this simply because you might normally expect to shake hands."

Maleah nodded. "I understand."

"This is not a scheduled visitation day, so there will be no other inmates seeing visitors. You'll have one hour with Browning, but if at any time before the end of that hour, you wish to leave, then simply tell one of the guards."

"Yes, thank you."

"I assume that if we need to visit Mr. Browning again, that could be arranged," Derek said.

"My instructions from the governor's office are that your visitation privileges are open-ended," Warden Holland replied. "All I ask is that you give us twenty-four hours' notice."

"Yes, of course," Derek said.

"And I should warn you, Ms. Perdue," Warden Holland said, "Browning will be in restraints during your interview."

"I assumed that was common practice for convicted murders, especially serial killers, but I have to admit that my knowledge of the penal system is limited."

"No, it's not common practice for inmates to be in shackles during visitation periods. But Browning is no ordinary inmate. His charm is deceiving," Warden Holland said. "We learned that early on. He can go from calm and cooperative one minute to aggressive and dangerous the next. He has attacked the guards and other inmates on numerous occasions."

"Thank you for telling us," Maleah said.

Claude Holland nodded and then motioned to the two uniformed guards standing at the back of the room. "Please escort Ms. Perdue and Mr. Lawrence to the visitation area. I'll call now and have Browning brought there to meet you."

Doing her best to concentrate not on where she was but on what she needed to do, Maleah walked quietly alongside Derek. Neither of them commented on their surroundings. The moment they entered the visitation area, her heartbeat accelerated, the sound drumming in her ears. There was no reason to be afraid, no reason whatsoever. She and Derek were perfectly safe.

Derek stood at her side, her shoulder brushing his arm. The two guards remained in the room, each stationed on either side of the door through which they had entered. She took a deep breath, held it, and then gradually released it, beginning with her belly and working upward to her throat. A yoga relaxation technique.

Two more guards entered the area, one on either side of the prisoner as they escorted him into the visitation area. Maleah stared directly at a handcuffed and shackled Jerome Browning. He looked older than the photos included in the Powell Agency files she and Derek had been given; but he was still tall, slender, and intriguingly handsome. Even dressed in prison garb of white shirt and pants and confined with restraints, he managed to exude an aura of worldly sophistication that totally surprised Maleah.

The moment he saw her, he smiled. A hard knot formed in the pit of her stomach. The smile was neither warm nor friendly. It was the type of smile she imagined would be on a cat's face when he had just spotted a delectable little mouse, one he looked forward to tormenting before devouring.

Chapter 6

Derek studied Browning closely, mentally comparing the information he had on the man with the man himself standing there before him. Browning was forty-nine and although he looked his age, he had the kind of features that aged well. In his youth, he would have been referred to as a pretty boy. No doubt, he had used his good looks and his charm to lure his victims, especially the female ones, to their deaths. Behind that handsome façade lay the mind of a cunning and diabolical killer.

One of the guards who had escorted their prisoner into the room indicated for Browning to take a seat. Without a moment's hesitation, he sat. His gaze never left Maleah.

Derek's gut tightened as his instincts flashed a warning—danger!

"I don't get many visitors," Browning said in a heavy Southern accent, his voice as smooth as glass. "Certainly none as pretty as you, Ms. Perdue."

Although Derek sensed Maleah tense, the action wasn't visible. He had to give her credit for not even flinching.

"And I'm unaccustomed to visiting murderers in prison," Maleah replied. "Especially ones as reprehensible as you are, Mr. Browning."

His chuckled softly. "Touché, my dear."

Maleah took the chair facing Browning, almost close enough to touch him, but not quite. She looked him square in the eye. They sat there staring at each other.

Derek barely controlled the urge to move in behind Maleah and stand at her back. His protective male instincts urged him to issue the man a warning. *If you mess with this woman, you'll have to deal with me.*

"Do you know why I'm here?" Maleah asked.

Browning's smile widened, showcasing a set of amazingly white, straight teeth. Apparently the state of Georgia provided great dental care for their inmates.

"I assume that you . . . or rather whatever agency you work for wants something they think only I can give them."

Derek was sure that Maleah wouldn't buy the man's I-don't-know-anything act.

"You know who I work for," Maleah said. "You were informed that Mr. Lawrence—" she inclined her head slightly backward toward Derek "—and I work for the Powell Private Security and Investigation Agency before you agreed to meet with us."

"Knowing who you work for and why you're here is not the same thing."

Maleah fixed her gaze on Browning. "I'll ask you again, do you know why I'm here?"

"We are allowed newspapers and magazines and television in here. And I occasionally have a visitor. People talk. I listen."

"What have you been listening to?"

"This and that. Whatever interests me."

"What interests you, Mr. Browning?"

That's it, Maleah, Derek thought. *Stay calm, keep things easy, remain completely in control. Don't let his evasiveness get to you.*

"Why don't you call me Jerome?" Browning's blue-eyed gaze traveled over Maleah, pausing on her breasts, which were modestly concealed by her lightweight blazer. "I'm more inclined to share confidences with people I'm on a first name basis with."

"All right, Jerome, what have you heard recently that interests you?"

He leaned back in the chair, spread his legs apart as far as the shackles allowed, and dropped his hand-cuffed hands between his thighs. "Well, Maleah . . . I can call you Maleah, can't I?"

She nodded.

Derek knew that Maleah hated the way Browning was ogling her, but she acted as if she didn't care, as if she wasn't even aware of what he was doing.

Smiling, he lifted his gaze back to her face.

"It's a pretty name for a pretty woman," Browning said. "Family name? Were you named after your grandmother?"

He's trying your patience. Derek wished he could tell her, but suspected she knew what Browning was doing. The man wanted to get a reaction out of her, wanted her to become impatient and lose her temper.

"We've just met, Jerome," Maleah told him. "We aren't at a stage in our relationship where we exchange personal information. Right now, today, our conversation is about business."

His smile disappeared as he cocked one brow and lowered his lids until his eyes narrowed to mere slits. "Whose business, mine or yours?"

"That's what I want you to tell me. I'd like to know if your business and Powell Agency business are related."

Forced and all the more deceptive, his smile returned. "What business could I possibly conduct in here? I'm considered a maximum security inmate. My privileges are limited. No way to get my hands on a scalpel. And as I'm sure you know, without the proper tools, I can't work."

"But you could teach, couldn't you, Jerome?"

Bull's-eye! Derek wanted to pat her on the back or high-five her. She was not only holding her own with Browning, but she was scoring points.

Browning couldn't manage to maintain his phony smile. The pulse in his neck throbbed. He clenched his perfect white teeth.

Silence lingered for a couple of minutes.

Then Browning recovered quickly and grinned. "Hmm . . . yes, I see your point. Those who can, do. Those who can't, teach." He sighed dramatically. "It's a sad state of affairs, don't you think, my dear Maleah, when a master must live vicariously through the accomplishments of an apprentice."

"And is that what you're doing?"

"What do you think?"

"I think you're enjoying our visit," she replied. "I think you like playing games. I think you will eventually tell me what I want to know. But not today."

"Smart and intuitive as well as beautiful." He straightened in the chair, deliberately rattling his manacles and gaining a guard's attention. Before the guard reached him, he settled quietly, his shoulders squared and his back straight.

"I don't believe there is any point in my prolonging this visit." Maleah rose to her feet and looked down at Browning. "My time is valuable, unlike yours. If you decide you want to be more informative, send word to the warden and Mr. Lawrence and I will come back for a second visit. Otherwise . . ."

"I'd be inclined to be more cooperative if you came alone." He glanced at Derek.

Son of a bitch! He sees me as a threat. He thinks that without my presence, Maleah will be more vulnerable.

"You cooperate with me and I'll cooperate with you," she told Browning.

"Give and take. I like that. You give me something I want and I'll give you something you want."

"Agreed."

"Come back tomorrow," he told her. "Alone."

Once Maleah drove away from the penitentiary, she glanced at Derek, who hadn't said a word since they had left the warden's office where she had arranged a second meeting with Jerome Browning. At ten o'clock tomorrow. Wednesday morning.

"Well, what are you waiting for?" she asked Derek. "I know you're dying to critique the initial interview. Tell me what I did wrong, how I screwed up, what I should have done differently."

"You didn't do anything wrong. I can't think of anything you should have handled differently. You were calm, cool, and in control every minute of the interview. You even managed to surprise Browning a couple of times."

"I can't believe it. Are you actually complimenting me?"

"I'm stating facts. You did a good job. Browning now knows that he's dealing with a worthy opponent. And never doubt that's how he sees you. For him, the game has begun. You may be ahead by a couple of points, but he learned a great deal about you today, far more than you learned about him."

Maleah gripped the steering wheel, breathed deeply

and told herself not to overreact to Derek's comments. "Are you saying that you think I revealed too much about—?"

"What I said was in no way a criticism. We had a file folder filled with info about Browning. We already knew a great deal about him. He knew next to nothing about us . . . about you."

"He'll be looking for my Achilles' heel, won't he?"

"Oh yeah, without a doubt. And if he discovers it, he'll use it like a sledgehammer to beat you into the ground. But only if you let him."

"Do you think he knows that Noah Laborde was my boyfriend?"

"Our copycat killer knows," Derek said. "It's possible that, if he and Browning have communicated, as we suspect they have, Browning is well aware of the fact that you were practically engaged to Laborde."

An overwhelming sense of doom threatened Maleah. She couldn't allow the foreboding thoughts and feelings to deter her from what she had to do.

They continued along Reidsville Road until they reached GA-30W, the highway that would take them back to Vidalia.

"How about an early lunch?" Derek asked.

"I'm not hungry."

"I am and you should be. You didn't eat much breakfast."

"I ate enough."

"Think of yourself as a warrior preparing to go into battle tomorrow. You need to be in tiptop shape mentally and physically. You're going to eat a decent lunch and dinner. And in the morning, you're filling up on protein—bacon and eggs."

Maleah groaned silently, but didn't reply. She knew that Derek meant well, that he wasn't trying to take control, that he really was thinking about helping her become battle ready for tomorrow morning's confrontation with Browning.

When she didn't say anything for several minutes, he asked, "Giving me the silent treatment?"

"Huh?"

"You're pissed that I dared to suggest—"

"You don't suggest, Derek, you command."

"Yeah, I suppose I do. Sorry about that. It's just that taking care of you is part of my job."

She practically stopped the SUV in the middle of the highway, slowing down so much that vehicles doing forty-five miles an hour flew past her.

"I shouldn't have said that," he told her. "I shouldn't have put it in those precise words. Let me rephrase—"

"Don't bother."

Suddenly realizing that doing twenty-miles an hour on a major highway could be hazardous, Maleah returned the Chevy to the allowed speed limit.

"I do not need you or anyone to take care of me." She kept her gaze focused straight ahead. If she looked at Derek, she might be overcome by the urge to slap him. "I'm an adult, not a child. I don't need or want anyone to fight my battles and take the hits meant for me. And I certainly don't need anyone overseeing my meals to make sure I eat properly."

"I realize that. What I should have said is that we're partners and partners depend on each other, right? I've got your back and you've got mine. Nobody's the boss. We're two equals doing a job and looking out for each other."

"Griff told you to take care of me, didn't he?"

Derek shrugged. "You know Griff."

"Yes, I do. He thinks I can't take care of myself."

"That's not it. He's concerned. After all, you're Nic's best friend and—"

"I'm going back to the prison alone tomorrow morning to see Browning." *Don't you dare tell me that I can't go without you!*

"All right."

"That was too easy. You agreed too quickly."

"You can see Browning without me. I'll wait in the warden's office."

"What's the catch?"

"The only catch is that we make a bargain."

"Uh-oh, I don't like the sound of that."

"You can see Browning alone, but you'll allow me to coach you before every visit."

"You mean you want to tell me what to do and what to say and—"

"I want to coach you, advise you, work with you."

"I'll think about it."

"It's not negotiable," he told her. "We strike a bargain or you don't see Browning alone."

Michelle Allen watched her seven-year-old niece Jaelyn as she swung across the monkey bars on her backyard swing set. Her brother's only child reminded her of herself in so many ways, and not just physically, although the resemblance was striking. But then she and Keith looked enough alike to be twins. She had always been a bit of a tomboy and enjoyed playing sports. She had excelled at basketball in high school and won a basketball scholarship to college. She'd been good, but not quite good enough for the WNBA.

"Watch me, Aunt Chelle," Jaelyn called to her. "I'm going to do a somersault in mid-air."

Michelle jumped to her feet. "Be careful. Don't fall." She raced toward the swing set positioned over an enormous bed of mulch, put there to protect Jaelyn if she fell. Keith and Shannon were conscientious parents and tried not to be overprotective. But it wasn't easy for them, walking that fine line, especially not with an only child, a child they knew would be their only biological offspring. And since at thirty-nine, Michelle doubted she would ever have children of her own, she felt a strong maternal protectiveness toward her niece.

Since Keith and Shannon didn't entrust their daughter to just anybody, they seldom had any alone time for just the two of them. When she was given a week off from work after her last assignment for the Powell Agency, Michelle offered to babysit her niece so that her brother and his wife could get away for a long weekend alone. They had left early Saturday morning and were due to return sometime tonight. A part of her was eager to return to work, to become involved with a new case, but another part of her hated to leave Paducah and the genuine pleasure she found in playing doting aunt to a child she loved as if she were her own.

Jaelyn performed a perfect mid-air somersault, caught hold of the overhead bars and lifted herself atop the swing set. Beaming with pride about her accomplishment, she tossed back her head and laughed. Michelle released the anxious breath she'd been holding and smiled adoringly up at her niece.

Michelle applauded. "Great job, sweetie. Now, come on down and let's go clean up for supper. Your mom and dad are due home later, so we'll want you fed and bathed and in bed before they get here. We don't want them to think I've been spoiling you."

"But you do spoil me, Aunt Chelle."

"That should be our little secret."

Jaelyn climbed down the side steps, taking her own sweet time. When her feet hit the ground, she raced straight to Michelle and threw her arms up and around her aunt's waist.

"I love you to pieces," Jaelyn said. "I wish you didn't have to leave when Mommy and Daddy come home. I wish you could live with us all the time."

Michelle leaned down, hugged Jaelyn and then lifted her off her feet for a forehead kiss. "I love you to pieces, too, angel pie."

As Michelle eased her niece back on her feet and grasped her little hand, Jaelyn giggled. "That's such a silly thing to call me—angel pie. Why do you call me that?"

"That's what my daddy used to call me," Michelle said. "You don't remember Papa Allen. He went to heaven before you were born."

"He was my daddy's daddy, too, wasn't he?"

"That's right. Your Papa Allen called me angel pie and he called your father pudding head."

"My daddy's a pudding head. That's so funny, but sometimes my daddy is funny. Mommy tells him he's being silly."

"Oh, he's silly all right."

Hand-in-hand, sharing aunt-and-niece conversation, they walked across the yard, onto the back porch and into the kitchen, both of them smiling happily. Tomorrow morning, she would return to Knoxville and return to work. But tonight, she would eat hot dogs and potato chips, oversee a seven-year-old's bath, watch the Disney Channel until eight o'clock, and listen to Jaelyn read aloud another chapter of *Could You? Would You?* before they exchanged good night hugs and kisses.

* * *

Tonight was the night. In a few hours he would slip the scalpel into his pocket, leave his room, and follow through with his plan for the fifth Copycat Carver murder. The closer it came to the actual moment when he would jab the scalpel into the side of the victim's neck and then slice across his throat, the more excited he would become. It had always been that way for him, even that first time, so many years ago. To say that he had been born to kill might be inaccurate. Surely no one was born to be a killer. But even as a child, he had derived a thrilling pleasure from capturing and killing animals. Birds and rabbits and squirrels. And then later on, neighborhood household pets. Cats and dogs.

He had been fourteen when he'd graduated from animals to human beings. He clearly remembered that day as if it were yesterday and not thirty years ago. They say you never forget your first. And that was certainly true for him. Renee Billaud had been a promiscuous sixteen-year-old with enticing tits the size of ripe cantaloupes. He had followed her into the woods where she had met a local man, a married man whose wife had been a friend of his grandmother's. He had watched them fucking, his penis growing steadily harder with each passing minute. As soon as the man had finished with her, he had zipped up his pants and walked off, leaving Renee lying on a bed of leaves beneath an enormous old oak tree. While her blouse was still unbuttoned, revealing her luscious breasts, and her skirt was still hiked up around her waist, he had come out from behind the bushes and stared her.

"What were you doing, you nasty boy, spying on me?"

He hadn't answered her. Instead, he had pounced on her. At first she had fought him like a wildcat, but once he'd managed to unzip his pants and free his penis, she had settled down and begun laughing when she realized he didn't know what he was doing.

"You've never done this before, have you?"

She had reached down, circled his penis with her hot little hand and guided him into her. He had pumped up and down only a couple of times before ejaculating. Renee had seemed to think his premature climax was amusing and proceeded to joke about what a poor lover he had been.

He would never forget the look in her eyes when he had tightened his hands around her neck and squeezed. And squeezed. Until she was gasping for air and struggling to loosen the death grip he had on her throat.

He had never known such pure pleasure as he did the moment she stopped breathing. A sexual orgasm paled in comparison.

Lost in a haze of sweet memories, he barely heard the tapping on his bedroom door. Already aroused and ready for action, he walked across the room, opened the door and smiled at the woman standing in the hallway. He had met her in the hotel bar last night and had struck up a casual conversation. She'd been one of the women he had noticed Sunday night. A woman on the prowl.

"Are you going to invite me in or do you want to do me out here and shock the other guests?"

He grabbed her arm, pulled her into his room, and kicked the door closed behind them.

Chapter 7

Maleah had needed time away from Derek. Time to clear her head. Time to think. Common sense told her that Derek was not her enemy, that she didn't need to do battle with him again and again just to prove a point.

And that point would be?

He could not control her. She would never allow anyone to have that kind of power over her, not ever again. Just when she thought she had finally come to terms with the terrors of her childhood and teen years, something or someone forced her to face those old demons.

Admit it, you're tempted to lean on Derek.

The thought of being even partially dependent on someone else for any reason terrified Maleah. And that irrational fear demanded she never relinquish the control she vigorously maintained over her life.

She had tried talking to her brother Jackson about their childhoods, about their stepfather, about the years they had lived under his tyrannical rule. But revisiting the past had proved painful for both of them.

"There's not a damn thing we can do to change what happened," Jackson had told her. "There's no need to dredge up the past. It's better left there, dead and buried with Nolan."

Her brother was right, of course. But sometimes she felt as if Nolan Reeves was reaching out from beyond the grave to influence her decisions. Deep inside her, the little girl who had lived in terror of her stepfather still existed. The little girl who had not known that her older brother had made a bargain with the devil in order to protect her. Nolan had punished Jack for every perceived misdeed by taking him to the old carriage shed and whipping him unmercifully. He had whipped the blood out of Maleah's legs and bottom only once. After that, although she lived in constant fear, he had never touched her again. What she hadn't realized at the time was that Jack had taken all her beatings for her.

She owed Jack more than she could ever repay. He had protected her as best he could and she would always be grateful. Jack's bargain with Nolan had saved her from more physical abuse, but not from Nolan's iron-fisted control over her life or his incessant verbal abuse.

Maleah had undergone therapy, paid for by Jack, when she'd been in college. The months of in-depth counseling had helped her immensely, enabling her to live a reasonably normal life. *Whatever normal is.* But nothing short of a lobotomy could erase the memories that still plagued her, often on a subconscious level.

"Damn you, Nolan Reeves. Damn your mean, black-hearted soul to hell."

Maleah's hands trembled. Her stomach lurched as emotions from her long-ago childhood resurfaced.

Don't do this to yourself.

Don't let your fears and uncertainties weaken you.

You have only one battle to fight, one enemy, one combatant that you have to outsmart and outmaneuver—Jerome Browning, not Derek Lawrence.

Checking her wristwatch, Maleah noted it was nearly eight o'clock. She had turned down Derek's invitation to join him for dinner that evening, but she couldn't avoid seeing him again tonight. They had made a deal—he would coach her on how to handle Browning and he wouldn't insist on accompanying her to the visitor's area at the prison.

She needed to freshen up and get her head on straight before Derek showed up at her door. He tended to be punctual, which meant she had less than ten minutes to throw cold water in her face, smear on a little lipstick and add some blush to her pale cheeks before he arrived.

Jerome usually spent the hours after dinner working on his handbook, a sort of *How to Get Away with Murder* manual. The idea had come to him nearly a year ago after he'd had a dream about the night he had been captured. In retrospect, he could see quite clearly the mistakes he had made. If he had it to do over again . . .

But there would be no second chances to get it right, only the opportunity to train others. He had no doubt that once he completed his work on the informative handbook, publishers would beat a path to his door. His book could make him even more famous than he already was. And how opportune that Maleah Perdue had come into his life today, just when he had begun plotting the chapter on manipulation.

The chapter heading would be: How to Use Others to Get What You Want.

And just what did he want from Maleah?

Jerome smiled.

Maleah was a delectable little morsel. She looked like nothing more than a sweet piece of blonde fluff. But looks could be deceiving. He knew that fact better than anyone. Hadn't he used his handsome face to his advantage all of his life? How many people had trusted him without question because of the way he looked? Poor fools. They never suspected that behind the pleasing façade, the mind of a genius existed, a mind capable of executing brilliantly complicated plans.

After being apprehended and charged with nine murders, hadn't he used his superior intelligence to avoid the death penalty? He had been in possession of a valuable commodity, one that both law enforcement and the families of six missing girls had been willing to bargain for on his terms. The whereabouts of those six teenage girls had been his ace in the hole. Not quite a get-out-of-jail-free card, but the next best thing.

He had been barely sixteen when he had killed Mary Jane Ivy, a meek little mouse of a girl who had lived down the street from him. He had never killed a person before that, although he had fantasized about it for years. During the next four years, he had killed five other girls. And he had gotten away with all six murders. No one suspected the good-looking high school jock, the boy voted most likely to succeed by his senior class. Not being found out had been almost as exhilarating as the kills themselves. Almost.

He had been locked up in this godforsaken hellhole for nine years now, with only occasional opportunities to participate in conversations that he found intellectually stimulating. A rare visitor from time to time. An intelligent, young minister certain he could save Jerome's soul. His former lawyer, who hadn't been in touch since his final appeal had been denied.

But tomorrow, Maleah would return for a second

visit, this time without her watchdog. He did not like the man with the dark eyes who had studied him as if he were a specimen under a microscope.

If he played this just right, he should be able to gain hours of pleasure from holding out a carrot stick in front of Maleah, letting her see it, smell it, lick it, even nibble a tiny bite.

Jerome laid his journal aside, fell back onto his cot and rested his hands behind his head. Closing his eyes, he visualized the way she would look tomorrow morning, all blond and golden and sweet. So very sweet.

"Ah, Maleah . . . Maleah . . ." He whispered her name. "Sweet Maleah."

The moment he tapped for the second time, Maleah swung open the door and much to his surprise actually smiled at him.

"Come on in." She waved her arm through the air, inviting him to enter.

He held out the plastic bag he had brought with him. She eyed the offering.

"Thin sliced turkey on wheat," he said. "Lettuce, tomato, and mustard only. No mayo. No onion." When she accepted his gift, he added, "A small bag of baked chips and an unsweetened tea, with several packets of Splenda."

He watched the play of emotions on her face and knew a part of her hated the fact that he remembered her likes and dislikes, that he knew she never used mayonnaise and ate only cooked onions. And she always preferred tea over cola, if tea was available.

She grabbed the sack. "Thanks. I appreciate your thinking of me, but I'm really not—"

"You've been skipping too many meals," he reminded her. "You need to eat."

He closed and locked the door behind him, then waited for her to blast him for daring to tell her what she should do.

But she surprised him again by taking the bag over to the desk, emptying the contents and saying, "You're right. I need to eat. And actually, I am hungry."

He eyed her suspiciously. It was on the tip of his tongue to ask her who she was and what she had done with the real Maleah Perdue.

"Sit," he told her. "Eat."

She pulled out a chair and sat; then she removed the paper wrapping from her sandwich and took a bite.

"I'll put on a pot of decaf coffee," Derek said. "Coffee will be good with our dessert."

She looked at the two small Styrofoam containers she had removed from the sack. "I usually don't eat dessert."

"It's Italian Cream cake."

Maleah moaned. "My favorite." She set aside the cake containers, tore the paper from the straw and inserted the straw through the hole in the lid of the iced tea cup.

Derek had observed Maleah on a daily basis while they had worked as partners on the Midnight Killer case and knew she struggled to maintain control over every aspect of her life. Being short and curvy, maintaining an ideal weight was a challenge for her. Under ordinary circumstances, he would never tempt her with a fattening dessert, but in an odd sort of way, tonight's meal paralleled the last meal served a person before they were executed the next day. In the morning, she would be walking into an arena to do battle against an opponent who would go for the jugular. He would do it subtly, hoping to take her unaware.

Derek rinsed out the coffeepot, poured in fresh bottled water, filled the reserve tank, and added the decaf provided by housekeeping. Once he set the machine to brew, he glanced at Maleah, who had a mouthful of the turkey sandwich in her mouth. He grinned.

"I spoke to Sanders this afternoon," Derek told her. "He wanted us to know that, by sometime tomorrow, they should have the names of everyone who has visited Browning and the dates of the visits."

Maleah swallowed, wiped her mouth on a paper napkin and said, "It's possible that our copycat killer and Browning exchanged letters and that Browning may have called him, but both the letters and the phone calls were probably monitored since he's a high-risk prisoner. Browning would have had to be very careful about what he said over the phone."

"Yes, he would have," Derek agreed. "My guess would be that if there has been any contact between the copycat and Browning, it started with a visit."

"I understand that my meeting with Browning in the hopes of bargaining with him for information is my top priority, but I don't want to be excluded from the investigation. I want to be part of every aspect of—"

"No one is going to exclude you."

"But if I'm at the prison every day—"

"Who said you'd be visiting Browning every day?"

"I just assumed—"

"You assumed wrong." Derek strode across the room, his gaze linked with hers as he approached. "You'll see him tomorrow, but after that, we will take it slow and easy. We want him playing this game by our rules, not the other way around."

"I understand." She nibbled on the sandwich.

Derek reached over, grasped the back of a chair by the windows and dragged it over to the table. After he sat, he picked up the bag of chips, opened it and offered it to her. She shook her head. He pulled out several chips and popped them into his mouth.

"When the time comes, I want to be the one who questions each of Browning's recent visitors," Maleah said.

"If we can locate them, and that's a big if, we will question them together, as partners. If the copycat visited Browning, I don't think he would have used his real name or given his current address, do you?"

"No, of course not, but the Powell Agency has a high success rate of tracking down people who do not want to be found."

"We're overlooking one other possibility—our copycat may not have visited Browning. He may not have ever been in contact with him."

"Then how could he possibly know so many details about Browning's murders, details that were never released to the press?"

"He could be in law enforcement."

Maleah frowned.

"Or he could have hired a PI or be a PI himself and found a way to dig up the info."

She shook her head. "I think Browning knows something."

"Browning wants you to believe he knows something."

After finishing off one half of her sandwich, she washed it down with the tea and dumped the rest in the wastebasket by the desk. She wiped her hands off on the napkin and tossed it, too.

"You're practically psychic when it comes to reading people." Maleah might not be Derek's biggest fan, but she respected his ability as a profiler and more recently as a detective. "Paint me a picture. In your opinion, does Browning have any personal connection to the copycat?"

"I'm intuitive, yes. Psychic, no. I leave all that paranormal stuff to Dr. Meng and her protégés."

"I'm surprised Griff didn't enlist Yvette or one of her protégés to interview Browning." Maleah eyed the cake container.

"I doubt Browning would have agreed to see anyone other than you. Griff knew the right person to send. Neither Griff nor I think it was a coincidence that the copycat chose to mimic the killer who murdered your former boyfriend. It's as if he chose you for a specific reason."

"Yeah, but the only problem is that we have no idea what that reason is."

"We can make some educated guesses."

"Such as?" she asked.

"Such as you're the copycat's ultimate target." When her face paled, Derek quickly added, "Or you were chosen because you're Nicole Powell's best friend. Or because the copycat is using your connection to Browning as a red herring to send us off on a wild goose chase."

"What's your intuition telling you?"

"The copycat and Browning have, at the very least, met and talked. I don't know if Browning is pulling the strings and the copycat is a disciple or if the copycat used Browning's knowledge for his own purposes."

"Neither Griff nor Nic were involved in Browning's capture and arrest, nor was I. Why would he be targeting the Powell Agency?"

"Excellent question. Griff has a theory, as does Nic. And I have several scenarios in mind, too, but we have absolutely nothing conclusive at this point."

"We need information from that son of bitch and he knows it." Maleah grabbed the cake container, flipped open the lid and eyed the cake hungrily. "He's going to want to bargain with me, to see what he can get out of me in exchange for what he knows."

Derek slid the other cake container over in front of him, then removed the cellophane wrap from two plastic forks and handed one fork to Maleah. She eyed the fork as if it were a snake and then grunted and snatched the fork out of his hand. He sliced his fork through the moist cake, balanced a bite on the fork and lifted it into the air, saluting her with the delicious morsel. She watched while he put the bite into his mouth.

"Just one piece of cake won't hurt you," he told her. "Think of the pleasure it'll give you. There's nothing quite like a sugar high to perk a girl up when she's down."

"I don't need a crutch of any kind. Not alcohol or drugs or gambling or shopping . . . or sugar!"

Without a moment's hesitation, she jabbed the fork into the cake and then shoved her piece of cake, container and all, across the table and into the wastebasket.

Stunned for half a second, Derek stared at her, then burst out laughing. My God, she had no idea that her biggest weakness, the crutch she relied on every day of her life, was being a major control freak.

When they returned from a moonlight stroll on the beach, they found a gift basket waiting for them outside their suite. Errol lifted the basket while Cyrene opened the attached card.

"It just says Happy Honeymoon." Eyeing the bottle of wine, the box of gourmet Swiss chocolates, the luscious in-season fruit and a sampling of imported cheeses,

Cyrene moaned with anticipation. "I can't think of anything better than a glass of wine before bedtime."

Hoisting the gift basket so that he could hold it with one hand, Errol reached out and unlocked the door to their suite. As his bride slipped past him, he whispered, "I can think of something better than wine."

Understanding the implication of his comment, she giggled and began undressing the moment he closed the door behind them and dumped the basket on the table in the entryway. Taking his cue from Cyrene, he unbuttoned his shirt and tossed it on the floor. By the time he loosened his belt, she had already stripped down to her panties.

He couldn't get out of his slacks and briefs quickly enough, but for a full sixty seconds, he stood and watched—totally spellbound—as his wife slowly, provocatively slid her bikini panties down, down, down, and off. His heart beat wildly. His penis hardened.

When he reached for Cyrene, she evaded his grasp. Instead, she raced over to the bed, the covers already turned down by maid service, and placed herself in the center. She arched her back, the action thrusting her breasts up and inviting him to touch and taste and enjoy. Errol kicked his briefs aside and moved toward the bed, never taking his eyes off the long, slender naked body of the woman he loved.

He straddled her hips and positioned himself over her. She lifted her arms up and around his neck, pulling him down until it was flesh against flesh. His penis probed for entry. She opened her thighs, lifted her hips and took him inside her body.

"Oh God, baby, you feel so good," he told her, his voice a husky moan.

"I love having you inside me," she said and then kissed him.

They made love for the fourth time that day and yet were as hungry for each other as they had been that morning. Errol wondered if he would ever get enough of Cyrene. Probably not. Even when they were old and gray, he would still want her, still love her, still be grateful that she had agreed to be his wife.

An hour later, shortly after midnight, they emerged from the bathroom where they had showered together. Errol belted his white robe and walked over to the entryway table while Cyrene slipped into a red lace teddy and sat on the edge of the bed to towel dry her curly hair.

He picked up the gift basket. "Want some wine now, Mrs. Patterson?"

"Wine would be lovely, Mr. Patterson." She glanced at the bedside clock. "We can toast to another glorious day of married life. It's after midnight, so if it's already tomorrow that means I've been Mrs. Errol Patterson for eleven days."

Errol removed the huge red bow and the clear cellophane wrapping from the gift basket, lifted the wine bottle and inspected it. "Hey, this is some of the good stuff. There's no twist-off cap." He chuckled.

"Only the best for us," she teased.

"I've got the best." He winked at her.

"Want me to get the glasses?"

"No need," he told her as he transferred the bottle to his left hand and retrieved the two long-stemmed wine glasses from the basket. "Want some chocolate or cheese or—?"

"I want it all," she admitted, "but I'll be a good girl and limit myself to one glass of wine."

He brought the bottle and glasses over to the bed. She took the glasses from him and held them while he rummaged in the nightstand drawer for the corkscrew that he had left there after opening the bottle of champagne the hotel had included in their "Welcome" package the day they arrived. After uncorking the wine, he poured each glass half full before placing the bottle on the nightstand.

He took one of the glasses from Cyrene. "Here's to our being this deliriously happy for the rest of our lives."

She clicked her glass to his, said, "Amen to that," and lifted the glass to her lips.

After he dimmed the lights, leaving the room bathed in moonlight, they sat in bed together, talking, laughing, sipping the wine, and making plans for their return to Tennessee. He knew that Cyrene was eager to decorate their new house in Farragut, a small town not far from Powell Agency headquarters in Knoxville. They discussed how lucky she was that there had been a teaching position open at a local elementary school. With school starting in early August, she would have about five weeks to put their new house in order.

Errol yawned. "Man, I'm getting sleepy. Must be the mixture of great sex and good wine." He removed the white terrycloth robe and flung it to the foot of the bed.

Cyrene sighed and nodded. "Must be. I can barely keep my eyes open."

Errol switched off the bedside lamp and then leaned over, kissed her, ran his hand from her shoulder to her hip and stilled instantly. The last thing Cyrene remembered was the sound of her husband snoring.

He had waited patiently. The lights in the luxury villa suite had dimmed over an hour ago, but he hadn't rushed in immediately. The odds were that Mr. and Mrs. Patterson had been sound asleep for most if not all of that hour, while he had been waiting and watching. But it was better to be certain.

Errol Patterson never left his wife's side. The two had been inseparable since they arrived in the Bahamas. He really didn't want to kill them both. Doing so would have meant deviating from the plan. The Carver had never murdered a couple.

His solution to that problem had been to send them a gift basket that included a bottle of expensive "doctored" wine.

He approached the French doors that opened onto the villa's private patio and pool. He stopped, listened, and peered through the doors into the darkened bedroom. Moonlight cast a glimmering path across the floor to the bed. After removing the small, carbide steel-bladed glass cutter from his inside pocket, he worked several minutes to make a precise round incision near the door handle. Once that was done, he pushed gently on the circle until it fell inward and hit the tile floor with a tinkling crash. He returned the cutter to his pocket. Without hesitation, he reached through the opening and unlocked the door from the inside.

He eased open the door, slipped into the room and managed to avoid stepping on the broken glass. Pausing to allow his eyesight to adjust to the darkness, he heard a mixture of sounds. Snoring. Deep breathing. The ocean waves hitting the nearby beach. The hum of distant music, no doubt coming from the resort's patio lounge that stayed open until 2:00 AM.

He walked over to the bed. Two bodies. One male. One female. Both deep in sleep. Sufficiently drugged.

He smiled.

The sheet rested at the woman's waist. Her breasts

strained against the sheer lace material of her teddy. He was tempted to touch her, but he didn't.

The kill would take only seconds, the death less than two minutes. But moving the body would require more time.

He reached inside his jacket pocket and removed the new scalpel, the fifth in a package of ten. Drawing closer to the edge of the bed, he studied the man's head and neck before choosing the exact spot—the jugular vein. With one quick, precise move, he jabbed the scalpel blade through the flesh and into the vein beneath. Blood gushed. He slid the blade down and across, slicing through the carotid arteries on both sides. He watched the life drain out of Errol Patterson's body.

I'm sorry to make you a widow while you're still on your honeymoon, lovely Cyrene. And I'm sorry that you'll awaken to a bloody bed and a dead husband.

Errol Patterson was a rather large man, probably six feet tall and weighing in at around one-ninety. But he could handle Patterson. He had maneuvered larger bodies.

He flipped back the bloody sheet, took hold of Patterson's ankles and dragged him off the bed and onto the floor. As his body hit the hard tile, it made a loud thud. He glanced up at the sleeping woman. She hadn't moved. Good.

He pulled Patterson's blood-splattered, lifeless body from the bedroom and into the bathroom. Then he turned on the tub faucets.

I never left them where I killed them. I moved the body, usually near a river or lake or stream. I even dragged a woman from her bedroom outside to her pool. There is something peaceful about water, don't you think?

Near the bathtub overrunning with water would have to do. He saw no point in dragging the body outside to the pool and certainly not all the way to the beach. No need to risk being seen.

Chapter 8

Cyrene woke with the worst headache of her life. She came to slowly, painfully, her eyelids flicking. Moaning as she stretched her neck, she tried to focus on the mundane task of keeping her eyes open. When she parted her lips, she realized that her tongue was stuck to the roof of her mouth and her throat felt parched. She remembered drinking a glass of wine with Errol last night after they had made love and showered together. Surely, she hadn't gotten drunk on a single glass. Had she drunk more than she thought she had?

"Errol . . ." She forced her eyes wide open, stared up at the unmoving ceiling fan and spread her arm across the bed, searching for her husband.

Dim early morning sunlight reflecting off the patio pool danced in waving patterns on the ceiling.

Ah, another day in paradise.

She ran her fingertips across the sheet and found that she was alone in the bed. Apparently Errol was already awake and had gotten up. He was probably in the bathroom. She could hear running water, but it didn't sound like the shower. Flipping over toward the side of the bed, she stretched her arms over her head, extended her legs and curved her feet backwards. When she rose from the bed, her bare feet encountered the cool tile floor.

Where are my house slippers?

Cyrene rounded the foot of the bed, intending to surprise Errol in the bathroom, but as she passed by his side of the bed, she caught a glimpse of something red on the sheets.

What in the world?

They hadn't spilled any wine in the bed, had they?

She moved closer, getting a better look at the dark red stains on the snowy white sheets.

How odd. It looks like blood.

Instinct kicked in, a primeval sixth sense that warned of danger.

"Errol?" She backed away from the bed. "Errol . . . Errol . . ."

Flooded with a barrage of frightening thoughts, Cyrene shook her head in denial, refusing to believe, trying to convince herself that nothing was wrong.

"Errol, where are you?" Silence. "Please, honey, answer me."

Silence.

As if her limbs were activated by some sort of remote control, her legs and feet moved, carrying her toward the bathroom. Gazing down as she walked, she noticed a smear of dried red liquid stretching from the bed to the bathroom.

Suddenly she went numb, unable to feel her hands and feet. The thunderous roar of her heartbeat threatened to deafen her. This wasn't real. It wasn't happening.

Standing in the bathroom door, she stared at the body lying on the floor beside the bathtub overflowing with water.

Errol? Oh my God, Errol.

His eyes were closed.

A thin red line marred the perfection of his smooth, clean-shaven neck and rivulets of dried blood descended from that red line like trinkets on a charm bracelet.

Cyrene stood perfectly still, her mind unable to process what she saw.

And then, in the quiet stillness of her honeymoon suite, Mrs. Errol Patterson screamed. And screamed. And screamed.

Maleah squared her shoulders and took a deep breath before entering the prison's visitation area. She didn't look back at Derek nor did she glance at the guard escorting her. After showering and dressing—khaki slacks and dark green tailored blouse—she had met Derek downstairs for breakfast. She had managed to down a cup of coffee and eat a few bites of blueberry muffin, hoping to quiet the tempest in her belly. Although she had done her best to assure her partner that she was not nervous and was ready for today's meeting with Jerome Browning, she sensed that he knew she was simply putting up a good front. And that she was doing it as much for herself as for him.

If you can act as if you are self-assured and confident, then you've already won half the battle.

She remained standing as she waited for the guards to bring Browning from his cell. Thinking about what she was going to say and wondering how he would respond, she heard rather than saw Browning enter the visitation area. When she looked directly at him, he stared back at her, that weirdly pleasant and completely unnerving smile growing wider and wider as he drew closer.

The guards instructed him to sit. He sat.

"Good morning, Maleah. I hope you had a pleasant night. I certainly did." He licked his lips. "I dreamed about you and woke this morning eager to see you again."

Is that the best you've got? she wanted to say. *A little sexual innuendo isn't going to unnerve me in the least. Not when you're in shackles and there are three armed guards in the room with us.*

"I slept quite well, thank you," she lied to him. "A restful, dreamless sleep."

"I assume Mr. Lawrence also slept well. Any man sharing your bed would sleep well after . . ." He didn't finish the sentence, but the implication was obvious.

Was he fishing to find out if she and Derek were lovers? Or was he merely hoping the comment would insult her? Either way, she had no intention of responding.

"We have an hour," Maleah said as she sat across from Browning. "I think we've wasted enough time on meaningless, uninteresting chit-chat."

"Is your love life meaningless and uninteresting?" His smile never wavered.

"Do you know why I'm here, Jerome? Why I'm wasting my valuable time even talking to someone like you?"

"Someone like me?" He laughed. "Someone handsome and brilliant and gifted. And if I may be so immodest, someone who has been told that he is a superlative lover."

Egotistical, maniacal, psychopathic monster! "You are someone who has murdered fifteen people." She

paused before adding, "That we know of. You are someone who will spend the rest of his life slowly rotting
away in prison."

He lifted his bound hands, gesturing toward his
heart. "You wound me with such harsh words." His
smile turned quickly to a frown, his expression one of
mock sadness.

"Do you know why I'm here?" She repeated her initial question.

"All work and no play makes Maleah a dull girl."

"You know why I'm here and what I want."

He stretched as languidly as his restrained body
could and glanced from the guard on his right to the
guard on his left, both men standing several feet behind him. "What am I going to do with such a dull, dull
visitor, gentlemen? All she wants to do is talk business."

Maleah eased back from the edge of the seat and
crossed her arms. "The warden has granted us an hour
today, Jerome. But if you're not in the mood to talk
about what I want to talk about . . ." She uncrossed her
arms, glanced at her wristwatch, tapped the glass face
and said, "Five minutes. That's as long as I'll wait for
you to tell me something that interests me."

Browning remained silent for four minutes. The silence in the large, nearly empty room echoed with the
sound of their quiet breathing. One guard cleared his
throat. Another coughed a couple of times.

"You're here because you think I might know who
has mimicked my unique modus operandi almost perfectly and has recently killed four people."

Finally.

"And do you know who he is?" she asked.

As if believing he now had the upper hand for the
time being, he smiled and shrugged.

"All right," she said. "You tell me what you want in exchange for answering my question."

"Ah, Maleah, my sweet beauty, you're very bright. You catch on quickly. Games are so much fun, don't you think?"

"You're wasting time," she told him.

"All right. I'll cut straight to the chase." He chuckled. "I want to know what color panties you're wearing."

Good God! Without blinking an eye, she said, "Beige. With lace trim."

He closed his eyes, licked his lips as if savoring a delicious morsel and sighed with a sickening sound of satisfaction.

"I assume the copycat killer is an admirer," Jerome said. "I assume he has studied my work. Perhaps, he's even communicated with me."

"Has he?"

"That's another question that requires payment."

Damn you, Browning.

"You haven't answered the first question yet. Not to my satisfaction." She looked him in the eye.

"I don't know who the copycat killer is," he said, and then hurriedly added, "Not exactly, but . . ."

"But what?"

"There are things I do know. Things that can help you find him."

"Why should I believe you?"

He grinned.

"Even if you answer every question I ask, how would I know whether or not you were lying to me?" she asked.

"You'd have to take me on faith. But if you do that, I can promise you that in time, you'll discover everything I tell you is true."

"Okay, let's say I take you on faith. But first, you'll

have to give me something right now, something to prove to me that I can believe you."

"He's going to kill again soon, if he hasn't already."

She snorted. "That's it? Sorry, Jerome, but you're going to have to do better than that."

"I'll tell you something about the next person he's going to kill, if you'll tell me something I'd love to know."

"My bra matches my panties," she said glibly.

"That information paints such an erotic picture in my mind," he told her. "But that wasn't my question."

"Then what is it?"

As nonchalantly as if he were asking her about her favorite flavor of ice cream, he asked, "Was he your first?"

She stared at him, puzzled by his question.

"Noah Laborde," Browning said. "Was he your first lover?"

She should have been prepared for this, but she wasn't. Damn it. She wasn't.

"You do remember Noah, don't you? Good-looking young man, fresh out of college. Quite an up-and-comer in the Atlanta business world about twelve years ago."

Get hold of yourself, Maleah. He's trying to rattle you. Don't let him get away with it. Show him what you're made of.

"Yes," she said.

"Yes, what?"

"Yes, I remember Noah Laborde. And yes, he was my first lover."

Browning smiled as if he thought he had won a great victory. He hadn't. But she had. He just didn't know it yet.

"He's going to begin varying the sex of his victims.

You won't know from one kill to the next if he will choose a man or a woman."

"We learned that from your files, so we assumed if he followed your lead, he wouldn't stick with two female kills followed by two males."

"Looks like you're a step ahead of me."

"Tell me something else, something I don't already know."

"Why should I? It's not my fault that I told you something you already knew."

"Ah, come on, Jerome. Fair's fair."

"You surprise me."

"Do I?"

"I believe I may have underestimated you, sweet Maleah."

"If you have, you wouldn't be the first." She stood up and glared down at him. "Pay your debt. Give me some information that I can use. If not, when I walk out of here today, I won't be back."

"You could be bluffing."

"Only one way to find out—call my bluff."

She turned around and walked toward the exit door, her escort following. Just as he unlocked the door and opened it, Browning called out to her.

"You'll be back. You won't be able to stay away."

She paused for half a second and then started through the door.

"The next victim won't be brown-eyed," he told her.

She kept walking without responding in any way. Keeping in step with her guard escort, she followed him back to the warden's office where Derek was waiting.

Derek took one look at her and knew the session with Browning had rattled her. But he also knew that she was okay. He could see the steely determination in her eyes and the stiffness in her spine. Whatever had transpired between her and Jerome, she had come through the battle with nothing more than a minor flesh wound.

She acknowledged his presence with a glance, then marched straight to the warden. "I won't be back tomorrow."

"Then you're finished with—?" the warden said.

"No, I'm not finished with Mr. Browning. Not by a long shot. But he needs to think that I am."

Warden Holland nodded. "I will need twenty-four hours' notice before your next visit."

She shook his hand, said thanks, and motioned to Derek that she was ready to leave. He tried to talk to her, but she told him flat out that she was in no mood for conversation.

"Not now. We can talk on the way back to Vidalia."

And so he waited, giving her the time she needed to decompress after game playing with a cunning madman.

When they reached the designated parking area, she said, "You drive." And then she tossed him her keys. He grabbed the keys mid-air, remotely unlocked the SUV and, gentleman that he was, opened the passenger door for her.

And then he waited until they were several miles from the penitentiary before he said, "The warden is going to have a list of all of Browning's visitors for the past year, along with the names and addresses of the people who have written to him and the names and phone numbers of the people he's called compiled and sent to me and to Powell headquarters as an e-mail attachment. He's promised we'll have the information by the end of the day."

"Great. We've finally got something to work with, don't we?"

"Yep." When she didn't continue their conversation, he asked, "Are you all right?"

"Yes, why wouldn't I be?"

"We'll have to talk about your interview with Browning. I'll need to know what he said, everything you can remember."

Maleah adjusted her seat so that she could lean further back. She rested her head on the cushioned leather and folded her hands together in her lap.

"He asked what color my panties were and I told him beige with lace trim and that I was wearing a matching bra."

"Son of a bitch." Derek growled the comment under his breath.

"He still didn't give me the copycat killer's name or a description of him. But he did say that he knew things about this guy that could help us find him."

"Did you believe him?"

"I didn't disbelieve him."

"He's playing you. He may not know a damn thing."

"He said if the copycat follows the Carver's MO, he'll alter the sex of his victims pretty much willy-nilly."

"Something we already knew."

"We didn't know that his next victim wouldn't have brown eyes."

"What?"

"He called out to me just as I was leaving. He said the next victim wouldn't be brown-eyed."

"How could he possibly know that?" Derek suspected that Browning wouldn't say something like that off the top of his head. If he wanted Maleah to come back to see him, he would try to impress her with his knowledge.

"I have no idea, but maybe we should check and see what color the first four victims' eyes were. Maybe there's a pattern."

"We'll contact the agency—"

Derek's phone rang. No music. Just a strong, routine ring tone.

With one hand on the wheel and his eyes fixed on the road ahead, he pulled the phone from his pocket, hit the On button and said, "Derek Lawrence speaking," without checking caller ID.

"I want you and Maleah at the Vidalia Municipal Airport as soon as you can get there," Griff Powell said. "There's a charter plane waiting to fly y'all to Atlanta. Nic and I will be taking off in the Powell jet within the next thirty minutes. We'll pick y'all up in Atlanta. We're flying from there straight to Nassau. The copycat struck again last night. He killed Errol Patterson. Errol's wife found his body in the bathroom of their hotel suite. She's under a doctor's care at the moment and heavily sedated. She's going to need all the help we can give her."

"We'll pick up our bags at the hotel and drive straight to the airport."

Succinct and to the point. Conversation ended.

"What's happened?" Maleah asked.

"The copycat killed Errol Patterson last night and his wife . . . his new bride . . . found his body this morning."

Chapter 9

Derek and Maleah boarded the Powell private jet in Atlanta. Nic met them the moment they arrived, but Griff was nowhere to be seen.

"He's in the bedroom making phone calls," Nic explained. "He's double checking with Barbara Jean about the arrangements for Cyrene's sister to fly in to Nassau as soon as possible. From what we understand, Cyrene is in no condition to return home alone and we felt it best for a family member to be with her."

Maleah had known Errol for several years, but only in a professional capacity. They had never worked a case together and she had probably seen him, at most, a dozen times. And she had never met his wife. With more than fifty agents employed by Powell's, some had never met and many knew one another only in passing. Agents were chosen for cases by their specific qualifications for the job and by their availability. Only when partnered with another agent or when pulling duty at Griffin's Rest together did the agents get a chance to form friendships.

It was not a surprise that when Nic introduced them

to Brendan Richter, the agent who had accompanied Griff and Nic, Maleah drew a blank. She had no memory of ever meeting the somber, auburn-haired Powell agent.

"Good to see you again, Richter," Derek said as he shook hands with the spit-and-polished man who looked as if he should be in uniform.

Maleah wondered if he had come straight out of the military.

"Likewise, Mr. Lawrence," Richter replied with a slight, almost indiscernible accent.

To Maleah's ear, the accent sounded German.

"That's right, you two know each other," Nic said. "Brendan is accompanying us to Nassau. He will be staying and overseeing Powell Agency concerns connected to Errol's murder."

"How long have you worked for our agency, Mr. Richter?" Maleah asked. She also wanted to ask how he and Derek knew each other, but she didn't.

When Richter looked at Maleah, his cold blue eyes inspected her with aloof detachment. "Six months."

He had answered her question without giving her any other information. "Are you retired military?"

"No, Ms. Perdue, I am not."

Seeing no point in continuing this line of conversation, she turned to Nic. "How much information do we have about Errol Patterson's murder?"

"Nothing really, except that he's dead and that his wife found him in the bathroom of their hotel suite. So far, Griff hasn't been able to find out anything else, no details."

"Then we don't know for sure that his throat was slit or that his body was mutilated?" Maleah asked.

"No, we don't know for sure, but Griff is convinced

that the Copycat Carver has struck again." Nic glanced at Derek. "What do you think?"

"I think Griff is probably right."

Maleah's mind whirled with various thoughts, combining information and mixing it until an idea hit. Suddenly, she said, "I know this is going to sound like a really stupid thing to say, but—Errol was African American, but he had green eyes, didn't he?"

Everyone stared at her. Her comment didn't make sense to anyone except Derek.

"Is there some significance to the fact that Errol was green-eyed?" Nic asked.

"Jerome Browning told me that the copycat's next victim would not be brown-eyed."

"Perhaps it was only a lucky guess," Richter said. "Or perhaps Mr. Browning chose his victims by eye color, eliminating those who had brown eyes, and he assumes the copycat killer will follow his lead. Do we know the eye color for the first four victims?"

"Shelley had blue eyes," Maleah said. "And so did Kristi."

"I don't know about Holt's brother or Ben's father," Nic said. "But I can find out."

"How would the copycat have acquired such a seemingly unimportant piece of information about the original Carver's victims?" Richter asked.

"Two ways," Derek told them. "Either he has access to police records or Jerome Browning told him."

"Neither Norris Keinan nor Winston Corbett were brown-eyed," Griff said from where he stood in the open doorway to the bedroom suite. "I had met both men in the past."

Everyone stared straight at Griffin Powell, his huge frame filling the doorway.

"My guess is that none of Jerome Browning's victims were brown-eyed." Griff came over, sat down beside Nic, and looked at Maleah.

"So the information he gave me is useless." Maleah wanted to hit something or someone, preferably Jerome Browning.

"Not entirely useless," Griff said. "If the copycat follows suit in this one area, then no brown-eyed Powell agents or brown-eyed family members are at risk. That means Nic is not in danger, nor are you and Derek." He glanced at Richter. "On the other hand, you and I, Brendan, are possible victims."

Before the conversation could continue, the pilot informed Griff that they were ready for take-off. Richter immediately moved toward the front of the cabin and isolated himself from the others. Maleah watched him pick up a leather briefcase beside the plush seat and place it in his lap before buckling his seatbelt.

While Nic and Griff put their heads together in a private conversation during take-off, Derek took the seat next to Maleah, but didn't say anything until they were airborne.

"Some of the information you'll get out of Browning will be useless, some only marginally helpful and some could even be misleading. But you never know when he'll let something slip and actually give us a diamond mixed in with all the rocks and pebbles he'll be tossing out."

"You're assuming that I'll actually go back to see him."

"You'll go back and you'll play his game."

"Think so, do you?"

"Know so."

"And if you were a betting man, who would you lay odds on to win, Browning or me?"

She held her breath, waiting for Derek's response. He looked at her and grinned. "I'd put my money on you, Blondie."

Maleah exhaled. She didn't know if she should believe him. He could have told her what he knew she wanted to hear, what she needed to hear in order to work up the courage to face Browning again.

"He mentioned Noah Laborde," Maleah said.

"Bastard." Derek murmured the word under his breath. "He didn't waste any time, did he? He was testing you. You know that, don't you?"

"Yes, of course, I know."

"How did you react when he asked about Laborde and how quickly did you recover?"

"You assume that I—"

"I know you. If he took you off guard, and I assume he did, then you reacted, even if only for a second."

"Okay, so I reacted," she admitted. "He might have seen me flinch, but that's all."

"He'll try to use Laborde again. I wouldn't put it past him to share the gory details of the kill. If he does, can you take it?"

Could she? Would she be able to listen to Browning describe how he had killed Noah without running from the room in tears or physically attacking the SOB?

"I don't know."

"You'd better know," Derek said. "You'd better be prepared. Once he's done his worst with it, he'll move on, so all you have to do is hold your own against him and survive the attack."

"I'm wondering if it's worthwhile to play his sick little game. Do you honestly think that Browning is going to help us?"

"Not willingly. Not without getting something out of it and since there are no more deals to be made through legal channels, we both know that what he wants is the pleasure of tormenting you."

"Lucky me."

Derek laid his hand over hers where she clutched the padded armrest. Her first impulse was to pull away, but she didn't. If she intended to continue interviewing Browning and survive the assignment, she would need Derek Lawrence.

There, she had admitted it. She couldn't do this alone.

Maleah flipped her hand over, grasped Derek's hand and squeezed. "Just don't go all macho-protective on me. I'm not some helpless female who—"

Derek chuckled. "Blondie, you are the least helpless female I know." He released her hand.

"And don't you forget it. And don't think that this changes anything between us or that we're going to wind up being friends. We're co-workers and partners on this case. That's all."

"Ah, shucks, Miss Maleah, I thought for sure that you and me would wind up getting hitched."

How he kept a straight face, she'd never know. But he did. She stared at him. Then, unable to stop herself, she smiled. "All right. I get your point. I made a big to-do over nothing."

He nodded.

Feeling somewhat relaxed, in large part to Derek, she glanced around the cabin. Griff draped his arm around Nic as she rested her head on his shoulder. Were they thinking about Errol and Cyrene Patterson and how less than twenty-four hours ago, the newlyweds were enjoying their honeymoon? Were they thinking about how life can turn on a dime, that you can be bliss-fully happy one moment and dragged down into the misery of hell the next?

Brendan Richter seemed totally absorbed in whatever he was doing on the laptop he had removed from the leather case.

Noting her interest in the new Powell agent, Derek said in a low, quiet voice, "Richter was with the Criminal Investigative Division of Interpol. We worked together when I was with the Bureau."

What an interesting coincidence that he should be leaving the Grand Resort just as the Powell entourage arrived. Although he had never met the famous Griffin Powell, he knew a great deal about him. Others might see him as strong and powerful, practically invincible. But they were wrong. Powell allowed his conscience to weaken him. He was a man on a mission to do good. He was loyal to his friends and benevolent to his employees. And he loved his wife. Loyalty was a weakness, as was kindness. But love was the greatest weakness of all.

They didn't notice him as they passed him in the lobby, Powell and his beautiful wife Nicole, along with Derek Lawrence, Maleah Perdue, and Brendan Richter. But then there was no reason for any of them to recognize him. He appeared to be nothing more than another tourist, an invisible man no one was likely to remember.

Richter and Lawrence were former law enforcement heavy hitters, but oddly enough, out of the three agents, Ms. Perdue possessed the most power at the moment. Ordinarily, she was a lightweight, a political science major with a desire to right wrongs, defend the underdog, and help the helpless. Using her connection to the Carver had been a stroke of genius, even though he couldn't take credit for the idea himself.

Without a backward glance, he waited outside for

the bellboy to load his suitcase into the hotel's van. He had a nonstop 3:00 P.M. flight to Atlanta.

Once seated inside the air-conditioned luxury van, he avoided direct eye contact with the other occupants.

"I can't get away from this place fast enough," the skinny, gray-haired woman sitting across from him said.

If she was talking to him, he would ignore her.

"I heard that the poor man was butchered like a pig," another woman replied. "They say there was blood everywhere."

"His wife probably killed him," someone else said. "It's usually the spouse."

"One of the maids told me that the wife had to be sedated and is under a doctor's care."

"She's probably crazy. Anyone who could cut a man to pieces that way . . ."

He settled into his seat, closed his eyes and mentally escaped from the chattering magpies. Since he had gotten no sleep last night, he would probably sleep on the plane. Once he arrived in Atlanta, he would make one phone call from the airport.

In the morning, he would rent a car and drive to Savannah, where the Copycat Carver's next victim lived.

Griff had called Derek's room and asked that he and Maleah join them for dinner in his suite that evening.

"Nic needs Maleah," Griff had said. "You know, another woman to talk to about things. Seeing Errol's wife . . . his widow . . . was difficult for Nic."

"When are you expecting her sister to arrive?"

"Tonight. I've arranged for a doctor to fly in with her and to accompany Cyrene back to the States."

When they arrived at the Powell suite, Derek could tell that Nic was still visibly shaken after seeing Cyrene

Patterson. Even though she had freshened up and changed clothes, she still looked shell-shocked.

Nicole Baxter Powell was a strong woman who had excelled in her position as a special agent for the FBI. She was definitely all woman, but she didn't have a silly, frivolous, or clinging bone in her body, like so many women he knew. But Nic had a kind heart. She genuinely cared about other people.

Derek lingered in the foyer with Griff, while Maleah and Nic went into the living room and exchanged hugs before sitting down on the sofa.

"I've arranged for you and Maleah to go with Richter in the morning for a meeting with the Chief Inspector and the inspector assigned to the Patterson case," Griff said. "I don't think you'll have a problem getting whatever information you want."

Derek nodded. "That's good. Once we know the particulars of Errol's murder, we'll be able to compare them to the details of the other four murders."

"I'm taking Nic home tomorrow. I didn't want her to accompany me on this trip, but she insisted. Why she has to be so damn stubborn . . ." Griff cleared his throat. "She thinks she has to be in the thick of things, getting emotionally involved and putting herself out there in harm's way."

"You know you wouldn't change her if you could."

"Damn right, I wouldn't." Griff glanced into the living room at the two women sitting side by side, deep in conversation. "Like I said, I'm taking Nic home tomorrow. But I want you and Maleah to stay here a couple of days and find out everything you can."

"Sure thing."

"Richter will be staying on for at least another week or two, keeping tabs on the police investigation and doing some independent investigating. Holt volunteered to go to Cullman to follow up on things there with Winston Corbett's murder. I think he, of all people, can persuade Ben not to try to do any investigating on his own."

"Agreed. And I think once Maleah and I finish up here, we should return to Georgia," Derek said.

"You think Browning really knows something about these copycat murders?"

"He knows something, but my gut tells me he doesn't know as much as he's pretending he does. Maleah's willing to play his cat and mouse game on the off chance he actually does know something and will willingly or inadvertently share it with us."

Griff moved closer to Derek and lowered his voice. "I plan to send Luke Sentell to London. He'll be traveling wherever the rumors take him, on to France and Switzerland and Italy."

"You haven't told Nic, have you?"

"No, not yet. She thinks I'm obsessed with the notion that I'm the killer's real target and this killing spree is somehow connected to my past . . . to Malcolm York."

"Is she right?"

Griff didn't respond immediately and then before he could reply, Nic called to them. "What are you two talking about in there?"

"I was filling Griff in on Jerome Browning," Derek lied as he entered the living room area of the suite.

"What a coincidence," Maleah said. "I was doing the same thing—filling Nic in on my visit with Browning."

"I ordered dinner half an hour ago," Nic said. "It should be here in the next few minutes."

"Anyone care for a drink?" Griff asked as he headed toward the bar area.

The room telephone rang. Griff paused and stared at the phone. Nic and Maleah stopped talking.

"It's probably room service calling about our dinner order," Maleah said.

When she stood, obviously intending to answer the phone, Griff told her he'd get it. He picked up the receiver and said, "Yes, this is Mr. Powell."

Whatever the person on the other end of the line said, Griff did not reply. Without uttering a word, he replaced the receiver.

"Who was it?" Nic asked.

Griff looked at her.

Derek suspected bad news of some sort.

"Griff?" Nic prompted.

"I don't know who it was, but the voice sounded male."

"What did he say?" Nic rushed to Griff's side.

Reluctantly, as if he considered lying to his wife, Griff finally replied, "He said 'If I don't decide to kill her first, your wife will make a lovely widow.'"

Chapter 10

The Assistant Superintendent, the Chief Inspector, and Inspector Yates Thompson, who was in charge of the Patterson murder case, met with Derek, Maleah, and Brendan Richter. Derek seriously doubted that even the inspector would have agreed to this meeting if not for Griffin Powell's considerable influence. How Griff went about getting what he wanted, Derek never asked, but he had a pretty good idea that his boss used whatever means necessary to achieve his desired goal.

After personally assuring them that everything humanly possible would be done to find the person who had killed Errol, the Assistant Superintendent shook their hands again, as did the Chief Inspector. Pretty much as he had thought, these two men had been commanded to put in an appearance, an order no doubt issued by the Commissioner of Police himself. But it was unlikely that they were expected to do more than that—show up, talk the talk, make assurances and appease the Powell agents.

"Inspector Thompson will answer any questions you have," the Chief Inspector said. "He will cooperate with you in any way possible and will keep you updated on the investigation."

Once his superiors departed, the tall, rawboned, ebony-skinned Thompson invited them to sit, which they did. But he remained standing.

"My orders are to cooperate with you," Thompson said. "And naturally, I will follow the Chief Inspector's orders, although I am unaccustomed to civilians involving themselves in police business."

"We understand," Richter said. "But Errol Patterson's murder is no ordinary murder case."

"So I have been told." Thompson glanced from Richter to Derek and then his gaze settled on Maleah. "You were Mr. Patterson's friends, yes?"

"Errol Patterson worked as an agent for the Powell Security and Investigation Agency, just as we do," Maleah replied.

Thompson nodded. "I understand other Powell agents have also been murdered in the past few months."

"Before Mr. Patterson was killed, yes, there were four others connected to our agency. We suspect all four deaths were the work of a serial killer," Derek said.

"One victim was an agent, one a secretary, one the brother of an agent, and the fourth the father of an agent," Richter told the inspector.

Thompson nodded again. "And these four people were murdered in a similar manner and you suspect the same killer in all three?"

"That's right," Richter replied, a note of aggravation in his voice.

Thompson tapped a file folder lying on his desk. "Mr. Patterson died almost instantly. His jugular was punctured, his trachea severed and his carotid arteries slashed." He paused, as if waiting for one of them to say something. When they didn't, he continued. "His wife found his body in the bathroom next to the tub which was filled to overflowing."

Derek and Maleah looked at each other, but said nothing.

"Were the others killed in a similar fashion?" Thompson asked.

"They were," Richter said. "Was there anything else, anything unusual about the body?"

Thompson's lips curved downward in a contemplative frown. "I assume you are referring to the triangular pieces of flesh cut from the victim's upper arms and thighs."

Yes, that was exactly what Richter had been referring to, that final piece of information that irrefutably linked Patterson's murder to the other four.

"Yes," Derek and Richter answered simultaneously.

"An autopsy will be performed," the inspector said. "And a toxicology screening has been ordered. Mr. Patterson was a large man in his prime, a security agent trained to protect himself and others, so how was it possible for someone to overpower him? And why did his wife sleep soundly while her husband was being murdered?"

"They were both drugged." Richter stated the obvious.

"We suspect so, yes."

Derek's opinion of Inspector Thompson as an investigator rose by several degrees.

"In the other four murders, the killer left behind no evidence that could help identify him or enable the police to track him," Derek said. "Is that true in this case?"

Thompson grunted. "Unfortunately, yes." He looked directly at Derek. "That is the sign of a true professional, is it not, Mr. Lawrence."

Thompson had done his homework, no doubt running a check on the three of them, which meant he knew that Derek was a former FBI profiler.

"Professional in the sense that he was no amateur," Derek said. "He is a skilled killer, which tells us that he's killed before, perhaps numerous times."

The thought that the copycat could be a gun-for-hire had crossed his mind, but that possibility was only one of several scenarios that he had considered. Until he had more evidence to back up any one theory, he had no intention of suggesting to Griff that the man they were hunting could be a professional assassin.

As if understanding Derek's assessment of the situation, Thompson simply nodded before inquiring, "Is there anything else you would like to know?"

"I think Ms. Perdue and I have what we need," Derek said.

"And you, Mr. Richter?"

"I would like to speak to the first responders on the scene," Richter said. "As well as any witnesses your people interviewed. I'll need copies of all the reports, photographs, and preliminary findings."

"Yes, of course."

"Mr. Lawrence and Ms. Perdue will be leaving Nassau tomorrow, but I will be staying on for several weeks, as the Powell Agency representative."

Inspector Thompson barely managed to hide his negative reaction. He quickly turned his frown into a forced smile as he shook hands with each of them.

"I wish you both a safe flight tomorrow." And then his dark gaze settled on Richter, each man sizing up the other. "I have the greatest respect for you, as a former ICPO agent, Mr. Richter. I suspect I may be able to learn a great deal from you."

Yes, Inspector Thompson had done his homework. Derek didn't doubt that the man probably knew what he, Richter, and Maleah had each eaten for breakfast that morning.

Nic knew her husband well enough to understand that he was not concerned about his own life, but was greatly concerned about her welfare as well as the lives of everyone associated with the Powell Agency. He was a man who took his responsibilities seriously. His primitive protective instincts made him a dangerous opponent when those he cared about were in danger, but those same instincts were his personal Achilles' heel, his only weakness. Griffin Powell's ability to love equaled if not surpassed the passion with which he hated. She admired his ability to stay calm under pressure, a trait she tried to emulate. But beneath that cool, controlled exterior, a violent rage smoldered just below the surface.

And it was that rage inside Griff that worried her.

They had calmly discussed the untraceable phone call he had received at the Nassau resort. She had struggled to match his restrained composure when faced with a threat against both of them.

If I don't decide to kill her first, your wife will make a lovely widow.

"He's taunting me," Griff had said. "He wants me to know that all roads lead to Rome, that every murder is leading him closer to me."

"Maybe he just wants you to think that. Maybe he's trying to steer us in the wrong direction."

"Maybe, but unlikely."

Nic still wasn't totally convinced that Griff was the ultimate target, that the copycat killings were connected to his past, to a dead man named York. Admittedly, that possibility frightened her far more than any other. Was that why she clung so doggedly to other theories?

At his request, she joined Griff in the agency's home office, an area inside their house that had been designed to allow Griff to oversee his vast empire without ever leaving Griffin's Rest. The Powell Building, located in downtown Knoxville, housed the inner workings of the agency, as well as the staff for the numerous Powell philanthropic endeavors. Each year, the Powell Empire required more and more employees, which meant that at the present time, approximately two hundred people and their families were at risk. Of course, those directly employed by the Powell Agency comprised only the tip of the iceberg. Indirectly, Griffin Powell employed countless thousands.

When she entered the state-of-the-art office suite, Nic paused in the doorway, allowing her gaze to travel around the room and pause on each occupant. Her initial thought—"round up the usual suspects"—would have made her smile if not for the seriousness of the situation.

Dr. Yvette Meng, the epitome of exotic elegance, stood away from the others, alone and infallibly serene. If her goal had been to be as inconspicuous as possible, she had failed. There was no way the dark-eyed beauty, whose very presence in any room commanded attention, could be overlooked.

Sanders stood behind Griff, who sat at the head of the conference table. She respected her husband's guard dog, which was the way she thought of the quiet, reserved man with the perpetual hint of sadness in his dark eyes.

Barbara Jean, her friend and confidant, glanced up from where she sat in her wheelchair at the far end of the table. She offered Nic an encouraging smile. One of the many things Nic loved about Barbara Jean was her optimistic outlook on life, which considering the tragedies she had endured was in and of itself a miracle.

Powell agents filled five of the ten chairs at the table, leaving the end chair—her chair—unoccupied. As she entered the office, she quickly noted which agents had been called in for duty at Griffin's Rest. Shaughnessy Hood, who had been with the agency since its infancy, a bear of a man at six-six and three hundred pounds; Luke Sentell, a former Black Ops commando, the most mysterious and most deadly member of the team; Saxon Chappelle, a Harvard graduate, who like Derek Lawrence possessed a borderline genius IQ. And then there were the two female agents: Feisty, petite Angie Sterling Moss, five months pregnant and presently on restricted duty. And Michelle Allen, an expert in martial arts, recruited after the death of her fiancé with whom she had owned a franchise of martial art studios throughout the state of Tennessee.

As Nic approached the conference table, Griff looked at her. The moment she took her seat, Griff broke eye contact with her and surveyed the others in the room.

"Starting today, from now until the Copycat Carver is apprehended, security at Griffin's Rest will be tripled and access both in and out of the estate will be limited. Those living here should be safer than any of the Powell employees living and working on the outside. Unfortunately, we have no way to predict who the copycat has chosen as his next victim."

An unnatural silence fell over the room.

"Luke will be leaving tomorrow for an assignment in London," Griff said.

Nic tensed. Griff had deliberately not discussed Luke's new assignment with her. She knew he had been trying to protect her, trying to postpone the inevitability that his actions would upset her, and trying to avoid yet another argument. But what she couldn't get through his stubborn head was how that type of protective maneuver only made matters worse in the end.

"Angie, you may choose whether you want to stay here at Griffin's Rest or if you prefer to take a temporary leave of absence. Talk it over with your husband and let him know that he's welcome to stay here with you."

"Yes, sir," Angie replied. "Thank you."

"I'm bringing in Cully Redmond," Griff said. "He will join you three—Michelle, Shaughnessy, and Saxon—who will rotate between the house here and Dr. Meng's retreat. You will be on duty twelve hours and off twelve, but you will not leave the estate."

Griff had made his decisions without including her in the process. Oh, she could call him on it and he would tell her that they *had* discussed the situation. They had, to some degree, but talking about something and making definite decisions on how to handle the problem were not the same thing.

She knew he was doing what had to be done, and she agreed with his decisions, even the one to send Luke Sentell to London. She also knew that he would move heaven and earth to protect those he loved. And in her heart of hearts, she knew that he loved her more than anyone or anything and that he would die to protect her.

Poppy Chappelle loved her grandmother, loved the big old house in Ardsley Park, Savannah's first suburb, a mere ten-minute drive from downtown, and loved her summers here with her father's family. She had been barely two years old when her parents divorced, so she couldn't actually remember a time when the three of them had been together. Her memories of her dad were sketchy, but she had a picture in her mind of a big, sandy-haired man who had laughed a lot and had called her "my little sugarplum." He and his latest lady friend had died when his single-engine Cessna had crashed on their flight back from Vegas five years ago.

"Miss Poppy," Heloise, her grandmother's housekeeper and companion for the past forty years called to her just as she reached the front door. "Your grandmother wanted me to remind you that she is expecting guests for dinner. You need to be home no later than five-thirty."

"I've already promised her that I won't be late. She knows that I'm going sailing with Court and Anne Lee this afternoon."

Heloise snorted. "Mr. Court and Miss Anne Lee are totally irresponsible. Your grandmother is sorely disappointed in those two."

"It's hardly their fault if they're spoiled brats," Poppy said. "Grandmother should blame their parents for their behavior, but she won't criticize Aunt Mary Lee the way she does my mother because she's her daughter."

"I have no intention of getting into a conversation with you about the dynamics of the Chappelle family. It's not my place to agree or disagree with you. I shouldn't have said anything about your cousins. I simply meant to remind you not to be late this evening."

Poppy rushed over to Heloise and hugged her. The dour-faced old maid who seldom smiled cleared her throat and patted Poppy's back.

"You're a good one, Miss Poppy. You and your uncle Saxon. You two are the best of the lot, if you ask me." She shoved Poppy away and gave her a push toward the front door. "You behave yourself with those hooligan cousins of yours and don't let them get you into any trouble."

"I won't. I promise."

A car horn announced her cousins' arrival. Poppy opened the door and stepped out onto the porch. She paused, glanced over her shoulder and waved at Heloise, then bounded down the brick steps and hopped into Court Dandridge's black BMW M6 convertible.

Maleah and Derek ordered dinner in her suite, the same luxury suite that Nic and Griff had occupied before their departure from Nassau that morning. Nic had insisted she use the suite since it was paid for through the end of the week. The butler, included with the suite, cleared away the table, stacked the dishes on a serving cart and wheeled it away.

"Will there be anything else, ma'am?" the prim and proper butler asked.

"Uh . . . no, thank you."

"Very well."

As soon as he pushed the cart out into the hallway and closed the door behind him, Maleah laughed.

"What's funny?" Derek asked.

"I'm glad I'm not rich. I don't think I'd ever get used to hot and cold running servants."

Derek stared at her, an odd expression in his black eyes. "You have to be the only woman I know who wouldn't love having servants to do her bidding."

"You need to get to know a better class of women."

He chuckled. "Yeah, maybe I do."

She eyed their twin laptops, provided by the agency, lying side by side where they had placed them on the coffee table when the butler had set the table for their dinner. "We should check to see if Sanders has any new info for us before we go over the list Warden Holland gave you."

"You check your e-mail and I'll pull up the file containing the list of Browning's visitors, telephone calls, and correspondence."

Maleah picked up her computer and took it with her over to the sofa. She kicked off her low-heel sandals, wriggled her toes, and settled at the end of the sofa. After flipping open her laptop, with an attached USB-Connect device, she logged on to her Powell Agency e-mail account.

"Nothing from Sanders," Maleah said.

After removing his sports coat, neatly folding it and laying it across the back of one of the chairs at the dining table, he got his laptop and joined Maleah on the sofa. They sat at opposite ends, leaving a wide space between them. Derek pulled up the file that Warden Holland had sent him about an hour ago. This was his first chance to take a look at the lists.

"Want me to read it to you or would you rather we take a look at this together?" he asked.

She shrugged. She wanted to read the info herself, but that meant close contact with Derek, something she usually avoided.

Grow up, will you, Maleah, she told herself. *He may have a Don Juan reputation, but it's not as if he's going to try anything with you. The guy is no more interested in you—in that way—than you are him. You're not his type. And God knows he's not your type.*

Who was she kidding? Derek Lawrence was every woman's type.

She scooted across the sofa until she sat beside him, only inches separating their bodies. He grinned. She faked a pleasant smile. He lifted his laptop and rested it between them, one edge on her left knee and the other edge on his right knee.

Look at the damn computer and stop thinking about Derek's knee pressed against yours.

"The first list has the names of all of Browning's visitors for the past year," Derek said.

They looked over the list, which turned out to be extremely brief.

"There are only three names," Maleah said.

"Albert Durham, Cindy Di Blasi, and Wyman Scudder," Derek read. "Scudder is listed as his lawyer. He visited him twice."

"The other two are listed as friends."

"Did the warden send Sanders a copy of this?"

"I don't know, but I forwarded it to him before lunch, just in case."

"Then it's too soon for us to expect Sanders to have found out anything about these people."

Derek grunted. "Let's move on to telephone calls."

"Same three names," Maleah said. "His lawyer and his two friends. One call to the lawyer, one call to Durham and one call every week to Ms. Di Blasi."

"Curious. I'm surprised Browning hasn't asked for conjugal visits."

"Don't make me sick. What woman in her right mind would willingly have sex with a psycho like Browning?"

"Different strokes for different folks," Derek told her.

Maleah groaned. "Don't remind me about how many screwed-up women there are in this world, women who willingly demean themselves. They make me ashamed of my own sex."

"Women don't hold a monopoly on stupidity. The world is full of pussy-whipped men being led around by the nose by heartless bitches who get their kicks out of emasculating the idiots."

Maleah snapped her head up and stared at Derek. Their gazes joined instantly, fusing together like two pieces of hot metal. Good God Almighty! She and Derek were two sides of the same coin. Why had she never realized that fact until two seconds ago?

"Uh . . . did we just say the same thing, sort of?" she asked, still partially puzzled by the revelation.

"Sort of," he agreed. "You have no respect for weak, spineless women who let men use them. I have no respect for weak, spineless men who let women walk all over them."

If you know what's good for you, you'll break eye contact with him. Do it now before something happens between the two of you that you will regret.

"We should look at the third list," she said, her voice softened by emotion.

"Right." He looked straight at the computer as he brought the next list up on the screen.

"Hmm . . . two names," Maleah said. "Albert Durham and Cindy Di Blasi. He received two letters from Durham and sent two replies to the man."

"Cindy has written to him every week for the past four months and he has replied to every letter." Derek went back to the first list. "Check out the dates. Durham visited for the first time five months ago, and then four months ago, Di Blasi visited for the first time. Why did they both start visiting Browning all of a sudden?"

"What about the phone calls?" Maleah asked.

They scanned the list of Browning's telephone calls again, checking the dates. "He called Durham two days after Durham's first visit."

"And he called Di Blasi two days after her first visit." Maleah pointed to the date. "Do you think there's a connection between Durham and Di Blasi?"

"There could be," Derek said. "It depends on exactly

who Cindy Di Blasi is and what her relationship with Browning is and how long they've known each other. She could be just one of those women who is fascinated by hardened criminals."

"And if she's not some wacko who's fallen in love with Browning?"

"We don't need to get ahead of ourselves and put the cart before the horse. Until Sanders does a background check and we know who these people are, we're wasting our time trying to figure how they're connected to Browning."

"Call Sanders and ask him to do a rush job on those background checks," Maleah told him. "And I'm going to get in touch with Warden Holland."

"Dare I ask why you're calling the warden?"

"He told me that he needed twenty-four hours' notice for me to see Browning again. I plan to talk to Browning again tomorrow afternoon."

When Derek didn't respond, she said, "Don't try to talk me out of it."

"I wouldn't dream of it."

"Good. I'm glad we're in agreement."

"We're not in agreement," he told her. "But I choose my battles wisely."

Ignoring his remark, she said, "The copycat killer is going to strike again. We all know it's only a matter of time. If there's one chance in a million that Browning knows something about the copycat, I'm willing to do whatever it takes to get him to tell me what he knows."

"And I'll do whatever it takes to keep you safe."

Their glazes clashed, but neither said anything, each knowing the other would not give an inch in a confrontation.

Chapter 11

Derek had misgivings about Maleah seeing Browning again, but had kept his concerns to himself. Although he hadn't tried to talk her out of coming to the penitentiary today, he had insisted on accompanying her. She tried not to think about how protective Derek was, chalking it up to just a generic masculine trait that all men possessed. It was nothing personal.

She had to admit that in some ways Derek reminded her of her brother Jackson. She suspected that as Jack had once done, Derek would volunteer to be her stand-in and take any beatings intended for her. And that, too, wasn't personal. The guy probably saw himself as hero material. After all, it was no secret that Derek Lawrence had a reputation with the ladies. Women tended to take one look at the guy and swoon at his feet.

She could not deny she understood why women swooned. He was incredibly handsome.

Good God, Maleah, is that ever an understatement.

Derek was drop-dead, eat-him-with-a-spoon gorgeous. And he was highly intelligent and rich and charming. And he made her laugh. But on the other hand, he could be an arrogant know-it-all. And his way-with-the-ladies was just a nicer way of saying he was a womanizer.

Maleah didn't want Derek or anyone else protecting her from the big, bad world. She no longer needed a big brother to run interference for her. She was fully capable of taking care of herself in every way. She was an excellent marksman, adept with both a handgun and a rifle. She had earned a black belt in karate, thanks to Michelle Allen's excellent tutelage. She earned a six-figure yearly salary as a Powell agent, so she certainly didn't need to depend on anyone else financially. And after several years of intensive counseling, she was in a reasonably healthy place mentally and emotionally.

Okay, so she still had some control issues.

The creak of an opening door followed by the clinking of chains against the floor brought Maleah from her thoughts and into the present moment.

Standing with her back rigid, her hands gripping and releasing repeatedly, she took several deep breaths and did her best to relax. Browning would instantly sense her nervousness and use it against her. He was the type of animal who would pick up the scent of fear and gladly use it against his opponent, quickly seeing them as easy prey.

Maleah was once again slightly disoriented by the man's good looks and air of sophistication, even in his simple prison attire. And once again she wondered how many people had been fooled by this man's physical appearance.

"How delightful to see you again, Maleah," Browning said as the guard indicated for him to sit. "You're looking quite lovely. That shade of teal brings out the green in your eyes."

She ignored his compliment. Odd that the salesclerk who had sold her the blouse had said exactly the same thing about the teal bringing out the green in her hazel brown eyes.

"Your copycat has killed again," Maleah said. Succinct and to the point.

"Has he? Male or female?"

"Male."

"Not brown-eyed."

"No, not brown-eyed. But then none of your victims were brown-eyed, were they?"

"My mother was brown-eyed. I loved my mother. She died when I was six, you know."

"Yes, I know. You were an only child. Your father married a woman with two daughters and a son. You tried to strangle one of the daughters. You were ten years old. Your father sent you to live with your mother's uncle."

His sickening sweet smile never faltered, but she noted the momentary flash of anger in his eyes. "Did you find my life story fascinating?"

"I found it instructive. Tracing your life from birth to the present allowed me to see the slow, steady progression of a psychopath from a boy who tried to kill his stepsister, to a teenager who killed six young women, to an adult serial killer who got his kicks from slitting his victim's throats and slicing pieces of their flesh from their arms and legs."

"Souvenirs. Little trophies that I could take out and look at from time to time."

"In order to relive each kill?"

"Something like that." He looked up at her. "Why don't you sit down, Maleah, or do you think standing over me gives you some type of psychological advantage? I assure you, it doesn't."

"Then what difference does it make to you whether I sit or stand?"

He shrugged. "I simply thought you might be more comfortable sitting. And it might be more pleasant for both of us if we're facing each other, eye to eye."

Maleah made an instant decision. She walked over and sat down in the chair facing Browning, the protection of two guards securely between her and any physical danger. But she and Browning were now at the same eye level. She squared her shoulders and calmly rested her loosely clasped hands in her lap.

"Now, isn't that better?" Browning asked.

"I have a question."

"Let me guess . . . hmm . . . You want to know what I did with my souvenirs. The police never found them, you know."

"I'm not interested in your souvenirs. It doesn't really matter where you stored them. Not to the police. Not to me. Not to anyone."

"He's not keeping them the way I did, is he?"

How the hell did he know that? "No, he isn't."

"Aren't you going to ask me how I knew?"

"If I did, would you tell me?"

Browning laughed, the sound as smooth as his silky voice. It was a practiced laugh, nothing about it genuine. "I find it curious that you have no interest in my trophies, considering the fact that I took eight little triangular souvenirs from Noah Laborde's body. I could tell you about that night, every detail, from the moment I punctured his jugular until I left him on the banks of the Chattahoochee River."

Noah's smiling face—young, handsome, sweet—flashed through her mind. "I want the answer to a question."

"Then ask your question." He seemed only slightly perturbed that she remained unfazed by his reminder that he had killed Noah.

"Who's Cindy Di Blasi?"

Browning stared at Maleah as if trying to see inside her head, wondering how much she already knew and what price she was willing to pay for his answer.

"Cindy is a lady friend."

"How did you meet her?"

"We have friends in common."

"How long have you known her?"

"For a while."

"How long is a while?" Maleah asked.

"That's four questions," he reminded her.

"And only three answers."

"A mutual friend on the outside hooked me up with Cindy. A guy gets lonesome for a little female companionship in a place like this."

"I'll bet."

"You could say that Cindy is my girlfriend." Browning winked at Maleah. "If Cindy finds out about you, she's going to be jealous."

"I won't tell if you don't."

Browning laughed again, just a hint of sincerity in the sound.

Maleah didn't buy any of it. Not the part about Cindy being a friend of an old friend. Or that she visited Browning, wrote him letters, and took his phone calls because she was now his girlfriend. Maleah didn't know who Cindy di Blasi was or what her real relationship was with Browning, but she intended to find out.

"Is Albert Durham a friend, too?" she asked.

Browning smiled. "An acquaintance. And before you ask, Wyman Scudder is my lawyer." He leaned forward, his piercing gaze unnerving and intimidating.

Maleah didn't flinch, didn't even blink. *Good try, you cunning son of a bitch, but no cigar. Not this time. That crazy, I'm-dangerous glare doesn't scare me.*

"Interesting," Browning said. "Nerves of steel, huh, Maleah? Makes me wonder just what it would take to unnerve you, just how hot the pressure would have to be to melt that steel."

He knew that she knew what this game was all about, that his ultimate goal was to see her fall apart completely. He would keep chipping away at her armor, searching for the weak spots.

"Sticks and stones, Jerome," she told him. "I'm not afraid of you."

He studied her for several minutes. She examined him just as thoroughly. Whatever he dished out, she could take, and then dish it right back to him.

"I'm glad that you're not afraid of me," he finally said. "Makes things all the more interesting, doesn't it? I'll be thinking about you during the time between your visits. Thinking about curling your long blond hair around my finger." He held up his right index finger. "Thinking about running my hands down your throat. Thinking about what I could do to make you afraid of me . . . very afraid."

"If you don't tell me something I consider useful in my investigation about Cindy Di Blasi or Albert Durham or the copycat killer, I won't be coming back for another visit."

"Oh, Maleah, you disappoint me. Resorting to idle threats?"

"Not a threat. Just stating a fact. I have no intention of wasting my time pursuing a dead end. And that's what you're becoming, Jerome—a dead end."

He tensed his jaw and narrowed his gaze. One hand curled into a tight fist. She had pushed the right buttons. Mentally patting herself on the back, Maleah rose to her feet.

"Leaving already?" he asked.

"Unless you want to answer my questions."

"Another time, perhaps."

"Perhaps."

"You'll come to see me again," he told her.

"Only if I get what I want before I leave today. And I'm on my way out right now, so you'd better hurry."

Silence.

She turned her back on him and walked toward the door where her escort waited. "I'm ready to go now," she told the uniformed guard.

The guard opened the door.

"Wait," Browning called to her.

She paused.

"Albert Durham is writing my biography," Browning said.

Maleah's breath caught in her throat. Durham was a writer? If so, then he had come to the prison to interview Jerome, to pick his brain for information. Was it possible that Durham was the copycat killer?

"Thank you, Jerome."

"You'll come back tomorrow?"

"Not tomorrow," she told him. "But soon."

Derek didn't immediately question Maleah about the interview. Outwardly, she seemed completely unaffected by today's encounter with Browning. She shook hands with Warden Holland, thanked him and requested a third interview for next Monday.

Why wait until next Monday? *Don't ask. She'll explain later.*

On the way to the parking area, Derek glanced at the overcast sky and commented about the weather. "Looks like rain."

Her gaze followed his. "Hmm . . ."

"I was thinking we could have a nice lunch at the Steeplechase Grill when we get back to Vidalia," Derek said. "I checked the place out online after the clerk at the hotel mentioned it was a great place to eat."

"Sure. Whatever." Maleah unlocked her SUV. "Have you heard anything from Sanders this morning?"

Derek opened the passenger side door. "As a matter of fact, he sent us the info we requested about Browning's recent visitors while you were chit-chatting with the guy."

Maleah shot him a screw-you glare before opening the door and sliding in behind the wheel. She waited until he got in before asking, "Do we have addresses? Phone numbers?"

"We have an address for Wyman Scudder. He isn't Browning's original attorney nor is he even with the same law firm or in the same city. Someone hired him six months ago to represent Browning's interests."

"Why would a man who confessed to murder, struck a deal with the DA, and exhausted all of his appeals need a new lawyer? It's not as if Browning has been screaming 'I'm innocent' for the past ten years."

"Scudder isn't exactly the best money can buy. According to Sanders's report, the guy's reputation as a lawyer isn't all that great. He's in debt up to his eyeballs, has an ex-wife who's still bleeding him dry after their divorce two years ago, and he was living in his office up until six months ago."

"Who retained Scudder for Browning and why? Sanders needs to get the Powell team to dig deeper and get us the answers."

"He's already on it."

Maleah started the engine and pulled out of the parking slot. "Is that all you've got on Scudder?"

"For now."

"What about Cindy Di Blasi?"

"Cindy Di Blasi is a mystery woman. Seems the Georgia driver's license that she used as ID for her visits to Browning is a fake. The street address on the license is for a church in Augusta. The phone number Browning called when he talked to Cindy was for a pre-paid cell phone. No way to track it."

"Interesting."

"Confusing."

"Do you think Cindy Di Blasi is an alias?"

"Could be," Derek said. "Using the description of the woman we got from the guards who remember her, the Powell team will compare her description, along with approximate age, to see if there's a woman by that name anywhere in the state of Georgia."

"Browning told me that Cindy is a lady friend and that a mutual friend hooked them up."

"And that mutual friend could be Wyman Scudder or—"

"Or Albert Durham."

"Albert Durham is a real person, not an alias. Sanders is checking out the info on the driver's license ID he used when he visited Browning. The man's a writer. He writes biographies about historical figures, presidents and generals, world leaders in various areas."

"This is becoming more and more curious, isn't it?" Maleah glanced at Derek. "Do you have a theory?" She refocused on the road immediately.

"I think we have three possible scenarios," Derek told her. "The Copycat Carver hired Scudder, Durham, and Cindy and has used them as go-betweens to contact Browning. Or the Copycat Carver is actually one of them—Scudder or Durham or Cindy."

"Cindy? I thought everyone was in agreement that the copycat is a man."

"Who said Cindy was a woman?"

Maleah snorted. "I say Cindy is a woman. Either a woman or a very small man. The guards said she was about five-two and maybe weighed a hundred pounds soaking wet."

"Yeah, Cindy is probably female. But that still leaves Scudder and Durham."

"Agreed. So, what's your third scenario?"

"Ah yes, my third scenario."

"Stop being so dramatic and just tell me."

Derek grinned. "Someone hired Scudder, Durham, and Cindy, as well as a professional killer to copy Browning's murders."

"This is the Griffin Powell theory, isn't it? Some mystery man over in Europe who is using the name Malcolm York is striking out at Griff by killing Powell agents and members of their families."

"It's one of three theories. At this point, I don't have a favorite. I don't know enough to make a judgment call. I don't even have a gut instinct pick."

Maleah remained silent for several miles, but Derek knew she was thinking, mulling things over, and deciding what she wanted to say.

"Browning was careful not to tell me anything I couldn't easily find out on my own," Maleah said. "That Scudder was his lawyer and that Cindy was his lady friend. But he did share something about Durham that seems odd to me."

Derek waited, allowing her to progress at her own speed.

"Just as I was leaving, Browning told me that Albert Durham was writing his biography."

"Why would a renowned biographer of historical figures choose to write the bio of a condemned serial killer?"

"What if he's not the real Albert Durham?"

"If he is or isn't the real Durham, you do realize that Browning probably believes he is," Derek said. "And Browning would have been inclined to share numerous details about the murders with his biographer."

"Which means Durham would have the info he needed to duplicate those murders."

"If we can find Albert Durham, we just might find the Copycat Carver."

Chapter 12

Wyman Scudder, you're a fool.

How many times had his ex-wife said those exact words?

She'd been right. Sheila had been right about a lot of things.

You're a fool. You're a drunk. You're a sorry excuse for a husband. You've ruined your life and tried to ruin mine, but I'm getting out while the gettin' is good.

Wyman lifted the open bottle of Wild Turkey 101 proof bourbon whiskey and poured his glass three-fourths full. The damn stuff had cost him sixty bucks, but he had the money, didn't he? It was nobody's business what he paid for his pleasures and a good bottle of bourbon headed his list of carnal delights. He lifted the glass to salute his ex-wife, his ex-associates, and his ex-life. He might have been on his way down six months ago, but not now.

"Here's to Wyman Scudder. Long may he live the good life."

He downed one long, glorious gulp, shivered, coughed, and then laughed. When he left his office today—a right nice office, if he did say so himself—he'd be going home to a Mill Creek Run apartment. After living in his old office for nearly a year, he had every right to celebrate his good fortune, didn't he? A new office on Third Street, a first-rate apartment, a good bottle of bourbon, and a new suit. He ran his hand over the quality material of his thousand-dollar pin-striped suit. It might be off the rack, but it was a damn expensive rack.

Wyman took a sip of the smooth whiskey and then another before placing the glass on a fancy soapstone coaster atop his desk.

He had a chance now to put his life back together and that's just what he intended to do. Screw Sheila. Screw his old law firm. Two years ago, both his wife and his firm had thrown him out as if he were yesterday's trash.

He'd show 'em just what he was made of.

You're a fool.

"Shut the fuck up," he hollered into the emptiness of his new office.

You've gotten yourself mixed up in something really nasty.

If anybody asked him who had hired him to represent Jerome Browning, he'd tell them the truth. He hadn't done anything illegal. He'd seen Browning only a couple of times, did what he'd been paid to do—consult with his client—and that was all there was to it.

If someone connects all the dots, what then?

Then you're screwed.

He could be considered an accomplice, couldn't he? An accomplice to murder? No, not just one murder. Five murders now.

But I didn't know. I swear to God, I didn't know what they were planning. If I had . . .

It was too late for ifs. He had taken the job, taken the money, and unless somebody put the puzzle pieces together, he'd get away scot-free, just as the others would. They would all get away with murder.

The Steeplechase Grill and Tavern was located in downtown Vidalia. Atop the signpost outside the restaurant, a wooden cutout of a comic laughing horse's head welcomed customers, setting the tone for the casual atmosphere inside the trendy establishment. Upon entering, the tantalizing aroma instantly whetted Derek's appetite.

"Nice place," he said as the hostess showed them to their table.

"Nice enough." Maleah climbed up and sat on one of the bar stools that graced a row of dark wooden tables.

They had arrived at 12:30 P.M., prime lunchtime in downtown Vidalia, so the restaurant was packed. He glanced around at the dark paneled walls, lined with metal signs, and then looked up at the whirling ceiling fans and down at the floral / leaf design in the dark carpet.

Maleah scanned the menu hurriedly, laid it on the table and tapped her fingers absently. Turning her head right and then left, she searched for a waitress. "We should have just picked up fast food and gone straight on to Macon."

"Settle down and relax," Derek told her. "It'll take us less than two hours to drive to Macon. It's not as if Wyman Scudder is going anywhere. In the grand scheme of things, taking an hour for a decent meal isn't going to matter."

She heaved a labored sigh. "You're probably right."

"Are you okay?"

"Yeah, sure, why wouldn't I be?"

"Half an hour with Jerome Browning, playing his sick little cat and mouse game, would have an adverse effect on anyone."

She stared at him, her eyes speaking for her, telling him that even though she hadn't walked away from the second interview with Browning without a few minor wounds, she had won today's game.

"You bested him, didn't you?" Derek grinned.

"I held my own. And yes, in the end, I won."

"He'll be all the more determined to draw blood next time."

She nodded. "I'm well aware of that fact."

The waitress appeared, all white teeth, freckled nose, and friendly attitude. "What can I get you folks to drink?"

"Sweet tea," Derek replied.

"Unsweet iced tea, please," Maleah said.

"Y'all know what you want or do you need a few minutes?"

Derek quickly looked over the extensive menu. One item caught his eye.

"I'd like the Charleston Chicken Salad," Maleah said.

"Yes, ma'am. And you, sir?" the waitress asked.

"A rack of baby back ribs, baked potato, fully loaded, and onion rings."

As soon as the waitress walked away to place their order, Maleah made a disapproving tsk-tsk sound with her tongue.

"You disapprove of my lunch choices?" he asked.

"It's your health and your arteries that you're clogging, not mine."

Derek grinned. He had learned months ago when not to argue with Maleah's reasoning, especially when she was right.

Despite the crowd, the service was good—fast and accurate. The waitress returned quickly with their drinks and a loaf of delicious brown bread coated with a hint of sea salt.

After their meals arrived, they ate in relative silence. Apparently Maleah thought that would save time and allow them to get off to Macon all the sooner. Halfway through eating the delectable ribs, Derek's phone rang. Using the wipes provided with his meal, he cleaned the barbecue sauce from his fingertips, retrieved his phone and noted the caller ID. The Powell Agency's number at Griffin's Rest.

"This is Derek Lawrence."

"Hi, Derek. It's Barbara Jean. Sanders received some updated info on Wyman Scudder he thought y'all should have immediately. I'll send a complete report via e-mail attachment later, and I'll text the new address, too, but I thought you needed to know that the address we had is incorrect."

"Okay, give me the correct address."

She called off the new address on Third Street in downtown Macon. "It seems that Mr. Scudder just signed a lease on a new office and a new apartment a few days ago."

"You don't say."

"What?" Maleah asked.

He waved her off, his actions requesting that she wait.

"Scudder has been making monthly deposits to his account," Barbara Jean said. "A thousand a month up until the first of June, when he deposited fifty thousand."

Derek whistled softly. "Now, why would anyone think a guy like Scudder was worth that kind of money."

"Sanders suggested that you and Maleah might want to ask him."

"Tell Sanders that he can count on our doing just that."

"We're still working on tracking down Cindy Di Blasi," Barbara Jean said. "And after you texted us with the info that Browning told Maleah Durham is writing his bio, which implies this guy really could be the real Albert Durham, we had some luck finding him. Or at least more info about him."

"No address or phone number?"

"It seems Albert Durham is a recluse and guards his privacy. He owns several homes, but keeps on the move a lot, travels abroad, works on extended vacations, that sort of thing. As soon as we come up with any information about where you can find him now, I'll be in touch. Until then, we're working under the assumption that the man who visited Browning is the real Durham. The info on the ID he used to enter the prison matches that of the real Durham, at least his physical description and date of birth. And the address is for one of Durham's homes."

"Thanks, BJ."

Barbara Jean laughed when he used the nickname he had given her—BJ. She was a good woman. A kind and caring woman. Sanders was a lucky man.

As soon as he slipped his phone back in his jacket pocket, Maleah snapped her fingers in front of his face. "Damn it, Derek, tell me."

"Scudder has a new office, a new apartment, and fifty grand in the bank."

Maleah's mouth dropped open, and then she smiled. "You can tell me the rest on the way to Macon." She laid her fork on the table, removed her napkin from her lap, tossed it alongside her half-eaten salad, and slipped off the wooden stool and onto her feet.

Derek eyed the remainder of the delicious ribs, gulped

down a swig of iced tea, and knowing better than to suggest they finish their lunch, he motioned to the waitress. When she was within earshot, he said, "We need our check, please."

Wyman Scudder had served his purpose and had been paid well for his services. Unfortunately, Scudder was a liability now, a loose end that needed to be tied up.

Scudder first; then Cindy Di Blasi.

Albert Durham wasn't a problem. Even if the Powell Agency could find the reclusive author, there wasn't a damn thing the man could tell them.

He had known the Powell Agency would eventually get around to interviewing Browning, which would prompt them to check out his recent visitors. However, they had moved a bit faster than he had anticipated. Too bad Scudder wouldn't get to enjoy his big payoff.

The walk from the Travelodge Suites on Broadway Street took only a few minutes and would have been rather pleasant if not for the rain. When he had left his hotel, the sky had been overcast. He had gone to his car to drop off his jacket and had picked up an umbrella. By the time he reached the corner of Walnut and Third, heavy droplets had begun falling. Now that he had reached the building that housed Wyman Scudder's new law office, a steady drizzle had set in.

After entering the lobby, he closed his black umbrella and headed straight for the elevators. While he waited for the Up elevator, the Down elevator opened and a man and woman emerged. The couple was so absorbed in their conversation with each other that they barely noticed him. Later on, if asked, they would say they had seen a black-haired man with a neat mustache and Van Dyke, wearing jeans and a short-sleeved plaid shirt. And perhaps one of them would remember that he had a large skull tattoo on his left arm.

He had learned long ago that a disguise should be simple and the effect subtle. Sometimes little more than a cap and a pair of glasses were needed to alter his appearance.

Scudder's office was on the third floor, a corner office that faced the street. The outer door was closed.

He knocked.

No response.

He tried the handle and the door opened to an empty outer office. No furniture. No secretary. Scudder hadn't had time to acquire either.

"Hello, anybody here?" he called out, wondering if perhaps Scudder had gone home early.

The door leading into the private office opened. A bleary-eyed, middle-aged man with a receding hairline and a slight paunch hanging over his belt stood in the doorway and stared at him.

"Who are you?" Wyman asked, his speech slightly slurred.

The idiot was drunk.

"A potential client, Mr. Scudder," he said using his best good old boy accent.

"Well, come right on in, Mr.—" Wyman squinched his eyes and studied his visitor. "Have we met before?"

"Might have, if you've ever been down to Perry. I got a motorcycle repair shop." He moved toward Wyman, who backed up into his office as his guest approached. "You got a motorcycle, Mr. Scudder?"

A perplexed look crossed Wyman's face. "No, I don't have a motorcycle."

He closed the door behind him. Wyman staggered toward his desk.

"Just how can I be of assistance, Mr.—?"

"Just call me Harold." He reached inside his pants pocket and pulled out the strong thin strip of nylon cord.

Wyman lost his balance and fell toward his desk, but he managed to steady himself by grabbing onto the edge of the only piece of furniture in the room other than a leather swivel chair.

"Yes, sir, Harold. Tell me why you need a lawyer."

"I don't need just any lawyer. I need you."

Before Scudder had a chance to turn and face him, he moved in for the kill. Quickly. Adeptly.

With the expert ease gained from years of experience, he walked up behind an inebriated Wyman Scudder and brought the cord over his head and across his neck before the unsuspecting fool realized what was happening. He struggled, but he was no match for a stronger, more agile, and sober man.

Halfway between Vidalia and Macon, the bottom fell out, and within minutes, Maleah could barely see the road. The rain came down in thick, heavy sheets, all but obliterating her view through the windshield. With little choice, for safety's sake, Maleah slowed the SUV to a crawl—twenty-five miles an hour.

"Maybe we should find a place to stop," Derek said. "At least until the worst passes."

"I'm okay," she assured him. "If it gets worse, I'll exit the interstate."

When he didn't respond, Maleah knew what he was thinking. Derek wished he was driving. Being the superior male, he could probably use his x-ray vision to see through the heavy downpour and his innate masculine abilities to maneuver the SUV through floodwaters.

After several minutes, Derek ended the awkward silence. "Do you know what puzzles me?"

"What? That I have managed not to wreck us?"

"Huh?" He laughed. "No. You're doing a great job. Better than I could do. I hate driving in heavy rain. Makes me nervous."

Maleah almost took her eyes off the road to glance at Derek, to see if he was mocking her. But she didn't. He sounded sincere, so she'd take him at his word.

"Okay, tell me what puzzles you."

"Why would someone hire Wyman Scudder, or any lawyer for that matter, to represent Jerome Browning, a man who confessed to murder and is serving consecutive life sentences?"

"I have no idea. You tell me."

"Let's say Albert Durham is our copycat killer. He wanted Browning to reveal all his little secrets so that he, Durham, could duplicate Browning's MO. Maybe simply telling Browning that he wanted to write the story of his life wasn't enough incentive for Browning to open up and share all."

Derek was right. Damn, he was always right! "I see what you're getting at. Durham promised Browning a new lawyer, maybe made him think Scudder could find grounds to reopen his case, as far fetched as that idea is. And he promised Browning a lady friend."

"Cindy Di Blasi. What are the odds that Cindy, or whatever her name is, gets paid by the hour?"

"A prostitute? Makes sense."

"Another thing that puzzles me is, if Durham isn't the copycat killer, why a writer with Durham's reputation would get involved with Browning. He's never chosen a convicted criminal as the subject of one of his biographies. If someone hired him to do it, why would he agree?"

"Maybe he needs the money."

"Possibly. But he'd have to know he was getting himself mixed up with something illegal."

"What if he's being blackmailed," Maleah said. "Or maybe Durham really is our copycat."

"Maybe he is. But if he is, why would he leave us a trail leading straight to him?"

"He wouldn't."

"We have too many unanswered questions."

"You're right. We need answers, so we start with Scudder. We know where to find him. He may be able to tell us something."

"I figure Scudder will talk for the right amount of money," Derek told her. "But I'm not sure how much he actually knows."

"Hopefully the agency will dig up more info on Cindy and Durham and once we've questioned Scudder and gotten some answers, we'll be able to move on pretty quickly to Cindy and Durham."

"It could take time to track them down, especially if they don't want to be found."

Maleah and Derek continued discussing the case, their conversation gradually dwindling down to an occasional comment by the time Maleah exited the interstate. The rain had slacked up to little more than a drizzle, but the pavement was slick and mucky with roadway residue. Muddy water filled the potholes and gushed across low-lying areas in the highway.

Following GPS directions, they watched for Mulberry Street, which crisscrossed with Third Street where Wyman Scudder's new law office was located.

Maleah noted the congestion ahead, but neither she nor Derek immediately realized that the next street was partially blocked by emergency vehicles, including a fire truck, an ambulance, and several patrol cars. As they drew nearer, she noticed a uniformed officer directing traffic. He stood in front of their destination.

"What the hell's going on?" Derek studied the situation while Maleah slowed the Equinox to a crawl. "Shit! It looks like something has happened in Scudder's building."

"Obviously I can't park here," she told him.

"I'm getting a bad feeling about this."

"Yeah, me, too."

"Let me out at the next corner," Derek told her. "You find a place to park while I see what's going on."

She hesitated, her competitive instinct interfering with her logical thought process. *You and Derek are partners,* she reminded herself. *You're playing on the same team.* "Yeah, sure."

Since traffic was pretty much bumper-to-bumper, it took Maleah a few minutes to maneuver the SUV into a position where she could come to a full stop. Without hesitation, Derek opened the door and jumped out and onto the street. Once the door slammed, Maleah moved forward and began her search for a parking place.

Five minutes later, out of sorts and perspiring enough to dampen her underwear, Maleah made it back to the cordoned-off area swarming with law enforcement and emergency personnel. She searched the crowd of curious onlookers for any sign of Derek, but didn't see him. Just as she stood on tiptoe and strained her neck in the hopes of gaining a better view, Derek came up alongside her.

"Looking for me?"

She released a startled gasp, but quickly recovered. "Damn it, I'm going to put a cow bell around your neck."

"Sorry."

She might have believed him if he hadn't chuckled softly.

"Well, what did you find out about all the hullabaloo going on?" she asked.

"A body was found on the third floor of that building." Derek pointed to the four-story office building in front of them.

"Don't tell me—"

The news crews in the crowd rushed forward as the ME's staff came out of the building carrying a body bag laid out on a stretcher. Questions zipped through the air like mosquitoes on a hot, humid summertime night as the reporters questioned officials on the scene. Their questions went unanswered as the officials ignored them.

"From what I've been able to find out, a young woman who had an afternoon interview for a position as a secretary for a lawyer in the building got quite a shock when she showed up for her appointment," Derek said. "She found her potential employer's body."

"It's Scudder, isn't it?"

"I couldn't get anybody to verify the victim's name, but when I asked if the dead man was Wyman Scudder, nobody said it wasn't. So, yes, I'm ninety-five percent sure it's Scudder."

Chapter 13

Derek had known that they wouldn't get any information by going through legal channels there in Macon. At least, not yet. The detectives in charge of the case had remained tight-lipped, as had the emergency personnel involved. He and Maleah had separated and moved through the crowd as discreetly as possible, both showing a casual interest in what was happening. Downtown Macon on a Friday afternoon buzzed with activity and the entire block swarmed with curiosity seekers. The police had sealed off the building and rounded up all the occupants for questioning. The one person Derek would love to talk to—the secretary interviewee—would be detained, questioned, and cautioned not to speak to the press.

Thirty minutes after they had parted company and circulated through the on-lookers, Derek and Maleah reconnected at the end of the block.

"Anything?" Maleah asked.

Derek shook his head. "Not much. I heard the name Wyman Scudder more than once. It seems to be the consensus that the victim was the newest renter in the building, a lawyer named Scudder."

"I tried speaking to the policemen in charge of crowd control, but that got me nowhere."

"They won't bring the secretary out the front way," Derek said. "Which means they'll take her out a back exit and possibly escort her to the police station or at the very least walk her to wherever she parked her car."

"Even if we knew the location of that exit, we have no idea when they'll bring her out. And it's not as if they're going to let us get anywhere near her."

"You're right, but we could get a good look at her and I could snap her photo with my phone."

"I don't think we should go the let's-play-secret-agent route," Maleah told him. "But I assume you weren't serious. I think our best course of action is to call Sanders and let the agency contact the Macon Police Department and see what information they're willing to share."

Derek grinned. "Ah, gee whiz, Mom, you won't let me have any fun."

She rolled her eyes. "Come on. Let's get out of here. You can call Sanders while I drive."

"Why don't we find a downtown hotel, check in and then go out for dinner while Sanders is working Powell Agency magic to get us the info we need about Scudder's death?"

Why not? She knew her easy acquiesce to his suggestion would surprise Derek, but in this instance she agreed with him.

"I'm okay with going out to dinner and possibly staying overnight." Zigzagging through the slow-moving traffic, they crossed the street together, Maleah a few steps ahead of Derek. "When you talk to Sanders, be sure to ask him about any updates on Cindy Di Blasi and Albert Durham."

"Yes, ma'am. Glad you thought of it."

"Bite me." Maleah snapped out the words.

Not slowing her pace as they left the bedlam behind them and walked up the block, she cut him a sideways glance. "We need to know for sure that Scudder was murdered, that he didn't have a heart attack or anything."

"Your gut instinct has to be telling you that he was murdered. I'd say what we really need to know is how he was murdered and if the police have any suspects."

Maleah led Derek to her SUV. "You think the Copycat Carver killed him?"

"Don't you?" Derek asked as he sat down in the passenger seat.

Maleah slid into the driver's seat, inserted the key into the ignition and started the SUV. "Probably. Apparently Scudder knew too much and could ID the copycat, so he had become a liability."

"Of course being murdered eliminates Scudder as a suspect. So, at least for the time being, that leaves Cindy and Durham as our only leads."

"I think there's a good chance that Durham is our copycat."

"I think you could be right," Derek said.

As she eased the Equinox into traffic, Maleah cast a quick glance in Derek's direction. "If we're right, then he'll go after Cindy next, won't he?"

"More than likely. And if Durham isn't our guy, then he and Cindy probably know who he is and that puts them both in danger."

"What we should be concentrating on is finding Cindy and Durham. If Sanders has any leads on either of them, I say we head out tonight. There's no point in our staying on here in Macon, is there?"

"Nothing except a decent meal and a good night's sleep."

"Call Sanders now," Maleah said. "There's no point in checking into a hotel until we know for sure whether we'll be staying or moving on tonight. I'll drive around for a few minutes while you call him."

Derek put a call through to Sanders's private number, used only by Powell agents. It was no surprise when Barbara Jean answered.

"We're in Macon," Derek said. "We just left a crime scene on Third Street. We're relatively certain that Wyman Scudder has been murdered. We need the agency to find out the particulars ASAP."

"I'll let Sanders know immediately and we'll get back to you with that info once we have it," Barbara Jean said.

"Anything on Cindy or Durham? If the copycat killed Scudder—"

"We believe we located Cindy. Her real name is Cindy Dobbins. She worked as a stripper for a while when she was younger. That's when she started using the name Di Blasi. She's been arrested half a dozen times in the past few years. Solicitation. Drug possession. Public intoxication," Barbara Jean said. "Check your e-mail. I sent you a complete report about half an hour ago, along with several arrest photos. Cindy's thirty-five. She looks fifty."

"Do you have a last known address?"

"We do, but she's not there. Hasn't been there in three weeks. We sent a local Atlanta contact to check it out."

"Do we know where Cindy was from originally?"

"Sure do. She was born and raised in a little wide-place-in-the-road town just over the Georgia state line, outside of Augusta. A placed called Apple Orchard, South Carolina. She's got a sister who still lives there."

"Maybe our little bird went home to roost," Derek said.

"The sister lives on Lancaster Road, number fourteen twenty. Her name is Jeri Paulk."

"Thanks, Barbara Jean. I'll fill Maleah in." He was pretty sure they would be heading straight to Apple Orchard, South Carolina. "By the way, anything else on Durham?"

"Durham owns three homes, a house in Tennessee, a condo in Aspen, and an apartment in New York City. But according to our investigation, he rents out all three. From what his agent told us, apparently he travels a great deal. The last time he checked in with her, he was in Virginia doing some Civil War research, but they haven't been in contact for nearly two weeks. It seems Durham doesn't own a cell phone."

"Doesn't this guy have any family or close friends?"

"He's a widower. No children. We're digging deeper to see if we can come up with relatives. According to his agent, the guy is a loner. He has dozens of acquaintances, but no bosom buddies."

"Got any recent photos of him?"

"Book jacket photo," Barbara Jean said. "I can send you a copy of that."

"What about his age? His background? Any military service?"

"Durham is sixty-three. No military background. The guy is an academic. He's got half a dozen degrees. Actually, he's Dr. Albert Durham."

"Doesn't sound like the type who'd get involved with a serial killer."

"Or become a copycat killer," Barbara Jean said.

After his conversation with Barbara Jean, Derek relayed all the information to Maleah. And just as he'd thought, she didn't hesitate to tell them they were going straight to Apple Orchard this evening. Checking online, Derek quickly found out that the small South Carolina town was a two-hour-and-forty-minute drive from downtown Macon.

"Let's at least stop for fast food on the way," Derek suggested.

She groaned. "You'd think you could skip a meal every once in a while."

"Drive-through will be fine."

She didn't reply.

Maleah headed the SUV north and continued in that direction on the interstate.

Poppy Chappelle had no idea she was being watched. Otherwise, he doubted the teenager would have removed her bikini top while she sunbathed in what she believed to be the privacy of her grandmother's backyard. No doubt, she and her cousins had spent the afternoon frolicking in the pool, but Court and Anne Lee Dandridge had left over an hour ago, only moments after he arrived. Poppy was now enjoying the late afternoon sunshine all alone while she stretched languidly on a padded chaise lounge.

It would be so easy to kill her. The grandmother probably hadn't come outside all day. He suspected the old woman took afternoon naps and avoided the June heat by staying indoors. The housekeeper had backed the late-model Mercedes from the garage fifteen minutes ago and headed toward downtown Savannah.

A brick fence flanked the back courtyard on either

side and connected to an eight-foot-high iron fence that ran across the back of the property. Towering crape myrtles heavy-laden with buds just beginning to burst open lined the fencerow. Although neatly maintained, an assortment of trees, shrubs, and flowers grew in profusion and partially obscured the view. He stood less than thirty feet from Saxon Chappelle's young niece, just beyond the unlocked back gate. He had parked his rental car blocks away, wore a ball cap and dark sunglasses, and had tossed his hand up and spoken to neighbors down the street as he passed by. If they remembered him, it was doubtful they could give anyone an even halfway accurate description of him. After all, he was just an average-looking white guy. His ability to appear quite generic had always given him an advantage.

He didn't especially like the idea of killing a sixteen-year-old, but she wouldn't be the first. In order to get the message across, he needed for the victim's death to matter. He supposed he could have chosen Saxon Chappelle's mother or his sister or the nephew or even the other niece, but his employer had seen Poppy's unusual given name as a sign, like a beacon glowing in the dark. She was the one.

Standing at the gate, he watched the rise and fall of Poppy's small, perky breasts. Her tiny rosebud pink nipples puckered as a warm breeze swept over her naked skin. He reached out and quietly lifted the latch. His pulse raced as the pre-kill adrenaline rush swept through his body, but it was only the first stage of the incredible high yet to come at the moment of the actual kill.

The urge to kill her now almost overwhelmed him.

But years of experience had taught him how to control his urges.

Wait. Now is not the right time. This is only a preliminary scouting trip.

"Poppy, what the devil are you doing?" a female voice demanded.

He dropped his hand away from the gate and took several careful steps backward while he searched for the source of the voice. An old woman, straight and tall, her white hair gleaming in the sunlight, came through the French doors that led into a back room of the two-story house.

Poppy reached down and grabbed her bikini top off the patio floor and hurriedly slipped it on before she got up and faced her grandmother. "I was sunbathing."

"In the nude?" the old woman asked.

"I wasn't nude. Besides, I'm all alone out here."

"In my day, a proper young lady—"

"Please, don't preach to me," Poppy said as she walked toward her grandmother. "I get enough of that from Mom."

Mrs. Chappelle sighed and shook her head, but when Poppy approached her, she opened her arms to give the girl a hug. "Your father was always testing my patience. He had a mind of his own and so do you. I can't tell you how much you remind me of him." She grasped Poppy's chin. "You're a Chappelle through and through. You'd do well to remember that."

"Yes ma'am."

"Well, come on inside and have a glass of the fresh lemonade Heloise made before she left to go shopping." Mrs. Chappelle took hold of her granddaughter's hand. "I do so love these weeks you spend with me every summer."

"So do I, Grandmother."

He waited until Poppy disappeared inside the house

before he latched the gate and turned to leave. As he walked away, the excitement coursing through his body began to fade ever so gradually, allowing his heartbeat to return to normal by the time he reached his car. He had checked out of the hotel in downtown Macon several hours ago and driven straight to Savannah without stopping. Two hours and fifty minutes. He had been careful to drive at the speed limit. The last thing he needed was to be stopped by the highway patrol.

Despite the desire to kill Poppy right then and there, he had not acted on impulse. He hadn't planned to kill Poppy today. In keeping to the Carver's timeline, he knew that the body should never be found before morning. There was no hurry, of course. He could come back tonight or tomorrow night or even the night after that, and kill her before dawn. When the moment was right, he would act. He would slit her throat, remove the small triangular pieces of flesh, and leave her body floating in her grandmother's pool.

You don't have to be satisfied with only one kill today, he told himself as he slid behind the wheel of his rental car. Humming softly, a favorite tune from childhood, he drove down the street and within minutes left Ardsley Park.

They traveled east on I-20, went through Augusta and exited off US 25 North going toward Newberry, but they left the main highway after less than fifteen miles. Derek had spent most of the trip reading aloud the reports that Barbara Jean had sent via e-mail attachments and they had discussed the information. A strong wind had blown in from the south, rocking the SUV and forecasting an oncoming storm. Keeping control of the Equinox, Maleah followed the road signs that led them straight to Apple Orchard, an unincorporated town in Edgefield County. Maleah had traveled around the U.S. and definitely throughout the South enough to recognize the signs of a dying small town. Apparently, the only remaining business was the mini-mart / gas station up ahead. To her left, the rusted hull of an old cotton gin near the railroad tracks rose into the eerily golden twilight sky like the giant carcass of an ancient beast. On the opposite side of the road, a centuries-old clapboard church stood vacant. Half the windows were broken and one of the double front doors, hanging precariously by a single hinge, thumped rhythmically in the wind.

They hadn't met a single vehicle in the past five minutes and she didn't see even one human being anywhere.

Derek hummed the theme from the old *Twilight Zone* TV show.

"Will you shut up," Maleah snapped at him as she slowed the SUV and turned off into the mini-mart parking lot. "Apparently there are very few street signs around here. We'll probably have to go in and ask directions."

"Actually, there are very few streets around here." Derek grinned.

Did he always have to have a smartass comeback? Okay, she knew that wasn't true. She was tired, frustrated, and hungry, but she shouldn't take it out on Derek. And yes, if she had driven through a fast-food place on the way here from Macon, as he had suggested, she wouldn't be hungry.

Talk about cutting off your nose to spite your face.

Why was she having so much difficulty accepting the fact that she didn't have to fight Derek for control? He was her partner, a co-worker she had learned to respect, and a man she was beginning to actually like. He deserved better from her.

Derek cleared his throat. "Want me to go in and ask directions or would you prefer to do it?"

"Why don't we both go in," Maleah replied. "I need to use the bathroom and I wouldn't mind picking up something to eat. Maybe a pack of crackers and a Dr Pepper."

She halfway expected him to mention his earlier suggestion about fast food, but he didn't. Instead, he got out, came around to her side of the SUV and walked alongside her toward the mini-mart. In the early days of their working relationship, he had acted like a real gentleman, but after she'd bitten his head off a few times, he had backed off. Occasionally, he still did little things like opening a door for her, and she had stopped reprimanding him for his good manners. She appreciated that a lot of men still treated a lady like a lady, but with Derek, she had seen it as condescension. But she had been wrong. So wrong. Derek didn't look down on her for being female or consider her a member of the weaker sex.

When they entered the Apple Orchard mini-mart, Maleah noted that the place was all but deserted. Odd, considering this was a Friday night. But then, the population might top out at less than a hundred people. Maleah spotted the bathroom and made a beeline in that direction while Derek meandered along at the back of the store where the giant coolers were located.

A few minutes later when Maleah and Derek approached the checkout, the young, bubble gum smacking clerk eyed them suspiciously. "Can I help you folks?"

"We're from out of town." Derek grinned at the girl, whose chin-length, dark brown hair was streaked with purple highlights. "We're looking for someone. We have her address and were hoping you could help us out with directions."

The plump, pug-faced clerk sported a shiny gold nose ring and a band of script tattoos circled each bicep revealed by her skimpy yellow tank top. A row of belly fat protruded between the end of the top and the waistband of her low-riding jeans. "Who you folks looking for?"

Derek smiled. Few women could resist his charm. "We're looking for my girlfriend's cousin." He glanced at Maleah to indicate she was the girlfriend. "Blondie hasn't seen her cousin since they were kids, but since we were on our way up to Columbia, another cousin suggested we look her up."

The girl smiled when Derek leaned over the counter and looked right at her. "You know a woman named Jeri Paulk? That's my girlfriend's cousin." Not taking his eyes off the clerk, he called to Maleah, who had gone in search of a canned cola. "Honey, what's that address your cousin Barbara Jean gave you for Jeri?"

"I know where Jeri lives," the girl said. "It ain't half a mile from here." She practically drooled while licking her lips, all the while looking as if she could swallow Derek whole.

Maleah scanned the refrigerated coolers across the back of the store, searching for a Dr Pepper while listening to the girl.

"Y'all remember passing an old church right before you got here?"

"Yes," Derek replied.

"Just go back and turn off on the road by the church. Jeri lives down the road a piece. You can't miss it. She painted the place bright blue last year. I told her that I'd bet the astronauts could see her place from outer space."

"Sure do thank you for your help," Derek said. "Honey, you got our colas and crackers?"

Maleah removed two canned Dr Peppers from the giant coolers and then grabbed a couple of packs of peanut butter and crackers off the shelves on her way back to the checkout counter.

After laying her items down, she said, "Yeah, thanks for helping us out. I sure am looking forward to seeing Jeri again after all these years."

"Sure, no problem." The girl rang up their order.

Maleah waited for Derek to pay for the items, then picked them up and headed out of the store. Halfway to the SUV, she handed him one of the colas and a pack of crackers.

"Thanks."

"Thank you," she replied. "That was a lot easier than I thought it would be. You practically had that girl eating out of your hand."

Derek chuckled. "What can I say, the ladies like me."

She punched him in the arm playfully and they both laughed.

They sat in the mini-mart parking lot long enough to devour the crackers and finish off part of their canned colas. Maleah started the SUV and went back the way they had come into Apple Orchard. She turned at the old church and headed down the narrow paved road that twisted and turned, carrying them farther and farther away from civilization. It was past sunset and darkness was fast approaching. Without lights along the road, Maleah had to rely totally on the Equinox's headlights to guide them. Just as Miss Purple-streaked-hair had told them, the bright blue house came into view less than half a mile from the mini-mart. Even in the encroaching gloom of nightfall, the small wooden house was visible. An older model Chevy truck and a late model Ford Mustang were parked in the gravel drive. Maleah pulled in behind the Mustang.

"So, what do we say to Jeri Paulk? Do we tell her why we're looking for her sister Cindy or do we make up some lie like we did back at the mini-mart?" Maleah asked.

"I suggest we play it by ear," Derek told her. "Let's see what kind of reception we get. If you're agreeable, let me take the lead and you just follow along with whatever I say. Can you do that?"

"Of course, I can."

They got out of the SUV and walked toward the porch. As they drew closer Maleah noticed the broken recliner, the vinyl ripped and the padding showing through, sitting beside two metal lawn chairs on the right side of the porch. Suddenly a dog reared his head up off the floor on the other side of the porch and barked. Maleah jumped. Derek cursed.

The dog kept barking, but didn't move toward them. The porch light came on and the front door flew open. A bear of a man wearing overalls and no shirt and carrying a shotgun in his meaty hand stood in the doorway. Behind his massive frame, a TV screen flashed and the sound of recorded laughter drifted outside.

"Get the hell off my property," the man yelled. "I know why you're here and you ain't welcome."

Maleah opened her mouth to respond, but before she could utter the first word, the man aimed the shotgun and pulled the trigger, sending a blast of buckshot in their direction.

Derek shoved Maleah out of the line of fire, tossed her onto the ground and came down over her. Eye to eye with her, his heavy weight a protective shield, Derek said, "Maybe we should have called first."

Chapter 14

Maleah didn't know whether to laugh, cry or just slap Derek in the mouth. During the process of rolling off her, he managed to unsnap her holster and remove her Glock pistol before she could. He aimed and fired. The bullet hit the tin sign hanging over the front door of the Paulk house. The pinging sound rang out over the dog's incessant barking.

"Unless you want the next one aimed directly at you, then don't fire that damn shotgun again," Derek hollered at the shooter.

"When did you damn bill collectors start carrying guns?" the man called out to Derek, then shouted at his barking mixed-breed dog. "Shut up, damn it, Pork Chop."

"We aren't bill collectors," Maleah said, as she grabbed for her gun still in Derek's clutch.

"We're from the Powell Private Security and Investigation Agency." Derek handed Maleah the Glock and whispered, "Don't holster that thing yet. You never know what Jethro there might do."

Jethro? If they hadn't been in such a deadly serious situation, she would laugh. Derek undoubtedly meant

Jethro Bodine, the big dumb character from the *Beverly Hillbillies* TV series of long ago.

"Are you folks lost?" the shooter asked.

"We're looking for Jeri Paulk," Maleah said as she rose to her feet, pistol in hand.

"That's my wife." The man lowered his shotgun, the muzzle pointed toward the porch floor. "I'm Lonny Paulk. What y'all want with Jeri?"

Derek stood, brushed the dirt and grass from his slacks and took a stand at Maleah's side. "We're looking for her sister, Cindy Dobbins. We think she might be in danger."

Lonny stepped out farther onto the porch and came over to the edge of the steps, shotgun still pointing down, and motioned to them. "Y'all come on up closer." He twisted his head and yelled over his shoulder, "Jeri, get your fat ass out here. There's some folks here who want to talk to you about that fuck-up sister of yours. Seems she's gotten herself into more trouble."

As they approached Lonny, Maleah noted several things all at once. He was as hairy as a grizzly, his greasy brown hair was pulled back in a ponytail and he emitted an unpleasant body odor. The man definitely needed, at the very least, a haircut and a bath.

Maleah paused when she reached the foot of the steps. Derek halted directly behind her.

"Who the hell's looking for Cindy?" A short, obese woman who was almost as broad as she was wide—about five feet—came out onto the porch. The first thing Maleah noticed was the woman's hair. It looked like bright yellow straw. She wore an oversized moo-moo in some hideous floral design of purple, hot pink, and turquoise that on a taller person would have hit them mid-calf. But on Jeri, the hem reached her ankles and floated over her small, broad feet and bright orange toenails.

"Are you Jeri Paulk?" Derek asked. "And is Cindy Dobbins, also known as Cindy Di Blasi, your sister?"

"Yeah, I'm Jeri and I got a sister named Cindy. What's this all about?" Jeri waddled across the porch to her husband's side.

"We're from the Powell Private Security and Investigation Agency," Maleah told them. "We're investigating a series of murders and we have reason to believe your sister Cindy is in danger. We're trying to locate her to warn her. We want to offer her our agency's protection."

"Who is it that you two are working for?" Jeri sized up Derek and apparently liked what she saw because she licked her lips and smiled at him.

Once again, if not for the gravity of the situation, Maleah would have laughed. "We're agents for the Powell Private—"

"I heard that part," Jeri said. "But who hired you?"

"Several murder victims were connected to our agency," Derek explained. "Our employer assigned us to investigate."

"How's my sister involved?"

"The killer that we're tracking is a copycat killer." Maleah watched for a reaction and when Jeri looked as if she understood, Maleah continued. "He's copying the style of a murderer known as the Carver. Your sister Cindy has been visiting the Carver, who is incarcerated in the Georgia State Prison. We want to question her."

"You said she might be in danger," Lonny said. "How?"

Derek leaned over and whispered to Maleah, "Cindy's here."

Maleah didn't know how Derek knew or why he was so sure, but she had learned not to question his instincts, which for the most part had proven to be infallible.

"Jerome Browning, aka the Carver, has had three visitors in the past year, one was a writer interviewing him for a book about his life, the other was his lawyer and the third person was Cindy." Maleah paused, giving Jeri and Lonny time to digest the info. "Browning's lawyer was murdered earlier today. We have reason to believe that Cindy could be next."

Silence.

Lonny turned to his wife. "I told you not to let her stay here. That woman is nothing but bad news. Every goddamn time she's around, trouble follows her."

Jeri planted her fat little hands on her ample hips. "She's my sister. What did you want me to do, tell her she can't come to me when she needs family? Lord knows I've put up with enough shit from that bunch of heathens you come from."

"Are you saying that Cindy is here?" Maleah asked.

A petite figure appeared in the doorway and stood behind the screen door.

"Cindy?" Maleah asked. "Are you Cindy Dobbins?"

The woman pushed open the door, came outside and moved past her sister and brother-in-law. "I'm Cindy Dobbins." She turned to Jeri. "You and Lonny go on back inside. I want to talk to these people alone."

"Are you sure?" Jeri asked Cindy.

Cindy nodded.

Jeri and Lonny went inside, but left the front door open.

"Y'all come on up here and take a seat." Cindy motioned for them to join her on the porch.

Maleah holstered her Glock and then walked up the steps, Derek directly behind her. Cindy sat in the dilapidated recliner. Maleah's first instinct was to wipe off the metal chair before sitting, but she didn't. When she sat, Derek came over and stood behind her. The yellow bug light shining down from the bare bulb in the ceiling cast a blaring amber glow across the porch

"Is Wyman Scudder really dead?" Cindy asked.

Maleah studied the slender, petite woman, who certainly looked older than thirty-five. But she wasn't a bad-looking woman, just old before her time. Hard living could do that to a person. Her short, curly hair had been dyed a dark burgundy red which made her pale face seem colorless. Without makeup and wearing jeans and a Harley-Davidson T-shirt, she didn't look like a prostitute, just a rode-hard-and-put-away-wet middle-aged country gal.

"Yes, Wyman Scudder is dead," Maleah said. "We're pretty sure he was murdered."

"How did you meet Mr. Scudder?" Derek asked.

"Look, before I answer any of your questions, I need to know that I'm not going to get in any trouble with the law." Cindy glanced from Maleah to Derek. "I got myself involved in something I wish I hadn't. But I didn't have no idea . . . I just needed the money. I've been out of the business for a while, you know. I've tried waitressing and working in the chicken plant and all sorts of odd jobs. I got a kid, see, and it ain't right that she's in foster care. The only way I can get her back is . . ." Cindy swallowed her tears.

"You have a daughter?" Maleah leaned forward toward Cindy. "What's her name?"

"Patsy Lynn. I named her after my mama."

"How old is Patsy Lynn?"

"She'll be eleven this October."

Maleah looked Cindy square in the eye. "Cindy, my name is Maleah Perdue, and I promise you that Derek—" she glanced at him "—this is Derek Lawrence. I promise you that we will do whatever we can to protect you and that includes protection from the police."

Cindy took a deep breath. "He paid me five thousand dollars. All I had to do was visit Jerome Browning at the Georgia State Prison and exchange a few letters and a few phone calls."

"Who paid you?" Derek asked. "Who hired you?"

"Wyman Scudder. I thought you knew."

"Are you saying that Wyman Scudder hired you and he's the one who paid you five thousand dollars?" Maleah asked. "You never met anyone else, were never contacted by anyone else?"

Cindy shook her head. "Nobody else. Just Mr. Scudder."

"Then you never met a man named Albert Durham?" Derek asked.

Cindy didn't respond immediately. Maleah sensed that the woman was giving her reply a great deal of thought.

"Cindy?" Maleah prompted.

"I never met him. But . . . Jerome talked about him. You know, when I'd go visit him. The first time I went for a visit, he said a man named Albert Durham was going to write a book about him and make him even more famous than he already was. Jerome liked the idea of the whole world knowing who he was and what he'd done."

"But you never met Durham?" Derek said.

Cindy shook her head.

"Can you tell us exactly why Wyman Scudder hired you?" Derek asked.

"Wyman was my lawyer, a few years back. We . . . uh . . . sort of had a thing. You know. For a while. I hired him to help me try to keep my daughter out of foster care. I couldn't afford to pay him." Cindy hung her head.

"When did Scudder first contact you about visiting Jerome Browning?" Maleah asked.

"About five months ago. He said he had a client who needed a friend, a female friend, to visit him every once in a while. I thought why not? I mean for five thousand, I'll do just about anything."

"What did you and Jerome talk about?" Derek asked.

"Everything. Nothing. Mostly about him. He liked to brag. And sometimes, he'd give me messages for Wyman."

"What sort of messages?" Maleah asked.

"Nothing really. Just things like, 'tell Wyman to come see me' or 'ask Wyman to tell Mr. Durham that we need to talk.' Stuff like that."

"You exchanged letters with Browning and spoke to him on the phone," Maleah said. "Do you still have those letters?"

"No, I ain't got them." She shook her head. "I turned each one over to Wyman as soon as I got it. They weren't really for me no how. That's what Wyman told me."

Maleah and Derek glanced at each other.

"What about the letters you wrote Jerome?" Maleah asked.

"I didn't write them letters. Wyman gave them to me, all typed out real neat like, and told me to write them out in my own handwriting and then mail them off to Jerome."

"Do you remember anything about what was said in those letters?" Derek asked.

"Not really. I didn't care. Weren't nothing to me one way or the other."

"I understand," Maleah told her. "But if you could re-member something, anything, about the content of those letters, it might help us."

"Would it help you find the man who killed Wyman?"

"Yes," she replied. "And the person who has already

killed five innocent people, using the same method that Jerome Browning used in his Carver murders. If you would come with us, let the Powell Agency give you around-the-clock protection, you could work with us to prevent this person from killing again."

"But how can I help you? I really don't know nothing."

"You probably know a lot more than you realize," Derek said. "The more you think about your visits with Browning and about the telephone conversations and the letters you exchanged with him, the more you might remember."

"You think so?"

Derek smiled. Cindy responded the way all women did to Derek's charm.

"You help us and we'll help you. Tell us what you want and we'll do our best to see that you get it."

Cindy studied Derek as if trying to decide whether or not she could trust him. She nodded. "Okay. You've got a deal, but I need to talk things over with my sister first and then pack a bag." Cindy got up and headed for the front door, then paused and asked, "I can let my sister know where I'll be and I'll be able to talk to her whenever I want, right?"

"Absolutely," Derek assured her.

As soon as Cindy disappeared inside the house, Derek and Maleah got up and walked out into the yard.

"Do you think she really can't remember anything or she's playing us to see what she can get out of us?" Maleah nodded toward the house.

"A little of both. I'm sure it didn't escape your notice that Cindy isn't the sharpest knife in the drawer."

Maleah grunted. "I noticed, and apparently it runs in the family."

"I figure if Griff can find a way to get Cindy's daughter out of foster care and if we can promise to return her daughter to her, she'll tell us everything she knows. And I can guarantee you that she knows more than she's told us."

When he had left Ardsley Park, he had fully intended to check into a downtown Savannah hotel and get a good night's sleep. He had planned to kill Saxon Chappelle's cute little sixteen-year-old niece tomorrow evening. But as fate would have it, he had decided to stop for a bite to eat and had carried his Netbook into the coffee shop café. While drinking an after-dinner cappuccino, he had removed a keychain flash-drive from his pocket, hoping it contained some useful information. After killing Wyman Scudder, he had downloaded the files from the man's computer before wiping Scudder's computer clean. It would take an expert a good while to restore those files, if it was even possible.

Just as he had hoped, Scudder had kept a current address and phone number for Cindy "Di Blasi" Dobbins.

Never put off until tomorrow what you can do today.

He laughed. He had put off killing Poppy Chappelle, but not without a good reason. He wanted her alone when he killed her. No witnesses. No collateral damage. Following in the Carver's footsteps as closely as possible didn't allow him much leeway.

He wasn't sure exactly how much Cindy knew, but if she knew anything at all that might help the police or the Powell Agency, she was a liability, just as Wyman Scudder had been. He no longer needed either of them, just as he no longer needed Jerome Browning. But Browning didn't pose a threat. He had used the convicted killer for his own purposes. And as smart as Browning was, his ego had prevented him from realizing the complete truth. However, by now, the Carver knew that Albert Durham would never write Jerome Browning's life story.

He could have waited until tomorrow to hunt down Cindy. Maybe he should have. But the moment he read the info from Scudder's file on Cindy, he realized that she was probably hiding out at her sister's place in Apple Orchard, South Carolina, and he had gotten an overwhelming urge to get the job done as soon as possible. And that's why he had driven straight from Savannah, a nearly three-hour trip. That's why he had set up about 250 yards into the woods, just far enough in so that he couldn't be seen from across the road at Jeri and Lonny Paulk's house. He had parked his car at a safe distance, but close enough to make a quick getaway. Hitting a small target, the size of a human head, at between 200 and 300 yards required the type of skill that he had acquired years ago and had used numerous times. He never became attached to a specific weapon, neither pistols nor rifles nor knives; instead he used whatever he considered perfect for the individual job. Tonight he had brought along a recent purchase—an M24 SWS.

One clean shot was all he needed. One shot directly into the kill zone where the bullet would sever the brainstem and cause instantaneous death.

He hadn't been there more than six or seven minutes now, watching and waiting for the right moment to strike. How long had the Powell agents been talking to Cindy? Lifting his Bushnell binoculars, he zeroed in on the Paulks' front porch. Cindy had gone back into the house and the Powell agents were standing in the front yard talking. Just what had Cindy told them? She couldn't have told them something of any real importance because her knowledge was limited. And with her out of the way, the agents would have no way to verify what, if anything, she'd told them.

Minutes ticked by, four, six, ten. The Powell agents hadn't left, which meant they were waiting for something or someone. During the wait, he had gone over his plan, preparing for several different scenarios, one that included having to kill the Powell agents as well as Cindy's sister and brother-in-law. Having to kill that many people would complicate the situation, make it messy. He preferred neat loose ends, all tied up, no usable evidence left behind. He always wore thin leather gloves that had been handmade in Italy, thus leaving no fingerprints. Whenever there was a possibility of leaving footprints, he made sure he wore inexpensive shoes that could be picked up at Wal-Mart. He prided himself on not making mistakes. Mistakes could be deadly. And he intended to live to a ripe old age.

When the front door opened, it was Lonny Paulk who came out onto the porch, not Cindy Dobbins. This time he wasn't carrying a shotgun.

"Cindy'll be out soon," Lonny told Maleah and Derek. "The wife ain't too happy about her going off with you two. She says we don't know y'all, don't know if we can trust either of you. But Cindy says she trusts you, so I reckon that ought to be good enough."

"We'll make sure Cindy is kept safe," Maleah assured Lonny. "She can call her sister every day if she'd like. We're not taking her prisoner."

"She says that the lawyer she hooked up with a while back got himself whacked and that the guy who killed him just might come after her next," Lonny said. "Any chance that me and the Mrs. might be in any danger?"

"I don't think you and Jeri have to worry. The killer

has no reason to harm either of you, especially once Cindy is no longer staying here with y'all."

Lonny turned halfway around and hollered into the house, "You two women stop your yakking and get out here. You're keeping these folks waiting."

When she glanced his way, Maleah noted the smile in Derek's eyes although he hadn't changed his expression in any way.

"Hold your horses," Jeri told her husband as she held the screen door open for her sister. "I needed time to say my good-byes to Cindy."

"I'm ready," Cindy said as she followed Jeri onto the porch.

Derek moved forward, reached up and took Cindy's small, seen-better-days suitcase while Jeri and Cindy walked down the steps and into the yard, the two women arm-in-arm. Maleah opened the SUV's driver's side door, slid behind the wheel and impatiently strummed her fingertips on the steering wheel. After placing the suitcase in the back of the Equinox, Derek stood outside the SUV. The sisters hugged each other and shed a few tears. Cindy released Jeri and walked toward Derek, who had opened the door for her and waited to help her up and into the vehicle.

Suddenly, halfway to the SUV, Cindy dropped like a stone falling through water and instantly hit the ground. The crack of rifle fire pierced the bucolic stillness just as the bullet entered Cindy's head. The sound was familiar in a rural area where hunting was a major pastime. But Maleah quickly realized that this nighttime shooter's prey had been human and that Cindy Dobbins had been killed by a skilled rifleman.

Jeri screamed at the top of her lungs.

Lonny mumbled, "What the hell?"

After reaching inside the SUV to grab the Beretta

Maleah kept under the seat as a backup weapon, Derek got to Cindy first and checked for a pulse. He looked up at Maleah, who rushed in behind him, and shook his head, then rose to his feet.

"Call nine-one-one," Maleah yelled as she flipped open her holster, pulled out her Glock, and headed across the country road.

Derek caught up with her just as she entered the woods. "Hold up," he told her. "We don't know where this guy is. It could take us a while to find him, if we can find him. Slow down and think this thing through."

"Damn it, Derek, while we're thinking, he could be getting away."

As if on cue, a car started somewhere nearby.

Without hesitation, they both rushed from the edge of the wooded area and ran up the road toward the sound of the vehicle's screeching departure. The red taillights winked mockingly at them as the car sped off in the opposite direction.

Maleah cursed under her breath as she turned and raced back up the road toward her SUV still parked in the Paulks' driveway.

"She's dead," Jeri wailed. "My sister's dead."

"Shot clean through the head," Lonny said, a look of shock in his eyes.

"Call 911, damn it," Maleah told them. "Get the sheriff out here." She jumped in the Equinox and revved the motor.

Derek barely got the passenger's side door open before Maleah started backing up the SUV. By the time he managed to jump inside the Equinox, she had the vehicle headed up the road, back toward the main highway.

Chapter 15

Derek noted that Maleah hadn't secured her seatbelt.

"I'm going to reach across and grab your seatbelt," he told her.

"Yeah, go ahead."

Once he buckled her in, he did the same for himself.

"I doubt the Paulks contacted 911," Maleah told him as she pressed her foot down on the gas pedal. "Call 911 and tell them what's happened and let them know that we are in pursuit of the shooter."

Knowing a reply was unnecessary, Derek hurriedly placed the call, gave them his name and then explained that there had been a shooting, the victim was dead, and her sister and brother-in-law were with the body. He rattled off the address and then explained that he and his partner, both Powell Agency employees, were pursuing what they believed to be the shooter's vehicle.

The 911 operator kept him on the line, asking questions as she began the process of contacting the proper agencies.

The scenery flashed by in a dark blur as they chased

the red taillights all the way back to the main highway. Maleah made the turn at eighty miles an hour. The SUV swerved and tilted as they rounded the curve and sailed into the oncoming traffic lane. Luckily, there wasn't another vehicle anywhere in sight, except for the getaway car.

Derek couldn't help being impressed with Maleah's driving skills. The Equinox had just hit ninety and was beginning to close in on the car ahead of them by no more than a hundred yards.

"Can you make out anything about the car?" Maleah asked. "Make? Model? Color? Car tag?"

"Not yet," he told her.

Staying on the line with the 911 operator by placing his phone between his ear and shoulder, he undid his seatbelt and climbed into the back of the SUV. Maleah didn't react. Remaining focused straight ahead, she kept driving in hot pursuit of the shooter. Derek plopped down in the backseat, spread his legs, reached into the floorboard and unzipped the black vinyl equipment bag. He rummaged around in the bag until he found what he'd been searching for—binoculars.

"I've given you all the info I can," he told the operator. "I'm going to hang up now."

He crawled over the console and back into the front passenger seat. After adjusting the Yukon night vision binoculars, he aimed them straight ahead.

"God damn it," Derek cursed.

"What is it? What's wrong?"

"He's playing with us, letting us get closer. There's no way in hell you're going to catch that bad boy."

"Bad boy?"

"Our shooter is driving a Dodge Charger. We're talking a Hemi V-8 standard on that car."

"Shit!"

Derek directed the binoculars toward the license plate. "It's a Georgia tag." He rattled off the number. "Bibb County."

"It's a rental, right? Otherwise he'd never let us get close enough to catch a glimpse of the tag. You can rent a Charger, can't you?"

"Sure can."

"Bibb County," Maleah said. "That's Macon. He rented a car in Macon, either before or after he killed Wyman Scudder."

"He wants us to know. Son of a bitch, he's telling us that he's tied up loose ends and—" Maleah mumbled a few choice curse words under her breath. "Damn, he's speeding up again."

"I'll call 911 back and give them the numbers I saw on the tag," Derek said. "I can't believe he's stupid enough to hand us that tag number on a silver platter."

"He's going to switch cars somewhere or he's got an accomplice waiting with another vehicle somewhere up the—"

"Watch out!" Derek yelled the moment he saw the pickup truck pulling onto the highway from a side road.

Maleah swerved to avoid hitting the truck, taking the Equinox all the way across the highway and onto the shoulder of the two-lane roadway. Derek's binoculars flew out of his hand and landed in the floorboard beneath Maleah's feet. Keeping her hands on the wheel and her wits about her, she managed to take charge of the quickly careening-out-of-control vehicle.

By the time she got the SUV leveled off and back on track, a couple of flashing blue lights coming from the opposite direction dove directly in front of her, effectively blocking her pursuit. She had no choice but to slow down and stop. Either that or deliberately ram into two patrol cars.

"Take a deep breath," Derek advised. "We have a lot of explaining to do. They don't know we're the good guys."

"I know. I know," Maleah said, aggravation in her voice. "These local guys just ruined any chance we had to catch the killer."

"No, they didn't. They're just the reason we ended our pursuit sooner rather than later." Once she cooled off a bit and could see reason, she would realize he was right.

In the meantime, they had to deal with local law enforcement and hope these guys would let them explain the situation before hauling them off to jail.

"Get out of the vehicle," a deputy called to them. "Slow and easy. And put your hands on your head."

Derek saw two deputies, pistols drawn and aimed, standing on either side of the Equinox, and one deputy directly in front, which mean the fourth was no doubt stationed at the rear.

"On the count of three, open your door and get out nice and slow," Derek told her. "And for once, would you please let me do the talking?"

Twenty minutes after he lost his pursuers, he drove into downtown Augusta. Once he realized they were no longer following him, he had slowed the Charger from a hundred to eighty and gradually down to the allowed limit. In retrospect, he knew he should have refrained from showing off by deliberately thumbing his nose at the Powell agents. But on occasion, he could not resist the urge to show lesser mortals that they were dealing with a smarter, superior, and more deadly opponent. There was no way they could ever best him.

He needed to ditch the rental car as soon as possible, but not before he was within walking distance of transportation. By now, it was likely that the Powell agents had given the Edgefield County sheriff's boys the license plate number and make, model and color of the vehicle. Using the GPS system, he'd gotten directions to the Greyhound bus station, which, as luck would have it, was now only five minutes away. When he reached the twelve hundred block, he pulled off the street and into the parking area for the Greene Street Presbyterian Church. After getting out, he popped open the trunk and removed a carrying case and a large suitcase. Then, working quickly, he disassembled the sniper rifle, carefully arranged the parts inside the carrying case, and placed the case inside the suitcase beneath his clothes and toiletries.

Before closing the suitcase, he removed his thin leather gloves and tossed them inside; then he closed and locked the bag. Whistling softly, the old familiar tune from his childhood, he clutched the suitcase handle and headed toward the bus station. Glancing at his lighted digital watch, he smiled. He had plenty of time to get there before the ticket counter closed at 11:59 P.M. He would go to Atlanta, take a day off to revise his plans, and then return to Savannah for the Copycat Carver's next kill.

By the time they were allowed to leave the Edgefield County sheriff's office, Maleah knew more about the sheriff and his department than she'd ever wanted to know. And she had gained a new appreciation for just how far Griffin Powell's sphere of influence reached, apparently all the way to Edgefield County, South Carolina. Otherwise, she and Derek would probably be behind bars.

Sheriff Gene Lockhart had taken charge of the murder case, the first murder in his county since he'd been elected. All three of the county's criminal investigators had been called in and two had been dispatched to the scene of the crime at the Paulk residence, along with the Chief Investigator and the forensic investigator. The third criminal investigator, Lieutenant Nelson Saucier, a middle-aged black man, with a wide smile and an intimidating stare, had been assigned to interrogate Maleah and Derek.

She had to give the man credit—he had assumed they were innocent of any wrong doing and had actually listened to what they had to say. And as soon as Derek had given him the license plate number and info about the Dodge Charger, he had issued an all points bulletin.

As difficult as it had been for her to keep her mouth shut, Maleah had done as Derek requested and allowed him to do most of the talking. There was no point in the two of them giving the lieutenant the same information. They were Powell agents working a case involving a suspected serial killer, a copycat murderer who was targeting their agency. Their investigation had led them to Apple Orchard in their search for a woman named Cindy Dobbins.

After patiently listening to Derek explain why they were on the scene when Ms. Dobbins was shot and why they were chasing the person they believed to be the shooter, Lt. Saucier interrogated them further, asking them question after question in rapid-fire succession. He expected answers from both of them and that's what he got, similar answers to each question, but not word for word identical responses.

The inspector had excused himself a couple of times, leaving them alone, but they had sat quietly and waited without indulging in conversation. The second time he had come back into the room, he'd handed each their driver's license and Powell Agency ID.

"Well, at least we know you're both who you say you are, but until I get the okay from Sheriff Lockhart, I'm afraid I'm going to have to hold y'all."

And so they had waited for what seemed like an eternity—well past dawn—before the sheriff, looking as if he, too, had been up all night—arrived at headquarters. He came in, introduced himself to Maleah and Derek and told them that they were free to go.

Maleah opened her mouth to speak, but didn't get out the first word before Derek grabbed her arm and said, "Yes, sir, thank you."

"Don't thank me," the sheriff replied. "Thank the attorney general. I've never gotten a direct order from the man, never even spoke to him before tonight."

"We'll be sure to let him know how grateful we are," Maleah said as Derek all but dragged her out of the sheriff's office and straight to where her SUV was parked.

"Give me your keys," Derek told her. "I'll drive."

She hesitated momentarily, then pulled her keys out of her jacket and tossed them to him. Before getting in on the passenger side, she stretched, tossed back her head, and stared up at the early morning sky. She ached all over, from head to toes. She was also sleepy and hungry and ill as a hornet. Despite the surprising competence of the sheriff's department, Maleah felt that too much time had been wasted on grilling her and Derek when that time could have been utilized in a better way. But then again, how could she fault local law enforcement, with their limited resources, for not catching their killer when the entire Powell Agency, with unlimited resources, had been unable to apprehend the Copycat Carver?

"Jump in," Derek said. "Let's get the hell out of Dodge while the getting is good."

Offering him a weak smile and a weary nod, she opened the SUV passenger door and hopped up and into the seat. While she adjusted her seatbelt, Derek started the vehicle, hurriedly checked his mobile phone and within two minutes, they were headed south. Struggling to keep her eyes open, Maleah began concentrating on the road signs and soon realized they were not headed back to Augusta.

"Where are we going?"

"Aiken," Derek replied.

"What's in Aiken?"

"A decent hotel that's not too far away."

"Is that what you were doing with your phone, checking for a hotel?"

"Aiken's closer than Augusta and I don't know about you, but the sooner I get something to eat and a few hours of sleep, the better."

"You won't get any argument from me."

"Will wonders never cease." He chuckled.

Although the trip from Apple Orchard to Aiken had been relatively short, Maleah had fallen asleep. She woke suddenly when Derek pulled the SUV under the entrance portico at the Holiday Inn Express in downtown Aiken.

"Get out and book us a couple of rooms," he told her. "I'll park, grab our bags, and meet you inside."

She shook her head to dislodge the cobwebs and without saying a word, got out and walked into the hotel. Before she reached the registration counter, the smell of the complimentary breakfast coming from the nearby dining area reminded her of how long it had been since she'd last eaten. *First things first,* she reminded herself, and went straight to the check-in desk. She explained to the clerk that she didn't mind paying full price for the two rooms for two nights—last night and tonight—although it was doubtful they'd still be here tonight. By the time Derek joined her, she had charged the rooms to her credit card and pocketed two room keys.

"They're still serving breakfast," she told him.

"Then what are we waiting for? I'm so hungry, I could eat a horse."

She led, he followed. After finding an empty table, he pulled over a third chair, dumped their bags into the chair and made a beeline to the coffeemaker.

As complimentary hotel breakfasts went, the food at the Aiken Holiday Inn Express wasn't half bad. Of course, Maleah was so hungry that anything edible would have tasted like a feast.

As they sat at one of the tables for two, each on their second cup of coffee, Derek reached over and flicked something off the side of Maleah's mouth. Momentarily surprised, she stared at him.

"Biscuit crumbs," he told her.

"Oh."

"Ready?" he asked.

"Huh?"

"Have you finished eating? Are you ready to go to our rooms and get a few hours of sleep?"

"Yes, I've finished eating. I'm stuffed." She had eaten far more than she should have, more than she normally did. As a general rule, she watched her diet and avoided big breakfasts, but this morning, she had indulged. Actually, she had overindulged. "And yes, I'm more than ready to go to bed."

Realizing that her comment could be misconstrued, she looked at Derek. He smiled and winked at her. Damn him. She felt a warm flush creep up her neck and color her cheeks. Crap. She wasn't the type who blushed, never had been, didn't want to be. But for some stupid reason, Derek had the ability to say or do things that caused her to feel slightly embarrassed.

"Your bed or mine?" His smile widened.

"Me in my bed and you in yours."

"Ah, shucks, Blondie, you're no fun."

"Shut up, will you? I'm too tired for your particular brand of humor."

He laid his hand over his heart. "You wound me, my darling."

Maleah groaned. "Damn it, Derek, grow up, will you?"

She scooted back her chair, gathered up her plate, cup and other items, and left him sitting there. After clearing the rest of the table and leaving a generous tip, he caught up with her at the garbage bin.

"Sorry," he said.

"No, I'm sorry," she told him. "I know you were just trying to lighten the mood a little. I shouldn't let you irritate me."

"I shouldn't kid around so much."

Maleah offered him a halfhearted smile as he picked up their bags and headed toward the elevator. She punched the Up button for the second floor and when the door immediately opened, she entered.

As the elevator ascended, she felt Derek staring at her.

"What?" she asked.

"Ever ask yourself why we seem to irritate each other so much?"

The doors opened. They got off the elevator.

"Because we're oil and water," she said. "If I say it's black, you say it's white. We're very different. And when you try to run roughshod over me, it irritates me."

"And do you think that I do that a lot, run roughshod over you?"

"Maybe." She paused outside her room, turned to him, gave him his key, and held out her hand for her bag. "This is my room. You're next door."

"I'll take your bag in for you."

She was too tired to argue, so when Derek took the key card from her, she didn't protest. He inserted the card into the lock and the instant the green light appeared, he turned the knob and opened the door for her. After entering, she flipped on the light. Derek followed her into the room and placed her bag on the floor.

"Sometimes you do run roughshod over me," Maleah said, finally admitting the truth. "I know you don't mean to and that you're usually unaware that you're doing it, but . . . Look, let's just drop it, okay?"

Derek set his bag on the floor beside hers. Instinctively, she stood her ground and watched him as he moved toward her. He came right up to her, looked down at her and grasped her chin. She struggled for half a second when he tried to lift her chin so that she had to face him, but quickly looked him right in the eye. If he thought he could intimidate her, he'd better think again.

He examined her face as if she were a bug under a microscope, studying each feature, searching for something behind her confrontational expression. The way he looked at her unnerved her.

"Well?" she said.

He reached out and caressed her cheek, his touch gentle and soothing. "Get some rest, Blondie. We can do battle another day."

She hesitated. Fraught with uncertainty, she waited. A moment passed, followed by another and then another, each one becoming tenser than the previous. Neither of them moved or spoke or even blinked.

He slipped his hand beneath her hair at the nape of her neck. Her breath caught in her throat. And then Derek broke eye contact and released her. She swayed, slightly unsteady on her feet, dazed by what had just happened.

But exactly what had happened?

She waited for Derek to say something, but he didn't. He gave her a quick nod, and as if he was slightly dazed himself, he turned and left the room. She didn't actually breathe again until she heard the door close; then she slumped down on the edge of the bed and sucked in huge gasps of air.

Luke Sentell sat at a sidewalk table in front of Le Bristrot du Peintre on avenue Ledru Rollin. The bistro, located in the heart of the 11th arrondissement between Bastille and Nation squares, was a ten-minute walk from the heart of downtown Paris. Dressed casually in jeans and a long-sleeved cotton polo shirt, he nursed a glass of Bordeaux, Cote de Bourg, as did his companion, an elderly French gentleman who called himself Henri Fortier. Luke neither knew nor cared what the man's real name was. They were not friends, not even friendly acquaintances or business associates.

Luke's French, although not flawless, was more than adequate, but Henri's command of English was excellent. Wishing to appear as nothing more than customers wanting a good meal, they each ordered. Luke chose the rib steak in cream sauce.

"When you return to America, you will please tell my old friend, Inspector Richter, that I send him my best," Henri said.

"Yes, of course."

Henri sipped his wine, all the while studying Luke, his gaze lazily inspecting his dinner companion. "Have you ever visited St. Jakob? It's a charming little village in the state of Carinthia, Austria."

"No, I've never been there. Do you recommend I visit sometime in the near future?"

"Yes, I highly recommend that while you're traveling in Europe, you add St. Jakob to your itinerary."

Luke nodded. "Could you suggest a hotel and perhaps a tour guide while I'm there?"

"Indeed. You must stay at the Inn Steinhof."

When the waiter brought their orders, Henri smiled at the young man, thanked him, and looked at his meal, eggplant lasagna with parmesan cheese.

As soon as they were alone again, Henri tasted a bite of the delicious concoction, sighed with satisfaction and then returned his attention to Luke.

"You must ask for Jurgen Hirsch. He will know where you need to go, what you will need to see."

Luke repeated the name quietly.

He would make reservations for the first flight from Paris to Carinthia tomorrow.

"And just where can I find Jurgen Hirsch?"

"When you arrive at the Inn Steinhof, leave a message for another guest, a gentleman named Aldo Finster. Simply state in your message that you are a friend of Henri Fortier and are looking for a reliable tour guide."

Luke nodded.

Henri smiled. "I think I shall order the orange tart for dessert."

Following his informant's lead, Luke, too, ordered dessert, but he ate only a few bites before saying goodnight. He had plans to make, a flight to book, and a report to send to Powell headquarters.

Chapter 16

The ringing telephone woke Derek from a sound sleep. He rolled over, kicked back the sheet, and noted the time on the digital bedside clock as he reached for his phone. 2:15 P.M. He had slept longer than he'd intended. Instantly recognizing the caller ID, he swung his legs off the edge of the bed and sat up as he answered.

"Derek Lawrence," he said, holding the phone with one hand and rubbing the back of his neck with the other.

"We think we have found Albert Durham." Sanders's voice seldom denoted emotion of any kind, always calm and even, regardless of the circumstances.

"Alive?" Derek said the first thing that popped into his mind.

"Yes, we assume he is alive," Sanders replied. "Of course, if you find him dead, then we will know he is not the Copycat Carver."

"Right. So, where is he?"

"He owns a home in Cleveland, Tennessee, but apparently he does not live there. There are renters residing there at present. He has an apartment in New York City, but it has been subleased for the next six months. And he has a condo in Aspen that he rents when he is not in residence."

"You've told me everywhere he's not," Derek said. "Do you know where he is right now?"

"Yes, of course. Otherwise, I would not have called you."

"So where can we find the guy?"

"He has rented a house on St. Simons Island, off the coast of Brunswick, Georgia."

"I'm familiar with St. Simons Island." Derek had spent many summers of his childhood vacationing there at the beach house owned by his family for several generations. The house had been built by his great-grandmother's uncle.

"I assume you and Maleah are no longer in Apple Orchard," Sanders said.

"We're in Aiken." Derek stood up and headed for the bathroom. "We're at the Holiday Inn Express."

"Hmm . . ." Sanders remained silent for a full minute, then said, "This puts you approximately two hundred miles from St. Simons. The quickest route should get you there in four hours. If you and Maleah leave within the next fifteen minutes, you could be there no later than seven this evening."

"Doesn't the agency have anyone closer who could check things out while we're en route?" Derek asked.

"We have already sent someone up from Jacksonville to keep an eye on Mr. Durham until you arrive."

"That's great. Give me the address and—"

"Barbara Jean has sent you the information you need. Check your e-mail."

"Right. Okay. Maleah and I will be on our way in a few minutes."

He should have known that Sanders would be one step ahead of him. The man had an uncanny sixth sense. If he didn't know better, he'd think Sanders had some psychic abilities of his own. In the past, Derek had often wondered why, if Dr. Meng possessed the empathic psychic talent Griff believed she did, Griff didn't put her gift to good use for the Powell Agency. When he had finally posed the question to his boss, Griff had explained:

"Yvette was once forced, by a madman, to use her special talents completely against her will. I would never use her in that way. I have rarely asked her to help me. How and when she uses her empathic abilities is her choice."

Derek used the bathroom, washed his hands and splashed cold water in his face. He had shaved and showered before lying down for a nap. His slacks and shirt had been wrinkled, so he'd folded them and placed them in a plastic bag. He put on a pair of jeans and a clean cotton shirt that he'd taken from his vinyl suitcase. Then he stuffed the bag containing his dirty clothes inside the suitcase and zipped it closed. He picked up the holster containing his personal weapon—an 8-shot 45 Colt XSE. He seldom carried a weapon, but considering what had happened in Apple Orchard, he had decided to take his pistol out of his suitcase. After strapping on his holster and lifting his jacket from the back of the desk chair, he felt inside the coat pocket. He hadn't realized until he had removed his jacket before taking a shower that, after he had opened Maleah's door for her, he had slipped her key back into his pocket.

He put a tip for the maid on the bed, left his room, vinyl carryall in hand, and walked the few feet to Maleah's door. He knocked softly. When she didn't respond, he inserted the key and unlocked her door.

Damn it, she hadn't put on the latch or double bolted the door. He entered, intending to remind her that she had neglected to take the proper safety precautions, but stopped immediately when he noticed the room was semidark. He set his bag on the floor, walked quietly over to the bed and looked down at a sleeping Maleah. She wore only her panties and bra, her hair was still partially damp, and she lay sprawled in the middle of the bed, the sheet covering one leg and hip.

He shouldn't be standing there looking at her. If she knew how much he was enjoying seeing her like this, she'd chew him out big time. But what man in his right mind wouldn't take advantage of the moment? After all, Maleah was a gorgeous woman, even if she seemed oblivious to the fact. Or maybe she was in denial. Most women wanted men to find them attractive. Not Maleah. For the most part, she wanted men to leave her alone. He didn't suspect sexual assault in her past as the reason. No, she wasn't afraid of men and didn't seem to dislike men in general. But she carried a major chip on her shoulder when it came to taking orders from a man, sometimes even Griff.

"Maleah," he called to her. "Hey, wake up, Blondie."

She stretched languidly, the movement shoving the sheet off her completely. When she turned flat on her back, Derek swallowed hard. Her breasts were high and round and full, straining against the pink lace bra. And beneath the sheer pink bikini panties, dark blond curls created a triangular patch.

"Maleah . . ."

She opened her eyes, looked up at him and smiled. "Hi."

"Hi yourself." He realized she was still half asleep.

Suddenly, as if just realizing Derek actually was standing there looking down at her and that she was half naked, she grabbed the sheet and pulled it up to her chin. Glaring at him, she asked, "How did you get in here?"

He held up the key card. "I accidentally put it in my pocket after I unlocked your door earlier."

"You should have knocked."

"I did. You were sleeping like the dead and didn't hear me."

"How long have you been standing there?"

He tried not to grin, but couldn't keep his mouth from curving into a closed-mouth smile. "Uh . . . not long."

"I assume you have a reason for invading my privacy this way." She jerked the sheet off the bed as she stood and wrapped it around her.

"Sanders called. Albert Durham is in St. Simons Island, Georgia."

"Is he alive?"

Derek chuckled.

"What so funny?"

"I asked Sanders the same thing."

"And his answer?" she asked.

"As far as we know Durham's alive. Sanders sent a Powell contact up from Jacksonville to keep an eye on Durham until we can get there."

"Give me ten minutes." Maleah disappeared into the bathroom, clutching the sheet just above her breasts as she dragged it with her.

Derek turned on a couple of lights, pulled a five-dollar bill from his wallet and laid it on the bed for the maid. He glanced around the room, checking for any personal items, and found none. Apparently, Maleah had left her suitcase in the bathroom after her shower.

Seven and a half minutes later, she emerged, completely dressed, her hair dry and swirled up into a loose bun, flyaway tendrils framing her face. She'd even put on some blush and lip gloss.

"How do you do it?" Derek asked

She stared at him. "How do I do what?"

"Manage to always look so beautiful?"

At first, she glared daggers at him, but then, as if unable to stop herself, she smiled and finally laughed. "I've learned not to take anything you say seriously. You get too much pleasure out of yanking my chain, don't you?"

"If you say so."

He opened the door and held it for her. Each carrying their own bag, neither in a talkative mood, they took the elevator down and quickly checked out.

By 2:40 P.M., they were headed for US-278 E.

Poppy loved her grandmother, the one constant in her life, the one person who never changed and seemed to love Poppy unconditionally. It wasn't that her mother didn't love her. She did. But she had other priorities. At forty, Vickie looked thirty, thanks to strict dieting, strenuous exercise and a little Botox here and there in strategic spots. Why her mom hadn't handed her over to Grandmother years ago, she'd never understand. Maybe as revenge against her husband's family, the people who had never approved of her as proper wife material for a Chappelle. Poppy did know that Grandmother had taken Vickie to court and an ugly legal battle had dragged on for nearly a year. But in the end, the court had awarded custody to Vickie, with generous visitation privileges for her grandmother. So, she had spent a couple of months every summer since then in Savannah, as well as every other Christmas, Thanksgiving, and birthday.

Sometimes, she dreamed of coming here to live per-

manently, but that wouldn't happen. When she graduated from high school, she would go off to college and
be in charge of her own life. It would be her choice
when to visit her mother and when to visit her grandmother. Her trust fund would pay for her college education, but the bulk of that small fortune would not be
hers to do with as she chose until she turned twenty-
five.

"Why such a sad face?" Grandmother asked.

"Ma'am?"

"Are you worried about something?"

"Oh, no, ma'am, just thinking about when I'm older
and I go off to college."

"That's a couple of years from now," Grandmother
reminded her. "I much prefer to concentrate on the
here and now, on today. Our guests will be arriving at
seven. You should go upstairs soon. A lady should take
all the time necessary to make herself presentable."

"Yes, ma'am."

"You are going to wear that lovely blue chiffon dress,
aren't you? I asked Heloise to lay it out for you and . . ."
Grandmother Chappelle smiled as if she had a delicious secret to share. "I took my sapphire earrings from
the safe. They're in your room, on your dressing table. I
would very much like for you to wear them this evening."

"Oh, Grandmother, the sapphire earrings. I couldn't.
I mean they were an anniversary gift from Grandfather."

"I'm not giving them to you, Poppy. I'm only loaning
them to you." Grandmother smiled. "But one day they
will be yours . . . when I'm gone."

Poppy threw her arms around her grandmother and
gave her a big hug. "I love you so much."

Staunch, prim and proper, stiff-upper-lip Carolyn

Chappelle hugged Poppy, then shoved her away and cleared her throat. She turned around, but not before Poppy saw the tears in her grandmother's eyes.

"I'll wear the blue chiffon," she said. She had seen the new dress Grandmother had bought for her and she hated it. It looked like something that girls wore forty years ago.

"And you'll wear the sapphire earrings."

"Of course I will."

Poppy rushed through the house and up the back stairs, taking them two at a time. She needed plenty of time to prepare for this evening, to psych herself up to "party" with the Chappelle family's friends. When in Savannah, her goal was always to make Grandmother proud of her.

For most of the four-hour trip, Maleah had concentrated on driving while Derek went over the reports from the agency, with updated information on Albert Durham, that included a recent publicity photo. The guy fit the general description of the man who had visited Browning at the Georgia State Prison. Derek shared the info with Maleah, giving her the condensed version, which left her too much time to think about other things. She couldn't forget the way Derek had looked at her that morning just before he left her alone in her hotel room. For half a second, she had thought he was going to kiss her. And she kept replaying in her mind the moment that afternoon when she had awakened to find Derek staring at her almost naked body. But what bothered her the most was that she kept hearing Derek ask, "How do you do it? Manage to always look so beautiful?"

Thankfully, those introspective moments didn't last

long. Powell Agency business kept them both occupied. Barbara Jean and Sanders had also sent updates on the Wyman Scudder and Cindy Dobbins murder investigations. The Macon PD weren't giving out any pertinent information, but the Powell Agency not only had been able to discover the secretary interviewee's name, but had already sent an agent to Macon to question her about discovering Scudder's body. The info on Cindy's murder had come straight from Sheriff Lockhart. As they had expected, no arrest had been made, and the killer was still at large.

So, where was the Copycat Carver right now? And who would be his next victim?

Derek had received several text messages from the agency's contact who had driven up from Jacksonville to keep an eye on Durham.

And Griff had called Derek. After their brief conversation, Derek had remained silent for a good while. Finally, Maleah's curiosity had gotten the better of her and she'd asked, "What did Griff want?"

Derek hadn't answered immediately, as if he had been debating about what to tell her. "The Powell Agency took a phone call from Jerome Browning a couple of hours ago. He left a message for you."

Maleah had braced herself. "What was his message?"

"Griff's handling it, so don't go ballistic, okay?"

"Damn it, tell me."

"Browning said to tell you that he's eager to see you again. And . . . he sends his regards to your brother Jack and his wife and son."

"That slimy, lowlife son of a bitch. He's threatening Jack and his family. My family!"

"Griff has talked to Jack and alerted him. And he's sending around-the-clock agents to guard Jack and Cathy and Seth. And like Griff said, so far the copycat hasn't warned us who he planned to kill next, so this probably isn't a warning from him, just part of the game Browning is playing with you."

"God, I hope Griff is right. If anything happens to—"

"It won't. They're safe. Griff is going to make sure of it."

With the combination of daylight savings time, St. Simons Island being in the Eastern Time Zone, and the date being late June, nightfall didn't occur until around nine o'clock. They reached the F.J. Torras Causeway in Brunswick before seven that evening, sunset nearly two hours away.

Derek knew that Maleah wanted to go to Dunmore, Alabama, where her brother and his family lived, that she wanted to guard them day and night, wanted to be the one to keep them safe. But he also knew that she would continue the investigation and allow Griff to send in other agents to Alabama because their best chance of finding and stopping the copycat was somehow connected to Jerome Browning. And Browning had chosen Maleah as the mouse in his cat and mouse game.

"Durham went fishing this afternoon." Derek relayed the latest information from their contact watching Albert Durham. "Since then, he hasn't left home."

"At least we know he's alive and well and we'll be able to question him."

"Yeah, but you know something's off about that," Derek said.

"Like the fact that Durham was relatively easy to find?"

"Right. If he's the copycat killer, he wouldn't want us to find him, would he?"

"It's possible that the copycat has been using Durham, too, just as he did Wyman Scudder and Cindy Dobbins."

"If that's the case, then Durham is in danger. The copycat will be coming after him next."

Maleah turned onto Demere Road, following the GPS directions toward Beachview Drive. "He was one step ahead of us in Macon and came in right behind us in Apple Orchard. If Durham isn't the copycat, but just another pawn in his sick game, then maybe we can save Durham's life."

"If Durham isn't the killer and the copycat knew where to find Durham, then why didn't he come to St. Simons Island straight from Apple Orchard?"

"Maybe he did," Maleah said as she turned onto Ocean Boulevard. "He may be here right now, watching and waiting for the opportunity to strike. It could be that the only thing standing between Albert Durham and certain death is our Powell contact who's watching him."

Derek shook his head. "If the copycat is already here, why didn't he kill Durham when the guy left home to go fishing? Even if he knows we've got somebody watching Durham, that wouldn't necessarily stop him. We were with Cindy last night when he killed her."

"Yeah, but he took us by surprise. That's not the case today."

"My gut is telling me that there's a missing piece to our puzzle."

"Maybe Durham is that missing piece," Maleah said. "Maybe he can fill in the blanks."

"We should be able to find out pretty soon," Derek told her when he saw the Beachview Drive rental come into view.

"Is that it?" She slowed the SUV in front of a pale peach stucco cottage overlooking the Atlantic Ocean.

"That's it."

She pulled into the narrow drive and parked behind the late model Mercedes. "Durham's car?" she asked, as she shut off the ignition.

Derek nodded.

"Where's our guy?"

"See the white panel van across the road?"

Maleah searched for the vehicle when she got out of her SUV, found it, and waited for Derek to join her before approaching the cottage.

Side by side, on full alert, aware of every sound, every scent, every flash of movement, Maleah and Derek walked up to the front door. Maleah rang the doorbell. Derek scanned the area from the rocky shoreline and sloping sandy beach to the wooded area behind the house.

They waited. No response. Maleah rang the bell again.

Derek heard movement inside the house.

"Somebody's in there," Maleah said.

Derek nodded.

And then the front door opened. A pair of inquiring blue-gray eyes looked each of them over quickly and then asked, "May I help you?" His voice had the raspy quality associated with a lifetime smoker.

"We're looking for Albert Durham," Maleah said.

"You've found him. I'm Albert Durham."

He vaguely resembled the debonair gray-haired gentleman in the publicity photo that had no doubt been airbrushed. Apparently Durham had shaved and gotten a fresh haircut before the photograph had been taken. But then, the man who stood in the doorway was on vacation, which probably accounted for the new growth of beard and the shaggy hair.

"I'm Maleah Perdue and this is Derek Lawrence. We're employed by the Powell Private Security and Investigation Agency," she explained as she and Derek showed the man their Powell Agency identification. "We're here to ask you a few questions about Jerome Browning," Maleah said.

"Who?"

"Jerome Browning, the serial killer known as the Carver. The man you interviewed for the biography you're writing."

"I have never heard of a Jerome Browning," Albert Durham said. "And I can assure you that whoever he is, I am not planning to write his biography."

"Are you saying that you have never visited Jerome Browning at the Georgia State Prison in Reidsville, Georgia?" Derek asked.

"I've never met this man Browning and I've never even heard of Reidsville, Georgia. And I have never visited anyone in prison, not in Georgia or anywhere else."

Chapter 17

Damn! Double damn!

Maleah believed Albert Durham. He didn't know Jerome Browning, had never met him, and was not writing his biography. One glance at Derek told her that he, too, believed Durham. So where did that leave them? Definitely with more questions than answers.

"Won't y'all come in," Durham said. "I have iced tea, fresh lemonade or I can stir up some cocktails, if you prefer."

"Thank you," Maleah said. "We'll forgo any refreshment, but we would like to talk to you about this mix-up."

Derek followed her into the large living room/dining room and kitchen space. The walls were pale yellow, the floor covered with beige tile, and the furnishings were a mix of new and antique, decent quality but not expensive.

"Have a seat." Durham indicated the sofa. He took the brown leather recliner.

They sat on the sofa, side by side, Maleah on the

edge of the seat cushion, Derek reclining, settled and relaxed.

"I suggest y'all start by telling me why you believed I was writing a serial killer's biography," Durham said.

"I've been to the Georgia State Prison to visit Jerome Browning, who during a murder spree a dozen years ago was known as the Carver," Maleah explained. "He told me himself that Albert Durham was writing his bio and had personally interviewed him."

"The description the guards gave us of the Albert Durham who visited Browning fits your general description," Derek added.

Durham rubbed his chin, scratching his fingers across several days' growth of gray-brown beard stubble. "I have no idea about this other Albert Durham. All I know is that I've never visited anyone in prison and until you mentioned his name, I'd never heard the name Jerome Browning."

"I don't want you to take this the wrong way, but . . ." Maleah paused, waiting to observe Durham's reaction and when his expression remained neutral, she continued. "If I give you the dates when a man calling himself Albert Durham visited Jerome Browning, do you think you could tell us where you were on those dates?"

Durham smiled. Maleah thought he had a nice face. Not handsome by any means. A bit weathered, as if he spent a great deal of time outdoors. And kind eyes. A soft blue-gray. The deep-set wrinkles of a longtime smoker crisscrossed his forehead and curved alongside his mouth and into cheeks.

"You want me to provide myself with an alibi," Durham said.

"Yes, I suppose that's what I'd like for you to do," Maleah told him. "That way we can verify there's no way you can be the Albert Durham we're searching for in connection to our case."

"Certainly. I understand. And if you'll give me those dates, I'll check my calendar. Since I keep a date book, I should be able to tell you what you need to know."

Maleah reached into her pocket and pulled out a notepad filled with scribbled notes. She called off the dates. Durham pursed his thin lips as he listened.

"The dates that you mentioned are easy enough for me to remember. I spent six weeks in Japan and was there on those dates." When Maleah and Derek stared at him questioningly, he added, "I was doing research on the subject of my next biography, Emperor Hirohito, who ruled Japan during World War II."

"An interesting choice for a bio," Derek said.

"My father was a WWII veteran and I've always been fascinated by that era," Durham said. "To verify where I was, I can let you take a look at my passport, and I can probably dig up credit card statements that show my expenses while in Japan, including hotels and restaurants."

"That would be great, Mr. Durham," Maleah said. "And I apologize for having to ask you to do this."

"No apology necessary, Ms. Perdue. If someone has been using my identity for any reason, especially to commit a crime, then I want them found and stopped as much as you do."

"More than likely the man we're looking for chose your identity because you're a biographer," Derek said. "For his own reasons, he needed to be able to pass himself off to Jerome Browning as a writer interested in gathering information for a biography."

Durham rose. "I keep my passport with me when I travel, even in the U.S. I never know when I might want to take a jaunt down to the islands for a few days. I can show you the passport, but I'm afraid I'll have to send you copies of my credit card bills when I return home."

"I'll leave you my business card," Maleah said. "I'll contact you if we need them and you can e-mail them to us."

While Durham disappeared into one of the bedrooms, Derek and Maleah stood and looked out the windows at the Atlantic Ocean.

"How do we even begin to find a man with no name, no face, and no ID of his own?" Maleah asked. "He used Durham's name and undoubtedly disguised himself to look like the real Durham."

"We'll start with a profile," Derek told her. "Now that we know who this man is not, we can begin figuring out who he really is."

"He's smart, whoever he is. Apparently, he fooled Browning, who may be a psychopath, but is far from stupid. And he's led us on a merry chase while he eliminated the only two other people who might be able to tell us something about him."

"With Wyman Scudder and Cindy Di Blasi both dead, that leaves only Jerome Browning. If Browning really has no idea that the Durham who interviewed him was a phony and had no intention of writing his bio, he may be willing to give up some information once he does know the truth."

"He won't give it up without a price," Maleah said.

"Yeah, with a guy like Browning, there's always a price to pay."

The real Durham cleared his throat as he returned to the living room. "Here you are." He opened his passport and handed it to Maleah.

She looked at the stamped dates for Durham's entry and exit from Japan, which proved he was out of the country on the dates that Albert Durham had visited Jerome.

"Thank you, Mr. Durham. We appreciate your cooperation."

"May I ask y'all a question?" Durham asked.

"Yes, certainly," Maleah replied.

"Why do you think this man who visited a convicted serial killer has been impersonating me?"

Maleah and Derek exchanged a how-much-do-we-tell-him glance.

Then Derek made the decision for them. "We believe that this man is copying Jerome Browning's MO and has become a copycat killer. By posing as a biographer, he was able to elicit details of Browning's murders from him, enough so that he could replicate those murders as closely as possible."

Durham's eyes narrowed, furrowing his brow. His mouth turned down in a pensive frown, deepening the grooves around his mouth. "And this man is using my name." He looked right at Derek. "My God, you have to find him."

"We're doing everything we can," Derek said. "The entire Powell Agency is working toward that goal—finding the copycat killer and stopping him before he kills again."

"How many people . . . ?" Durham swallowed. "How many has he killed?"

"Five."

"Did one of the victim's families hire your agency?" Durham asked.

"In a way," Derek said. "You see, each victim was connected to our agency, either an employee or a relative of an employee."

"Then finding him is as important to you as it is to me. It's personal."

"That's right."

Durham nodded. "I wish there was more I could do

to help you, Mr. Lawrence . . ." He glanced at Maleah. "And you, Ms. Perdue."

"We appreciate your cooperation," Maleah told him.

Durham studied Derek for a minute and then said, "Derek Lawrence. Hmm . . . why does your name sound so familiar?"

Before Derek could respond, Durham snapped his fingers. "Derek Lawrence, former FBI profiler. You're a writer, too. You've written half a dozen true crime novels. I've read several of them. They're intriguing. You're quite a good writer, Mr. Lawrence."

"Thank you."

"Could I interest you two into staying and going out to dinner with me this evening?" Durham asked. "There is this marvelous seafood place—"

"I'm afraid we can't stay," Maleah said. "We appreciate the offer."

"Yes, yes, of course. I understand. Duty calls."

Durham continued talking to Derek about writing as Durham walked them to the door and followed them outside to Maleah's SUV. Then they shook hands and said their good-byes.

As soon as they were on the main road, Maleah asked, "Where to now?"

"You're actually asking for my opinion?"

"We're partners, as you keep reminding me. I'm consulting you about our next move."

"You didn't consult me before you declined Albert's offer to take us to dinner."

She shot him a quick, questioning glance. "I didn't realize we had time to waste."

"We're going to have to eat anyway," Derek reminded her. "I suggest we find a place to stay here on the island tonight and get an early start in the morning."

When she opened her mouth to protest, to suggest they travel through the night, he cut her off. "We need rest, Blondie. We're both exhausted. We've been on the road—"

"All right, all right."

"We won't waste our time. We'll order room service and work through dinner, if that will make you happy."

She shot him a menacing glare. "You don't want to know what would make me happy."

Derek laughed. "Probably not. But remind me sometime to tell you what would make me happy."

Groaning, Maleah clutched the steering wheel tightly.

Ignore him. Ignore him. Ignore him.

Derek wondered who now oversaw their family's vacation home there on St. Simons. His mother? His sister? Or perhaps one of his uncles? He hadn't been inside the oceanfront "cottage" since he was a teenager, but if he thought no one was using it right now, he'd take Maleah there tonight. Stupid thought. First of all, he didn't have a key to the place. And he doubted the same island couple who oversaw the upkeep of the house and grounds all those years ago were still alive since they had been in their sixties when he was a kid.

Forget the family place and just check into a decent hotel.

"I need to stop at a gas station and fill up," Maleah said. "We're down to less than a quarter of a tank."

"While you're doing that, I'll find us a place to stay tonight."

"Fine."

Five minutes later, Maleah stopped at one of the Friendly Express stations on the island and Derek called to book them rooms at the King and Prince, a

beach and golf resort. He wouldn't mind luxury accom-
modations for a change and he thought Maleah could
use a little pampering about now.

After swiping her credit card, Maleah placed the nozzle in the mouth of the gas tank and set the pump on
automatic. She opened the door and asked, "Want
something to drink? I'm getting a Coke."

"A Coke's fine. Want me to—?"

She noticed he was still on the phone. "I'll get them.
You finish your call."

By the time she returned with their colas and placed
them in the cup holders inside the SUV, the pump had
shut off, indicating the tank was full. After hanging the
pump nozzle back on the hook, she hopped into the
Equinox, removed a small bottle of hand sanitizer from
the console storage bin, and hurriedly cleaned her hands.

"Was your phone call to Sanders?" she asked.

"No. I haven't gotten in touch with him yet. I was getting us a room for tonight."

She started the engine. "Where to?"

He gave her the directions. When they arrived a
short time later, he was surprised by her reaction. Other
than giving the resort a quick once-over as they drove
up, she didn't react in any way. He had thought for sure
she would bitch about their staying at such a luxurious
hotel.

Their side-by-side rooms were identical, both with
king beds, both with oceanfront views and decorated in
a cool, soothing color combo of cream, white, blue, and
gold. After dumping his bag in the closet, he returned
to her room. She came to the door when he knocked,
but didn't invite him in.

"I thought we could go ahead and order in, eat in
your room or mine, and then get down to work," he
said.

"I want a nice long soak in the tub," she told him. "Would you please order for me? Any seafood dish is fine. Shrimp, salmon, whatever. And a salad. No dessert. Iced tea."

"I'll place the order before I hop in the shower," he said. "Your room or mine?"

"It doesn't matter."

"I'll have them deliver to my room and I'll call you."

"Fine."

She closed the door in his face.

Smiling, he shook his head.

Maleah, Maleah.

He had never known a woman who irritated him the way she did. Or intrigued him as much. Or made him want to turn her over his knee and spank her. He chuckled as he unlocked his door. She'd skin him alive for that thought. And he had to admit to himself that if he ever got his hands on her, spanking wouldn't be on his Top Ten list of things he wanted to do.

No sooner had he entered his room than his phone rang. He answered as he closed and locked the door.

"Good evening," Barbara Jean said. "I have an update for you."

"We have an update for you, too," he told her. "Ladies first."

"Thank you." She went over some mundane basic facts with him about both recent murders. Derek made mental notes of anything he felt might be significant in compiling his profile of the copycat killer. "Sanders wanted you to know that he's discussed all the information with Griffin and Nicole. For the present, Sanders is in complete charge of the copycat case. Griff's focus is on locating the source of the rumors about Malcolm York. He's in touch around the clock with Luke Sentell."

"I assume if there was any news on that front—"

"Yes, of course, we would inform you and Maleah. But for now, all we know is that Luke is in Austria following a lead."

"We're staying on St. Simons tonight and heading out in the morning, probably going back to Vidalia for Maleah's next scheduled visit with Jerome Browning."

"What about Albert Durham? Did y'all find him?"

"Yes, we found him," Derek said. "The only problem is that the man we talked to this evening is the real Albert Durham. The man who visited Browning at the state penitentiary is a fake. He assumed Durham's identity and posed as a biographer to get Browning to share details about his kills."

"I'll let Sanders know."

"Please do."

"Derek?"

"Yes?"

"When Maleah sees Browning again . . ." Barbara Jean paused as if wanting to choose her next words carefully.

"I'll take care of her. I promise."

"She wouldn't appreciate the fact that I asked or that you agreed. Our Miss Maleah sees herself as a tough cookie. She doesn't want to need anyone, but I learned long ago that in one way or another, at some time in our lives, we all need someone."

"So far she's held her own with Browning," Derek assured Barbara Jean.

"I have no doubt that she has, but . . . Well, let's just say that Nicole and I worry about her as if she were our little sister. And we're counting on you to rein her in if you see these interviews with Browning get out of control."

"Do you and Nic honestly think I can rein in Maleah?"

"We think you are probably the only man who can."

Before Derek had time to digest Barbara Jean's final comment, she said good-bye.

What the hell had Barbara Jean meant when she had said *we think you're the only man who can?* It wasn't as if he had any power over Maleah. He wasn't her father, brother or mentor. And he certainly wasn't her lover. They were barely friends. Maybe not even friends. Not enemies. Not exactly adversaries, because they *were* on the same side. And they were definitely more than acquaintances. Damned if he knew how to label their relationship.

Standing in the center of his room, Derek took a deep breath. Then as he walked across the carpeted floor, he tossed his phone onto the bed. He picked up the guest book that contained the menu and hurriedly scanned the items available for dinner. Noting that room service ended at 10:00 P.M., he lifted the hotel phone, dialed room service, and ordered.

Moving toward the bathroom, he began stripping out of his clothes, dropping them haphazardly on the floor as his went. Naked, his clothes strewn from bedroom to bathroom, Derek turned on the shower and then grabbed the guest soap and toiletries. As he lathered his hair and the steamy warm water pelted his body, he tried to figure out just what kind of relationship he did have with Maleah.

They were coworkers. They were partners, albeit reluctant partners.

Yeah, that was it—they were reluctant partners.

So, why would Nic and Barbara Jean think he, of all people, would be able to rein in Maleah? If he said or did anything that even hinted of trying to control a situation, she overreacted. If ever there was a woman over whom he had absolutely no control, it was Maleah Perdue.

Chapter 18

With her eyes closed, Maleah lay in the tub, bubbles up to her chin and soothing warm water surrounding her tired body. As hard as she tried to empty her mind, to concentrate on her breathing so that she could relax, her mind wouldn't slow down and allow her a few precious moments of peace. She didn't want to think about anything or anyone. She didn't want to worry herself sick about her brother Jackson and his family. The thought that they could be in danger had crossed her mind ever since Winston Corbett's murder, but she had managed to subdue her concerns in order to do her job. But no longer. Not now. Not after what Derek had told her.

Browning said to tell you that he's eager to see you again. And . . . he sends his regards to your brother Jack and his wife and son.

But did Browning actually know who the copycat had targeted as his next victim or did that evil bastard just want them to think he knew?

Logic told her that the best way she could help her brother, his wife, and son was to continue her visits with

Browning. For the time being, he seemed to be their only link to the killer. Pure emotion urged her to go home to Dunmore, to place herself between her brother and his family and any danger that might come their way. But Griff had already sent in other agents—one each to guard Jack, Cathy, and Seth. Knowing the danger they were in couldn't be good for Cathy or the baby she was carrying. If anything happened to that innocent little life . . .

Maleah slid down into the tub until her head hit the water, separating the thick bubbles into two big mounds on either side.

Stop thinking, damn it, stop thinking.

She sunk lower until she submerged her entire head under the water.

Jack and his family are safe. And you're going to do what you have to do—see Jerome Browning again.

Maleah rose from the watery grave, rivulets of soapy water racing down her head, across her shoulders and over her bare breasts. As she grappled around at the bottom of the tub searching for her washcloth, she shook her head sideways to dislodge any water trapped in her ears.

"Always shake your head," Jackson had told her the first time he'd given her a swimming lesson. "Like this." He had demonstrated the motion for her. "It'll help get the water out of your ears. I don't want my kid sister getting swimmer's ear."

She loved Jack more than anyone on earth. He was not only her brother. He was her hero.

"Oh, Jack, I'm sorry that my being a Powell agent has put you and your family in danger."

Tears gathered in her eyes. God, how she hated weak, weepy women. Women like her mother. She would never be like that. She would never let some man beat her into the ground and walk all over her. Even if it meant spending the rest of her life alone, she would never willingly give any man the power to hurt her.

After finally finding her washcloth, she brought it up from the bottom of the tub, wrung out the excess water and wiped her face with the damp cloth. She had no idea how long she'd been in the tub, thinking, trying not to think and fighting the almost overwhelming urge to cry. But the once hot water was now tepid and her fingertips were puckered, so she figured she had been in the tub too long.

She rose from the water, stepped out onto the bathmat and reached for a thick, fluffy towel. She draped a towel around her wet hair and then retrieved another and dried off, from face to feet. As she slipped into her clean panties, she debated about putting on a bra, but quickly dismissed the thought of going braless. After all, she didn't want Derek to think she was trying to be provocative.

If only she didn't have to see Derek again tonight. If only he wasn't her partner on this case. But he was her partner and for a very good reason—his expertise as a profiler could prove invaluable. And she did have to see him again tonight. They had work to do.

While she dressed, she reminded herself that Derek really was not a problem. He was her partner. She needed him as much as he needed her. Like it or not, they were a team.

Once she'd gotten to know him, when they had worked together on the Midnight Killer case, Maleah realized that some of her preconceived notions about Derek were wrong. But some were dead on. He was arrogant. But only occasionally. Most rich, handsome, intelligent men were. He was a womanizer who went through women as if they were Kleenex. Stupid women.

And from the first day they met when he had tried to charm her, she had begun putting up a protective barrier between them. No way was she going to fall for a guy who thought he could sweet talk any woman he wanted into his bed. But what she hated most about Derek was the way he tried to boss her around and make all the decisions for her. Or at least he had in the beginning. Now, he actually made an effort not to go all macho he-man on her, delegating her to the role of helpless female.

No, Derek was not the major problem in her life right now.

Jerome Browning was the problem.

She needed to know whatever Browning knew.

She had to find a way to make him talk.

And she would do it, no matter what the cost to her.

Alone on the patio, Nicole stared up the night sky filled with countless tiny, sparkling stars, distant light peeping through pinpricks in a heavenly black canvas. An overwhelming sense of doom settled over her, a foreboding feeling of desolation and danger. But she was safe. Everyone within the protective walls of Griffin's Rest was safe. So why did she feel as if she were dying by slow, excruciating degrees?

God, Nic, don't be overly dramatic. You're not dying. You're worried and upset and pissed at your husband.

If she didn't love Griff so damn much, she would have packed her bags and left long before now. She would have put some distance between her and Griff, for her own sanity. But she had tried that before, spending time away from him, and in the end, she always came home. Home where her heart was. Home to the man she loved more than life itself.

And the bittersweet thing about loving Griff was knowing that he loved her in the same wildly, desperately passionate way.

She didn't doubt his love or his loyalty.

And yet she didn't trust him to be totally honest with her.

In her gut, she knew he was keeping something from her, something possibly so terrible that he couldn't bear for her to know.

But Sanders knew.

And Yvette knew.

Tears lodged in her throat. She wouldn't cry. Crying was pointless. It served no purpose other than to give her a splitting headache.

Griff had left the house less than an hour ago. He had asked her to go with him. She had declined. Before leaving her, he had searched her face as if seeking her approval. He didn't need it. He did as he pleased. If she had asked him not to go, he would have gone anyway. And he would have asked her to understand.

But how could she understand?

Her husband loved another woman.

How many times had Griff told her that his love for Yvette was that of a brother for a sister, of one battle-weary comrade for another, of a friend for a friend? She believed he meant what he said.

And yet she wondered what would happen if he ever had to choose between the two women in his life, the two women he loved. The bond he shared with Yvette and Sanders, a bond he told her had been forged in hell, could not be broken and it was a bond she couldn't share. She had not lived on Amara, a captive of billionaire madman Malcolm York. She had not shared their particular torment and torture and inhuman treatment.

At best, she was a sympathetic outsider to their god-damn holy Amara trinity of wounded souls.

She had lived through her own particular hell when she had been kidnapped by a psychopathic serial killer who had hunted his victims as if they were animals. After she escaped from her captor, Griff had told her about the time he had spent on Amara. Knowing that he truly understood what she had gone through had helped her not only recover and believe she could return to a normal life, but it helped her trust Griff. Trust him with her life. Trust him with her heart.

It had taken quite some time after they married for her to realize that he had not told her everything about his experience on Amara, and that he had no intention of ever telling her.

"We made a pact, Sanders, Yvette and I," Griff had told her. "We would never tell another living soul everything we endured and that only with the other two's permission would we ever discuss any part of our experience with someone else."

Sanders and Yvette had allowed him to share a part of their story with her. To help her heal. And she knew that the threesome had agreed to bring Derek Lawrence, Luke Sentell and the Powell Agency lawyer, Camden Hendrix, into the inner circle that also included her. Their knowledge was limited, even more so than hers; but they knew that Griff, Sanders, and Yvette had killed Malcolm York, a monster who had tortured and murdered numerous people on his private Pacific Island of Amara.

Griff had not wanted her to tell Maleah, but she had finally made him understand that she badly needed to confide in her best friend. During the past few years, Maleah had become the sister she never had.

Nic rose from the chaise lounge, walked off the patio and onto the pathway that led from the house to the lake. Suddenly she sensed his presence, a gigantic form coming out of the shadows. She didn't bother to turn around and look his way. Griff had assigned Shaughnessy Hood as her personal bodyguard and she was never to leave the house without him. Ignoring her protector, she made her way down to the peacefully serene riverbank.

Damn it, Griff, why did you have to go to Yvette? Why did you feel it necessary to check on her in person? You could have called her. It's not as if Michelle Allen isn't at her side night and day, protecting her just as Shaughnessy protects me.

Room service arrived and set up their dinner on the balcony overlooking the ocean as Derek had requested. He phoned Maleah and she arrived promptly just as the waiter left. He took one look at her, hair hanging to her shoulders in soft blonde waves, a pale pink cotton sweater loosely covering her hips that were encased in white jeans, and wished she were any other woman on earth. If she wasn't Maleah Perdue, the personification of I-am-woman-hear-me-roar, he would move heaven and earth to get her into his bed tonight.

"What's the matter?" she asked.

"Huh?"

"You're looking at me funny. Do I have toothpaste on the corner of my mouth? Or did I forget to zip my jeans?"

"No toothpaste, no unzipped jeans," he said. "Come on in. We're having dinner on the balcony. I hope that meets with your approval."

"Isn't it a bit too warm to eat outside?"

"Actually, it's not." He took her hand in his. Surprisingly, she didn't jerk away from him. "It's a beautiful, balmy evening."

When they reached the door, she paused. "Dinner by candlelight? Isn't something that romantic wasted on us?"

He opened the door, held it, and quickly ushered her onto the balcony. "It's not romantic, just pleasantly civilized."

She glanced down at the candle lanterns and the covered dishes. "What am I eating tonight?"

"Madame will begin with a traditional Caesar salad, followed by Creole Florida black grouper topped with creamy Cajun crab and shrimp sauce over a bed of sautéed baby spinach."

"Oh my God, that sounds delicious."

Acting the gentleman, he helped seat her and then took his place across from her. "I know you said not to order dessert, but . . ."

"I am not eating dessert," she told him.

"It's triple chocolate cheesecake."

"You sure know how to torture a girl."

"Honey, dessert every once in a while is not going to ruin that gorgeous figure."

She snapped up her head and stared at him. He knew what was coming. She was going to tell him not to call her honey. She had chastised him repeatedly, but every once in a while, he simply forgot.

But then, to his surprise, she said, "Thank you for the compliment, even if you didn't mean it."

"You're welcome." He waited a few seconds before adding, "And I meant it."

She removed the cover from her meal and sighed. "This looks wonderful."

He followed her lead, revealed his twelve-ounce rib

eye, and lifted his knife and fork. For the next twenty minutes, they ate in relative silence, occasionally exchanging a few words.

While Derek enjoyed his slice of cheesecake, Maleah excused herself to go inside and make a phone call.

"I want to check on Jack," she said.

"Give him and Cathy my best."

"Yes, I'll do that."

After Derek finished with dessert, he blew out the candles inside the glass lanterns on the small table and waited around outside on the balcony for another five minutes, giving Maleah her privacy. He understood how concerned she was about her brother and his family. She had every right to be worried because they had no way of knowing where the copycat killer would strike next. And that was the reason he had asked Griff to assign agents to discreetly guard his mother as well as his sister and her family. There was no way the Powell Agency could provide private protection for every employee's family, but considering Derek's personal connection to Browning now, Griff had agreed that it was wise to guard Derek's family.

By the time he went inside, Maleah was ending her conversation. "Derek sends his best," she told her brother as she smiled at Derek. "Yes, I'll tell him. That works both ways, you know." She laughed. "Take care, big brother."

Maleah slid her thin phone into the front pocket of her jeans.

"What did Jack want you to tell me?" Derek asked.

"Oh, he said as my partner, he expects you to have my back."

"Ah. And you told him that it works both ways. You've got my back, too."

"Isn't that the way a partnership works, each partner takes care of the other?"

"Yes, ma'am, I believe you're right."

"Should we call down and ask them to clear away our dinner dishes?" She glanced at the remains of their delicious meal still on the balcony.

"I'll take care of it before I go to bed," he told her.

"All right then, partner, let's get to work." Maleah pulled out the swivel chair from the desk and indicated for him to sit. When he did, she plopped down on the blue and white striped sofa directly across from the desk.

He turned to face her. "Barbara Jean called earlier this evening."

"And?"

"Nothing really. She just gave me bits and pieces of information that she thought might help me work up a profile on the copycat."

"Would you mind sharing the information with me?"

He quoted Barbara Jean almost word for word and waited for Maleah to respond. When she didn't, he added, "You should know that, at least for the time being, Sanders is completely in charge of the copycat case. Griff is preoccupied with proving his theory that someone calling himself Malcolm York is behind the murders. Luke Sentell is in Austria, following a lead."

"I hope Griff is wrong," Maleah said. "Besides, don't you think it would be a truly odd coincidence if it turns out that someone impersonating Malcolm York is behind the murders, considering the fact that we now know someone is impersonating Albert Durham?"

"Stranger things have happened."

"Do you think the fake Albert Durham and the elusive risen-from-the-dead York could be the same person?'

Derek got up, walked around the white coffee table and sat down beside Maleah. She turned sideways and faced him.

"It's possible," he said. "Anything is possible."

"A lot of help you are."

He shrugged.

"Do you think you can put together a profile with what little information we have?"

"I'm going to try. We have to start somewhere and as we learn more about our copycat killer, I can revise the profile if necessary."

"Will it help to talk it out, to discuss—?"

"Absolutely. Some good back and forth discussion between the two of us could help," he told her. "We'll combine your thoughts and mine on the subject of our copycat killer."

"You talk. I'll listen and comment."

"The Copycat Carver is an odd bird." Derek leaned back against the thickly padded sofa cushions and spread out his arm, bringing his fingertips within touching distance of Maleah's neck. "He's gone to a great deal of trouble to copy Jerome Browning's MO and yet he deliberately sent the pieces of flesh he re-moved from the victims' bodies to you instead of hiding them away somewhere the way Browning did. Why?"

"Why did he send them to me or why did he alter Browning's MO in respect to the pieces of flesh?"

"Either. Both."

"The reason he didn't stick strictly to Browning's MO was because he wanted to send me a message and what better way of doing that than by giving me what would have been the Carver's most prized possessions."

"Very good reasoning."

"Thanks."

"We've agreed that for some reason, it's important to

the copycat for you to be personally involved in this case. That's why he chose Browning to emulate."

"Because Browning killed Noah Laborde, my former boyfriend." Maleah looked at Derek, concern in her hazel brown eyes. "But the question is why me? If Nic or Griff is the real target, then . . ." She paused for a full minute. "Could it really be that simple? Is he making me jump through hoops simply because he can and he wants Nic to know he can control her best friend? And what better way to hurt Nic than through me, right?"

"It's definitely what Griff thinks and it does make a crazy kind of sense. If tormenting Nic and Griff is his objective, then he's punishing them for some reason. He's going to strike again and again, possibly getting closer and closer to his ultimate target with each kill, eventually discarding the Carver's MO."

"If that's the case, then what are the odds that he'll try to kill me before he moves on to Nic and Griff?"

Chapter 19

"It's not as if we didn't already know that both of us or either of us could be targeted as one of the killer's next victims," Derek said. "My guess is that he'll gradually deviate more and more from the original Carver's MO, so having brown eyes eventually won't protect us."

"Your putting my thoughts into words makes it seem more real." Maleah eased back into the comfort of the sofa.

He squeezed her shoulder. "I try not to think about it. Besides, my guess is that your being jerked around by Browning is what the copycat killer wants, not your death. At least not yet."

"Maybe." She looked into Derek's black eyes. Her stomach tightened. "What about you? What's your role in all this craziness?"

"I'm the profiler. He knows my background. I'd lay odds on it. And it's just possible that he wants me to profile him."

"Why would he—?"

"He's giving me clues to who he is and it's up to me to decide which clues are true and which are false."

Absently, Derek massaged her shoulder, his touch seeming instinctive, as if he was barely aware of what he was doing. She knew she should pull away, tell him to stop. But she didn't. She leaned back against the sofa cushion and closed her eyes.

From the moment she had met Derek, she had been aware of the tension between them. And spending so much time with him these past few months had increased that live wire, just-below-the-surface unease she felt when he was anywhere near her. But on the other hand, as they had become better acquainted, her initial opinion of him had altered, at least somewhat. She had a greater respect for him, for his intelligence and his wit. She'd even gotten use to the way he kidded her.

"We're dealing with two, maybe three, separate people," Derek told her. "The copycat is playing Browning, using him, and it's possible that Browning isn't aware that he's been used. I'm not sure how much Browning knows, if anything."

"That's my job, isn't it, to find out what Browning knows." She opened her eyes and glanced at Derek.

"Yeah, that's your job and we both know he's not going to make it easy for you."

The gentle, continuous touch of his hand on her shoulder changed from soothing to arousing. She didn't know if that was his intention or just her reaction, but either way, she had to put a stop to it. Without making a big deal of it, she slowly pulled away from him.

"You said there were three separate people involved. There are Browning and the Copycat Carver. Who is the third person?"

"I said *possible* third person."

"Okay, if you want to split hairs, who is the *possible* third person?"

"Two scenarios," Derek explained. "First, the Copycat Carver is the man behind everything. He's working alone targeting Powell agents and members of their families, probably as a direct act of revenge against Griff and / or Nicole."

Maleah nodded. "And scenario number two is?"

"Someone else is the brains of the operation and he or she is the one controlling the copycat and Browning while keeping his or her hands clean."

"That's Griff's theory—the Malcolm York imposter is the Svengali puppeteer pulling all the strings."

"And Griff could be right. If he is . . ."

Maleah waited for Derek to finish his thought, but when he didn't, she asked, "If Griff is right, then even if we track down the copycat and stop him, this won't be over, will it?"

"We know Browning is a psychopath and my guess is that the copycat is, too. Working up a profile on the copycat is possible, but the third person—if there is a third person—is an unknown. He could be a she. He could be anywhere in the world, making it almost impossible for us to find him, especially if he has unlimited resources."

"How likely is that scenario?" Maleah asked, hoping Derek would dismiss it as an unlikely theory.

"I'd say between the two scenarios, it's fifty/fifty."

"Damn," Maleah mumbled. "So how do we find out exactly who and what we're dealing with?"

"You know the answer to that question."

"We have to find the copycat."

"That's our job. Yours and mine, working as a team, with the power of the Powell Agency behind us," Derek said. "And it's Luke Sentell's job to find out if the Malcolm York imposter is a real person or if rumors about him are just that, rumors, and nothing more."

Maleah yawned. "Sorry."

"You're tired. Maybe you should go back to your room and get a good night's sleep."

"No, I'm okay. I thought you were going to use me as a sounding board, bounce your thoughts off me."

He grinned. Her stomach did a wicked flip-flop. As if realizing the effect he had on her, he chuckled.

Damn it! Damn him!

"If you say one thing . . ." she warned him.

"Oh, honey . . . er . . . sorry. Scratch that endearment. Not honey. Let me rephrase."

"Just skip it, will you. Stop smiling at me. Get serious."

"A little levity isn't a bad thing, not when it's easy to get sucked into the kind of darkness these evil bastards inhabit."

She stared at him. "Is that how you see them, the Carver and the copycat, as evil?"

"In a sense, yes, they are evil. Not the they're-possessed-by-the-devil kind of evil, but evil in an all too human way. Psychopaths and sociopaths have mental disorders. Some can be treated through therapy and medication, if diagnosed. Some become killers. It is believed that these people lack a conscience and feel no remorse or guilt."

"Do you agree with psychiatrists who believe that sociopaths are a result of environment and psychopaths are a result of heredity?"

"There's too much controversy in the mental health field regarding the differences between sociopaths and psychopaths for me to take sides on that issue," Derek said. "Most clinicians use the 'antisocial personality disorder' diagnosis these days to describe both."

"And yet you refer to Browning and the copycat as psychopaths."

"Browning's doctors put that label on him, not me. But I do agree. As for the copycat, I'm going on gut instinct. This guy has to be highly organized. He thinks ahead, plans ahead, doesn't do anything erratic or unplanned."

"Even if someone else is telling him what to do, as would be the case in scenario number two?"

"If there is a third person who is in charge, he would hardly choose a loose cannon to do his dirty work, would he?"

"You're right. He would choose someone capable of taking orders, and someone who wouldn't draw attention to himself by acting in an irrational manner."

"It's not uncommon for many killers to show signs of both the psychopath's and the sociopath's characteristics, but each usually leans more in one direction than the other."

"You believe that our guy leans more toward the psychopath's characteristics, right?"

"Right. So my profile starts there. The Copycat Carver is organized, possibly obsessively organized. He will be difficult to catch because he does nothing on the spur of the moment. He plans each step of his kills and makes sure he leaves behind no clues."

"And he certainly has no problem using other people, without remorse or guilt, to achieve his goals."

"Our killer is probably above average in intelligence, just as Browning is. The victims are strangers to him, just as Browning's Carver victims were strangers. Browning deviated from the psychopath's norm by leaving the bodies in plain view."

"And the copycat has done exactly the same thing."

"He is a copycat."

Maleah nodded. "I know. It's just . . . Damn it,

there's something off about this whole thing. I can't put my finger on it, but it's there, if only I could figure out what it is."

"I agree. That's why the more I think about everything, the more I'm beginning to wonder about the copycat's role in these murders."

"What do you mean?"

"He's obviously intelligent, organized, mobile, skilled, has no ties to his victims, and no problem using murder to tie up loose ends. To date, he has mimicked Jerome Browning's murder MO five times. He strangled Wyman Scudder with the skill of a trained solider and he shot Cindy Di Blasi with the expertise of a professional."

"That's it, isn't it?" Maleah realized that the truth had been staring them in the face all along. "The copycat *is* a professional."

"Yes, I think he is. He's not a typical serial killer, actually not even a true copycat killer. He is, most likely, a hired killer."

"A hit man."

"Yes, an assassin, bought and paid for by our *third person.*"

"Then Griff's been right all along, hasn't he?"

"Maybe."

"What do you mean maybe?" she asked.

"Even if our guy is a professional assassin, that doesn't mean someone calling himself Malcolm York is his boss. Anyone with a grudge against Griff—or Nic for that matter—could have hired him."

Maleah yawned again. "Sorry, I guess I am getting a little sleepy."

"Let's call it a night."

"No, not yet. I should be good for a while longer. I can't stop thinking about your profile of the copycat or

the fact that we agree he could be a professional killer."
Maleah kicked off her shoes, brought her bent left leg
up on the sofa and crossed her right leg over the left.
Relaxing her shoulders between the sofa back and the
padded armrest, she faced Derek. "So, tell me how you
go about profiling a professional killer?"

"One size doesn't fit all," Derek said. "Although I believe it's the consensus of law enforcement and psychiatrists that for the most part, all professional assassins
have at least one thing in common—the thrill of killing."

Maleah shivered. The thought that anyone could derive pleasure from murdering another human being
was an alien concept for her. "Are all professional killers
psychopaths?"

"No, not in the strictest sense. For some of these killers
it's a matter of showing their control because having
that kind of power—power over life and death—gives
them an unparalleled rush, an excitement they can get
no other way."

"My God, that is so sick, but you say all of them aren't
mentally ill, that they aren't crazy."

"Each of us has within us the ability to kill," Derek
said. "Given the right circumstances, you or I could and
would kill. The difference is that most of us would not
derive pleasure from the act. It would be in self-defense
or to protect someone else. Or as soldiers do every day,
we would be willing to kill or die for our country, for a
cause we believe in."

"But a soldier killing in wartime is different."

"Yes, it is. And yet . . ."

"What?"

"Nothing. Just . . ."

"Something you want to share?" She stared at him.
He shook his head. "No, not really."

When she continued staring at him, he glanced away, breaking direct eye contact. "When I was in my late teens and early twenties, I bummed around the world on my own, putting as much distance between myself and my family as I possibly could. Not long after I turned twenty, I found myself flat broke. I was damned and determined not to touch my trust fund, so I did something really stupid."

"I can't imagine your doing anything stupid. Not you." Without giving her actions a thought, she reached up on the sofa back and laid her hand over his.

He tensed the moment she touched him. She eased her hand away.

"I joined a group of guys I met up with when I was in Europe, some real badasses, and I thought I was as mean and tough as they were so I sort of bluffed my way into their circle. They were mercenaries of a sort, most of them former soldiers. They weren't all that particular about who joined them. As long as I kept my mouth shut and did what I was told, we got along fine. I spent nearly ten months with them." He looked into her eyes. "You've never killed anyone, have you, Maleah?"

"No, I haven't. But I have been in several situations where I've had to return fire. And a few years ago, I was shot and spent some time in the hospital."

"I remember. I was working strictly freelance at the time. I consulted on that case. Rick Carson was the Powell agent in charge."

"That's right."

They sat there in silence for a few moments before Derek said, "I have killed. I've killed more than just one person."

"When you were working with those mercenaries?"

"Yeah. The first time I killed a man, I was scared to death. We'd been hired by a family to rescue a kidnap victim. I thought of myself as one of the good guys and the man I killed as one of the bad guys. The second time I killed a man, I wasn't quite as scared and eventually, it got easier. And finally it became too easy. I began hating myself. That's when I got out, changed my life around and came home to the U.S."

Maleah looked at Derek Lawrence with a greater insight into the person he really was, not the man she thought he was. Why he had chosen to share with her what was obviously painful memories about his youthful walk on the wild side, she didn't know. But she was glad he had. Seeing him now, all sleek and sophisticated with his expensive haircuts, his designer clothes, his air of casual elegance, she never would have thought—not in a million years—that he had ever been a soldier of fortune when he was very young and apparently very stupid.

She would never again be able to look at him and see only an arrogant playboy.

"I really don't know you at all, do I?" She couldn't take her eyes off him because she felt that she was seeing him for the first time.

"Sure you do, hon—" He broke off mid-word. "You know me. Sometimes I feel as if you can see straight through me." He grinned, the motion forced and self-mocking. "Now, you know me a little better. I've given you more weapons in your arsenal of reasons to dislike me."

"Is that what you think, that I look for reasons to dislike you?"

"Don't you?"

"No, of course not."

"Tell me one thing you like about me," he challenged.

"I'm not playing this game with you." She sat up straight and halfway rose to her feet.

He grabbed her upper arms and forced her back down on the sofa. "Just tell me one thing you like about me and I'll let you go." He kept a tight hold on her.

She didn't fight him, didn't even squirm. "I like your silver Corvette."

His lips twitched. "That's something I own. Try again."

His tenacious hold loosened ever so slightly.

"I like . . ." Her mind went blank. He was staring at her with such intensity, as if her answer meant a great deal to him. But that wasn't possible, was it? Derek didn't really give a damn what she or anyone else thought of him.

"You like what?" he asked. "My good looks? My winning personality? My magnificent body? My keen intellect?"

"Yes." She swallowed hard.

"Yes, what? Be specific."

"Yes, I like your looks, your body, your intellect and your personality, too, except for the macho he-man part that fights me for control and tries to put me in my place."

What is the point of lying? He already knows how I feel about him.

"And what do you believe I think your place is?" He slid his left hand down her arm and slipped it around her waist, then moved his right hand up to circle the back of her neck.

Keeping her eyes focused on him to show him that he didn't intimidate her, she replied, "You think I should be a helpless, needy female who can't survive without a big strong man like you to lean on, to support me, and to make my decisions for me."

When Derek laughed, she felt as if he had thrown ice water over her head.

"What's so damn funny?"

"You are, Blondie. You have no idea how wrong you are. Would I like to see you all soft and feminine, yeah, sure I would. But you could never be helpless and needy. That's not who you are, thank goodness. You're tough, outspoken, and independent. And those are things I like about you."

She stared at him with wide-eyed disbelief.

"And FYI—I like your pretty face, your gorgeous body, and your sharp mind." With his hand at the back of her neck, he drew her closer and closer.

He's going to kiss me. God help us both! What do I do?

You resist, you idiot, that's what you do.

But she didn't resist. "What about my personality?" she asked, her voice husky with emotion.

"I like your personality, except . . ." He brought his mouth close to hers.

"Except?" she asked, her lips parting in anticipation.

"I forget," he told her.

And then he kissed her. A tender marauding that claimed her mouth.

Mercy Lord.

She kissed him back. Kissed him with equal hunger and need and passion. Not until that very moment did she realize exactly how much she had wanted Derek to kiss her.

Chapter 20

Had he lost his mind? Kissing Maleah Perdue was insanity. A huge mistake. But damn it all, he couldn't remember the last time he had wanted anything half as much. While his thoughts went wild with warnings, he deepened the kiss. As if she were a drug he had become instantly addicted to, he wanted more. But the moment his tongue touched hers, Maleah shoved against his chest, trying to push him away from her. When she managed to free her mouth from his, she gasped for air.

"We can't do this," she said breathlessly. "It's crazy. We're crazy!"

He released his hold on the back of her neck and eased his arm from around her waist. Breathing hard, he stared at her flushed cheeks, her swollen lips, and disheveled hair. Apparently, without realizing what he was doing, he had threaded his fingers through her hair.

"Do I need to apologize?" he asked, knowing full well that she was going to lay all the blame on him. And maybe she should. After all, he had started the whole thing by kissing her, hadn't he?

Maleah shook her head. "I don't know what happened." She jumped up. "But it was as much my fault as yours." She refused to look directly at him. "I should go back to my room."

When she turned and headed for the door, Derek got up and followed her, catching up with her just as she reached for the door handle.

He laid his hand on her shoulder. She tensed.

"It was bound to happen sooner or later," he said. "There's been some sort of sexual tension between us since the day we met. That kiss was a good thing. It defused the tension, so we don't have to deal with it anymore."

She glanced over her shoulder, right into his eyes, and saw the truth. Who was he trying to kid? He was lying. They both knew it. That kiss hadn't defused a damn thing. The exact opposite was true.

"Right," she said, agreeing with his lie.

He reached around her, his arm brushing her side as he opened the door. She offered him a weak, we're-fine smile and walked out into the hall.

"See you in the morning," he said.

"Yeah, see you in the morning."

He stepped out into the hall and watched her until she disappeared into her room. Then he went back into his room and closed and double locked the door.

Cursing under his breath, calling himself every kind of fool, he stomped across the carpeted floor and went outside on the patio. After taking several deep gulps of fresh nighttime sea air, he sat down in one of the lounge chairs and looked out over the ocean.

Time for some hard truths, buddy boy.

He was attracted to Maleah. Not just her pretty blond looks or her hourglass-shaped body. He liked that she was smart and independent and aggressive. Hell, he even liked the way she stood up to him, challenged him, and wouldn't let him get away with anything.

Maleah was her own woman. She wasn't waiting for some man to come along and make all her dreams come true. She didn't expect a future husband to provide her with everything his money could buy. Not like Happy, who had married his father for his family's vast wealth and proceeded to make the man's life a living hell. At least that's the way he remembered his parents' marriage. And not like his sister Diana, who had jilted the guy she had really loved in order to marry the man Happy had chosen for her. A man with the right pedigree, social standing, and bank account.

Maleah was nothing like his mother or his sister. And maybe that was the reason he liked her so much. Too damn much.

You've got to let this thing go. You may want her . . . hell, she may even want you . . . but it just won't work. Not for either of you.

Okay, so things would be a bit awkward in the morning, but if they both just pretended it had never happened . . . But could they? Could he forget what it felt like to have her in his arms, how much he wanted far more than just a heated kiss? Even now, his body still wanted her.

How would Maleah feel about having sex? No strings attached. No deep, long-lasting emotions involved. Just screwing until they worked "it" out of their systems.

It? Primitive desire. Animal hunger. Lust. Call "it" whatever you want.

Maleah sure as hell wasn't the first woman he'd ever wanted that way and she certainly wouldn't be the last. But . . .

But Maleah wasn't just any woman and that was the problem.

Derek mumbled a few self-loathing obscenities as he got up, went inside and undressed for bed.

The Inn Steinhof, located in downtown St. Jakob, possessed the old world charm one associated with rural Austria. The three-story white building provided spacious, comfortable en suite rooms. Breakfast was provided and dinner was available for an additional charge. There were tables outside for shaded summer seating and a small bar and grill was located on the main floor, just off the lobby area. Upon arrival, Luke had done as Henri Fortier had instructed and left a message for Aldo Finster, whom Luke had been told was away hiking and would return the following day.

Long ago, Luke had learned the value of patience.

And so he had waited for Finster to return to the hotel. Half an hour ago, one of the maids had delivered a note from Finster, inviting Luke to meet him in the lobby in an hour.

When Luke arrived in the lobby, he casually scanned the area, and in less than a minute, spotted the person he assumed was Finster. He was a small, plump, balding gentleman in his late forties, his blue eyes appearing quite large behind a pair of thick bifocals.

Luke approached the man. "Herr Finster?"

"Yes, I am Aldo Finster." He smiled. "And you are Mr. Sentell." He held out his hand.

Luke shook hands with Finster.

"You are enjoying your stay in St. Jakob?" Finster asked.

Luke nodded.

"Will you be here long?" he asked.

Finster's command of the English language was excellent, although his accent was quite pronounced.

"Long enough," Luke replied.

Finster nodded. "I know an excellent restaurant just down the street. A short walk. Shall we go now?"

Luke nodded again.

Once they exited the hotel, Finster said, "You know Henri Fortier, I believe."

"Yes, I know Henri."

"He suggested you ask me to put you in contact with a tour guide, yes?"

"Yes."

"I know someone who would be perfect for you, Mr. Sentell. He has an excellent reputation for providing tourists with whatever they want."

"Then you can arrange for me to meet this tour guide."

"Most certainly. There will be a small fee, of course."

"Name your price."

"Sixty-two thousand euro." Finster continued walking, his smile widening as he glanced at Luke.

"This guide must be exceptional." Luke paused.

Finster stopped and looked squarely at Luke. "I can assure you that his knowledge of Austria is priceless."

"Then by all means, make the arrangements as soon as possible."

"You understand that this will be a cash transaction," Finster said.

"I'll have your money for you in a couple of hours."

"Excellent, excellent." Finster began walking again. "Perhaps we should forgo lunch today while we each attend to business."

* * *

Maleah had ordered coffee, cold cereal, and fresh fruit for breakfast and her meal was served promptly at eight. She was already dressed and ready when the waiter delivered her food. So far that morning, Derek hadn't gotten in touch with her. She suspected he was putting off the inevitable, just as she was.

Grow up, will you. It was just a kiss.

Yeah, but what a kiss.

As she sipped on her second cup of coffee—she had practically inhaled the first cup—she eyed her phone lying on top of her packed suitcase alongside her shoulder holster.

Go ahead and call him.

And say what?

Say good morning. Ask what time he wants to leave the hotel. Suggest that we should drive straight back to Vidalia, Georgia, to prepare for my next interview with Jerome Browning.

There was no reason to mention the kiss. Derek probably wouldn't say anything about it. No doubt he wanted to forget that it had happened just as much as she did. But the problem was could either of them ever forget?

You overreacted. That kiss wasn't as incredible as you thought it was.

She marched over to the bed where she had placed her suitcase.

Just pick up the phone and call him.

She reached down, grasped the phone and held it in her hand.

Aggravated with herself for hesitating, she said aloud, "Put on your big girl panties and do it."

She hit the preprogrammed number and held her breath as she waited for him to answer.

"Good morning, Blondie," Derek said.

"Good morning. I . . . uh . . . was wondering—"

"I'm ready to hit the road whenever you are," he told her. "I had my breakfast delivered half an hour ago. Have you eaten?"

She glanced at the untouched cereal and fruit on her breakfast tray. "I just now finished. I can be ready to leave in about ten minutes."

"Okay."

"I'll knock on your door when I'm ready to go."

"Sounds fine. That will give me time to check in with headquarters."

Everything was going to be all right. Derek sounded like his usual self. Apparently, she was the only one with a problem, the one who had stammered and acted all morning-after stupid.

"Derek?"

"Huh?"

"I think we should head straight back to Vidalia. I really want some prep time before I go back to the penitentiary for another interview with Browning. I'm going to need your help."

"We're thinking alike," he said. "I've already called the Hampton Inn where we stayed and reserved rooms for the next three nights. And while you're driving today, I'll start putting my thoughts down on paper and we can discuss strategy."

"Thanks, Derek."

"You're welcome, Blondie."

Poppy didn't go to church except when she stayed with Grandmother in Savannah. Her mother wasn't a religious person. Actually Vickie didn't believe in God. She said religion was for idiots and senile old fools like her grandmother. But Grandmother wasn't an idiot nor was she senile. And Poppy actually enjoyed Sunday morning services at the First Presbyterian Church. Aunt Mary Lee was Episcopal now, having converted when she married Uncle Lowell. The Dandridges had been Episcopalian for generations, just as the Chappelles had been Presbyterian.

"I thought we'd have lunch out here," Grandmother called to Poppy from the sunroom. "It's just the three of us today. I told Heloise not to worry with anything much. No sense heating up the house on such a warm day when we aren't expecting company."

"I made chicken salad before we left for services this morning." Heloise came out of the kitchen carrying a tray that held a pitcher of iced tea and three glasses. "And there are teacakes left over from yesterday. I thought they'd be good with ice cream and some fresh sliced peaches."

"What can I do to help?" Poppy asked.

"Why don't you set the table," Heloise said. "The everyday dinnerware will be fine, won't it, Miss Carolyn?"

"Certainly, certainly." Grandmother waved her hand in dismissal as she sat down in one of the big wicker chairs.

Although the Chappelles were no longer wealthy, Grandmother continued to live a comfortable lifestyle. She still played bridge with her snooty friends, still maintained a membership at the country club, still resided in the home where she had raised her family, and still kept a housekeeper, although after all these years, Heloise was as much friend as servant.

"The old bat has no idea that if it wasn't for Saxon putting money in her bank account on a regular basis, she'd be living from hand to mouth," Poppy's mother had told her. "The crazy fool thinks she's still rich."

Sometimes her mom wasn't a nice person.

Poppy often wished she could live with Grandmother all the time, not just during the summer. But when she had mentioned the idea to her mother, she'd gone ape-shit and threatened all sorts of things, including telling Grandmother the truth about her finances— that she was actually flat broke and living off her son's charity. When she turned twenty-five and had full access to her trust fund, she would help Uncle Saxon take care of Grandmother.

Sometimes Poppy hated her mother.

Luke paid Aldo Finster in cash. In exchange for the sixty-two thousand euros, Luke was escorted to a parked car outside his hotel that evening around eight o'clock. The driver got out, opened the door for Luke and waited while Luke slid into the backseat.

"Good evening, Mr. Sentell," the car's backseat occupant said.

"Jurgen Hirsch, I presume?"

"As good a name as any other and one I use on occasion."

"I understand from Herr Finster that you're the ideal tour guide for me."

In the shadowy darkness of the car's interior, Luke's eyesight adjusted, enabling him to see more clearly. Jurgen Hirsch, blond, muscular and probably no older than he, studied Luke, his gaze focused on Luke's face.

"There is someplace in particular you wish to go, someone you wish to see?"

"I'm looking for a man who calls himself Malcolm York."

Dead silence.

Luke waited, his gaze riveted to his companion's.

And then Jurgen Hirsch's lips tilted upward in a cold, calculating, unemotional smile. "I, too, have heard the rumors about a man by that name. But it is my understanding that Malcolm York is dead and has been for sixteen years."

"Then there is nothing you can tell me about him that I don't already know, but perhaps you can tell me more about these rumors."

"You are very persistent, Mr. Sentell."

"I'm fifty thousand dollars persistent, Herr Hirsch."

Hirsch laughed. A look of amused curiosity glimmered in his icy blue eyes. "Have you ever heard of Anthony Linden?"

"Who hasn't heard of Linden, the infamous former MI6 operative who went rogue. What does Linden have to do with Malcolm York, other than both men are dead?"

"Ah, but that is what makes their association so interesting," Hirsch said in his lightly accented English. "Rumors are that Anthony Linden is alive and well and has been working as a professional assassin for the past ten years."

"And?" Luke knew where this was going, a gut feeling he didn't like.

"Rumors abound, of course, but the most recent rumor circulating among my associates is that Linden is working for York."

"An interesting rumor, especially since both men are presumed dead."

"Sometimes rumors have a basis in facts. I have no proof that the billionaire Malcolm York who lived on the Pacific Island of Amara is alive, but I know for a fact that Anthony Linden is very much alive because I had drinks with him six months ago, the night before he left for America."

* * *

Griff took Luke's call at 2:30 Eastern Time that afternoon. When their brief, private conversation ended, Griff called Sanders into his study and then closed and locked the door.

"Do you remember a man named Anthony Linden?" Griff asked.

"A former SIS agent, I believe. He was permanently terminated ten years ago."

"It seems that Linden may be alive and well and is reported to have been in the U.S. for the past six months."

Sanders didn't react, didn't even blink. "And did Luke ascertain what the presumed dead Mr. Linden is doing in the U.S.?"

"It seems Linden is now a professional assassin."

Sanders's eyes widened. He clenched his jaw.

"Luke was told that Linden is working for Malcolm York," Griff said.

Sanders's nostrils flared as he released a deeply inhaled breath. "How reliable is Luke's source?"

"As reliable as fifty thousand dollars can buy. It seems that the source claims to have had drinks with Linden the night before he left for America. Luke assumes that his source and Linden are in the same business."

"If Anthony Linden is alive and if he is in the U.S., sent here in his profession as an assassin, you and I know that the man who hired him is not Malcolm York. York is dead."

"Is he?" Griff asked.

"You know he is."

"Yes, of course I know he is. He was dead when we left him on Amara. No one could have survived what we did to him, not even an inhuman demon like York." Griff looked at Sanders for affirmation, needing to hear him say the words, to vanquish the ghost that haunted him. Malcolm York was dead and yet . . .

"What York did to us, and to many others, lives on in each of us, like an incurable disease," Sanders said. "But York is dead. He was dead long before we chopped off his head."

Chapter 21

The trip from St. Simons Island to Vidalia took close to two and a half hours. Maleah drove straight through without making any stops. When they arrived at the Hampton Inn that Sunday afternoon, they went to their separate rooms. Although they had both acted as if last night's kiss had never happened, that singular event stood between them, an invisible wall of uncertainty. After making a concentrated effort for months to persuade Maleah to like and trust him, why had he done something so monumentally stupid? Any fool would have known that by kissing her, he would alter their fragile friendship.

If he could take back the kiss, would he?

Maybe.

But when he had kissed her, she had kissed him. Crazy thing was that he suspected she had enjoyed the kiss as much as he had, that it had affected her as strongly as it had him.

As he settled into his room, he tried to stop thinking about Maleah as anything other than his partner on a Powell Agency case. He unpacked his suitcase, hung up his clothes, and placed his shaving kit on the bathroom sink counter. He picked up the ice bucket and took it with him when he left the room in search of the refreshment center. He returned to his room with a full ice bucket and four canned colas, two in his jacket pockets and two balanced atop the bucket.

After placing three colas in the mini-fridge and the ice bucket on the desk, he upended a glass from the paper coaster, filled the glass with ice and popped the tab on his Coke. Then he removed his jacket and shirt, as well as his shoes and socks, stripping down to his T-shirt and bare feet. After setting up his laptop, he grabbed the glass of cola, along with a pad and pen, and relaxed on the sofa. Kicked back, sipping on the cold drink, he propped his feet up on the coffee table.

On the drive from St. Simons Island, he and Maleah had avoided any mention of last night. She had focused on driving; he had checked e-mails and text messages and given his full attention to the copycat killer case. They hadn't talked much and when they had, their conversation had been limited to strategic planning for tomorrow.

Maleah had a ten o'clock interview with Browning in the morning. She understood that the first goal was to find out if Browning knew that his visitor Albert Durham was not the real Durham, the real biographer. If the fake Durham had fooled Browning, then it might be possible to coax him into betraying any confidences the two men had shared. But he wouldn't give the info to Maleah without equal payment in return. He would want his pound of flesh. And he would want to strip it off Maleah himself, inch by inch.

If Browning knew that his visitor had been a fraud, his knowing that would change everything. That could mean the two men were co-conspirators, working together, each getting something they wanted from their alliance. If that were the case, then Browning wouldn't be inclined to offer any info to Maleah. Not unless she could up the ante and offer him something that the fake Durham couldn't.

Derek could only imagine what price Browning would demand.

Would Maleah be willing to pay the price?

Would he let her?

Listen to yourself, Lawrence! Would you let her? How the hell do you think you could stop her, short of knocking her out and tying her up?

While he jotted down first one thought and then another, anything and everything that came to mind, he finished off the first Coke. Just as he got up, refilled his glass with ice and reached into the fridge for a second can, someone knocked on his door.

He set the can beside his glass on the table and padded barefoot across the carpet. When he peered through the peephole, he smiled. He hadn't expected to see her again until morning.

He opened the door. "Hi."

"May I come in?" Maleah asked, her chin high, her gaze direct.

He stepped aside to allow her room to enter. "Yeah, sure, come on in."

When she scanned him from head to toe, he realized she was taking in his completely casual appearance. "I was settling in for the evening."

"I apologize for disturbing you." She was still dressed just as she had been when they had arrived at the hotel. Navy slacks, tan jacket, and sensible low-heel shoes.

"You're not disturbing me," he told her as he closed the door. "Would you like a Coke?"

She eyed the glass filled with ice and the unopened cola can on the desk. "Do you have another?"

"Two more as a matter of fact." He moved past her toward the desk.

"Then, yes, thank you, I'd like a Coke."

"Have a seat." He busied himself preparing a second glass with ice and then split the Coke between the two glasses. He walked over to where she sat on the sofa and offered her the drink.

Before joining her on the sofa, he opened the fridge and retrieved a second cola, popped the tab and set the can on the coffee table beside Maleah's glass. When he started to sit down, Maleah reached out and picked up the notepad he had left lying on the sofa.

"Take a look," he told her. "I was just putting down some thoughts on your meeting with Browning in the morning. See if there's anything you think you can work with, anything that strikes you as doable."

She read over the page of notes, and then set the pad on the coffee table before lifting her glass and sipping on the cola.

"First and foremost, you have to find a way to figure out if Browning knows that the Albert Durham who visited him is a fake," Derek said.

"I figure a direct approach is best," she said. "I think I should lead off with the news that we spoke to the real biographer, Albert Durham, and that the man who visited him and passed himself off as a writer wanting to tell the world Browning's life story is a phony."

"I agree. Watch him closely for his initial reaction. After those first few seconds, he'll hide what he's feeling and thinking. Browning is smart. He'll figure out what you want almost immediately."

"And that's when the games begin."

"Yeah, I'm afraid so."

"What if I can't read him well enough in those first

few minutes to figure out if he already knew Durham was a phony?"

"You'll get an initial gut reaction in those first few seconds," Derek told her. "Go with your gut, let it lead you into what you'll say next. Don't listen as much to what Browning is saying as to what he isn't saying. Read between the lines. And be aware of his body language."

"I know the basics, of course, but . . . Just this once, I wish you could be there, in the room with me. You're the expert."

He reached out, instinctively planning to touch her, but stopped himself mid-reach when she scooted away from him. Ignoring his action and her reaction, he dropped his hand to his side and said, "You know enough. It's mostly common sense and an ability to read people. Browning isn't going to willingly give away anything. He's going to lie and not only with his words."

"Are you saying he'll know I'm watching his body language and will fake that, too?"

"He may try, but the more intense the conversation, the less likely he'll be concentrating on what he's doing because he'll be too involved in what he's saying."

"I wish I had time for a body language refresher course."

"How about I give you one?" Derek suggested. "Why don't I order pizza delivery for supper, get a couple more Cokes and more ice and we'll settle in for the evening?"

"Sounds like a plan." She downed half a glass of cola as she stood. "I want to get out of these clothes and into some jeans. Give me thirty minutes." She set her glass on the coffee table. "Don't get up."

He watched her walk to the door, his gaze moving from her slender neck, exposed because her hair was up in a bun, and down over her trim, toned body. When she walked through the door, he leaned back on the sofa and huffed out a get-hold-of-yourself breath. He had to concentrate on business, not his partner's shapely butt.

It was that damn kiss!

He'd always been aware of how attractive Maleah was, but now he couldn't seem to think about anything else.

Well, you'd damn well better get your mind on helping Maleah survive tomorrow's interview with Jerome Browning. She's going into battle and the more weapons and armor she has to defend herself, the better.

Maleah had tried not to think about the kiss, but the harder she tried to forget it, the more she thought about it. How many times had she replayed Derek's words: *It was bound to happen sooner or later. There's been some sort of sexual tension between us since the day we met. That kiss was a good thing. It defused the tension, so we don't have to deal with it anymore.*

Although they had both known that comment was a lie the minute he said it, they had spent the entire day pretending it was the truth. They had acted as if nothing had happened, as if the tension between them no longer existed, when in fact the exact opposite was true. She was more aware of Derek as a handsome, desirable man than she had ever been. How ridiculous was that? She had convinced herself that he was everything she disliked in a man and had denied the physical attraction that sizzled between them.

You'll hate yourself if you have sex with him.

Where the hell had that thought come from? She wasn't going to have sex with Derek. Not tonight. Not ever. She didn't have indiscriminate sex just because her hormones went into overdrive. Doing something stupid and impulsive just wasn't who she was. She chose her sexual partners with care and that was why there had been very few men in her life. For her, a sexual relationship was based on specific factors: mutual respect, a certain amount of admiration, physical attraction, and love. Not the forever-after, let's-get-married kind of love, but the friendship I-like-you-a-lot kind of love.

She and Derek were partners, working together to solve a mystery, to identify and stop a killer targeting the Powell Agency. Now was most certainly not the time for them to explore all the explosive tension they each were trying so hard to deny. Later on, when this job was over and everyone associated with the Powell Agency was safe, they would have to face whatever it was between them. The ever powerful "it" that had taken on a life of its own when Derek had kissed her.

You kissed him back! she reminded herself for the hundredth time.

Hurriedly, Maleah removed her clothes, down to her underwear, slipped on her white jeans and baggy pink cotton sweater, and then slid her feet into a pair of pink Yellow Box flip-flops. After applying fresh blush and pink lipstick, she removed the pins from her hair and ran her fingers through it.

There. I'm presentable. But I don't look as if I'm trying to impress him.

As an afterthought, she rinsed with mouthwash and rubbed some scented lotion on her arms and hands before leaving her room.

After the second knock, Derek opened the door. "I found a Pizza Inn in the Yellow Pages. It's not far from here and they'll deliver in about an hour. I thought we'd have an early dinner since we skipped lunch."

She breezed into his room, hoping her body movements expressed casual confidence. She wanted him to

believe that she was completely comfortable eating dinner with him in his room, just the two of them alone.
She wanted him to know that the kiss they had shared
last night was the farthest thing from her mind.

"In about an hour is fine," she told him. "I am getting a little hungry."

"How does taco pizza sound? I know how you love
Mexican food."

"Taco pizza sounds delicious." She picked up Derek's
notepad off the coffee table and sat on the sofa.

"Don't shoot me, but I ordered dessert." He grinned.
"It's cinnamon stromboli."

"You, Derek Lawrence, are a wicked, wicked man.
You're trying to make me fat."

He laughed. "I like my women with a little meat on
their bones."

As if suddenly realizing how what he had said might
be misconstrued, he stopped laughing and searched
her face. "Not that you're one of my women. Or that I
think of you as one of many. Or—"

"Shut up while you're ahead," she told him.

"I really stuck my foot in my mouth that time, didn't
I?" He came over and sat down beside her.

"Don't worry about it. I realize that if I hadn't overreacted so many times in the past and repeatedly bitten
your head off, you wouldn't be concerned that I might
take offense at every innocent remark."

His brow wrinkled as he narrowed his gaze and
stared at her. "Once again, I have to ask who are you
and what have you done with the real Maleah Perdue?"

She laughed. "Oh God, not another imposter. Now
you're dealing with three fakes—the Malcolm York imposter, the Albert Durham imposter, and the Maleah
Perdue imposter. How did you find me out so quickly?
What did I do to give myself away?"

"Are you laughing at me?"

He smiled again and she noted how his whole body had relaxed. Body language. As if suddenly remembering what she was doing here in his room, all alone with him again, she said, "I'm here for my refresher course in body language, not for our mutual amusement."

"Who says we can't have a few laughs before, during, and after class?"

"We've had our before laugh, so let's get down to business." She flipped open his notepad, found the first blank page and clicked the ink pen. "If I recall correctly, some negative gestures include legs or arms crossed, more space than necessary between people, although I want as much space as possible between Jerome Browning and me."

"A general rule of thumb when you're trying to decide if someone is lying or telling the truth is to compare their gestures with what they're saying. If someone is saying yes and at the same time shaking their head, then odds are the gesture is true and the word is false."

"Okay, that makes sense."

"Unfortunately, we don't know how skilled Browning is in the art of using body language. He could use it as adeptly as a gambler who has learned how to bluff with expert ease."

"If it turns out that he's that good, I don't think a mini-brush-up course is going to help me." Maleah tapped the tip of the ink pen on the pad.

"Deciphering body language is not an exact science. Use it for what it is, an effective tool that isn't always infallible."

"I understand."

"Look for certain signs," Derek told her. "And remember to take nothing at face value, not what Browning says or what he does."

"I'm ready." She tapped the notepad with the pen again.

"People who glance to the side quite a bit are usually nervous, lying or distracted. Browning will most likely look you right in the eye, trying to intimidate you, but once you're deep into conversation, he may revert to acting in a more normal fashion."

"Got it." She scribbled down the info. "Next."

"Okay. Arms crossed over his chest means defensive. Touching or rubbing his nose could mean he's doubting you or he's lying. Rubbing his eye is a sign of doubt. Rubbing his hands together equals anticipation."

"Slow down."

"Sorry."

She scribbled hurriedly, then said, "Go on."

"You need to remember not to over-evaluate his gestures. It's easy enough to read them wrong, especially if he's playing you. Keep reminding yourself that you can't trust anything he says or any of his body language."

"Gee whiz, coach, is there any way I can win this game?"

Derek grinned. "Not if you play fair."

"Who said I intended to play fair?"

"You'd better not. If you do, he'll chew you up and spit you out in little pieces. Protect yourself at all costs."

"Yes, sir." She saluted him. They both laughed. "Now, back to Body Language one-oh-one."

For the next fifty minutes, they discussed body language, mind games, and went over techniques used to control emotions.

"If he says something that triggers a deep emotional response, there is a danger you'll lose track of the conversation. If this happens, recognize what's going on before you let it get out of control."

Maleah nodded. "I know the signs—rapid heartbeat and breathing, as well as a desire to scream. I can handle this. Some yoga deep breathing techniques usually work for me."

"If the deep breathing alone doesn't work, try refocusing for a few seconds," Derek suggested. "Just think about how you're normally in complete control."

"I can do that, too."

"And when you end the interview, you really need a debriefing. You can do that yourself or I can help you. If you can talk it out with me—"

"I will. My guess is that I'll need to vent. Besides, you'll need to know everything about the interview anyway."

A knock on the door interrupted his response. Instead he said, "That's probably the pizza delivery."

Griffin would have preferred not including Nicole in his private conversation with Sanders and Yvette. But he had allowed too many secrets to come between them and cause Nic to doubt him. The last thing he wanted was for her to feel excluded, especially when he shared confidences with Yvette. If only he had told her the complete truth in the beginning, before they married. Sanders had advised him to be completely honest with Nic; but Yvette, who had sensed Nic's jealousy, had warned him that there was one secret he should never share with his future wife. And in all honesty, he hadn't told her everything because he'd been afraid he would lose her. And losing Nic would be like losing his own life. She was his life. After knowing her, loving her, living with her, he knew that without her, he would cease to exist.

Even now, after Yvette and her protégés had been at

Griffin's Rest for nearly two years, Nic still had a problem with Yvette living nearby. He had tried in so many
different ways to reassure her, to make her understand
that she had no reason to be jealous of his love for
Yvette. But if he were honest with himself, he would
admit that it was the lies he had told Nic, the secrets
that he had kept, that made her distrust him. And yet
despite everything, Nic was still with him, loving him
and standing by his side.

Sanders had chosen to walk over to the home that
housed Yvette and seven young men and women who
possessed rare psychic gifts. He had gone on ahead,
half an hour before Griff asked Nic to join him. Yvette's
"students" were misfits, people who didn't fit into main-
stream society because they were remarkably different.

"You should talk to your wife first," Sanders had advised Griff. "She does not want to believe that the copycat murders are connected to your past. But with the
information Luke has discovered, combined with what
Meredith Sinclair told us that she was able to sense after
Kristi's and Shelley's murders, Nicole has to accept the
truth."

"Nic told me that Meredith could be wrong, even
though we all know that the girl's psychic abilities are
incredibly accurate."

"Nicole instinctively dislikes anything to do with your
experiences on Amara. She does not know the whole
story and yet on some instinctive level, she senses that
there is a secret you are keeping from her, a secret that
could destroy your marriage."

Griff refused to consider the possibility that Nic
would ever leave him, at least not permanently.

But if she ever found out about . . .

He had to make sure that never happened.

On their walk to Yvette's home, he told Nic only that

he wanted them to all be together when he told them about Luke Sentell's most recent report. If he could spare Nic, he would. But he had alienated her too many times in the past by excluding her because he wanted to protect her.

Michelle Allen opened the door when they arrived. Griff had assigned her to live there at Yvette's sanctuary as the in-house bodyguard for Yvette and her students.

"Dr. Meng is waiting for you in her office," Michelle said. "Sanders is with her."

After exchanging pleasantries with Michelle, Nic slipped her arm through his and said, "Let's do this."

Just as they reached the entrance to Yvette's private office—adjacent to her living quarters and separate from the rooms on the opposite side of the house where her protégés lived—a young student came rushing out into the hall.

When she saw Nic and Griff, she stopped dead still and stared at them, her mouth wide and a startled expression on her face.

Yvette stepped out into the corridor and placed her hand on the girl's shoulder. "It's all right, Shiloh. We'll talk later this evening. Go back to your room now and meditate."

"Yes, ma'am." Shiloh rushed past Nic and Griff.

Yvette smiled, her gaze traveling slowly from Griff to Nic. "Shiloh did not realize that Sanders was here or that I was expecting more visitors. She simply needed to talk, which we will do later."

Griff knew how hard Nic tried to like Yvette and how hard Yvette tried to be Nic's friend. His love for both women had put each of them in an untenable position.

Once the four of them were inside Yvette's office, Griff closed the door. He looked at Nic first, and then at Yvette and finally at Sanders.

"I received a call from Luke Sentell yesterday. I shared the information with Sanders immediately. I've waited until today to tell both of you because I wanted to consider every possibility and every implication. And I've been using Sanders as a sounding board, as I so often do.'"

"We are not going to like what you have to tell us, are we?" Yvette said.

"I agree with her on that—it has to be bad news," Nic said.

"The rumors are still rumors," Griff said, "but where there is smoke there is usually fire." He paused, collecting his thoughts, considering what he had to say. "As we already know, there is supposedly a man somewhere in Europe who calls himself Malcolm York. We also know he cannot be the York that we—" he glanced quickly from Sanders to Yvette "—killed on Amara. What if any connection this Malcolm York has to the other one, we don't know.

"Luke's contact, who may or may not be a reliable source, sold Luke information concerning a man named Anthony Linden, a former MI6 agent who went rogue and was eliminated approximately ten years ago. According to official records, he chose suicide over capture. But it seems that not only has York risen from the dead, but so has Linden. And York hired Linden, a professional assassin, and sent him to America six months ago. Or so the story goes."

"Oh my God," Nic said. "This is ridiculous. The entire thing sounds like a plot invented by someone who is completely insane."

Griff's gaze met Yvette's.

They knew, he, Yvette, and Sanders, how completely insane Malcolm York had been. Diabolically insane.

"Are we to believe that this pseudo Malcolm York has

sent a hired killer to murder people connected to the Powell Agency?" Yvette asked. "And he is a professional assassin, who according to official records is dead?"

"It's all too far fetched to believe," Nic insisted, her gaze traveling the room, searching the others' faces for any signs of disbelief. "Please tell me that none of you actually believe this story."

"Far fetched or not, we can't dismiss the possibility," Griff said.

"Good God, Griff, you think it's true, don't you?" Nic glared at him. "You think somehow, someway, York is reaching out from beyond the grave to seek revenge."

"No. I don't believe that Malcolm York is reaching out from beyond the grave," Griff said. "But I do believe that a real live person is using York's name."

"But who?" Nic asked. "And why?"

"That's what we have to find out," Griff replied. "That's why I want to send Meredith to London as soon as possible to join Luke." He looked at Yvette. "He'll need her from here on out. Will you speak to her and persuade her to help us?"

Yvette didn't respond immediately. Griff could see that the idea of sending the emotionally vulnerable Meredith Sinclair to aid Luke in his dangerous investigation bothered Yvette greatly. She was extremely protective of her protégés, the way a mother would be of her children.

"The choice is hers," Yvette finally said. "But if she agrees, then I believe I should go with her."

"No, it's far too dangerous for you to leave Griffin's Rest."

"I can't let Meredith go alone."

"You can and you will, if she agrees. Luke will take care of her. He understands her special needs. He won't let anything happen to her."

Chapter 22

Maleah had barely managed to force down a piece of toast and drink a cup of coffee that morning. Her stomach was tied in knots. She had put up a brave front, but suspected that Derek knew just how nervous she was. As she waited for the guard to bring in Jerome Browning, she tried to collect her scattered thoughts. Her mind reeled with information overload. *Focus, damn it, focus. Remember what Derek told you—don't over-think anything, just go with your gut instincts.*

The moment she heard the door open, she squared her shoulders, took a deep breath and stood tall and straight. The guard escorted a handcuffed and shackled Browning into the room. As on the previous visits, Browning was neatly groomed, clean-shaven, hair trimmed. His dark complexion appeared even darker against his prison uniform of white shirt and pants.

When he saw her, he smiled. "Hello, Maleah. How nice to see you this morning. May I say how lovely you look."

"Thank you." She approached the chair facing the one in which the guard placed Browning. Using the advantage of height, she stood and looked down at him. "I told you that I would come back to see you this week."

"So you did." As he looked up at her, his smile widened. "I appreciate a lady who keeps her word."

Enough chit-chat. She wouldn't waste another second on pleasantries.

"My partner and I met Albert Durham on Saturday."

She watched Browning's face for a reaction and saw nothing to indicate he was surprised or concerned. His smile didn't waver. He didn't even blink.

What had Derek said about someone not blinking? Did it mean he was lying? But lying about what? His calm reaction to her statement?

Don't over-analyze.

Assume nothing.

"And how was he? Well, I hope," Browning said.

"Quite well. And confused about why we had tracked him down to ask about his relationship with you."

"Was he? Odd. I never found Albert to be confused about anything."

Browning kept his gaze focused on Maleah's face.

Unwavering eye contact. That meant Browning's thoughts about what she had said were positive. Either that or it meant he didn't trust her enough to take his eyes off her.

Damn it! All this reading body language shit was driving her nuts and defeating the purpose of gauging Browning's reactions and reading between the lines of what he said or didn't say.

Remember, gut instinct, first and foremost.

"I'm afraid the Albert Durham you know isn't the real Albert Durham, the writer who has published more than a dozen biographies," Maleah told him. "Whoever the man was who visited you under the pretense of writing your life story was a phony."

Browning lifted his cuffed hands, tented them together and rubbed the tips of his index fingers across his chin. "Was he, indeed? How utterly fascinating."

Rubbing the chin meant disbelief. Right? Didn't Browning believe her? Who knew? Hell, maybe his chin itched.

"Did you know he was a phony?" she asked.

"How could I have known?"

"He could have told you who he really was and what he wanted from you."

"He wanted to write my biography because he found me to be a fascinating subject."

"Is that really what he told you?"

Browning eyed the empty chair across from him. "Why don't you sit down, Maleah, and make yourself comfortable. I'm tired of straining my neck to look up at you. And our sitting face to face is so much more intimate, don't you think."

She remained standing. She wasn't giving him what he wanted without getting something in return. "Did Durham really tell you he was going to write your bio? And if he did, did you believe him?"

"He did. And I did."

She sat down then, keeping her back straight as she crossed her arms.

Browning studied her pose and then widened his eyes. He was observing her body language as closely as she was his. *Got you!* she wanted to scream. She had deliberately crossed her arms, an indication that she had put up a barrier between them, to see how he would react. Now she knew that he would play her, not only verbally, but with his gestures.

"Tell me about your conversations with Durham," Maleah said. "What did the two of you talk about during his visits?"

"We talked about my favorite subject—me." He chuckled.

"About your favorite color, your favorite food, your favorite music—"

"About my favorite way to kill."

"He wanted to know the details, didn't he, because he wanted to copy the Carver's MO?"

"That's your theory."

Changing her tactics just a bit, Maleah asked, "Are you pleased with your protégé? That is how you see him, isn't it? You taught him everything you know. You instructed him on how to kill."

Browning laughed.

Her gut instincts told her that the laugh was genuine, that for some reason, her comments had amused him.

"Do you want me to guess why you find what I said so entertaining?"

"I find you entertaining, Maleah. Oh so sure of yourself. So confident and self-contained. A lady who doesn't allow anyone to control her." His gaze raked over her in a sexual way, pausing first on her lips and then on her breasts. "But that wasn't always the case was it? Not when you were a little girl . . . when you were a teenager."

What the hell did he know about her personal life? Was he simply guessing? Or did he actually know something?

"I'm not here to discuss me," she said. "I'm here to discuss you and your association with Albert Durham."

Browning shrugged. "But, sweet Maleah, I find you as fascinating as you find me. So, if you give me what I want, I'll give you what you want. You tell me what I want to know and I'll tell you what you want to know."

"What do you want to know, Jerome?"

"Oh so many things about you, my dear."

"My favorite color is pink. My favorite food is any-thing chocolate. My favorite song is—"

He burst out laughing; and all the while his gaze never left her face. "And your favorite way to fuck is? Do you like to be on top? Or do you secretly prefer for the man to dominate you? What was Noah Laborde's fa-vorite position? I'll bet he enjoyed your riding him like a bucking bronco, didn't he?"

Damn you, you son of a bitch. Damn you to hell. That's exactly where monsters like you belong, in the hot, burning tortures of everlasting hellfire.

"Is that what interests you, Jerome, other people's sex lives?" she asked in a calm voice. She was still in complete control. "You have no sex life of your own so you get your kicks living vicariously through hearing about how other people fuck."

His jaw tightened. His gaze narrowed. His nostrils flared.

Oh yes, she had pissed him off. That taunting verbal arrow had hit its mark.

After several tense moments, he visibly relaxed. He had suffered nothing more than a flesh wound. He was ready for battle again.

"Noah was a handsome young man. The two of you must have made a striking couple." Browning leaned forward ever so slightly. "Why didn't you marry him?"

"I didn't love him enough to give up my freedom," Maleah answered honestly and quickly turned around and asked for payment in kind. "Did you think of Durham as your protégé? Is that why you agreed to share the details of your kills with him?"

"Durham is an admirer, not a protégé. The way Elvis Presley admired Roy Orbison's voice, Durham admired my skills. I think of us more as colleagues than teacher and student."

As she absorbed what she instantly knew was significant information, she did her best not to act so damn pleased. Did he realize just how much he had told her? "Then you knew, from the very beginning, that Durham wasn't a writer?"

"Did I say that?"

"Yes, I think you did."

"You're free to interpret what I say any way you please."

"You knew all along, from his first visit, that the man really wasn't Albert Durham and that he wasn't interviewing you for a biography," Maleah said. "You lied to me."

"If you say so."

He looked at her, his gaze moving from one eye to the other and then traveling slowly up to her forehead, his gesture indicating that he was taking an authoritative position. She understood that at that precise moment, he felt he was in charge and she was subservient to him.

"Did you also know that the phony Durham was not a novice at killing?"

"What makes you think Durham wasn't a novice?"

"Are you saying he was?"

"Perhaps." He nodded his head. "Perhaps not." He shook his head.

He was having fun at her expense. He knew she had initially been trying to read his body language and now he was mocking her.

"Tit for tat, Maleah. You give, I give. Don't forget the rules."

"Noah was my first lover," she said, giving him the answer to his much-too-personal question about her sexual relationship with Noah. "He was a gentle, considerate lover and not much more experienced than I

was. We were young and in love. We were good together."

"Young and in love. How sweet. But you weren't in
love enough to marry him, isn't that what you said?"

"Yes, that's what I said."

"How did you find out about his death?" Browning
rubbed his hands together, anticipation evident in the
gesture.

"His sister called me."

"Were you shocked?"

"Yes."

"Sad?"

"Yes."

"But not devastated. Not broken hearted."

"I was shocked and sad and angry. But no, I wasn't
devastated by Noah's death. I hadn't seen him or spoken to him in well over a year. We had both moved on. I
still cared about him and wanted him to have a good
life. It did break my heart to think he would never
marry and have children and reach his full potential in
his profession."

"I took all that away from him." Browning steepled
his fingers.

She understood that he wanted her to admit that he
had possessed the power of life and death over Noah.

"Yes, you took it all away from him."

"Do you hate me, Maleah? Do you wish you could rip
out my heart? Or perhaps you wish you could slit my
throat the way I slit Noah's throat." He lunged toward
her so quickly that she barely had time to react and draw
away from him before the brawny black guard grabbed
his shoulders and forced him back into the chair.

He sat there, his breathing accelerated, his pulse
throbbing in his neck, his cheeks flushed. And then his
lips lifted upward forming a self-satisfied smile.

Maleah struggled to control the unexpected fear that surged through her, telling herself that the only reason she was afraid was because she hadn't anticipated Browning's actions.

"I hate what you did to Noah and to your other victims," Maleah finally managed to say. "I hate that there are people like you in the world. I think you should have been executed for your crimes and should be rotting in hell right now."

Browning sighed as if her answer had given him some sort of deeply gratifying satisfaction. How sick was that!

"After his first visit, I suspected Durham was not who he said he was," Browning told her. "On his second visit, when I confronted him, he did not try to lie to me. He told me he respected me too much. And that's when we made our bargain."

"What was the bargain?"

Browning shook his head and made a clicking noise with his tongue. "I gave you what you paid for. No freebies."

"Of course not. What was I thinking?" She rose to her feet.

Browning looked up at her. "You aren't leaving so soon, are you?"

"Game playing wears me tee-totally out." She planted her hands on her hips. If he wanted to continue their game, she was ready, but she was damn tired of being jerked around. "If you want me to stay—"

"Sit back down, Maleah." Browning's voice was harsh, almost angry.

She ignored him.

"Please, sit back down," he said.

"Give me a reason."

"Durham—or whoever the hell he is—wanted details

about my life as the Carver. In exchange, he offered to hire me a new lawyer and provide me with a female friend."

Maleah sat. "You have no idea who he really is?"

Using his clenched fists, Browning drew an X across his chest. "Cross my heart and hope to die."

He was lying, damn him. He was lying through his pearly white teeth.

"There had to be a reason you suspected he was not a novice at killing. Was it something he said? Did he—?"

"You want an awful lot for no more than you're willing to give me."

"I do want a great deal, but I'm willing to pay for it. I just don't want you jerking me around, giving me tidbits when I've paid for the entire meal."

"You really have no idea how expensive certain items are, do you, my lovely Maleah?"

"I have a good idea. You want me to open up a vein and bleed all over the place."

"Yes, that, too," he admitted. "I want your blood . . . your sweat . . . and your tears. Your tears most of all. So, do we have a deal? I can give you the real Albert Durham, served to you on a silver platter."

"How do I know you aren't lying? You just told me a few minutes ago that you have no idea who he is. Remember? Cross my heart and hope to die."

"You won't know if I'll be lying to you when I tell you about him," he agreed. "But isn't it tempting to give me what I want in exchange for the possibility that I can tell you who is killing people connected to the Powell Agency and maybe even why he's doing it? Also, I could tell you why he chose to copy my kills, but I suspect you already know that."

"Yes, I already know."

"Think about my offer. You have twenty-four hours.

If you're willing to pay the piper, I'll play you a beautiful tune." He glanced up at his guard. "We're finished here. I'm ready to leave."

The guard looked at Maleah. She nodded.

Browning stood. "See you tomorrow, sweet Maleah." He winked at her, then turned and fell into step alongside the guard.

The man once known as Anthony Linden finished a series of push-ups, lifted himself from the hotel room floor, and grabbed a bottle of water from the nearby table. He had run five miles in the warm Savannah sun this morning before returning to the hotel to exercise. His body was a well-maintained machine. With perspiration moistening his face and chest, he looked at himself in the mirror. For a man of any age, he was in remarkably good shape. For a man of forty-five, his body was in excellent condition. He picked up a towel from the edge of the bed and wiped his face and chest, and then draped the towel around his neck.

After twisting off the cap, he brought the bottle to his mouth and downed half the contents before pausing. He continued sipping from the bottle as he walked into the bathroom.

He was expecting a guest in less than an hour, just enough time to shave and shower.

He sat on the commode, removed his running shoes and damp socks, and then stood and stripped out of his jogging shorts. After turning on the shower—hot and steamy—he yanked a towel and washcloth from the rack. He laid the towel on the closed commode lid and took the washcloth into the shower with him. He had left his razor and shave cream on a ledge in the shower when he had cleaned up last night.

He took his time shaving, careful not to nick himself, and afterward washed his face, rinsed it, and then lathered his body. As he thought about his expected guest, his penis hardened. Before a kill, he liked to have sex. If he had any pre-kill rituals, they would be to eat a good meal and have a good fuck.

After drying off, he slipped on a dark blue silk robe and slid his feet into a pair of black house slippers. His profession as a death technician paid well and afforded him all of life's little luxuries, including a high-priced call girl.

Just as he poured himself a glass of whiskey, he heard a soft knock on the door. He checked the clock on the bedside table. Right on time. He appreciated punctuality.

He opened the door to an attractive brunette, long legged, slender, her breasts high and firm, obviously the result of implants.

"Mr. Hambert?"

"Yes, please come in, Ms. Smith."

He closed and locked the door behind her. When she turned around and smiled, he downed half his whiskey in one gulp, set the glass on the coffee table and then unbelted his robe.

"Do you want me to undress now?" she asked.

"No, not yet," he replied.

She nodded.

He removed his robe and tossed it on the nearby chair. His hard, erect penis projected outward.

"Come here," he instructed.

She came to him. He took her hand and brought it to his erection.

"Get down on your knees."

She did.

He clutched either side of her head. "Open your mouth."

"I really don't need instruction. I've done this before," she told him.

"I want complete control. I decide how much you take into your mouth and how far I shove my dick down your throat. Do you understand?"

She nodded. "Yes, I understand."

"After I come, clean me with your tongue."

"Yes, of course."

When she licked him from tip to shaft, he closed his eyes and savored the feel of her wet tongue on his penis. First a blow job, just to release the tension. And later, after lunch, he'd make the little whore really earn her money.

Chapter 23

While Derek had waited patiently in the warden's office, he had struggled to concentrate on the crossword puzzle in yesterday's *Savannah Daily News*. Warden Holland had picked up the copy off his desk and offered it to Derek before he'd left for an early lunch.

"Don't worry about her," the warden had said. "Ms. Perdue is just fine. There are two guards present at all times and Browning is handcuffed and shackled."

"I'm not worried about her physical safety."

"Yeah, well, something tells me that Ms. Perdue can hold her own against that wily bastard."

Derek hoped the warden was right. In a fair fight, he'd put his money on Maleah every time. But Browning wouldn't fight fair. He was a no-holds-barred kind of opponent. He'd use whatever methods necessary to get what he wanted.

And just what did he want from Maleah?

Did he want to hurt her? Humiliate her? Make her beg for mercy?

Yes, all of the above. He was the type who derived pleasure from killing, and since he couldn't kill Maleah, he would have to settle for emotionally wounding her. The thrill of the kill would be replaced by the thrill of complete control.

Staring at the folded newspaper in his hand, the puzzle facing him, he turned his ink pen backward and tapped the end against his teeth. In the past half hour, he'd filled in less than a dozen slots. Ordinarily, he would be finished with at least a third of the puzzle by now.

Immediately after he heard the sound of footsteps, the door swung open and the guard escorted Maleah into the warden's office. Derek jumped up, tossed the newspaper into the chair and pocketed his pen.

"Thank you," Maleah told the guard, and then turned to Derek. "Let's get the hell out of here."

"I'm ready," he said.

She went back out the door and down the hall before he caught up with her. He wanted to ask if she was all right, but didn't. Instead, he fell into step alongside her and kept his mouth shut. When she was ready, she'd talk. Until then, he'd wait.

They were a good five miles away from the penitentiary before Maleah spoke again. "I stink at reading body language."

Of all the things he thought she might say, that hadn't been one of them. "He played you, didn't he?"

"Like a fiddle."

"But you knew enough to realize he was playing you. Give yourself credit for that."

"He wanted to play a game of 'you show me yours and I'll show you mine,' but he wanted to see twice as much of mine as he was willing to show me of his."

"He thinks he can get you to pay double for everything he gives you. He's playing hardball, just as we expected he would."

"It's not even two for one. It's more like he'll give me one for every three I give him." She clutched the steering wheel so tightly that her knuckles turned white.

"What did he say about Durham?"

"At first he claimed he didn't know what I was talking about, but then he gradually changed his story. He said that he and the fake Durham made a deal. He gave Durham details about his kills and Durham provided him with a new lawyer and a lady friend to visit him. By the end of our conversation, he told me that not only had he already known the Albert Durham who visited him was a fake, but that he could tell me who he really is and why he's killing people associated with the Powell Agency. He even claimed he could tell me why the copycat chose to copy his kills."

"We know why—because of you," Derek said. "By choosing to emulate Browning's kills, he accomplished more than one goal. He deliberately connected his MO to the murder of a Powell agent's former boyfriend, but not just any Powell agent. He chose Nicole Powell's best friend. And he offered Browning more than a new lawyer and a woman to visit him. He offered Browning a special gift—someone who had loved one of his victims— you."

"So, I'm the prize, huh?" Maleah loosened her tight grip and ran her cupped hands over the steering wheel from the top to the bottom and then halfway up again.

"Offering to bring you to Browning was the copycat's ultimate bargaining chip, the one thing Browning wanted above all else—a new victim."

Maleah shivered. "Lovely thought."

"There's something else to think about," Derek said. "What if Browning has already told you everything he actually knows?"

"Are you saying that Jerome Browning is a diversion,

that the copycat is using him, that we're wasting our time concentrating on Browning?"

"Yes and no. It's all a sick game to Browning. How much he actually knows, we can't be sure. My gut's told me all along that Browning knows very little about the copycat, who he is or what his motives are. The copycat could have told Browning to string us along, to divert our attention. Then again, Browning might know something that he doesn't even know he knows."

"But if there's even a slight chance that he knows anything that can help us track down the copycat, it's worth whatever we have to pay, right?"

"What you have to pay, you mean. He wants his pound of flesh from you."

"He wants my blood, sweat, and tears," Maleah said. "Mostly my tears."

"That's what he told you?"

She nodded.

"Don't go back to see him." At that moment, Derek would have liked nothing better than ten minutes alone with Browning. Man-to-man.

"What?" Maleah cast him a quick sideways glance.

"He's stringing you along. He has no idea who the copycat is. He can't give you the fake Durham's real name because he doesn't know it. And there's no reason why the copycat would have shared anything about the reasons for his kills, especially if it turns out that he is a professional assassin, as I suspect."

"But you said Browning may know something he doesn't know he knows."

"Are you willing to put yourself through more of Browning's shit on the off chance you'll learn something useful?"

That's it, try to talk her out of it. You know Maleah, the harder you push, the harder she'll push back. You're using the wrong tactics.

"Damn it, Derek, I'm not some fragile hothouse flower that can't withstand a little rough treatment. You've got me confused with my mother. No one controls me, tells me what to do or manipulates me. I'm not afraid of Browning."

Her mother? What is she talking about?

"Never underestimate someone who kills for the thrill of it," he told her.

Groaning, Maleah gritted her teeth.

"And as for confusing you with your mother, need I remind you that I never knew the lady," Derek said. "But if she was a fragile woman, easily controlled by others, then you learned a valuable lesson from her, didn't you?"

"I didn't mean to say that about my mother. It just slipped out. And yes, I learned from her example the type of woman I did not want to be."

"Parents can teach us all sorts of lessons, both positive and negative. You learned from your mother what kind of woman you didn't want to be and I learned from my mother and father what kind of man I didn't want to be."

Maleah glanced at him, a puzzled expression on her face. "I know it's none of my business, but—"

"Happy Lawrence is a man-eater. Apparently, she's the polar opposite of your mother. There's nothing fragile or vulnerable about Happy. She's made of carbon steel. She's a master manipulator. She wields a great deal of power and has no problem destroying anyone who stands between her and what she wants, even her own husband."

"My God! You sound as if you hate her."

"There was a time, years ago, when I hated her," Derek admitted, realizing he had already said far more than he should have. He never discussed his mother with anyone. "Now I'm apathetic toward Happy. I see her as seldom as possible, but since she is my mother, I show her the proper respect when I'm forced to be around her."

"And your father?"

"He's dead. He died when I was a kid." Derek never talked about his dad either, but for some reason he felt compelled to add, "He was a weak, spineless mama's boy who went from letting his mother run his life to letting his wife put a ring through his nose and drive him to drink and suicide."

"Oh, Derek . . ."

He forced a fake laugh. "You see, Blondie, I'm as fucked up as you are. Childhood scars and all. You've got control issues. I've got commitment issues."

"We're quite a pair, aren't we?"

"Flip sides of the same coin, huh? Maybe even soul mates."

Now where had that stupid thought come from—soul mates? Get real, Lawrence, Maleah's not the type to fall for romantic nonsense.

"I don't believe there is such a thing as soul mates," she said quite matter-of-factly. "Flip sides of the same coin, possibly. I do know one thing, the more I get to know you, the more I realize you're not who I thought you were. All I've allowed myself to see is that rich, handsome playboy image you deliberately project to the world. That's not who you are at all, is it?"

"Nope. No more than the I-am-woman-hear-me-roar image you project is all there is to you."

"That's not just an image, you know. It's actually part of who I am . . . or who I try to be."

"Yeah, I know. That rich playboy image is part of who I am, too, but only a small part. I use it as a protective shield between me and the rest of the world."

"Especially women?"

"Guilty as charged."

"You have no intention of ever being like your father and allowing a woman to put a ring through your nose, right?"

Derek chuckled. "Right. And you don't intend to ever be an easily dominated, fragile hothouse flower."

Maleah smiled. "God, you've profiled me, haven't you? And yourself, too."

"Yeah, I guess I have. But can't you see the weird two sides of the same coin analogy? Male and female. For both of us, it's all about control and commitment. We both see making a commitment to another person as giving up control."

"But it is, isn't it? At least for people who have such a strong need to be totally in control of their own lives. I know other people can make marriage work. My mother and father did. Jack and Cathy have."

"Nic and Griff," Derek suggested.

"I'm not sure about those two. I think maybe it's a constant struggle for control with them."

"But neither controls the other. They're both too strong to allow that to happen."

"I don't know. Should being in love and maintaining a healthy marriage be that much of a struggle?"

"For people such as Nic and Griff who are aggressive and independent and passionate, I can't imagine it being any other way. It would be the same for us." Now why had he said that? "I didn't mean—"

"For us?" Maleah asked, almost choking on the question.

"Not for the two of us together," he corrected. "I

meant if you or I were married to someone our equal—
also aggressive, independent, strong, and passionate—
it would take work to make a relationship work."

"Oh . . . yes, I see what you mean."

"Hey, it's past lunchtime," he said, intentionally
changing the subject. Their conversation was becoming
too much like true-confessions to suit him. "Why don't
we stop somewhere for a quick bite to eat. You barely
touched your food at breakfast."

"Is food all you ever think about?"

"Ah now, Blondie, that's a loaded question."

She groaned. "Forget I asked. You men are all alike.
Food and sex."

"Food and sex. Sex and food. Yeah, that pretty much
sums up all of us men."

Maleah laughed.

God help him, he loved the sound of her laughter.

"Please come in," Griffin said. "And close the door
behind you."

Sanders did as Griffin had requested.

His old friend stood by the windows, his gaze absently fixed on something outside, his rigid stance ex-
pressing the depth of his anxiety. Sanders knew Griffin
almost as well as he knew himself. They understood
each other in a way no one else did, not even Yvette.

"Who is he?" Griffin asked, his voice barely more
than a whisper.

"I would think he is someone who knew Malcolm
York, perhaps admired or even loved him."

"To our knowledge, York had no family, other than a
few distant cousins. His parents were dead. He had no
siblings, no nieces or nephews. And no children." Grif-

fin turned and faced Sanders. "Is it possible that someone could have actually loved a monster like York?"

"Perhaps this person was an admirer, someone who
knew York quite well."

"It couldn't be anyone from Amara, could it?" Griffin settled his gaze directly on Sanders. "We didn't leave
any of the guards alive and the other prisoners hated
York as much as we did."

"Perhaps he is someone York encountered in his
travels? Or he could even be one of the guests who visited him on Amara."

"Are there any of those special guests still alive?"

"At last count, only two," Sanders replied.

"How long has it been since Byrne contacted us?"

"More than two years. At that time, he had tracked
down Sternberg."

"Then you're right, there are two of York's associates
who are still alive. Otherwise, Byrne would have been in
touch."

Griffin went to the portable bar, picked up a bottle
of The Macallan, the twenty-five-year-old Scotch whisky
his favorite, and poured the amber-red liquor into two
glasses, filling each halfway. He held out a glass to
Sanders.

"Of the six frequent visitors to Amara, only Bouchard
and Mayorga haven't been found and eliminated," Griffin said. "Here's to Byrne finishing his life's mission
sooner rather than later."

When Griffin saluted Sanders with his glass, Sanders
returned the gesture. Each took a hefty sip of the full,
smooth whisky that drank like a fine brandy. The combination of smokiness and oakiness gave the aged single malt its unique flavor.

Griffin sat in one of the two large leather chairs

flanking the fireplace and continued drinking. Sanders sat across from him, the two men silent for several minutes.

"Is it possible that either Bouchard or Mayorga could be passing himself off as Malcolm York?"

Sanders nodded. "Perhaps, but would either put himself in the line of fire, knowing that Byrne is hunting for him?"

"If I remember correctly, Bouchard was an arrogant son of bitch. He's the type who would think he could outsmart Byrne while taunting us."

"And I always thought Moyorga was stupid. Stupid enough to think neither we nor Byrne could find him."

"We need to find Byrne."

"He can't be found, unless he wants to be."

"Get word out to the proper channels and see what happens."

"Yes, of course." Cradling the glass of whisky in the open palm of his right hand, Sanders circled the edge with his left index finger. "There is one possibility that we haven't discussed," Sanders said.

Griffin nodded. "Are you referring to Harlan Benecroft?"

"I am."

"I thought we agreed years ago that the man is harmless. He was terrified of York. He had as much reason to want York dead as we did."

"He may have feared York and steered clear of you when you were collecting York's fortune for Yvette, but he was York's cousin and in his own pathetic way was as mentally unstable as York."

"Benecroft doesn't have the balls to pass himself off as Malcolm York."

"Luke is on his way to London," Sanders said. "Why

not have him check on Benecroft, if for no other reason than to exclude him?"

"You find Byrne. Have Richter get in touch with his Interpol contacts and while he's doing that, call in some favors with the CIA and MI6. I'll get in touch with Luke." Griffin downed the remainder of his Scotch. "Will it ever end? Will we ever be free of York?"

"The evil that men do lives after them," Sanders paraphrased Shakespeare. "The good is often interred with their bones."

"There was no good in York. He was evil personified."

Chapter 24

"I have a lead on Anthony Linden," Luke Sentell told Griffin Powell. "Someone who knows someone who can verify that Linden is alive, and this person may possibly be able to give us a description of the man."

"If only they could tell us exactly where Linden is right now."

"Have Dr. Meng or one of her underlings look into her crystal ball and see if they can locate him," Luke said sarcastically.

Even though Luke had seen Dr. Meng and Meredith Sinclair work their woo-woo magic, he still wasn't a true believer. Not the way Griff and Sanders were. He didn't quite trust anything beyond his five senses, definitely nothing in the sixth sense realm.

"You must be a little psychic yourself to have mentioned Yvette and her protégés just now."

Uh-oh. Luke got a sinking feeling in the pit of his stomach. "Why do you say that?"

"Because I'm sending Meredith Sinclair to you on my private jet first thing in the morning," Griffin told Luke. "One of our agents will accompany her. You know

Saxon Chappelle. Once they arrive, he'll turn her over to you for safe keeping."

"Damn, Griff, you know how I despise babysitting Ms. Sinclair. Once was enough for me. She's more trouble than she's worth. If you want her in Europe doing her magic act, then why not leave Chappelle here to look after her?"

"Meredith works best without distractions, which means the fewer people involved the better. You know that one-on-one is the best situation for her. And for whatever reason, her senses seemed to be fine tuned whenever you're nearby. It's as if you boost wherever signals are coming through to her. Apparently you're some sort of conduit."

"I've been called a lot of things in my life, but never a conduit."

"Hell, you know what I mean. Meredith's psychic gifts are all over the place most of the time, despite all the work that Yvette has done with her. But add you into the equation and she suddenly becomes focused and working on all cylinders."

"Yeah, lucky me. Have you ever thought maybe she's afraid of me and that's what fine tunes her sixth sense? At least when she's around me, she acts like she thinks I'm the devil himself. Maybe Dr. Meng should try a little tough love with her prize student."

"That's between Yvette and Meredith. She'll be in London by late tomorrow. I'm expecting you to work with her, regardless of your personal animosity. And it goes without saying that I know you'll take good care of her."

"I won't coddle her," Luke said. "Damn it, Griff, you know what happens, how after one of her so-called psychic episodes, she's a basket case."

"Handle her the best way you can. I don't know how

much she can help us, but at this point, I'm willing to try anything and that includes using an emotionally fragile psychic if there's even a slim chance she can help us find our imposter and put a stop to these murders."

"You're the boss," Luke said reluctantly.

"Humph." Griff snorted. "I may pay your salary, but we both know I'm not your boss. You may follow orders, but you always do things your own way. And that's not a criticism. It's one of the reasons I hired you. I like a man who can think for himself."

Luke had great respect for Griff. If he didn't, he wouldn't be working for the man. And he believed in what Griff stood for and in the way he tried to help others. There weren't very many true champions of the people left in the world. Griffin Powell was one of them. It sure as hell didn't matter to Luke that the Powell Agency cut corners and circumvented the law on occasion to accomplish their goals—to do what was right.

"I don't suppose there's any chance that Dr. Meng could come with—"

"No," Griff said. "It's too dangerous for Yvette to leave Griffin's Rest right now."

"I work best alone. You know that. Babysitting Ms. Sinclair is going to slow me down."

"That could be, but it's also possible that she'll be able to help you, maybe steer you in the right direction in your search for the pseudo York. But before she arrives in London tomorrow, I need for you to check on Harlan Benecroft. Let's make sure he's still contained, that he's still non-lethal."

"That pompous ass? You can't possibly believe that Benecroft is posing as York, can you?"

"He certainly wouldn't be on my Top Ten list, but we need to rule him out completely."

"Better to be safe than sorry, huh?"

"Yeah, something like that."

"Sure, I'll check on him, but I have a feeling that it will probably be a waste of my time. I'll put in a few calls first thing in the morning and get back to you as soon as I know anything."

"While you've got your ear to the ground, there are two other names you should listen for, discreetly of course—Mayorga and Bouchard."

"All right."

Luke didn't ask for more information. If Griff thought he needed to know more, he would tell him.

Sanders had spoken privately to Brendan Richter. As a former Interpol agent, Richter understood the necessity for discretion. Ciro Mayorga had been on Interpol's Most Wanted list for a number of years, but he had escaped capture just as he had eluded Raphael Byrne's swift and sure form of judgment. But sooner or later, Rafe would find him. Mayorga's crimes ranged from drug trafficking to money laundering. The warrant for his arrest had been issued in Spain ten years ago. Yves Bouchard had also managed to stay under the radar, steering clear of national and international law enforcement agencies that knew but could not prove his involvement in human trafficking. When Rafe Byrne eventually caught up with Bouchard, his execution would be immediate, no arrest, no trial, and no sentencing required.

Sanders had known Rafe as a beautiful, slender, wide-eyed boy of seventeen when Malcolm York had first brought him to Amara. He had been certain that the angelic teenager would not survive a week. And he wouldn't have, if Griffin Powell had not taken the boy under his wing and done his best to protect him.

The day they had killed York and fought their way through several of the ten guards he kept on duty around the clock, they had freed the four captives who were still alive, but they had been unable to find Rafe. The men they had freed had joined them in annihilating their sadistic overseers. Eventually, they had found Rafe in one of the dark dungeon cells, chained, beaten beyond recognition and starved to the point of emaciation.

Of the five men who had left Amara with them, two had committed suicide less than a year later. One had died in a car accident in Barcelona and another in a skiing accident in Aspen more than ten years ago. Only one was still alive.

Raphael Byrne.

Weeks following their escape from Amara and after Rafe had undergone several surgeries to repair his battered face, they had visited Rafe in the London hospital where he was recovering. There had been no resemblance, physically, mentally and emotionally, between the seventeen-year-old boy York had brought to Amara and the twenty-year-old man who had made a solemn vow to them that day. In a deadly calm voice, he had sworn he would hunt down and kill all six men who had visited York during the three years Rafe had been on Amara. The six men—Tanaka, Di Santis, Klausner, Sternberg, Mayorga, and Bouchard—who had hunted him by day, as if he were a wild animal, and had amused themselves with him at night, each in their own way.

Maleah was beginning to like Derek Lawrence.

And liking him wouldn't be a problem if she didn't

also find him terribly attractive. She'd been able to handle the unwanted physical attraction between them as long as she had disliked him. But now, everything between them had changed, at least for her. And to make matters worse, she felt certain that he was dealing with the same problem. He had shared a part of himself with her today, a part she suspected he seldom shared with others, just as he had told her about his youthful exploits as a solider of fortune. Why had he exposed himself to her that way? Why had he given her more than just a glimpse of the real Derek, someone as flawed and imperfect as she was, someone with battle scars from a miserable childhood, someone who, like she, was all too human?

After they had shared lunch on their return to Vidalia earlier today, she had escaped as quickly as possible. She had needed to get away from Derek and work through her unsettled feelings before facing him again. Her excuse for begging off a work session had been only a half-lie. She'd told him that she wanted to call Jack and Cathy and then take an afternoon nap. She seldom if ever took an afternoon nap unless she was sick or had been up half the night. She hadn't taken a nap, but she had called her sister-in-law.

"Seth is enjoying summer vacation," Cathy had said. "He's working part-time as a lifeguard at the community center pool and he has half a dozen girls chasing after him."

"Like father like son."

Cathy had laughed. "Oh, believe me, he's more like Jack than I ever realized."

"So how is my little niece?"

"You and Jack. You're both so sure the baby is a girl."

"She is. Just wait until you get that next ultrasound. I'm positive you'll find out the baby is a girl."

Hearing Cathy's voice, so cheerful and positive and seemingly unafraid, had gone a long way in reassuring Maleah. But she still couldn't completely shake her fear that the copycat might choose a member of her family as his next victim.

It was only a matter of time until he killed again.

After a thirty-minute conversation with Cathy, she had flipped on the television, zipped through the channels, and turned it off three minutes later.

Now, she had to find something to do. But if she went over the copycat killer files one more time, she would scream her head off. She had practically memorized everything they had on record about Jerome Browning, as well as information about Wyman Scudder, Cindy Di Blasi, and the real Albert Durham.

If only they had some information about the fake Durham. But at this point, the man was a complete mystery, except for Derek's preliminary profile. However, having so little info to work with made Derek's job more difficult.

Pacing the floor, wishing she really could take a long nap, she nearly jumped out of her skin when her phone rang.

Please don't let it be Derek. I can't deal with him right now. I need to put just a little time and space between us, between the realization that I like him—like him a lot—and seeing him again.

When she noted the caller ID, she sighed with relief. "Hello, Nic."

"Hey, are you okay? You sound odd."

"I'm fine. I was lost in thought and the phone ringing startled me."

"How are you? Really?"

"You want the truth?'

"Always," Nic told her.

"I'm thinking seriously about selling my soul to the devil in the hopes he'll give me some information that will help us find the Copycat Carver. And as if making that decision isn't enough to deal with in one day, I've just discovered that I genuinely like Derek Lawrence and . . ." She wasn't sure she could admit, even to her best friend, how she really felt about Derek.

"And what?"

"And I've got the hots for the guy." She could tell Nic anything, couldn't she? They were best friends. Nic would understand.

Nic laughed.

"Do not laugh at me. This isn't funny."

"I already knew," Nic said.

"Knew what? That I'd do whatever it takes to get information out of Jerome Browning or that I had the hots for Derek?"

"Both actually, but I was referring to your having a thing for Derek. You do know that he's got it bad for you, too, don't you?"

"Having feelings for Derek complicates my life and I don't like it. So, before you say another word, I'm telling you right now that I refuse to become another notch on his bedpost."

"You'd never be that, just as I wasn't for Griff," Nic said. "You and Derek remind me so much of Griff and me in the early stages of our relationship."

"Bite your tongue."

"Want my advice?"

"I have a feeling you're going to give it to me whether or not I want it."

"Have sex with him."

Maleah growled through her clenched teeth.

"And don't sell your soul to the devil for info from Browning," Nic told her.

"Derek said the same thing."

"Then listen to the man. Not only is he smart, but I suspect he has your best interests at heart."

"Save your breath. I'm going back to the prison tomorrow to see Browning again. It may be my last visit, but I have to try one more time."

"If I thought you'd listen to me, I'd try to talk you out of your decision, but I know you too well to even try. No one can talk me out of doing something once I've made up my mind. You and I are both as stubborn as mules." Nic paused for a moment and then said, "Griff is sending Meredith Sinclair to London tomorrow in the hopes she can help Luke."

"I bet Luke's thrilled. Is Yvette going with Meredith?"

"No, Griff believes it's too dangerous for Yvette to leave Griffin's Rest."

"He's probably right."

"Listen, Maleah, I have some rather important news for you and Derek. Griff and Sanders are both busy handling other matters, so I've been delegated to touch base with you two and give you the latest information."

"Please tell me you have good news to share, or at the very least information that can help us."

"It's information that possibly confirms Derek's tentative profile of the Copycat Carver as a professional assassin."

Maleah sucked in her breath.

"A contact in Austria sold Luke information concerning a man named Anthony Linden, a former MI6 agent who went rogue. He supposedly killed himself ten years ago instead of allowing the authorities to capture and imprison him. But apparently the rumors of his death were greatly exaggerated."

"Meaning that Anthony Linden isn't actually dead."

"So it would seem."

"And this information is important to us because?"

"Because this same contact told Luke that the man rumored to be impersonating Malcolm York hired a very-much-alive Linden, who is well-known in certain circles as a professional assassin. And York sent Linden to America six months ago."

"That's quite an interesting story, one I'm sure Griff has bought into, right?" Maleah said. "But what about you? Are you buying it?"

"It's plausible. It's possible. I don't know if it's true, but . . ." Nic's voice trailed off into complete and utter silence.

"Nic?"

"Oh God, Maleah, if the copycat continues killing, if we can't find him and stop him soon, I don't know how Griff is going to bear it. He's not sleeping. He's lost his appetite. He's drinking too much. He's preoccupied and edgy and keeps shutting himself off in his study, sometimes alone, sometimes with Sanders. I try to talk to him, try to convince him that he's not responsible for all these deaths, but it's as if he doesn't even hear me."

"I wish I knew what to tell you," Maleah said, her heart aching for her dear friend. "Griff's a strong man. He's not going to fall apart. You know that when he shuts you out, he thinks he's protecting you. Nic, you know he loves you."

"If he would only tell me everything, all the horrible things about Malcolm York and Amara, then maybe I could help him. Whatever secrets he's keeping from me are part of what's tearing him apart. He knows that the real York is dead, and yet . . . Oh, Maleah, I wish that the copycat killer would turn out to be someone seeking revenge against me because of one of my cases when I worked for the Bureau. Or if the copycat is a professional killer, then I wish someone with a grudge against the Powell Agency and not someone from Griff's past hired this man to exact revenge against the agency."

"We can't rule out either of those possibilities. Not yet. That's one reason I have to go back to see Browning. If only I could persuade him to tell me what he knows."

"If he actually knows anything. And you do realize that the odds of that are very low. Besides, all the evidence is beginning to stack up in favor of Griff's theory."

"I'm sorry, Nic. I'm so very sorry."

"There's nothing for you to be sorry about. None of this is your fault. I'm the one who's sorry that the copycat deliberately involved you by choosing to emulate the murderer who killed Noah Laborde."

"If Griff's theory is correct, then someone very badly wants to torment Griff by whatever means necessary, even going so far as to strike out at his wife's best friend."

"Don't go back to see Browning again. I have a very bad feeling about it. Please, Maleah . . ."

"I have to go. Don't worry about me. I'm tough." Maleah faked a laugh. "Besides, I have Derek. If Browning chews me up and spits me out in little pieces, Derek will put me back together."

"Oh, Maleah."

"Hey, you take care of yourself and that husband of yours. I'll be fine. I need to hang up now and go fill Derek in on the news from Luke."

"Call me tomorrow, after you see Browning."

"Okay, if it'll make you feel better, I'll call."

As soon as they said their good-byes, Maleah went to the bathroom, freshened up and changed into a pair of faded navy sweat pants and an oversized yellow, navy, and white striped T-shirt. After slipping into a pair of navy Skechers, she slid her room key into her pants pocket and left her room.

Maleah stood outside of Derek's closed door. Once she had worked up enough courage to knock, he opened the door in two seconds flat.

They stared at each other, neither of them saying a word.

He wasn't wearing a shirt. Swirls of thick black hair formed a perfect T across his upper chest and disappeared into his unsnapped jeans.

Why oh why did he have to look so good? All lean and muscular, handsome and sexy, he was dark, tantalizing temptation wrapped up in a to-die-for package.

Say something, you idiot.

Say what? I want to jump your bones?

Tell him about Nic's phone call. Give him the latest information from Luke Sentell. Don't keep standing here staring at him. Just open your damn mouth and say something.

But when she opened her mouth to speak, Derek forcefully grabbed her shoulders, pulled her into his arms, and kissed her.

Chapter 25

Derek drove his tongue into her mouth, deepening the kiss, taking her breath away. Capturing her neck and threading his fingers through her hair, he pulled her into his room and kicked the door shut. Without conscious thought, going strictly by instinct, she wrapped herself around him and lost herself completely in the kiss. His lips were firm and warm, his tongue moist and hot.

He walked backward, taking her with him step-by-step, his hands roaming over her shoulders and back, and then delving lower to cup her butt. Her femininity clenched and unclenched in an age-old preparation for mating, as her mouth worked feverishly against his.

When he toppled them over and onto the bed, she went with him willingly, as hungry for him as he was for her. Changing the dynamics of the kiss, he eased his tongue from her mouth and nibbled on her lower lip. She moaned deep in her throat as he slid his hands between them and lifted the edge of her T-shirt, exposing her naked belly and the lace bra covering her breasts. The moment he lowered his head, his breath scorching her skin, she forked her fingers through his hair and brought his mouth to her breast. He suckled her through the thin material and then flicked his tongue across first one hard nipple and then the other.

Squirming, her body throbbing, she rubbed herself against him and felt how much he wanted her.

"Oh, baby . . . so sweet . . ." He shoved his hand between her thighs and palmed her mound. "We're going to be so good together, honey, so good."

Baby? Honey?

Generic terms, endearments he had probably used countless times with numerous women.

He had not called her Maleah. He hadn't even called her Blondie.

Her vow to Nic echoed inside her head, softly at first, but growing louder with each passing second. *I refuse to become another notch on his bedpost.*

Gradually coming to her senses, she shoved against his chest. His deliciously warm, hairy, muscular chest.

Stop this right now. You are not going to have sex with Derek Lawrence.

"Get off me," she told him, her voice a ragged whisper.

"What's wrong?" He lifted his head and stared at her. "Did I hurt you?"

Yes, you mortally wounded me. With words. Baby. Honey.

"No, you didn't hurt me." She shoved him up and off her.

He rolled over onto the bed while she sat up, took several deep, steadying breaths and started to stand. He reached out, grasped her wrist and held her in place on the edge of the bed.

"Look at me, Maleah."

Now he remembers my name.

"What just happened?" he asked.

She looked everywhere but at him. "We almost made a terrible mistake."

He sat up so that they were side by side. He cupped her chin and turned her to face him. "Why did you stop what was happening between us? You were into it as much as I was, wanted me as much as I wanted you—as much as I still want you. You can't deny the truth."

"I'm not denying anything." When she looked at him, it was all she could do not to give in to her baser instincts. God, how she wanted him!

"Then please tell me what just happened? What did I do wrong?"

How did she answer that question? With a lie? The truth? A half-truth? "You didn't do anything wrong. I just came to my senses before it was too late." Unable to continue direct eye contact for fear he would know she was lying, she averted her gaze.

He squeezed her chin. She glared at him, and then jerked out of his grasp and got up. "Put a shirt on, will you? You shouldn't have come to the door half naked."

"Are you afraid if I remain partially unclothed, you won't be able to keep your hands off me?" he asked jokingly as he rose to his feet.

"I'm not the one who grabbed you and kissed you," she reminded him.

He came up behind her, lowered his head and kissed the side of her neck. Shivering at his touch, she closed her eyes and stood perfectly still as he whispered in her ear, "The moment I opened the door, I knew what you wanted. You were begging me to kiss you."

Snapping around with the intention of blasting him for his accusation, she didn't realize until it was too late just how close his body was to hers. Her breasts collided with his chest as her belly encountered his erection.

She sucked in her breath and shoved against him. Smiling at her, he stepped backward.

"I wasn't. I didn't . . ." *That's it, Maleah, lie to him again.* "Despite what you think, I knocked on your door to tell you that Nic called me with information."

He looked at her questioningly. "Business first, huh?"

"Yes. No. Damn it, you know what I mean. Business only."

"Ah, Blondie, do I have to keep telling you that you're no fun?"

When she glared at him, he laughed as he walked over to the dresser, opened a drawer and removed a white T-shirt. While he slipped into the garment, Maleah pulled out the desk chair and sat. He turned around, his gorgeous chest now covered, and grinned when he saw that she had avoided sitting on the sofa.

"You sure do blow hot and cold, don't you?" He flopped down on the sofa, propped his feet up on the coffee table and crossed his arms over his chest. "You went from not being able to keep your hands off me to not even wanting to sit by me."

"Will you please drop it? If you want me to take full responsibility for what happened, then I will. You're irresistible. I fought my attraction to you for as long as I could. I took one look at your magnificent bare chest and went wild. Pick your fantasy, Mr. Lawrence. But that's it. I am not going to discuss what happened."

He ran his gaze over her slowly, appraisal in his eyes, as if she were an object on the auction block and he was considering a purchase. "Okay. I'll go along with however you want to play this. Let's chalk it up to just one of those things."

"Thank you."

"You're welcome."

She couldn't tell if he was sincere or if he was making fun of her.

Silence hung between them for several minutes, then she cleared her throat and said, "Griff received information from Luke Sentell that, if proven true, could substantiate your theory that the Copycat Carver is a professional assassin."

Uncrossing his arms, his eyes widening with interest, Derek leaned forward and said, "As much as I like being proven correct in my assessments, I know I'm not going to like this new information, am I?"

"Probably not." Now that they were discussing their current case, Maleah relaxed. As long as she kept her relationship with Derek strictly business, she'd be fine. "I have no idea how Luke made contact with this man, but I assume it all boils down to who you know. Griff has contacts all over the world. And we have a former Interpol agent working for the agency now, as well as Luke, who is rumored to have been a Black Ops agent."

"Is there a reason why you're taking the scenic route with this information instead of—?"

"Sorry. I was thinking out loud." Maleah forced herself to look at Derek. "Luke paid this person, some man in Austria, for the info, and as of right now, he has no way to verify the validity of what he was told. But supposedly there is or was a man named Anthony Linden, a former MI6 agent who went rogue and became a hired killer. When the authorities caught up with him about ten years ago, he reportedly killed himself rather than be captured."

"Let me guess—Linden didn't kill himself. He's alive and well and still working as a professional assassin. And for some reason Luke believes Linden may be our copycat killer."

She marveled at how easily Derek connected the

dots. She snapped her fingers. "Just like that, you put it all together. So, how about making an educated guess as to why Luke and Griff think Linden is our guy."

"Hmm . . ." Derek stroked his chin. "The mystery man who calls himself Malcolm York and Anthony Linden are somehow connected, right?"

"Right. Supposedly Linden is working for the mysterious Mr. York, who sent him to America six months ago."

"Six months ago, shortly before Albert Durham visited Jerome Browning for the first time, and less than two months before the Copycat Carver began his murder spree by killing Kristi Arians."

"Is Griff right? Is all of this happening because of him, because the fake Malcolm York is exacting revenge for the real York?"

"Your voice is trembling," Derek told her. "That happens when you're upset and worried. Tell me what's really going on with you."

Maleah hated that he knew her so well. Damn his extraordinary powers of observation. "I'm concerned about Nic . . . and about Griff, too, because she's worried sick about him."

"If I promise I won't bite, will you come over here and sit by me?" He patted the sofa cushion. "We're friends now, aren't we? Talk to me. About your concerns for Nic and Griff and about anything else that's troubling you."

She eyed him suspiciously.

He lifted his arms in the air on either side of him. "I promise I won't touch you."

She rose from the chair in a slow, languid move and walked toward the sofa. "I have to go back to see Browning tomorrow."

"No, you don't. You do not have to see him ever again."

"I do. If he knows—"

"He doesn't know squat," Derek said. "The copycat, whoever he is, Anthony Linden or John Doe, didn't share any big secrets with Browning. Why would he?"

"But you said that maybe Browning knows something he doesn't even know he knows. Maybe he can—"

"Damn it, Maleah, he can't help us." Derek reached for her, then stopped dead still and clenched his hands into fists.

She released a relieved breath. If he had touched her, she didn't think she could have resisted the urge to throw herself into his arms.

"Nic said that Griff isn't sleeping or eating and he's pulled away from her. He blames himself for what's happened. He thinks it's somehow his fault that five people associated with the agency have been murdered."

"I don't claim to know any more about Griffin Powell than you do, but I understand him as one man understands another. Any man, especially one as powerful as Griff, hates to admit that something in his past has come back not only to haunt him, but could be the reason for five murders. And although he would never admit it, Griff's scared out of his mind that something might happen to Nic. He's the type who wouldn't want the woman he loved to see any weaknesses in him, not even if *she* was his major weakness."

"He would rather withdraw from her, even risk alienating her, than to share his fears with her and let her help him? That is so wrong."

"Yeah, I know, but we men are strange creatures."

"Would you do that?" she asked. "I mean assuming

you loved someone the way Griff loves Nic, would you put up barriers to prevent her from—?"

"I'm not Griff. I haven't lived his life. I don't have his secrets. I didn't say he and I were alike. I said I understood him as one man understands another." He gazed into her eyes. "You and Nic are best friends. You've shared confidences and probably know each other better than anyone else does. You understand her, right?"

Maleah nodded.

"But even though you and Nic are both strong, independent women, you're also different. There are things she has lived through that you haven't and vice versa. I can't see you letting the man you loved keep secrets from you. If he did, you'd walk away, wouldn't you?"

She stared at Derek, wondering if he, too, had more deep, dark secrets, ones he had never shared with anyone. "She's tried leaving him, but she always comes back. Love makes us weak and it certainly can make fools of us all."

"Have you ever loved anyone like that?" he asked.

"No. Have you?"

"No."

They sat there staring at each other for several minutes and finally Derek said, "Okay, Blondie, if you're damned and determined to visit Browning again in the morning, then we need to talk about it. I'll take on the role of Browning and play devil's advocate, no holds barred, and we'll see how you react."

"You want to see just how thick my skin is, don't you?"

Derek grinned. "When it comes to sparring with Browning, I suspect your skin is thick enough. But I happen to have firsthand knowledge as to just how really soft and smooth your skin is."

When she reached over and socked him on the arm,

he held up his hands in a surrender gesture. "For the record, I want it to be noted that you touched me first."

She socked him again, harder the second time.

"Ouch. That hurt."

"Good. I wanted it to hurt."

"You're a hard-hearted woman, Maleah Perdue."

"Yes, I am, and you'd do well not to forget it."

Derek burst into laughter.

"Why are you laughing? Why aren't you—?"

He leaned over and without laying a finger on her, he kissed her. She mumbled and spluttered and then placed her hands on his chest to push him away. But suddenly, he lifted his head and smiled.

"Any plans for seduction that you might have for tonight will have to be postponed to another time," he told her. "We've got work to do, woman. And work always comes first."

She stared at him, completely confused for a few seconds. Then she realized his intention had been to lighten the mood. "You're the most aggravating, infuriating man I've ever known."

"And that's what you like about me, that and the fact that I'm such a good kisser."

Maleah groaned. Derek was right. He was a good kisser.

The modified Georgian-style Chappelle house in Ardsley Park had been built in the center of the lot and set back off the street. Two towering palms graced either side of the brick walkway and two overgrown holly bushes the size of small trees flanked the white brick structure. No doubt, in its day, the house had been impressive, and it was still a lovely old home. A wide variety of eclectic styles created a diversity of houses in the area, which stretched from Bull Street on the west to Waters Avenue on the east, and from Victory Drive north to Derenne Avenue south. He could leave the Chappelle home after he finished his job and be on I-16 in about ten minutes. By daylight that morning, he would be more than halfway to Atlanta.

While Poppy had attended church with her grandmother and the housekeeper on Sunday, he had broken the lock on the outside entrance to the basement at the side of the house and had slipped inside without any trouble. As luck would have it, the old woman hadn't put in a security system, so he had been able to go upstairs and take his time familiarizing himself with all the rooms. Twelve in all, not counting bathrooms and two sun porches.

Mrs. Carolyn Chappelle's room had been easy to spot. It was the largest bedroom which also included a sitting area in front of heavily draped bay windows overlooking the front lawn. The antique furniture, polished to shining perfection, overfilled the space, making the room feel cluttered. In comparison, the housekeeper's eight-by-ten room, that probably had originally been the nursery, was sparsely furnished and excessively neat. Wooden shutters covered the single window. He had checked each of the other bedrooms, searching for Poppy's room, and when he found it, he wondered if it had once belonged to her aunt Mary Lee. Two large windows overlooked the pool and enclosed patio. Feminine to the point of being frilly, the white French Provincial furniture, lace adorned drapes and bedding, and floral wallpaper seemed, as did the other rooms in the house, to be trapped in a time long past.

Moonlight illuminated the predawn sky and cast shadows over the lawn. Tree branches swayed in the warm summer breeze, their tips scratching at the upstairs windows on the east end of the house. Security lights at the back of the house kept the pool area well lit, but the basement door, the lock now broken, lay hidden in darkness behind a row of red azaleas.

He had parked his rental car in the driveway. If by any chance some neighbor happened to be awake at this hour and looked out a window, he or she would see a nondescript sedan and possibly assume the Chappelles had an overnight visitor. He had no intention of returning the rental and there was no way it could be traced back to him, only to the real Albert Durham. He would leave the car at the Atlanta airport tomorrow. With the time difference between the U.S. East Coast and London, his employer would be enjoying a late breakfast when he reported in, once he was on the road. After he spoke to his employer, he would make flight arrangements. This morning's kill would be number six, the exact number he had been paid for by wire transfer to his Swiss account, which had been opened under one of his many aliases.

He was known by many names and yet he remained nameless. He was a man of a hundred disguises and yet he remained faceless, unidentifiable. In his world, he was known only as the Phantom, except by a precious few who had once known him as Anthony Linden. But he was not Anthony Linden and hadn't been in more than ten years. For all intents and purposes, Anthony Linden was dead.

Poppy woke with a start, her mouth dry and her cotton sleep shirt damp with perspiration. She kicked back the light covers and lay there, her eyes open, her heartbeat racing. She stared up at the shadows dancing on her ceiling. She'd had the most god-awful dream.

You shouldn't have watched that old Twilight show marathon on TV last night with Heloise.

Her nightmare had been a convoluted jumble of scenes, none of which had made the least bit of sense. Headless zombies creeping toward her. Pig-faced people hovering over her. Outraged men and women chasing her down the street, screaming at her, accusing her of being an alien from outer space.

Poppy shuddered.

I'm not afraid. I'm not afraid. Bad dreams can't hurt you. No, but they can sure scare the bejeezus out of you.

She wished her bedroom—Aunt Mary Lee's old room—wasn't at the opposite end of the hall from Grandmother's and Heloise's rooms. She certainly had no intention of walking up that long, dark corridor. The old house moaned and groaned enough as it was without her padding down the hall and making the wooden floors creak.

She could turn on the light, get up, and read a few chapters in the paperback romance novel on her nightstand. Or she could go downstairs to the den and watch TV or grab a snack in the kitchen.

Just close your eyes and try to go back to sleep.

The odds were if she went back to sleep, she wouldn't dream again. Not if she thought about pleasant things. *Think about going sailing with Court and Anne Lee on Wednesday afternoon. Think about Court's friend Wes Larimer.* Anne Lee had promised that Court would invite him to join them.

"I think Wes likes you," Anne Lee had told her. "If Mother wasn't best buds with his mother, I'd go after him myself. But God forbid that Wes and I hook up and make our moms happy."

"He's cute, isn't he?"

"Do Chihuahuas shiver? Girl, Wes Larimer is cream of the crop."

Think about Wes. And who knows, maybe you'll dream about him instead of weird characters out of an old TV show.

Poppy closed her eyes and imagined Wes putting his arm around her and kissing her. It would be explosive, like fireworks lighting up the sky. They were alone on Court's sailboat, just the two of them. The ocean was smooth, the sun was warm, the breeze balmy.

"Oh Court, kiss me again," she mumbled to herself and then yawned before dozing off to sleep.

He moved through the Chappelle house as quietly as smoke rising from a chimney. He turned off the slender flashlight he held, pocketed it and took the back stairs two at a time, being careful to tread lightly. Even when the old staircase creaked occasionally as his weight pressed on the carpeted runner, he didn't pause. Those living here were accustomed to the odd sounds that the nearly eighty-year-old house made in the night. When he reached the landing, he glanced down the corridor toward Mrs. Chappell's suite and across the hall to Heloise McGruger's bedroom. Both doors were closed.

He turned and went in the opposite direction, straight toward the young girl's room decorated in fancy ruffles and lace. Unlike the older ladies in the house, Poppy slept with her door partially open. A thin line of moonlight seeped through the narrow opening and painted a pale yellow-white line across the threshold and onto the floor beneath his feet. He reached out, grasped the crystal knob and slowly eased open the door all the way. His eyes had adjusted to the darkness so he could see quite well with only the moonlight brightening the bedroom just enough to reveal the furniture's silhouettes.

Poppy Chappelle lay beneath a ruffled canopy, one arm and one leg tangled in the top sheet and light-weight blanket. The upstairs central air unit kicked on, sending a rush of cool air from the ceiling vent. He stood over her bed and watched her while she slept. So very young. So pretty.

Such a pity he had to kill her.

He didn't choose the victims. His employer did.

He was simply an employee following orders, a pro-fessional doing his job.

Easing up to the edge of the bed, he rubbed his glove-encased hands together, collected his thoughts and prepared for the kill. He slipped his hand into an inside pocket, removed the disposable scalpel from the small carrying case and returned the case to his pocket.

I'm sorry, little girl.

A momentary calmness came over him, steadying his hand and clearing his mind. The rush of excitement would come later, with the act itself. The moment the knife entered her body, he would experience an unpar-alleled exhilaration. He always did.

He watched her for another minute, noted the rise and fall of her tender young breasts as she inhaled and exhaled.

And then he plunged the scalpel into her jugular. Blood gushed.

A mental and emotional orgasm began to build in-side him. He sliced the sharp blade across her neck, from one carotid artery to the other, effectively cutting her windpipe in the process.

She died almost instantly, without a sound, never having opened her eyes.

His hands were steady, his outward demeanor calm. But a soul-deep enjoyment burst wide open inside him and sent climactic pleasure through his entire body.

Mimicking the Carver's MO, he worked quickly, cutting triangles from her upper arms and thighs and stuffing the tiny pieces of flesh into the small insulated bag he had brought with him.

He took no pleasure in the mutilation of a body, but he was under orders. This was business, a necessary part of the job assignment.

At the foot of the staircase, the grandfather clock struck four times. He would be gone well before daybreak. And it would be morning before anyone discovered Poppy's body.

Leaving his victim lying in her bloody bed, he walked across the room, opened the widow, and lifted the screen. Then he returned to the bed, picked the dead girl up into his arms and carried her to the window.

From the height of the second floor, he glanced down at the moonlight shimmering across the pool. Keeping a firm grip, he held her body out the window as far as he could reach and then released her. She sailed down, down, down, and hit the side of the pool. While her legs crashed onto the patio, her head and the upper two-thirds of her body sank into the water. Then the weight of her head and upper body submerged in the pool gradually dragged her legs into the pool and she slowly disappeared beneath the water's surface.

Chapter 26

Maleah sipped on the coffee, black with one packet of Splenda, that Derek had brought her. When she had opened the door to him a few minutes ago, her expression had been filled with questions and doubts. Knowing what she wanted and needed this morning, he had set the tone for their day. Back to business as usual. Partners working on a case, their once adversarial relationship now bordering on friendship and definitely based on mutual respect. There would be time later, tomorrow or the next day or a week or month from now, for them to explore the reasons behind the sexual tension driving them both crazy.

"Anything you want to go over with me this morning?" he asked as he sat down on the sofa, snapped open the lid flap on his insulated coffee cup and took a sip of his black coffee.

"I don't think so. I believe we pretty much took care of every possible scenario last night." She joined him on the sofa.

"More than likely, Browning is going to tell you

about how he killed Noah Laborde and the pleasure he derived from what he did. We assume he doesn't know anything else about your personal life, and if we're correct, that means he's going to use Noah. He sees your former boyfriend as your Achilles' heel."

"I'm prepared for whatever he tells me." She took several sips from the cup before placing it on the coffee table. "I'll give him what he wants. I won't try to completely control my emotions. If he wants to see me cry, I'll cry."

"I have to remind you that this may all be for nothing. You may give him exactly what he wants and get only useless information in return."

"I know. I'm willing to take that chance."

Derek nodded. "Barbara Jean contacted me about half an hour ago. Our orders are to head back to Knoxville after your visit with Browning."

"Why? Has something happened? Has the copycat—?"

"No, and since the trail is cold and we have no new leads to follow, Sanders wants us back at headquarters to sit in on a top-level powwow, the two of us, Griff, Nic, Sanders, BJ, and Dr. Meng."

"Any idea what this big powwow is about?" Maleah asked.

"BJ didn't say, but I suspect Griff wants to discuss his theory about who the copycat is, who hired him and why."

"And as Griff so often says, all roads lead to Rome."

"In this case, Rome being Malcolm York."

"Rome being Griff's obsession with the pseudo York, if he actually exists."

"I don't think any of us can dismiss the real possibility that someone who calls himself Malcolm York exists," Derek told her. "And if we accept that possibility, we also have to be prepared to accept the possibility that York hired a professional assassin to carry out some diabolical plan against Griff."

"Have you actually bought into Griff's theory?"

"I'm keeping an open mind and you should, too."

"You're right," Maleah agreed. "If all of these copycat murders are a part of some elaborate scheme to exact revenge against Griff, then we're up against far more than a single killer. Even if we find the copycat and stop him, that won't be the end of it."

"You're right. It won't end until York, whoever he really is, is found."

Miss Carolyn was an early riser, as was Heloise. They enjoyed leisurely cups of coffee each morning in the small den adjacent to the kitchen, the television tuned to WJCL, channel 22, the local ABC affiliate. Her employer, whom she thought of after all these years as a dear old friend, watched only *Good Morning America*. She had been a huge Charlie Gibson fan and bemoaned his exit from the show, but had found consolation in watching him on the evening newscast until his retirement.

"I prefer to get my evening news from a man," Miss Carolyn had said. "But I like Diane Sawyer well enough. She's a smart lady. And as long as they keep Robin Roberts on *Good Morning America,* I'll keep watching that show, too. I like her."

Miss Carolyn was nothing if not opinionated and always believed her opinion was superior to and more important than anyone else's.

Little Miss Poppy was not an early riser. She often slept until well past ten, sometimes as late as noon, much to her grandmother's displeasure.

"These young people sleep away the best part of the day," Miss Carolyn often said.

With the breakfast dishes neatly stacked in the dishwasher—she had a precise system of where to place each item—and the television turned off until the local mid-day news, Heloise began lunch preparations. Since it was only nine-thirty and lunch wouldn't be served until noon, she had more than enough time to bake a blueberry pie, using the fresh berries she had bought at the Farmer's Market. And she intended to use last night's leftover chicken to make chicken salad, which she would serve with some of the buttery croissants she had picked up at the bakery.

Wearing her wide-brimmed sunbonnet and carrying her gardening gloves, Miss Carolyn came through the kitchen and paused at the back door. "If you need me, I'll be in the garden. I want to prune the roses before it gets so hot. I can't abide these ungodly humid days. I don't remember it ever being this miserable in late June. When I was a girl summertime weather didn't hit until the Fourth of July."

Heloise didn't bother pointing out to Miss Carolyn that the Fourth was only a few days away.

After Miss Carolyn was halfway out the door, she stopped, glanced over her shoulder and said, "When Miss Lazybones gets up, please tell her that I expect her to be here for lunch today because her great-aunt Sarah will be joining us." She sighed heavily. "The woman is an absolute bore, but she is family. She was married to my dear brother Courtland for forty years."

"I'll be sure to remind her."

"Oh, is the pool boy coming today? If he is, I need to speak to him."

"Yes, ma'am, this is Tuesday and he comes every Tuesday. He should be here any time now."

"I can see the pool from the rose garden, so I'll keep an eye out for him."

Heloise smiled as she removed the blueberries from the refrigerator. Miss Carolyn had her good qualities and her bad. But being a perfectionist and expecting everyone else to live up to her high standards did not endear her to the people she referred to as "the hired help." This included the young man who cleaned the pool each week.

Heloise gently dumped the berries into a colander she had placed in the sink, turned on the water and used the sprayer to wash the berries.

A bloodcurdling scream startled Heloise. Who was screaming? The sound was coming from somewhere outside, wasn't it? *Oh mercy God, it's Miss Carolyn.* She must have fallen. Or she had come across a snake in the rose garden.

Heloise wiped her damp hands off on her apron as she headed for the back door, running as fast as her old legs would carry her. She searched the rose garden for any sign of Miss Carolyn, but quickly realized the screams were coming from the pool area.

And then she saw Miss Carolyn, soaked through and through from head to toe, on her knees, slumped over something—no not something, someone—lying at the edge of the pool.

Merciful Lord!

Heloise rushed through the open gate leading from the garden to the pool. "I'm coming, Miss Carolyn. I'm coming."

As she drew nearer, Miss Carolyn stopped screaming and looked up, her eyes glazed with shock. When she glanced down at the person Miss Carolyn was holding in her arms, Heloise barely managed not to scream herself. Apparently Miss Carolyn had jumped in the pool and pulled Little Miss Poppy's body from the water. But it was more than obvious that the child hadn't drowned. Someone had slit her throat and hacked out pieces of flesh from her arms and legs.

Salty bile rose up Heloise's esophagus. She was on the verge of vomiting. *Help me, Lord. Help me.*

"Call nine-one-one," Miss Carolyn said in a choked voice. "We have to get her to the hospital as soon as possible."

"Oh, Miss Carolyn . . ."

Heloise would call 911, but knew there was nothing anybody could do to save Poppy Chappelle.

Maleah thought she had prepared herself for the worst, and had believed she could listen to Browning describe in detail how he had murdered Noah and still remain in control of her emotions. She'd been wrong. Nothing had prepared her for Browning's self-satisfied smile or his giddy excitement as he recalled, step-by-step, the last moments of Noah's life.

While he relived what for him had been an exhilarating experience, Maleah envisioned, with sickening horror, Noah Laborde's death.

"Can you imagine it, Maleah? Noah's shock? When he woke that morning, he had no idea it would be the last day of his life. What must he have been thinking in those final few seconds before he died?"

Maleah swallowed.

I'm still in control. I'm shaky. I'm nauseated. I'm angry. But I'm not defeated.

She could give Browning a little of what he wanted— her blood, sweat, and tears—without pretending. What she felt at that precise moment was all too real.

"I—I can imagine." The tremor in her voice was not

faked. "Noah must have been shocked by what happened and so very afraid of dying."

Browning chuckled. "I'm sure he was. He knew that I possessed all the power and he was powerless. He knew that I had taken his life away from him."

"That's what it was all about for you, wasn't it—power and control?"

"God, yes! You have no idea . . ." He paused, leaned forward and glared directly into her eyes. "But then again, maybe you do. You're a lady who prides herself on being in control, aren't you?"

A red warning flag popped up in Maleah's mind. How could Browning know that she had dealt with control issues most of her life?

He can't know. He's only guessing.

When she didn't reply to his question, he smiled. God, how she hated his smile.

"What would it take to snap that tight control you maintain?" he asked. "I would love to see that happen. I'd enjoy breaking you, taking your power away and controlling you."

Maleah understood that for Browning, killing another human being was far more about power and control than about their pain, but the rush he experienced when he took a life was probably the same as a sadist who physically tortured his victim.

"I'm not good at play-acting," she told him. "You know how difficult it was for me to listen to you tell me the details about Noah's murder. What more do you want from me?"

"Ah, yes, it was difficult for you. I noticed your misty eyes, but there were no real tears, no weeping. I heard the tremor in your voice, but you didn't scream with uncontrolled outrage." Browning leaned back in his chair and studied her for a moment. "It wasn't enough. No, not nearly enough. I want much more."

"So do I," she told him. "Up to this point, I've been doing all the giving and you've been doing all the taking."

"All right, then. If you want payment for the pleasure you gave me, I'll pay up. After all, fair's fair." He tilted back his head, pursed his lips and hummed. Then he lowered his head and looked at her. "I don't know Durham's real name. He didn't tell me and I didn't ask. But he was younger than he appeared to be. Being a keen judge of human beings, I'd say that his disguise added ten or fifteen years to his appearance. The man you're looking for is probably in his forties. He was average height and build, but he was muscular, his body well-toned. Look for a man who keeps his body in tip-top shape."

Although she was slightly stunned that Browning had willingly given her the information, when he stopped talking, Maleah managed to ask, "Do you recall anything else about his physical appearance? Moles, scars or tattoos? Were his arms hairy? Did he speak with an accent of any kind?"

"No visible moles or tattoos," Browning said. "His arms had a fine dusting of light brown hair, his eyebrows and lashes were the same color and his eyes were blue. Of course he could have been wearing contacts. As for an accent . . . well, he wasn't from the South. He had more of a Midwestern accent, as if he had practiced the way he talked, trying to make his speech pattern as nondescript as possible, you know, the way English and Australian actors speak when they're mimicking an American accent."

"Do you think he was British?"

"Possibly."

"What about—?"

"That's all for now. If you want more, you'll have to give me more."

Maleah nodded, understanding that he was ready to put her through Act Two of *Her Torture for His Pleasure*. And she had no choice but to take on the starring role.

Derek paced back and forth in the warden's office, unable to sit down, let alone relax. Everything in him wanted to rush down to the interview room, barge in and rescue Maleah from Browning's evil machinations.

Not an option.

All he could do was wait. And worry.

The waiting was difficult, but the worry came all too easily. He repeatedly reminded himself that Maleah was a big girl, strong, tough, tenacious, her soft underbelly well protected. But she would not come away unscathed. He had warned her that if she revealed even a hint of weakness, Browning would go in for the kill.

Derek didn't know what the hell was wrong with him. It wasn't like him to go all chest-beating, manly-man protective where a woman was concerned. Any woman. He honestly couldn't remember ever feeling like this. When they'd been kids, he'd run interference between his kid sister and his mom and even between his older brother and Mommy Dearest a few times. But he'd done that more to piss off their mother than to protect either sibling.

For the past forty-five minutes, Claude Holland had done his best to engage Derek in conversation, but had soon realized keeping Derek's mind off Maleah's visit with Browning was an impossible task. Finally, the warden had settled down to business as usual, made a couple of phone calls, went over various paperwork, and drank three cups of coffee.

Derek decided he would give Maleah thirty more minutes and if she hadn't returned to the warden's office, he'd go get her. His gut told him that Browning had been playing her—playing them—and today's interview would be a burnt run. No matter what happened, not even if Maleah retrieved some usable info from Browning, she was not going to return to this damn place for a repeat performance. This would be her final visit with the Carver. If he had to hogtie her and guard her night and day, he would. She'd have to understand. A guy could take only so much waiting and worrying.

When his phone rang, he paused mid-stride and checked caller ID. A knot formed in his stomach. He had already talked to Powell headquarters this morning, via Barbara Jean, whom he affectionately called BJ. This call was from Sanders.

"Yeah, what's wrong?" Derek asked.

"There has been another copycat murder," Sanders said.

Derek's stomach knots tightened. "Who?"

"Saxon Chappelle's young niece, Poppy. She was only sixteen."

"When? Where?" Derek cursed under his breath. "Hell, I don't suppose it matters, does it?"

"She was visiting Saxon's mother in Savannah for the summer. Her grandmother found her in the backyard swimming pool this morning."

"This was kill number six and we're no closer to nabbing this guy than we were weeks ago."

"Is Maleah with you?"

"No, she's still in with Browning, doing her damnedest to get something out of him. Why?" Derek asked. "Do you want us to leave here and head straight for Savannah?"

"No, we are sending Holt Keinan to Savannah today. As we speak, Saxon Chappelle is over the Atlantic on the Powell jet, accompanying Meredith Sinclair to London. On his return, he will be taken directly to Savannah and Holt will meet him. Griffin still wants you and Maleah to return to Griffin's Rest as soon as possible."

"Can you tell me what's going on?"

"You and Maleah are the only two employees, other than Luke Sentell, who are privy to all the information we have accumulated on the Copycat Carver, a man named Anthony Linden, and a mystery man who is calling himself Malcolm York. I believe Griffin wants the two of you included in a strategic planning session."

"All right, then, as soon as Maleah finishes up here, we'll go back through Vidalia, check out of our hotel, and head your way."

"Very good. I will tell Griffin that we can expect you this evening."

"Sanders?"

"Yes, sir?"

"How's Griff?"

Several seconds of contemplative silence followed. And then Sanders replied, his voice a reflection of the man's stoic personality, "You will be able to ask him yourself when you see him tonight."

Without so much as a by-your-leave, Sanders ended their conversation. Well, what had he expected? He should have known better than to ask the man anything personal regarding Griffin Powell. Sanders guarded Griff's privacy as strongly as he guarded his own.

They were both men with secrets. Dark, deadly secrets.

What had really happened on Amara sixteen years

ago when Griff and his cohorts had killed Malcolm York? Derek knew only the basic facts—Griff had been kidnapped at twenty-two and held captive by a sadistic madman for four years before he, along with Sanders and Yvette, both also York's prisoners, had revolted and killed York. The details Griff had given him had been, at best, sketchy, huge chunks of info not included. If Nic knew more about the events that took place on Amara, she had not shared them with Maleah, who seemed to know little more than he did.

"Has there been another copycat murder?" Claude Holland asked Derek.

He had forgotten that the warden was still in the room. "Yes, I'm afraid there has. This time, he's killed a sixteen-year-old girl, the niece of one of our agents."

"I'm so sorry," the warden said. "Let's hope that Ms. Perdue has some success in getting Jerome Browning to tell her everything he knows."

"I don't think Browning knows a goddamn thing," Derek said. "But Maleah just won't give up. She was damned and determined to give it one more try."

Warden Holland shook his head sadly. "I hate to say it, but I agree with you, and I'm afraid Ms. Perdue is going to come away from this latest interview with little more than a few mental bruises."

He had been waiting for nearly six hours and was beginning to grow restless. When he had reported in after he left Savannah before daylight this morning, his employer had applauded him on a job well done, then instructed him to check into a hotel in Atlanta and remain there until he got in touch with him again.

"I am finalizing my plans and should have further instructions for you before noon Atlanta time."

During the past few months while he had been carrying out the copycat murders, as soon as one kill had
been accomplished, he had been given the information
about the next victim. But not this time. Was the Copycat Carver's reign of terror over?

Stripped naked, down to his bare skin, the real man
revealed, he lay on the king-size bed in the four-star
hotel and stared up at the ceiling. When on an assignment, he always wore disguises and only in moments of
solitude such as this did he allow himself such indul-
gent freedom. Even with the expensive whores he
bought for a few hours of pleasure, he didn't remove
his wig or colored contacts or, if using them, the fake
mustache and beard. He kept his body in perfect condition, lean, muscled, healthy. He kept his head and
chest shaved and since he was not an excessively hairy
man, he had only a sprinkling of light brown hair on his
arms and legs.

When his phone finally rang, he didn't rush to answer it. *Let him wait.*

He picked up between the fifth and sixth rings.

"Yes?"

"I'm afraid you've been compromised. Or should I
say that Anthony Linden has been."

"How did that happen?"

"Not to worry, not to worry. The leak will be
plugged."

"Give me a name and I will take care of it myself."

"No, no, you're too valuable to me where you are.
Someone else can resolve that problem. I need you
there in America to handle something extremely deli-
cate for me."

"Another kill?"

"Actually, no. I want you to pick up a guest for me
and bring her with you when you return to London.

There will be a private jet waiting for you in Nashville. You and my guest will be the only passengers."

"Am I to bring her directly to you?"

"No, I have arranged for a lovely, private retreat where I want her guarded night and day."

"You're giving me a babysitting assignment?"

"I'm putting you in charge of a mission that will allow me to continue with my attack against the Powell Agency. Your job will be to deliver my guest safely to London. I wouldn't trust anyone else with such an important task. As soon as she is delivered, another payment will be transferred to your bank account."

"Half now and the other half once I deliver her."

"If you prefer. I don't quibble over unimportant details with people who have proven themselves to me the way you have."

His employer gave him the necessary details, including the name of his "guest" and her present location.

"I'll need twenty-four to forty-eight hours to put a plan into motion."

"Very well, but I need this done in no more than forty-eight hours. If you can pick her up and deliver her by tomorrow morning, I'll add a bonus to your payment."

Chapter 27

Even if the general description that Browning had given her of the copycat matched that of Anthony Linden, former MI6 agent, there was no way they could be certain the two were the same person. So far, the information Browning had given her was pretty much useless, just as Derek had warned her it would be. If he was right about how little Browning actually knew, then she would be wasting her time if she continued playing his game.

But what if he actually does know something that will help us? What if I give up now and walk away? If I do that, I'll never know for sure and I'll always wonder if I could have done more to stop the copycat killer.

She had to stay a while longer. She couldn't give up. Not yet. She had to keep trying. But at what cost?

Browning wanted to see her suffer. He wanted to stick the knife into her, figuratively speaking, and then twist it.

"Have you decided?" Browning asked. "Are you staying or going?"

His eyes all but sparkled with anticipation.

You son of a bitch!

"I'm staying," she told him.

"Ah, that's my girl. Just as I had hoped—a fighter to the bitter end."

"I want a show of goodwill," she told him. "I'll make a statement and all you have to do is reply yes or no. Agreed?"

Smiling as if she had just handed him a get-out-of-jail-free card, he shrugged. "Maybe. If I agree and I give you this one thing, then you swear that you'll answer all my questions, no matter what I ask?"

She hesitated, contemplating what he might ask her. But she knew she had to take the risk. "Yes, I'll answer whatever you ask. But for every answer I give you, you give me one in return. Agreed?"

"Agreed. Now, the next move is yours, Maleah."

"The copycat chose the Carver's kills as the model for his murders because he wanted a connection between the killer he mimicked and a Powell agent," Maleah said. "He chose you because you killed Noah Laborde, who had been my college boyfriend."

Browning's smile widened. "Yes, of course. Any idiot could have figured that out. But you needed to hear me confirm it, didn't you?"

Yes, of course she had known. And yes, she had needed to hear him confirm it. But his confirmation of that fact didn't necessarily confirm that Durham or Linden or whoever the hell the copycat was had shared this information with Browning. As he'd said, any idiot could have figured it out.

"Now, we get down to business." She met his eager gaze, despising him, but determined to show no reluctance. "You've already told me you don't know the copycat's real name, and that you knew he wasn't the real Albert Durham. Is that the truth?" When he opened his mouth to speak, she held up her hand in a Stop signal. "You also implied that you know why the copycat is killing people associated with the Powell Agency. I want you to tell me why. What's his reason?"

"That's really *the* question, isn't it? The one you'll pay any price to know."

"You're such a smart man, I'll bet you already know the answer to your own question."

"Do you trust me to tell you the truth?" he asked.

"No, of course I don't trust you."

Browning laughed. "You must have been a pretty little girl, all blond curls and pink cheeks. Did you smile a lot? Laugh a lot? Were you happy as a child?"

Those were not the questions she had expected him to ask, but she answered them all the same. "When my father was alive, I smiled and laughed a lot and I was very happy."

"And after your father died? He did die, didn't he?"

"Yes, he died when I was quite young." *But how did you know?*

"Poor little Maleah."

She didn't flinch and never broke eye contact.

"Was your mother as beautiful as you are?" Browning asked in a low, seductive tone.

"My mother was very beautiful."

"Was she a good mother? Was she a good role model? Did you want to grow up to be just like her?"

"She was the best mother she knew how to be," Maleah said honestly. "Why do you want to know these things about my mother?"

Browning slowly twisted his neck around and around, as if trying to loosen aching muscles. Then with his head down, his chin almost touching his chest, he rolled his eyes up and then lifted his head slowly.

In that moment, she realized she had said the wrong

thing, that her reaction to his questions about her mother had triggered his curiosity. Unwittingly, she had played right into his hands.

"I want to know everything about you," he told her. "And where better to start than learning about the woman who gave birth to you."

Maleah did not like where this conversation was heading. Her gut instincts told her that somehow, someway, Jerome Browning knew things about her that he couldn't possibly know.

Shake it off. All those doubts and fears and uncertainties. Browning doesn't know anything about your personal life. He's guessing. He's smart. He picked up something in your reaction. The tone of your voice. A glint in your eye. An unconscious gesture of some type. Don't give him any more ammunition to use against you.

"I loved my mother," Maleah told him. "She was gentle and kind and sweet and—"

"And you swore you'd never be like her."

She simply stared at Browning without responding and then quickly realized that her reaction had spoken for her. So far, in this stupid game, she was losing.

"Gentle, kind, sweet women tend to need a man around to take care of them," Browning said. "Did you have a stepfather?"

Don't go there. Please, don't go there.

There was no way he could know anything about Nolan Reeves, her mother's sadistic second husband.

"Yes, I had a stepfather."

"Was he a good man?"

"No."

"You disliked him?"

"Yes."

"Hated him?"

"Yes."

"Ah, Maleah, being worthy of your hatred must indeed be a sweet, sweet thing. I envy your stepfather. How wonderful it must have been having all that power over you when you were a helpless little girl."

Her heartbeat accelerated, the sound of her racing pulse drumming inside her head. *Don't give him one damn thing. Keep everything on an even keel. You can do this. You know you can.*

"Did he rape you?" Browning asked, excitement in his voice.

Perspiration dampened her forehead and hands. She swallowed hard. "No, he never raped me."

"Fondled you inappropriately?"

"No."

"Ah, nothing sexual. That means he must have beaten you. There are men like that, sadistic men who enjoy inflicting pain." Browning burst into laughter. "I'm going to tell you something that I've never told anyone else, not even Albert Durham, my so-called biographer. I didn't want his kills to be exactly like mine, so I failed to mention that before I killed, I waited for a few seconds before I plunged the scalpel into the jugular because I needed to see the fear and agony in their eyes. Just for a moment."

She sucked in a deep breath and released it slowly. "If I answer your last question, I'll expect you to give me more than your rambling memories that mean nothing to me. I'm not interested in your kills, only in why the copycat is killing Powell agents and members of their families."

"Then answer my question first. Did your stepfather beat you?"

"Yes."

"Often?" He was practically licking his lips over the prospect of hearing the gory details.

"Sorry to disappoint you, but he beat me only once."

"Only once?" Disappointment in his voice, Browning frowned.

"Yes, only once, but it was a severe beating. I had bruises and welts on my back and legs and buttocks and I could barely stand after he finished."

There, you son of a bitch, are those details gruesome enough for you?

"Why only once? Did you mother intervene?"

"No." Maleah stood her ground and stared the devil down. "And if you want any more answers, then I'll need a few from you."

Browning studied her as if trying to decide whether or not the pleasure he derived from tormenting her was worth the price she was asking.

"Durham and I actually played our own game," Browning admitted. "He came to understand that he wasn't dealing with an ordinary person, that I was his intellectual equal and therefore deserved his respect. Once I realized he was not the real Albert Durham, I demanded payment for my services."

"You asked for a new lawyer and a female visitor . . . what else?"

"Information."

"And he was willing to tell you whatever you wanted to know? I can't believe—"

"No, of course not. But I didn't ask for very much. We understood each other, so he was willing to give me what I required. He knew that the information I requested would in no way harm him. I asked him why he had chosen me. And he told me what I believed was the truth. After all, who was I going to tell?"

"And he explained why—because of your connection to Noah Laborde, who was the former boyfriend of a Powell agent."

"Not in those exact words."

Maleah glowered at Browning, her patience growing thin.

Stay calm. Pace yourself. Let him have all the time he needs.

"Explain," Maleah said. "Give me his exact words."

Browning ran his tongue over his teeth, licked his lips, and sighed dramatically. "I'm afraid that I don't recall his exact words."

"Then paraphrase."

"He told me that he admired my work. I thanked him. I asked him why he had chosen me. He simply said, 'You killed a man named Noah Laborde.' I said yes. And when I told him that I didn't understand the significance, he told me that I didn't need to understand."

"Did he ever mention the Powell Agency or Griffin Powell by name? Did he tell you or did you sense that he was a professional?"

"That's two questions," Browning reminded her. "Neither of which you've paid for, my dear."

She nodded as dread spread through her like quicksilver, fast and poisonous, because she knew what was coming next.

"Why did your stepfather beat you only once?" Browning asked, the glint of anticipation sparkling in his eyes again.

Maleah knew she could lie to him, perhaps even convincingly, but she couldn't fake the emotion that went along with lying. And it was an emotional reaction that Browning wanted from her. *Blood, sweat, and tears.*

"Because my big brother made a bargain with our stepfather to take both his own beatings and mine."

Browning's eyes widened with exhilaration. "How noble and heroic of your brother. But you must have felt terribly guilty allowing someone else to take your punishment while you got off scot-free."

Answer him, damn it. No, wait. Let him see how much his question affected you, how it brought back painful memories.

"What's wrong, Maleah?"

"Nothing." *That slight tremor in your voice was a nice touch. Browning had to know it was real and not faked.*

"Then answer me."

"I didn't know . . ." Maleah admitted. "Not until years later. All I knew was that my stepfather never beat me again."

"But you were afraid of him, weren't you? Why was that?"

"You already know the answer. I'd think it would be obvious to you."

"Ah, but I want to hear you say it . . . in your own words."

"Yes, I was afraid of him, deathly afraid. Afraid for my mother and my brother and for myself. He was a cruel, heartless bastard." With tears misting her eyes, she looked right at Browning. "He never beat me again, but he berated me every chance he got. Once a day and twice on Sunday."

Browning chuckled. "It's good to see you're able to maintain a sense of humor about such a tragic childhood. That shows just how tough you are now, doesn't it, Maleah? And you pride yourself on being tough, on being strong and in control."

"Damn straight about that," she told him, not trying to conceal the anger in her voice. *He wants emotion—I'll give it to him.* She shot up out of her chair and looked down at him. "Did the copycat ever mention either the Powell Agency or Griffin Powell by name?"

Browning didn't respond.

"Answer me, you goddamn, sadistic, lowlife son of a bitch. I paid for your answer and you're going to give it to me."

Angling his head sideways, he rolled his eyes upward and glanced at her. "What a delicious thing your anger and hatred is, my dear Maleah. I can't tell you how much pleasure you're giving me."

"Tit for tat, Jerome. I give to you. You give to me. If you try to change the rules of the game now, I'm out of here so fast that—"

"He never mentioned Griffin Powell by name," Browning said.

"What about the agency?"

"No. The name Powell never came up, not the man or his agency."

"Then the only name the copycat ever mentioned was Noah Laborde?"

"That's right."

Once again, Browning had given her information that was all but useless.

"Did you ever suspect or did the copycat ever imply that he was a professional, that he was working for someone else?"

"That's the sixty-four-thousand-dollar question, isn't it?" Browning stretched languidly, rotating his shoulders slowly and then twisting his head from side to side.

"What's the going exchange rate between sixty-four thousand and my tears?" she asked, knowing what he wanted.

"A few more insights into the real Maleah Perdue," he said. "And one small stipulation."

"What small stipulation?"

"I want to taste them."

"You want to taste what?" Dear God, he couldn't mean what she thought he did.

"Your tears. I want you to come close enough for me to wipe away your tears with my tongue."

No way in hell was this monster going to put his mouth on her!

"It's not going to happen," she told him.

He shrugged. "It's your choice. But I can answer your question with certainty. And maybe, just maybe, I can give you even more."

She didn't believe him about the even more part and wasn't sure she believed that he could or would answer her question. But she was close, so very close, to ending this. She couldn't stop when she had made it almost to the finish line.

"If I cry, then you tell me what I want to know first and if your answers are worth anything to me, you can use your fingertip to wipe my tears."

"Hmm . . . a compromise." He nodded. "Agreed."

"Agreed."

"Sit back down, Maleah. Let's get all comfy cozy."

She sat, crossed her ankles, and folded her hands together in her lap. She didn't try to hide her apprehension. Allowing her emotions free rein was the only way she could give Browning what he wanted. A large part of the pleasure he was seeking would come from knowing how difficult it would be for her to relinquish control over her emotions.

"Your stepfather, did he beat your mother?"

"Yes, I believe he did. I know he slapped her quite often whenever she did anything that displeased him."

"And what do you think it was like for her during sex? Did you ever think about how he must have brutalized her? I'll bet you could hear her crying, couldn't you?"

Memories that she had kept buried deep inside her

subconscious broke through the barrier of her iron control, memories that she didn't want to recall.

"Yes, I heard her crying, but . . . I was too young and innocent at the time to know why."

"But when you were older and you knew all about sex, about what goes on between a man and a woman—"

"I tried not to think about it."

"No, of course not. You wouldn't let yourself, would you? No man would ever hurt you. No man would ever dominate you, control you, beat you into submission." He paused, as if waiting to see if one of his accusatory arrows had hit their mark. "And yet here you are giving me something you've never given another man."

She clenched her teeth, hating Browning, hating herself.

Finish it. Give him everything he wants. Pay the price. And then get the hell away from him.

Maleah brought the memory up from the dark corners of her soul. Her naked mother running down the hall, her face bloody and bruised. Nolan catching her, shoving her down on the floor and—

Thirteen-year-old Maleah had heard her mother's screams, gotten out of bed and opened her door. Jack had been gone for only a few weeks. He had joined the army and left her all alone in the family's house of horrors.

Maleah hadn't realized she was crying, not until she heard Browning's deep intake of breath, so satisfied, so pleased with himself.

She looked at him through her tears.

"Did you ever try to help your mother?" Browning asked.

"No."

After all these years, she still felt guilty that she hadn't done more to save her mother. But even as a teenager, she had been terrified of Nolan Reeves, of the threats he had made to kill both her and her mother if she ever interfered or told anyone "lies" about him.

"Your stepfather beat your mother, raped her repeatedly, abused her terribly and you did nothing," Browning said.

Tears threatened to choke Maleah. Emotions long bottled up inside her rose to the surface. It took all of her energy to hold them at bay.

Enough!

She had paid his price. She had given him her tears. Now, by God, he'd give her whatever information he had or . . . Or what?

"Tell me," she managed to say, her voice a mere whisper.

"Thank you, Maleah." Jerome Browning leaned back his head, closed his eyes, and released a heavy, orgasmic sigh. "It's been a long time since a woman has given me so much pleasure."

Every instinct she possessed urged her to attack, to rip out the monster's heart and throw it to a pack of wild dogs. At that very moment, she hated Jerome Browning almost as much as she had hated Nolan Reeves.

"Tell me, damn it," Maleah demanded.

"Of course, my dear. I am an honorable man who always pays his debts. You give to me and I give to you."

"Then give, you sick son of a bitch."

"He referred to himself as a death technician and an international contractor. I like those terms, don't you?" Browning's gaze sparkled with amusement, but he didn't smile when he said, "As a professional courtesy, one skilled death technician to another, the man you refer to as the Copycat Carver did not deny it when I asked him if he was a professional hit man. As far as I'm concerned, his silence was a confirmation. He knew that as well as I did."

Maleah swiped the tears trickling down her cheeks.

"Save just a taste for me," Browning reminded her and then ran his tongue across his upper lip.

Ignoring his comment and gesture, she asked, "Do you know anything at all about who hired him and why?"

"Perhaps."

"I've paid you in full, so don't try to play me. Not now. It's too late in the game," she reminded him. "You still owe me."

Browning hesitated for a moment before replying. "Why would you think he would have shared that kind of information with anyone, even with me? He is no sloppy amateur. He kills people for a living. And he's quite good at it, isn't he?"

Instinct told her that Browning did know something else and she was determined he share that info with her, no matter how insignificant. "I want the rest of the information I paid for."

"Yes, of course. A deal is a deal." He couldn't take his gaze off the tears clinging to her lashes and seeping from the corners of her eyes. "Sometimes, during his visits, we talked philosophy, past experiences, things like that. We exchanged confidences the way people in the same profession do. It's not often that you meet someone who is your equal, perhaps even slightly superior. Of course, he didn't mention names, but . . ."

Maleah waited, allowing him this one final moment of victory.

He savored the moment, let it drag on and on, and she knew what he wanted.

"But what, Jerome?" She jumped up, leaned over

him and glanced at the guard out of the corner of her eye, trying to nonverbally ask him to stay put. "You can't tell me anything, can you? You've been stringing me along all this time. You really are a son of a bitch, aren't you? And I hate you." She balled her hands into fists and held them in his face, letting him see how much she wanted to pummel him. "I hate you, hate you, hate you, hate you!" she shouted.

"My copycat is a very proud man and if he has one flaw, it's that he's boastful." The words flowed out of Browning like water from a dam that had just burst wide open. "He liked to brag about how rich and powerful those who have employed him are. As I said before, he couldn't mention names, but he did tell me that he has worked for political leaders and crime bosses throughout the U.S., Europe, and around the world. That makes him an international contractor. His current employer is a billionaire who owns a private island retreat where he enjoys some of the perks of his business."

A billionaire? A private island retreat.

"Exactly what are those perks?"

"Human trafficking," Browning said with such delight that it was all Maleah could do to stop herself from actually striking him. "A smorgasbord of human delights. Whatever your pleasure. Male or female. Child, teen or adult. Dark or fair. Experienced or virginal."

The description of a billionaire who made his fortune from human trafficking and who owned an island retreat sounded all too familiar.

Malcolm York.

The real Malcolm York.

But that isn't possible.

The real York is dead, has been dead for sixteen years.

"A deal's a deal." Maleah leaned close enough for Browning to touch her.

Smiling, he lifted his cuffed hands, and then slowly and very tenderly wiped a tear from the corner of her eye. As she lifted her head, she watched as he placed his index finger on his tongue, licked his finger and then sucked it into his mouth.

Maleah turned and, without a backward glance, walked away.

When she reached the guard who had been assigned to escort her to and from the interview, he opened the door for her. At that precise moment, Browning called her name.

"Maleah?"

She paused, but didn't turn around or look back.

"It was good for me," he told her. "Was it good for you?"

The sound of his laughter followed her as she hurried away from him as fast as she could.

Chapter 28

The moment he saw Maleah, Derek sensed she was on the verge of collapse. Not that anyone else would even notice. She managed to hide her emotional stress remarkably well, especially considering what he suspected she had just endured at Browning's cunningly cruel hands. What Derek wanted to do and what he did were two entirely different things. He wanted to grab her, hold her, and tell her it was all right to fall apart because he'd be there to take care of her. What he actually did was walk over to her, give her a casual glance, and ask her if she was ready to leave.

"Yes, I'm ready," she told him, her voice deceptively calm.

They both shook hands with Warden Holland and thanked him.

"Will you be scheduling another interview?" the warden asked.

Derek wanted to shout "no way in hell."

"No. This was the final interview," Maleah said, absolute certainty in her voice.

As they walked together out into the parking area, he

waited for Maleah to speak first and was prepared to take his cue from her on how to proceed. If she wanted to talk, he'd talk. If she wanted to be quiet, he'd keep his mouth shut. If she needed time alone when they returned to Vidalia, then he would give her some time alone. But within a few hours, he would have to tell her about Saxon Chappelle's niece. Only sixteen. *Sweet sixteen and never been kissed.* He hoped the lyrics to that old song weren't true in Poppy's case. He hoped the girl had been kissed at least once by a young boy who had made her toes curl.

Sixteen was far too young to die.

As Derek and Maleah approached her Equinox, she pulled her keychain out of her pocket and tossed it to him. He caught the chain mid-air, keys jangling together when he grasped the large silver "M" to which the chain was fastened.

"You drive, okay?" Maleah did not make eye contact.

"Yeah, sure," Derek said.

For a woman who usually insisted on driving her own car and even the rental cars they had used in the past, a woman hell-bent on always being in control, handing over her keys and asking him to drive meant only one thing. Maleah didn't trust herself to drive. Outwardly she appeared to be completely fine, but it was obvious to Derek that she was far from all right.

This was the second time she had asked him to drive after a visit with Browning. The first time, her request had taken him by surprise. This time, he had known she would ask. He had expected her to come out of this final interview in bad shape. What he didn't know was just how bad it really was.

He unlocked the doors before they reached the SUV, and then he opened her door. But he stopped himself just short of actually touching her, despite wanting to hug her to him and then ease her gently into the passenger seat. By the time he rounded the hood and slid behind the wheel, Maleah had put on her seatbelt and sat there ramrod straight, her fisted hands crossed at the wrists and resting in her lap.

As soon as they were on the road, he asked, "Want some music?"

"Not especially."

"Want to stop for—"

"No, please, I don't want anything. Not right now. Nothing except peace and quiet. All right?" She leaned back her head and closed her eyes.

"Yeah, sure."

They spent the next twenty-one miles in complete silence. Derek kept his eyes on the road, not once glancing at Maleah. But she was all he could think about. If only she'd make a sound. A gasp or a sigh or even a hiccup or a sneeze. It was as if she had hit some sort of mute button inside her.

Less than thirty minutes after leaving the penitentiary, Derek turned in at the Vidalia Hampton Inn, parked the SUV and killed the engine. When Maleah didn't open her eyes or say anything, he came damn close to grabbing her and shaking her. But the minute he looked at her, really looked at her, his heart stopped. God in heaven!

"It's going to be okay, Blondie," he told her in the calmest, most reassuring tone he could muster. "It's going to be okay."

He undid his seatbelt, got out, pocketed the keys, and rushed around to her side of the SUV. When he opened the door, she sat there unmoving. He reached in, unhooked her belt, and very gently reached down and peeled back the clenched fingers of her right hand. She had clutched her hand so tightly that her short, neat nails had dug into her flesh so deeply that her palm was bleeding. He repeated the process with her left hand and found it to be in the same condition.

"Ah, Maleah, sweetheart . . ." He pulled a white monogrammed handkerchief from his inside jacket pocket, wiped the bright red droplets of blood from each palm and wrapped the handkerchief around her right hand. "Come on, let's get you out of here and into the hotel."

When he grasped her shoulders and turned her sideways, she opened her eyes and stared at him. After slipping his arm around her waist, he lifted her up, pulled her out of the SUV and straight into his arms. Then he eased her down onto her feet.

She looked up at him. "Thank you."

Keeping his right arm around her waist, he caressed her cheek with a gentle backward swipe of his left hand. "You're welcome. Come on. You need to lie down and rest for a while."

She nodded and then followed him into the hotel and down the corridor to the elevator. He kept his arm around her, supporting her, sensing that without him, she would spiral down to the floor and curl up in a ball. He didn't bother asking her for the key to her room; instead he walked her straight to his room. He unlocked the door and led her over to his freshly made bed. She didn't protest when he eased her down onto the edge of the bed. But when he moved away from her, intending to take off her shoes before getting a washcloth to clean her hands, she reached out and grabbed him. The bloody handkerchief wrapped loosely around her right hand slipped off just as she gripped his shoulders.

"Don't leave me, Derek. Stay, please. I—I . . ."

"I'm not going anywhere," he told her. "I just want to take off your shoes so you can lie back and relax. Then

I'm going to get a warm washcloth and wash your hands. Okay?"

"I won the game," she said. "Browning told me everything he knows."

Derek lifted a stray tendril of glossy blond hair that had escaped from the soft bun atop her head and wrapped it behind her ear. "I never doubted for a minute that you would beat him at his own game." *But at what price to you, Maleah?*

"I need to tell you what he said, everything about—"

Derek tapped his index finger over her lips, effectively silencing her. She gazed up at him with questioning eyes.

"You can tell me everything. Just not right now. You need to rest for a few minutes. You need to let me take care of you. Just this one time. All right?"

She nodded. "All right. Just this one time."

He smiled. "That's my girl." And in that moment, Derek Lawrence admitted an undeniable truth—he thought of Maleah as his. His girl. His woman. His to care for and protect.

Heaven help us both!

Derek knelt in front of her, removed her sensible pumps, set them under the bed, and then lifted her feet and legs. He turned back the covers at the head of the bed, stacked one pillow on top of the other and gently eased Maleah down until her head rested on the double pillows.

"I'll be right back," he told her.

A few minutes later, he returned with a warm, damp washcloth and his shaving kit. He sat on the edge of the bed and tenderly washed her hands. And then he took out a tube of salve from his kit and rubbed the soothing cream into the shallow nicks her nails had made in her palms.

She lifted her hands, one at a time, inspected them and said, "Thank you. I didn't realize what I was doing. I was just trying so damn hard not to fall apart."

He leaned down, kissed her forehead and said, "I know, Blondie. I know."

"I'm all right. Really. I'm just a little shell-shocked."

He set his shaving kit on the floor, dumped the washcloth on top of it, and then turned his attention back to Maleah. "Tell me what you want right now. Tell me what you need."

"What I want and what I need aren't the same," she told him. "I want to forget everything Browning said to me, every question he asked, every innuendo, all the memories he made me dredge up from my childhood. I want to pretend that I didn't let all those horrible memories make me feel the way I did when I was a child and a teenager. Helpless. Frustrated. Frightened." She grabbed Derek's hands and curled her fingers around them. "What I *need* is to exorcise whatever remains of those old demons. I thought I'd done that in my twenties during a few years of therapy sessions, but apparently, the roots of those memories were buried a little deeper than I realized."

"Then talk to me. Let's dig up those roots and burn them to ashes."

"If anyone had ever told me that I'd be asking you, of all people, to be my father confessor, I never would have believed it," she said, the corners of her mouth lifting in an almost smile.

He eased his hands from her death grip, tapped her playfully on the nose, and then sat down beside her. He focused on her eyes. "Anything you say will stay between the two of us for as long as we live. You already know my ugly secrets. You know that I despise my own mother, my money-grubbing, social climbing mother who drove my weak, spineless father to drink and eventually to suicide. And she's never felt guilty about it a day in her life. And you know that when I was young and stupid, I did some pretty awful things. You know that I've killed people."

He took her hands in his and held them so loosely that she could easily pull away. The last thing he wanted was for her to feel trapped by his superior male strength.

"Nothing you ever did could be half as bad as what I did." He lifted her right hand, kissed it, then lifted the left and kissed it.

She pulled her hands out of his and eased up into a sitting position, her back against the headboard. "When my father was alive, we were all so happy. Mama and Daddy and Jackson and me. Then my father died when I was just a little girl. And my mother, my weak, lonely, needy mother, married a monster."

"My mother was married three times, but both of my stepfathers were decent guys. I sort of felt sorry for them. If anyone was a monster in those marriages, it was my mother."

"Nolan Reeves was a sadist." Maleah clutched the sheet on either side of her hips. "He abused my mother every way a man can abuse a woman—physically, sexually, emotionally, mentally. And he beat Jack unmercifully for years, until Jack got big enough to stand up for himself. I think by the time Jack left home and joined the army, Nolan was halfway afraid of him. He wasn't as mean to Mama for a couple of years before Jack left. But then, later, when Jack was gone . . ."

Derek circled her wrists, moved his hands downward and opened her clenched fists. He held her hands. She closed her eyes and breathed deeply.

"When I was thirteen, I saw them," Maleah said. "I saw my mother running from Nolan. She was naked, her body and face were bloody and bruised and . . ."

She gulped several times. "He caught her and threw her on the floor and . . . and . . ."

Derek squeezed her hands tenderly.

"I didn't do anything. I just stood there in my bedroom door, frozen to the spot and scared out of my mind," Maleah told him. "I closed the door, got back in bed and covered my head with a pillow so I couldn't hear her crying while he raped her."

Tears trickled down Maleah's cheeks.

"You were a child, even at thirteen. There's nothing you could have done."

"I know that. As an adult, I know. But on an emotional level, that thirteen-year-old girl blames herself for not trying to stop him." Her gaze locked with Derek's. "He . . . he told me that if I ever interfered in what was a private matter between my mother and him or if I ever told anyone our family's private business, he would kill Mama and me."

Derek pulled her gently into his arms and held her. She wrapped her arms around him and laid her head on his shoulder. And while she cried, he tenderly stroked her back and whispered reassurances.

"That's it, honey. Let it all out. I'm here. I'll take care of you. No one can hurt you." More than anything, he wanted to take away her pain. If he could, he would suffer it for her.

During their flight from Knoxville to London on the Powell jet, Meredith had, thus far, kept to herself as much as possible. Her escort, Saxon Chappelle, had not pressed her to carry on a conversation, not even when they had eaten a meal together. She greatly appreciated how considerate he was. From the moment he had shaken her hand and said, "Please, call me Saxon," she had sensed that he was a good man. She instinctively trusted him and felt at ease around him, neither of which was true when it came to a great many people.

She suspected that he had been told enough about her so that he knew when she touched him she would be able to "read him" to a certain extent. And that's why he had immediately shaken hands with her, to reassure her, to let her know he was a decent human being.

Even when she couldn't see Saxon and wasn't touching him, she occasionally could pick up on his fleeting thoughts, flashes of memory, and even his feelings. And the same held true for the pilot and co-pilot. Saxon loved his mother and worried about her. A young girl named Poppy kept slipping in and out of his thoughts. She was his niece and he worried about her, too.

Meredith wasn't sure if it was the pilot or the co-pilot who kept thinking about women. Their breasts. Their legs. Their hips. Kissing them. Fondling them. She had deliberately shut out those sensual thoughts. They were far too personal and absolutely none of her business. It wasn't that she wanted to invade other people's privacy. She didn't. But she couldn't help it. For as long as she could remember, she'd had "the gift." Her Granny Sinclair had had the "second sight," too, and people in their small Louisiana town had called her a witch. Some people even accused her of practicing Voodoo. It had been Granny who had learned about Dr. Meng and made plans to send Meredith to the woman who was now her mentor. She'd been seventeen when Granny died and old lawyer Dupree had read Granny's will.

"She wants you to go to London," Mr. Dupree had told her. "To a doctor over there, some woman named Yvette Meng. She managed to set aside money for your plane ticket and enough for you to live on for at least a year, if you live frugally."

In the six years since she had become one of Dr. Yvette Meng's protégés, Meredith had progressed from a frightened, awkward, hostile and misunderstood girl to a cautious, curious, often outspoken woman who was still, on occasion, quite awkward, especially around the opposite sex. Men were not attracted to her. She wasn't pretty. She was short, plump, and plain. And covered in freckles. Her hair was carrot red, wild and curly and untamable. The best she could do with it was pull it back into a ponytail. And even if a man could get past her lack of beauty, he would certainly be put off by her ability to read his mind.

But she couldn't actually read minds.

She sensed thoughts.

And when she touched someone, she could feel what they were feeling.

Yvette had told her that she had never known anyone whose "gifts" were as varied or as strong as Meredith's were.

"You are very special," Yvette had told her. "Once you learn to harness and control your abilities, there is so much good you can do."

And that was why she was on the Powell jet, heading to London, straight into the arms of a man she feared. From the moment she had met Luke Sentell, she had known he was a killer.

As hard as she had tried not to think about Luke during the flight, he kept creeping into her mind. She had read for a while, watched a movie, taken a nap, and meditated. Without those quiet, still, soul-refreshing moments of meditation, she didn't believe she could survive.

And now they were over the Atlantic, on their way to a city that held so many good memories for Meredith, memories that included her first meeting with Yvette and her introduction to other gifted people. When Yvette had moved her academy/sanctuary from London and resettled all of them in the U.S., at Griffin's Rest, Meredith had hated leaving London. But eventually she had become accustomed to her new home in the U.S. and oddly enough now dreaded returning to London. When they landed at Heathrow, Luke Sentell would be waiting for them. No doubt he would whisk her away, via a limousine, to some fancy London hotel where he would keep her a virtual prisoner while he watched her, pushed her to the brink of exhaustion, and guarded her from the outside world. She would force herself to delve into the unknown mystical realm of her mind and use her psychic gifts because Yvette had asked her to help Griffin Powell. And if she failed to give Luke the results he wanted, he would move her to another city, to another country, to wherever he thought she might "pick up the scent" of their prey. He treated her as if she were nothing more than a hunting dog.

She had been sent to London on a mission and Saxon Chappelle would hand her over to Luke, a man she neither liked nor trusted, so that she could help him find a man named Malcolm York.

Chapter 29

Maleah awoke disoriented and confused. She was lying in bed, fully clothed, and cuddled against Derek Lawrence. The last thing she remembered was weeping in his arms. Apparently, she had cried herself to sleep. When she looked directly at him, he looked back at her and smiled. Her mind told her to disengage her body from his, to lift her head from where it lay nestled on his shoulder and to move her arm from around his waist. But she didn't change her position by more than a fraction as she leaned back her head and tilted her chin so that they wouldn't be practically nose-to-nose.

"How long have I been asleep?" she asked.

"Not long. A little over an hour."

"Have you been awake the entire time?"

He nodded.

"Why didn't you—?"

"I enjoyed watching you sleep," he told her. "And you were exhausted. You needed some rest."

She eyed him speculatively. "You enjoyed watching me sleep?"

His grin widened. "Yeah. Did you know you make

funny little noises in your sleep? You fell asleep in my arms, the two of us sitting up, so I just eased us down onto the bed and when I did that, you whimpered and cuddled up against me."

She lifted her head from his arm and scooted away from him, putting a couple of feet between them. "I need to tell you about my interview with Browning."

"Your final interview," he told her.

"Yes, my final interview." She sat up and leaned back against the headboard, determined to return her relationship with Derek to business only. "Browning and the copycat killer made a bargain. We already figured out that the copycat agreed to provide Jerome with a new lawyer, a female visitor, and a new victim, one he couldn't actually kill, only emotionally torment."

"And you were that victim." Derek grumbled unintelligibly, no doubt a few choice curse words. "I'd like to have five minutes alone with Browning."

Maleah laid her hand on Derek's shoulder. His gaze connected instantly with hers.

"I'll condense things for you," Maleah said. "It seems Browning and the copycat formed a rather unique relationship, one killer to another, during their phone calls, letters, and visits. The copycat never told Jerome his real name, but when Jerome asked if he was a professional, he didn't deny it."

"Which was as good as an admission, right?" Derek sat up beside her.

"Right."

She noticed that several buttons in the center of Derek's shirt were open, leaving the material gapping. Had she done that—unbuttoned his shirt in her sleep?

Concentrate on what you need to say and not on Derek.

Keeping strictly to the facts and not elaborating,

Maleah told him about her conversation with Browning and the information he had given her.

"Browning said that the copycat is an international contractor, his word—contractor. And his current employer is a billionaire who owns a private island retreat, where he enjoys the perks of his business."

"And his business is human trafficking." Derek frowned. "The description sounds familiar, doesn't it, too familiar."

"Are you saying Browning was lying?"

"No, I'm saying that maybe the copycat was lying to Browning, knowing he would pass along false information."

"If you're right about that, then Browning actually gave me nothing. I paid for more useless information."

"I didn't say that. For all we know, everything Browning told you is the truth."

"But you said—"

"I said maybe the copycat was lying to Browning. Maybe he wasn't. But any way you look at it, you came away with one very important piece of information."

"Okay, maybe I'm slightly addled from my mini-emotional meltdown and mid-day nap, but you're going to have to enlighten me. My brain isn't—"

"The copycat, whoever he is, knows something about Malcolm York, either the original York or the pseudo York rumored to be in Europe somewhere at present."

"You're right," Maleah said, suddenly feeling more like her old self by the minute. "And this info adds more weight to Griff's theory that the copycat murders are connected to his past and to both Malcolm Yorks."

"I think we can safely assume that Griff's theory is correct. I have little doubt now that the copycat is, as we suspected, a hired assassin."

"An assassin hired by the fake York, right?" Maleah got up, brushed off her wrinkled slacks and searched for her shoes. "We should contact Griff right away and let him know." She found her shoes halfway under the bed, dragged them out, and slipped into them.

"First of all, yes, logically, we can assume that the man who calls himself Malcolm York hired the copycat, but we need more proof before we can be certain." Derek buttoned his shirt and got out of bed. "Secondly, there's no need to call Griff because we'll see him this evening. I got a call from Sanders while you were in with Browning this morning. It was bad news."

"And you're just now telling me about it?"

"I thought it could wait," Derek said. "All things considered."

"You mean considering the fact that I came away from the interview with Browning an emotional wreck."

"You just needed a little time to recover, honey. You should be proud of yourself. You held your own against a psychopathic monster."

"If you say so." *He's right, damn it. You might have come away with a few battle scars, but for all intents and purposes you won the game. And you survived.* "What's the bad news from Sanders?"

"The copycat struck again."

Oh God, no. "Who?"

"Saxon Chappelle's sixteen-year-old niece."

Maleah sucked in an agonized breath. How could anyone kill a young girl who was little more than a child?

"Poppy Chappelle was spending the summer with Saxon's mother. The grandmother found her this morning."

"They didn't let Saxon go to Savannah on his own, did they?"

"Saxon may not even know yet," Derek told her. "He left early this morning to escort Meredith Sinclair to London. But once he hands her over to Luke, he'll return to the U.S. tonight. Griff sent Holt Keinan to Savannah."

"Griff wants us at Griffin's Rest by tonight because he's circling the wagons, isn't he?"

"Yeah, probably."

"Then let's get the show on the road. I need to go back to my room and grab my suitcase and then we can check out."

"Take your time, Blondie. I'll check us out. You can meet me in the lobby. But first, wash your face, put on some lipstick, and comb your hair. You look like you just got out of bed."

The Berkeley Knightsbridge, a five-star luxury hotel, was located on Wilton Place, in the heart of residential Belgravia. From this location, they were only moments from the hustle and bustle of Knightsbridge and not far from Buckingham Palace, Hyde Park, and Belgrave Square. During the years Meredith had spent in London with Yvette and her fellow misfits, they had lived in comfort, but not in splendor. She suspected that Griffin Powell had arranged for the two-bedroom suite at this luxurious hotel just for her. He understood the type of sacrifice she was making in order to help him find and stop a killer and no doubt wanted to compensate her for the mental and emotional pain and anguish. Meredith was doing this out of a sense of loyalty to Yvette, but also because she, too, did not want to see another innocent person die.

"We can order room service for dinner," Luke Sentell told her as he escorted her into the spacious living room, which was both elegantly sophisticated and yet beautifully understated.

The moment she walked into the room, the image of a woman appeared in her mind. Blond and attractive. Possibly the interior designer. Someone who liked a clean, lean and yet classic look.

"Thank you, but I'm not hungry," Meredith replied.

"I've given you the master suite," Luke told her as he walked across the living room and opened the bedroom door. "I'll put your suitcase in here and if you'd like to rest for a while—"

"I'd like to call home and speak to Yvette. I'm concerned about Saxon Chappelle." Meredith glowered at Luke, whose stoic stare slightly unnerved her. "You could have been a little less blunt when you told him his niece was the Copycat Carver's latest victim."

As if ignoring her comment, Luke disappeared into the bedroom for a couple of minutes. Once again, as she had done in the past, she tried to sense something in Luke Sentell other than his steely determination to protect himself from her probing. On the outer edges of his consciousness, she picked up on rigid control and single-mindedness, both aspects of his apathetic personality.

Deciding not to make an issue of his rudeness, she surveyed her surroundings. The cool taupes and grays and beiges used with the dark, gleaming wood in the room soothed Meredith. She preferred the gentleness of neutral colors, the peacefulness of muted tones.

"I assume you can unpack for yourself," Luke said as he emerged from her bedroom.

"Yes, certainly."

"I told Chappelle the facts. If I had put my arm around him and shed a few tears, do you honestly think it would have helped him any?"

"No, but you were so cold and matter-of-fact."

Luke grunted. "Make your call to Yvette while I order our dinner."

"I don't want anything," she told him.

"Well, I do." His scrutinizing gaze raked over her with cold precision. "You need to eat something to build up your strength before you start earning your keep."

"I'll be sure to eat a substantial breakfast."

"You'll eat a substantial dinner, too, because I intend for us to begin work tonight."

"Tonight?"

"Yes, tonight."

"But—"

"I realize that you're probably tired from your long flight and more than a little pissed about getting stuck with me as your babysitter, but the sooner we locate Anthony Linden, the sooner we will be able to stop him from killing anyone else. Do you understand?"

"Yes, I understand. I just didn't realize you had anything available here at the hotel for me to use to connect with Linden."

"I do."

"Then let me freshen up and unpack while you order dinner. And as soon as I call Yvette, I'll be ready."

She didn't bother asking him what he had in his possession that had at some time belonged to Anthony Linden. She would know soon enough. Even something as insignificant as a cigarette lighter or an unlaundered handkerchief could be used as a catalyst to connect her with the person or persons who had used the specific object. The fewer people who had handled the object, the more precise her revelations.

"Do you have any preferences about dinner?" he asked. "Protein of some type, right?"

"Yes, protein," she told him. "For strength and stamina."

"And if I remember correctly, no wine, no liquor of any kind. Just water."

"That's correct."

Meredith found herself unable to break eye contact with Luke, his steel-gray eyes holding her attention like metal to a magnet. A whirlwind of energy spun around them, cocooning them together inside a kinetic force neither could control.

Trust me. I'll take care of you.

Luke hadn't spoken, but Meredith had heard his thoughts.

But that was the problem. She wasn't sure she could trust him. "If I go in too deep, you're the only one who can save me."

"Yes, I know." He turned, walked away and entered the foyer that led to the entrance to the second bedroom that was attached to and yet separate from the rest of the suite.

Prompted by the incentive of a bonus, he had wasted no time in making arrangements to pick up the special guest for his current employer. Locating her had not been a problem, but removing the obstacles in his path would require quick, decisive action. Complicated by the presence of a private security agent who made rounds outside the home every two hours, as precise as clockwork, and disarming the home's security system had taken a while longer than he had anticipated. He was pretty sure the guard wasn't a Powell agent. He wore a uniform of some kind and Powell agents didn't wear uniforms. His guess was that the family had hired him for protection in case the Copycat Carver targeted one of them.

Unlike the Chappelle home in Savannah, there was no outside basement entrance, leaving him with only the windows and doors on the first and second levels of the house as a means of entry and exit. With a guard on duty, probably stationed downstairs, his best bet was to find a way to enter through an upstairs widow. And since time was of the essence if he wanted that big bonus, he needed to check out the house's interior quickly and pinpoint her bedroom. But with only three occupants, other than the bodyguard, it should be a relatively simple matter. All he'd have to do was look into the bedrooms to find her. At this time of night, she would be alone. And her room would no doubt be distinctly decorated.

With a few twists, he locked the carbon steel talons of the compact grappling hook into position and sent the hook sailing up and atop the sloping roof at the back of the house. Testing the connection and finding it secure, he began his ascent up the lightweight nylon rope. Once on top of the roof, he made his way carefully over to the nearby single window, one he assumed would take him into a bathroom. He removed the glass cutter from his pocket, along with a suction device, and removed a section of the windowpane without breaking it. He reached through the opening, unlocked the window and raised it high enough to allow him enough space to slip inside the house.

As he had assumed beforehand, he now found himself inside a small bathroom, well lit with a decorative hot pink glitter nightlight. How lucky for him that he had, no doubt, entered through her bathroom window. Not having to search the entire upstairs to find her simplified his job enormously. The bathroom door stood wide open. With practiced stealth movements, he entered the bedroom silently, not making a sound. Another nightlight identical to the one in the bathroom cast a pink glow across the carpeted floor and moonlight streaming through the sheer striped curtains illuminated the wicker bed in which she slept.

He reached into his pocket, removed a small vial and a linen handkerchief and then opened the vial and soaked the linen with its contents as he crept closer and closer to the bed. She lay there in all her beautiful blond innocence, never knowing the part she would play in a madman's diabolical scheme. But this specific madman paid extremely well. And it wasn't his place to judge the people who employed him to do their dirty work.

He leaned down, placed the ether-soaked handkerchief over her nose and mouth and positioned his other hand in the center of her chest to hold her in place if she woke. Her eyes flew open. She stared up at him for a few moments and then closed her eyes as the anesthetic took affect. He reached inside the inner pocket of his snug-fitting jacket, removed an envelope and laid it beside her pillow. Without hesitation, he flung back the covers, lifted her up and into his arms and retraced his steps through the bathroom. He eased her through the window, placing her solidly on the roof before he climbed out and joined her. The moonlight struck the tiny pink sequins outlining the ruffles on the hem of her gown.

After checking below on the ground, he hoisted her up and positioned her beneath his arm, clamping her securely between the inner curve of his elbow and his ribcage. Mindful that one wrong move could result in him dropping her to the ground, he grasped the nylon rope and descended with careful precision. Once on the ground, he lifted her up and across his shoulder, like a sack of potatoes, and then ran up the alley toward the car he had parked there less than twenty minutes ago.

A private jet would be waiting for them in Nashville. In two and a half hours, he and his employer's special guest would board the jet and be ready for take off to London by daybreak.

Chapter 30

Meredith glared at Luke across the breakfast table. Despite having kept her up until the wee hours of the morning, he had knocked on her bedroom door at precisely seven-thirty and informed her that room service had just delivered their breakfast.

"I ordered the full English fry-up," he had told her. "Eggs, bacon, sausages. Plenty of protein, along with baked beans, mushrooms, and fried bread. I expect you out here and ready to eat in ten minutes."

Knowing that if she didn't join him for breakfast within a reasonable time, he would come in and get her, she had grabbed a quick shower, washed her hair, and slipped into a pair of ratty sweat pants and a soft cotton T-shirt. Leaving the towel wrapped around her damp hair, she had arrived at the table less than ten minutes after he had summoned her.

"Eat hearty," he said. "We have a lot to do. Maybe after a good night's sleep, you'll be working on all cylinders this morning."

He had been referring to the fact that last night when he had placed what Luke had told her had been a set of cuff links owned by Anthony Linden in her hands, she had drawn a blank. It was if no one had ever handled the cuff links, other than Luke. After more than an hour of useless efforts to use the links as a conduit to previous wearers, Luke had told her to go to bed.

Now, as he sipped on his breakfast tea, she watched him until he set down his cup and looked at her. "What?" he asked.

"I've eaten all that I can. I'm fueled and ready to perform, hopefully on all cylinders," she told him. "But if all you have for me to use is those cuff links, then forget it. For some reason, all I picked up when I handled them were some vague faces of various people. One I believe actually made the gold links and another was the jewelry store salesman. And you. I saw you tossing the cuffs back and forth in your hands."

Luke's lips twitched as if he were about to smile. He didn't. "The cuff links never belonged to Anthony Linden. I purchased them new yesterday."

She stared at him in disbelief. "Why would you—? Damn you! You were testing me. Was that your idea or were you instructed to—?"

"Testing you with the cuff links was entirely my own idea."

"Why?"

"Because although I've seen you in action a few times, I find it difficult to believe in what you and Dr. Meng and her other protégés do."

Without giving any thought to what she was doing, Meredith shoved back her chair, stood, picked up a piece of the soft fried bread on her plate and flung it at Luke. It hit him mid-chest, the grease staining his navy blue polo shirt.

"What the hell," he grumbled.

"Don't you ever do something like that to me again."
She planted her hands on her hips.

"Go get dressed," he told her. "I'll change my shirt
and then I'll bring you something that actually belonged to Anthony Linden."

"Are we going out somewhere today?" she asked.

"Probably not."

"Then I'm dressed for the day," she informed him.
"I'll go dry my hair and be right back."

Luke shrugged. "Suit yourself."

After slamming her bedroom door, Meredith debated
whether or not to change clothes. She had brought
along a pair of jeans, dress slacks, and several nice
blouses. But fifteen minutes later, with her hair dry and
pulled back in a loose ponytail, she stormed back into
the living room wearing the same sweat pants and T-shirt.

The table had been cleared, with only a fresh pot of
tea now in the middle of a tray that held two clean cups.
Luke sat on the sofa in his khaki slacks and a navy and
red striped button-down shirt, the short sleeves revealing his muscular arms.

"Sit down here beside me," he ordered her.

She sat, obeying without question, although reluctantly and with great reservation. He glanced at the
round coffee table in front of the sofa. There beside a
clear glass vase filled with white lilies lay a rectangular-
shaped box.

"Open it," Luke said.

She did. Inside, she found a handgun.

"What's this?" she asked.

"It's a SIG Sauer—"

"No, I don't care what make and model the weapon
is," she told him. "I hate firearms of any kind. If this is
another one of your tests—"

"It's not a test. That pistol is supposed to have be-

longed to Anthony Linden and has never been owned
or used by anyone else."

When she simply stared at the gun for several minutes, Luke apparently grew aggravated with her. He removed the pistol from the box and held it out to her. "It
isn't loaded."

"I should hope not." She opened her palm and held
out her hand.

The very instant he placed the gun in her hand and
the cold metal touched her skin, she cried out.

"What's wrong?"

She heard Luke's question, but despite the fact that
he was sitting right beside her, he sounded as if he were
in another room. As people's faces flashed through her
mind like images from a television screen, moving at
top speed, she sensed that all those people were dead.
Three men, two women, and a child. When she closed
her eyes, she saw only black emptiness and felt an odd
rush of adrenaline soar through her body. And then the
rapid fire of a pistol echoed inside her head.

"Oh God," she whimpered. "He killed them. All of
them."

"You're getting something about Linden. What is it?"

"He's killed so many people with this gun. I saw
them, six of them. One was just a boy."

"We already know he's a killer, that he's a professional hit man. I need for you to move on from that and
try to tell me something we don't know. Try to focus on
finding the son of a bitch, not taking a gruesome walk
down memory lane."

"Don't . . . please . . ." *Leave me alone. You don't understand. I have very little control over what I see and what I
feel.*

She wrapped her fingers over the butt of the gun
and clutched it tightly.

"He has a good job and he likes it. He likes it a lot," Meredith said. "The money he earns affords him a lifestyle he enjoys. He tells himself that he kills for the money, but . . . he kills for the pleasure, too."

Although she felt Luke's hands on her shoulders, felt the non-too-gentle shake he gave her, only her body was in the room with him. She tried harder to concentrate on the man who had owned the gun, on his present location. Where was he right now?

The face that appeared to her kept changing. Dark hair, light hair, red hair, bald. Blue eyes, brown eyes, hazel eyes. Mustache, beard, clean shaven, sideburns. Glasses. No glasses. The image of his features wasn't clear. It kept changing too quickly for her to describe him.

"He wears disguises."

"Meredith, concentrate completely on where he is right now, this very minute," Luke told her as he ran his hands down her arms and then released her. "Any other information is useless to us."

Concentrate. Concentrate.

I'm trying. I'm trying.

Suddenly she felt weightless. She floated above the earth as if she had wings. Clouds surrounded her, white and fluffy. She loved the sensation of flying and had had visions, for as long as she could remember, of leaving her body and soaring into the heavens.

And then all of her feelings of joy disappeared and a dark, foreboding fear claimed her. The hum of an engine grew louder and louder, and louder still, until it drowned out every other sound, every thought, every feeling.

She gasped for air, trying to escape from the onslaught of the roaring engine, and fought her way back to rejoin her mind with her body. Her head ached. Her stomach lurched with nausea.

As she slowly opened her eyes, the gun she had been clutching dropped from her weak hand and hit the floor. "He's on an airplane."

"Right now?" Luke asked. "Is he on an airplane right now?"

She stared at Luke. "Either now or very recently. He's coming toward me."

"What do you mean by that?"

"He's coming toward me," she repeated half a second before she collapsed in a heap at Luke's feet.

When Maleah and Derek had arrived at Griffin's Rest late yesterday, they had found a high level of anxiety that spread from the very top and filtered its way down through every employee. If they thought security had been tight when they left there the last time, they found out as they drove through the security gates just how much tighter it could be. Barbara Jean had met them at the front door, and Maleah had noticed Brendan Richter hovering in the background.

"My God, you'd think we were being invaded," Maleah had said as she entered the foyer. "Is all of this because of Saxon Chappelle's niece?"

"Partly," Barbara Jean had replied as she'd glanced from Maleah to Derek. "Sanders is waiting for you in the office. He needs to speak to you now." She had looked up at Maleah. "Nicole wants to talk to you. She's upstairs in her sitting room."

After that, Maleah hadn't seen Derek again last night. How long he spent in the auxiliary Powell office headquarters there at Griffin's Rest, she didn't know.

Nor did she have any idea where he'd slept or if he had slept. She had spent more than two hours with Nic, after being allowed entrance into Nic's bedroom suite by her private guard dog, Shaughnessy Hood. One look at her best friend and she had realized just how bad things were with her and Griff. Nic had looked like death warmed over.

"If you think I look bad, you should see Griff," Nic had said. "He was in rough shape before Poppy Chappelle was killed, but now . . . Oh, Maleah, I'm worried sick about him. I haven't seen him all day. He hasn't ventured out of his den and my guess is that by now he's drunk himself into a stupor and passed out."

Unlike the other Powell agents who were assigned a bedroom in the house when they rotated shifts at Griffin's Rest, Maleah had her own room, a perk of being Nic's best friend. Since she spent almost as much time here as she did in her Knoxville apartment, she kept several changes of clothes in the closet and an assortment of toiletries in her private bathroom.

When she had finally gotten in bed well past midnight, she had tossed and turned for nearly an hour before dozing off to sleep. And she had awakened at a little after six, feeling a bit groggy and sleep-deprived. Her first thought had been about Derek. She had wondered if he was awake and if he was, had he already gone downstairs for breakfast. Odd that she should have had such an overwhelming desire to see him, talk to him, be with him.

Now less than an hour later, freshly showered, dressed for the day in tan twill slacks and a black, short-sleeved cotton sweater set, she found herself taking more time than usual to apply her makeup and fix her hair.

This is ridiculous. You're primping like a teenager getting ready for the prom.

She stared at herself in the vanity mirror, her long hair framing her face as it fell in layers down to her shoulders. She had even taken great pains to use a curling iron to style her hair.

All because you want Derek Lawrence to find you attractive. And don't you dare try to deny it.

She couldn't deny it. Not to herself and not to the reflection staring back at her from the mirror. "All right, so what's the big deal? Why shouldn't I want to look my best this morning?"

While in the midst of having an in-depth conversation with herself, Maleah heard a repetitive rapping at her bedroom door. It might be Nic, even though she hoped her friend was in bed with her husband, the two of them getting some much needed rest. But more than likely Griff was still in his study and Nic had lain awake half the night worrying herself sick about him.

When she opened the door, she halfway expected to see either Nic or Barbara Jean, but instead Derek stood there, a dead serious expression on his handsome face.

"Good morning," she said.

"How are you today?" he asked.

"I'm fine, all things considered. How about you?"

"I've been better," he admitted. "May I come in?"

"Sure." She moved back so that he could enter, and then she closed the door before asking, "What's wrong?"

"I was up until after one this morning," Derek said. "Helping Sanders with Griff. He . . . uh . . . he drank a little too much. We managed to walk him into the bathroom connected to his study, put him in the shower and finally got him into a clean pair of jeans and a T-shirt.

Sanders sent me on to bed around one-fifteen. I think
he sat up all night while Griff slept it off on the sofa."

"I was with Nic until well after midnight. She wasn't
drinking, but she wasn't in much better shape. She's
worried about Griff and she figured he was drinking."
She stared at Derek. "Tell me why a man who professes
to worship the ground his wife walks on shuts her out
the way Griff does Nic when he needs her the most. The
way he's acting is killing her."

"I've told you that big strong men don't like to appear weak in front of their women. No matter how mis-
guided his actions, Griff's intention is to protect Nic.
He didn't want her to see him the way he was last
night."

"Men! I don't understand any of you."

"That works both ways, Blondie. We men don't understand you women either." He looked her over and
smiled. "You sure do look pretty this morning."

She felt the warmth of a blush creep up her neck.
Turning away from him, she picked up a pair of small
pearl studs off her dresser. "Thank you for the compliment." She slipped one stud and then the other through
the holes in her ears before turning back around to
face Derek. "Have you been downstairs yet?"

"I went down for a cup of coffee about fifteen minutes ago. Sanders and Barbara Jean are in the kitchen
preparing pancakes and sausage. I spoke to Griff briefly
before he came upstairs to see Nic."

"Then they're together now?"

Derek nodded. "Griff has a meeting planned for ten
this morning in his office here at the house."

"Who's being invited to this meeting?"

"Only the people Griff and Nic trust with their
lives—Sanders, Barbara Jean, you, me, and Yvette."

She hadn't realized that her expression had altered in any way at the mention of Dr. Yvette Meng, not until Derek said, "Making a face like that is a dead giveaway, you know. It implies that you don't like Dr. Meng."

"It's not that I dislike Yvette. I don't. She seems like a very nice lady, but . . ."

"But what?"

"Her presence here at Griffin's Rest creates problems for Nic, for her marriage."

"It shouldn't," Derek said. "Yvette Meng isn't a threat to Nic's marriage. If ever a man was completely in love with his wife and totally dedicated to his marriage, that man is Griffin Powell."

"Is that your professional opinion?"

"That's my gut instinct. If there was anything more than friendship between Griff and Yvette, it's in the past, and Nic needs to believe that."

"So you do think there was something more than—?"

"Whoa there, Blondie. Don't put words in my mouth. I said *if* there was."

Maleah felt the need to defend Nic. "I think Nic has every right to feel the way she does. How would you like it if the woman you loved moved a dear old friend, who just happened to be male, into your home? And you knew with absolute certainty that she loved this man?"

"There's love and then there's love," Derek said. "I'm surprised that a woman such as Nicole Powell would be so insecure."

"Loving someone the way she loves Griff can make a woman vulnerable, even someone like Nic."

"Yeah, love can make us all vulnerable," Derek agreed. "And to answer your question—no, I wouldn't like it if the woman I loved brought an old friend whom she loved into our lives on a daily basis, had him practically living at our back door, especially if I thought they had once been lovers. But I'd deal with it somehow, if the only alternative was giving up the woman I loved."

"That's what Nic is doing, what she's been doing ever since Griff built the sanctuary for Yvette and her pro-tégés here at Griffin's Rest."

"You disagree, don't you?" Derek asked. "What would you do? How would you handle the situation differently?"

Maleah hesitated, uncertain just how honest she should be with him. *To hell with it.* "If I were in Nic's shoes, I'd tell Griff to choose. He could either have Yvette living within a stone's throw of us, a constant presence in our lives, or he could have me. If he didn't move her out, then I'd leave."

"Why do you think Nic hasn't done that?"

"I think the answer to that would be obvious."

"Enlighten me."

"No." She had already said too much about her best friend's personal life. Her only excuse was that it had become so easy to talk to Derek.

"Nic's afraid that if she demands he make a choice between Yvette and her, he might choose Yvette," Derek said. "That's the reason."

Maleah didn't confirm his assessment of the situation, but she wasn't the least bit surprised that he had zeroed in on the exact reason.

"I'm hungry," she said, deliberately changing the subject. "Let's eat breakfast. I love Barbara Jean's pancakes."

Derek nodded, and then opened the door and offered her his arm. "Shall we?"

She slipped her arm through his. "Derek?"

"Hmm . . . ?"

"I don't think I ever thanked you properly."

"For what?"

"For looking out for me after that last interview with Browning." It had been on the tip of her tongue to say, thank you for taking such good care of me. For holding me, comforting me, letting me draw strength from you.

"Hey, no problem, Blondie. That's what partners do, right?"

"Yeah, right."

Why was it that she wished he'd said he had done it because he cared about her and not just because they were partners?

The phone rang at precisely at 7:30 A.M. that morning.

"Well, hello there. What a nice surprise to hear from you. How are y'all doing? How's—?"

"Listen very carefully," he said. "You are going to receive a phone call later today with instructions on what you have to do, and if you don't do exactly as he tells you to do, she's going to die."

"What are you talking about? Who's going to call me? Who's going to die?"

The caller explained about the kidnapping, that the person they both loved had been kidnapped, taken from her bed in the middle of the night, and a note had been left on her pillow. Someone had managed to break in through an upstairs bathroom window, go into her bedroom and abduct her without anyone being the wiser.

Whoever had taken her was not an amateur. He had to be a professional.

Had the Copycat Carver taken her? If so, why had he changed his MO? Why had he kidnapped her instead of killing her? It didn't make any sense.

"You understand, don't you?" the caller asked. "If you don't do what he tells you to do, we'll never see her alive again. Please, please tell me that you'll do whatever he asks you to do."

"Yes, of course I will."

"Swear to me."

"I swear."

The reality of the situation was difficult to grasp. This was a nightmare of monumental proportions. Life or death. But no matter what the instructions or how difficult the assignment, the orders would be carried out. There was only one choice—to do whatever was necessary to save her life.

Chapter 31

The private jet had landed safely at Heathrow. He and his employer's guest, both equipped with false IDs, including passports, zipped through customs without a problem. When she had awakened en route, frightened and confused, he had explained in simple terms what had happened, what was going on, and what he expected her to do. And quite amazingly, she had not screamed or cried. Undoubtedly, she was suffering from a mild form of shock, which actually worked in his favor.

As a general rule, he didn't hire out as a kidnapper. Too many things could go wrong. Murder for hire, on the other hand, was his forte. A quick, clean and simple kill. If the money had not proven to be irresistible, he would never have taken on the current assignment.

Until they had cleared customs, he didn't draw an easy breath. Anything might have happened. But he had warned her that he would kill her if she did not co-operate. He had learned long ago that fear was a great inducement in gaining obedience, especially from fe-males.

After picking up a hired car, he placed her in the

backseat, forced a couple of sleeping pills down her throat and told her to lie down and keep quiet. She had choked on the pills and had coughed and cried. When he had wiped the tears from her cheeks, she had gazed at him with fear and wonder.

"Be a good girl and you'll come out of this alive. Understand?"

She had nodded, but said nothing.

Using the GPS system provided with the rental vehicle, he had no trouble navigating through the city and after less than an hour, he drove through the thousand-year-old town of Harpenden, located in Hertfordshire. Tourists as well as London residents no doubt flocked here because of the town's traditional English village atmosphere.

A few miles out of town, they arrived at their destination, a secluded house surrounded by trees and isolated from any prying neighbors. He parked the rental behind the house, opened the back door and lifted her into his arms. She would probably sleep for several more hours, possibly the rest of the day.

As he had been told, he found the back door unlocked and the key lying on the kitchen table. He carried her through the kitchen and down a narrow hall until he located a small bedroom with only one window. After laying her on the double bed, he covered her with a quilt. He checked the window and found that it was sealed shut with countless layers of paint that had been applied over the years. Leaving the door open behind him, he returned to the kitchen, pulled out a chair from the table and sat. Checking his mobile phone, he found there was decent coverage here in the country. He dialed the number that he had memorized and waited for his employer to answer.

"You've arrived safely with my guest?"

"We're at the house. I didn't encounter any problems."

"How is my guest?"

"Right now, she's sleeping."

"Then now is the perfect time for you to make another phone call. Memorize the instructions I will give you and repeat them word for word."

"Very well."

He listened as his employer told him in quite succinct terms about his plan and the message he was to relay, word for word.

"Now, repeat it back to me."

He did as he had been instructed.

"Yes, you have it precisely. As soon as we end our conversation, make the phone call. Be sure it is understood that you will call again for an update and to give further instructions."

"I understand and I'll stress the importance of following your instructions to the letter."

"Yes, yes. And in the meanwhile, take good care of my guest. She's very important, at least for the time being."

"Yes, sir."

His employer never bothered with pleasantries nor did he. Their association was strictly business.

He would enjoy a cup of tea, but first things first. He walked down the hall, checked to make sure she was still sleeping soundly and then returned to the kitchen. Standing by the windows overlooking the private garden in back, he dialed another memorized number.

"Hello." Such a nervous, frightened voice.

"Listen very carefully," he said. "I will not repeat these instructions. You are to do exactly as I tell you. If you do not—"

"Don't hurt her. Please. I will do whatever you want me to do."

"Good. If you cooperate fully, then she has a good chance of coming through this unharmed."

Luke Sentell had spent the day waiting for Meredith Sinclair to recover from whatever kind of spell she'd had that morning. He didn't pretend to understand what made the woman tick, any more than he could believe without question the validity of her psychic abilities. If he couldn't see it, smell it, hear it, taste it, or feel it, it didn't exist. Not in his world. Not for any normal, logical human being. And yet he had seen Meredith work her hoodoo on several occasions and without fail, her visions—or whatever the hell you wanted to call them—had proven to be accurate.

He sorely wished that his path had never crossed with Meredith's, that Griffin Powell had not chosen him to accompany them on his initial European manhunt when rumors about Malcolm York had first begun circulating. His boss had brought Meredith along, using her as his bloodhound, hoping she could sniff out who had started the rumors. Griff had assigned him as Meredith's personal bodyguard. The job had quickly become a combination of babysitter and nursemaid. Whenever Meredith had come out of one of her trances, she would sleep for hours, as if whatever she had experienced had zapped every ounce of her energy.

A really crazy thing had happened on that first partnership with Meredith, and every subsequent time they had been together. For some unknown reason, whenever he was around, his presence seemed to fine tune her sixth sense. He had no idea why. Considering he was a skeptic, you'd think having him around would have an adverse effect. Instead the opposite was true. He had to accept the truth—it was what it was. And that's why he was here with her now, the two of them stuck with each other on another manhunt.

That morning, after she had fainted and fallen in a heap at his feet, he had lifted her and put her on the sofa. Trying to wake her had been pointless. He knew from past experience that the best thing to do was simply let her rest until she came out of it on her own. She had slept for hours and when she awoke, she had gone to her room after telling him that she needed to be alone for a while.

Here it was after three in the afternoon and she was just now emerging from her bedroom and gracing him with her presence. When he glanced up at her from the copy of the *Daily Telegraph* he'd been reading, he was surprised to see her looking so well. Her eyes were bright and clear, her cheeks had color, and her voice was quite strong when she said, "I'm ready now."

"Do you want something to eat?" He folded the newspaper and laid it on the coffee table. "It's nearly three-thirty and you skipped lunch."

"No, I'm fine, thank you. I just want to try again. I've spent time concentrating on what I saw and felt this morning, trying to make sense of it all."

"And did you?"

"Only partly," she admitted. "When I told you he was coming toward me, I wasn't sure what I meant, but now I know. This man who calls himself Anthony Linden was in flight, coming here."

"Here as in London or here as in this hotel?"

"Here as in London."

"Are you sure?"

"As sure as I can be," she told him. "I'm never a hundred percent sure of what I see and feel. All I can do is let it happen and afterward try to figure it out."

"So, you're guessing about Linden being in London."

"I suppose you could call it guessing."

"What would you call it?"

"Sensing."

"Humph."

"I'm well aware of the fact that you consider me a freak of nature, Mr. Sentell. And you think I'm mentally disturbed, that anyone who claims to be gifted is actually crazy."

"There you go again, putting words in my mouth."

She glared at him, her hazel green eyes sparkling with anger. "We're wasting time with this conversation. I'm ready to go to work. Where's the gun?"

Where's the gun? The first thought that went through his mind was that she wanted to shoot him. He barely managed not to smile.

"The gun isn't going to help you," Luke told her. "You've been there, done that. You probably got everything from handling the gun that you could. Right?"

"Possibly, but I need something to connect me to Anthony Linden if I'm going to find him."

"Then let's go where you think he's been. If he flew into London, the odds are that he came through Heathrow." Luke glanced at her wrinkled sweats and T-shirt. "Change clothes. We're going out."

"We're going to the airport?" she asked.

"Yep."

"That's a great idea."

"Yeah, I thought so."

* * *

When Maleah and Derek arrived together at Griff's office, a first-rate, state-of-the art complex housed within his home at Griffin's Rest, they passed by several agents who flanked the open door to the auxiliary headquarters for the Powell Agency. Brendan Richter nodded and spoke to them. He had been assigned to keep tabs on Barbara Jean and act as backup for Sanders. Shaughnessy Hood, a giant of a man and the only agent physically larger than Griffin Powell himself, threw up a hand as they walked past him. Griff had given him the task of guarding Nic twenty-four / seven. On the opposite side of the door, Cully Redmond watched them approach.

"Morning," Cully said.

"When were you called in off patrol?" Derek asked.

"About an hour ago," the big, robust redhead replied. "Sanders assigned me temporarily to Dr. Meng because Michelle came down with a stomach virus this morning."

"How's Michelle doing?" Maleah asked.

"I haven't seen her, but Sanders said it's probably just a twenty-four-hour bug and she'll be right as rain by tomorrow."

"That's good."

Derek cupped Maleah's elbow and escorted her into the office. Apparently they were the last to arrive. As soon as they entered, Sanders closed the door and took his usual place, standing directly behind Griff. Derek had decided quite some time ago that Griff and Sanders were closer than brothers, the bond between them stronger than any blood tie could ever be.

Seated at the head of the table, Griff presided over the small group. Not for the first time, Derek was struck by Griffin Powell's commanding presence. More than the fact that he was a large, tall man was the air of confidence and the demeanor of authority that radiated from him.

Having been fascinated by human nature all his life and with a natural aptitude for the subject, he found himself more often than not making mental mini-profiles of others, in both social and professional settings. This ability came to him so naturally that he often didn't realize what he was doing until his mind had already formed an opinion.

Nic sat on Griff's right. Usually, she sat at the other end of the conference table. Her having moved closer to her husband could mean nothing more than this meeting would be comprised of a small group. But Derek surmised that not only did Nic need to be near Griff, but that she wanted to send a strong message to everyone in the room that she was Mrs. Griffin Powell, always at her husband's side.

BJ sat in her wheelchair on Nic's left. Barbara Jean Hughes possessed an ageless beauty, which meant she would still be attractive at eighty. And despite her being a paraplegic, she exuded a *joie de vivre* he admired and envied.

The exotically beautiful Dr. Meng, her head bowed and her hands folded together in her lap, sat beside BJ. He sensed a deep sadness in Yvette. She wore that melancholy like a thin shawl about her shoulders, an accessory to her soul, not the soul itself.

Maleah rushed ahead of him, went straight to Nic, and gave her friend's arm a reassuring squeeze before sitting beside her.

Maleah Perdue was a special lady.

Blondie.

His Blondie.

Without realizing what was happening, Maleah had, as the old saying goes, gotten under his skin. Although it wasn't something he wanted, he actually found the fact that he cared about Maleah rather amusing.

Care about her?

It's more than just caring.

Admit it, Lawrence, you're in love with her.

He watched her hovering over Nic and sensed her desperate need to console her friend. Maleah might be a control freak, but God help her, she was a caretaker, the two traits often related. Sister traits. And even if she didn't know it—which he suspected she didn't—Maleah had the capacity to love deeply. He had seen that manifested in her feelings for her brother Jackson, his wife Cathy, and their son Seth, as well as in her love for her best friend, Nic.

Would she, considering her deplorable childhood, ever trust any man enough to love him with that same depth of emotion and loyalty?

Any man?

Damn it, Lawrence, that's enough introspection for one day. You've admitted that you're in love with Maleah. You don't need to figure out anything else right now. Things like whether or not she loves you and if she does, do the two of you have a future together. Considering you both have an aversion to commitment, marriage is probably out of the question.

So what's wrong with an affair?

Determined to refocus on business, Derek surveyed the room's occupants again, quickly scanning everyone before he took the seat beside Maleah, which put him directly across from Yvette Meng.

Yvette lifted her head, a fragile smile on her full, red lips, and looked at him with large, luminous brown eyes.

"How are you this morning?" he asked, simply being polite.

"I am well, Mr. Lawrence. And you?"

"Just fine, ma'am."

When Maleah pivoted around in her chair and glanced from Derek to Yvette, Yvette lowered her head again, as if sensing Maleah's disapproval.

No doubt Yvette Meng had endured men's lust and women's envy all of her life. Men saw her as a sex object; women saw her as a rival. And yet if you looked closely, you would realize that Yvette was heartbreakingly alone, separate and apart from all others, and by her own choice.

Obviously Griff hadn't called the meeting to order yet. He seemed preoccupied, his gaze unfocused as if he was deep in thought. Ever the stoic solider, Sanders stood with his arms crossed over his chest. On the defensive. Always guarding Griff as if it was his sole purpose in life.

Knowing what little he did about the years Griffin had spent in captivity on the island of Amara with Sanders and Yvette, Derek understood the bond comrades-in-arms shared. But the depth of their relationship went beyond the norm. Derek could only imagine under what circumstances their three souls had joined.

Griff lifted his head, cleared his throat and looked from one person to another, beginning and ending with Nic.

"We asked a great deal of Maleah," Griff said. "She interviewed Jerome Browning, the original Carver." He looked directly at Maleah. "Nic told me about the information you shared with her last night. Thank you for what you did."

Maleah simply nodded.

Derek reached out and took her hand in his. She gripped his hand tightly, but kept her gaze focused on Griff.

"I realize that we can't automatically take Browning's word for anything," Griff said. "But I believe he was telling the truth when he told Maleah that the Copycat Carver is a professional assassin, just as we suspected. Derek had come to this same conclusion while working up a profile of the killer."

All eyes on Griff, everyone remained silent, waiting for him to continue. Derek understood now why only the ones present in the room had been included in this private meeting. Griff intended to keep the circle of intimate knowledge as small as possible. Across the Atlantic, Luke Sentell and Meredith Sinclair were searching for the truth—and the whereabouts of two men who were presumed dead. Maleah had confronted the copycat killer's mentor and paid a high emotional price for information that confirmed the worst case scenario. She had every right to be here. Derek had been included today because of his status as a profiler. Nic was here because she was Griff's wife.

And then there were three.

The Amara Triad, as Nicole Powell referred to her husband, Sanders, and Yvette.

"Jerome Browning informed Maleah that the copycat killer had bragged about his billionaire employer," Griff said. "He did not mention the man by name, but he did tell Browning that the billionaire owned a Pacific island and enjoyed the perks of his profession—human trafficking."

"It is not possible," Yvette said, a slight tremor in her soft voice. "He lied. Either the copycat lied to Browning or Browning lied to Maleah."

"I don't believe Browning lied," Griff said. "I believe that the man the copycat killer works for is passing himself off as Malcolm York."

"But who is he and why is he pretending to be York?"

Yvette asked. "And why would he want to avenge the real Malcolm York's murder?"

"That's what we have to find out," Griff told her. "The first step is to locate Linden, if he is the copycat, and stop him before he kills again. Once he's eliminated, we'll have a brief window of opportunity to find this pseudo-York before he hires another assassin."

"Do you think he plans to continue killing people associated with the Powell Agency?" Maleah asked.

"I do," Griff replied. "I am his ultimate target . . ." Griff paused, glanced over his shoulder at Sanders and then at Yvette. "My guess is he wants to draw out the three of us. What his reasons are, I don't know. What his connection might have been to Malcolm York, I don't know. And why he's striking out now, after sixteen years, is a complete mystery."

"It would seem that we are at his mercy," Yvette said. "But I refuse to believe that we cannot stop him."

"We will stop him," Nic said, her gaze colliding with Yvette's.

Griff reached out and grabbed Nic's hand, bringing her attention away from Yvette and to him. "Less than half an hour ago, Luke Sentell contacted me with news, interesting news, if true. Meredith believes Anthony Linden is now in London."

"If Meredith senses Linden's presence, then you can be sure that he is there," Yvette said.

"Why would Linden, if he's the copycat killer, go to London?" Maleah asked. "Is it possible that he's chosen Luke or Meredith as his next victim?"

"I think that's highly unlikely," Griff replied. "Certainly not Meredith since they were en route to London less than a day apart. And I can't imagine anyone being able to find Luke Sentell unless he wanted to be found."

"Then why would the copycat go to London?" Derek asked. "Unless his employer recalled him."

"That would be my guess," Griff said. "The only problem is that we have no idea why he would have recalled him. If this fake York intends to continue killing people connected to the agency, why rein in his pit bull?"

When Luke had carried an obviously unconscious Meredith through the hotel lobby and to the elevator, people had stared at him as if he were a murderer.

"I'm afraid my wife can't hold her liquor," he had explained, smiling like an idiot.

They had spent half an hour at Heathrow before Meredith passed out from sheer exhaustion. She would probably sleep soundly the rest of the evening.

He laid her across the foot of the bed and removed her shoes. Then he turned down the covers and placed the fully clothed Meredith beneath the sheet and lightweight blanket. She looked about fifteen lying there, her face void of makeup, her hair fiery red against the white pillowcase. He lifted her head enough to maneuver his index finger beneath the tight band holding her ponytail in place, and with one quick snap freed her thick mane of wild curls.

"Sleep tight, Orphan Annie," he said as he paused in the doorway.

He closed her bedroom door and returned to the living room. After sitting down and pulling his thoughts together, he called Griffin Powell.

"Luke?"

"Yes. Are you free to talk?"

"I'm alone at the moment. Nic and I have been in a meeting with Maleah and Derek. Sanders and Yvette, too, of course, and Barbara Jean. I've filled them in about the possibility that Linden is in London."

"Linden's not in London."

"But I thought Meredith was sure he was there."

"She was and he was," Luke said. "I took her to Heathrow this afternoon and she picked up his scent almost immediately. She says he was there at the airport sometime recently, perhaps only hours before we arrived, and he wasn't alone. But she doesn't know who was with him, only that his companion was female."

"If Linden is not in London any longer, then where is he?"

"Good question."

"Didn't Meredith pick up on anything else, get any sense of which direction—?"

"Of course she did," Luke said. "North of London, possibly northwest."

"She couldn't be more specific?"

"She was trying . . . before she passed out."

"Is she all right?"

"Yeah, I think she's fine. You know what happens to her after she has one of her visions. She's sleeping now and I expect she might sleep through the night."

"Do you think she can find Linden?" Griff asked.

"Maybe. Of course my brain is telling me no way in hell."

"Your gut, Sentell, what's your gut telling you?"

"That there is a fifty/fifty chance she'll lead me straight to Linden."

Silence. Long and drawn out, only the sound of Griff's deep breathing.

"I'll take those odds," Griff said. "And Luke, when you find Linden, you know what to do."

"If he is the professional you believe him to be, I

won't be able to make him talk. He'll die before he'll break."

"No, he won't talk. He will never reveal any information about his employer."

"Then what you want is for me to simply eliminate him."

"Yes, when you find the bastard, kill him."

Chapter 32

After Griff ended the morning meeting, which had lasted about forty-five minutes, Maleah had taken a walk around the property, something she often did to clear her head. Derek had insisted on going with her, and after Griff told her that no one left the house alone, she reluctantly agreed to let Derek tag along. Much to her surprise, he had not insisted on conversation, which was the last thing she had wanted or needed. What she had needed was time alone, but apparently unless she secluded herself in her room, that wasn't an option anytime in the near future. And being a girl who loved the outdoors, the thought of spending the rest of the day cooped up inside would have made her agree to having Genghis Khan as her companion.

Her life had suddenly, in the past couple of weeks, become extremely complicated. For most of her adult life, she had been able to enjoy a certain amount of peace and privacy in her personal life, which counterbalanced her exciting and often dangerous job as a Powell agent. But both her personal life and professional life were at risk. Until the Copycat Carver was caught, no Powell agent or family member was completely safe. It wasn't enough that she had to worry about her own life, but she lived in fear for her family. Then to make the situation worse, teaming up with Derek again had created an unexpected problem, one she wasn't sure how to handle. Somehow, someway, the impossible had happened.

She had fallen in love with Derek Lawrence.

Derek Lawrence, the rich, spoiled, pampered, womanizing playboy she had disliked from the moment they met.

But that was just it—the real Derek was a different man entirely. Oh, he was rich, a millionaire many times over, and he did have a reputation with the ladies that he couldn't deny. But he was not spoiled or pampered and his playboy image had been greatly exaggerated, probably by Derek himself.

He had allowed her to see a side of him that she suspected not many even knew existed. Few people would believe that the debonair, sophisticated Southern charmer's youthful past included a nefarious secret.

By the end of her long walk—with Derek—she had come to the conclusion that she could handle only one major problem at a time. She'd just have to put her feelings for Derek on the back burner. Being in love was a foreign concept to her. She had spent her entire life trying to avoid repeating the mistake she had made with Noah—becoming involved in a committed relationship that could lead to marriage.

After lunch, which she and Derek had shared with Nic, Griff, Sanders, and Barbara Jean, she had returned to the Powell Agency office there at Griffin's Rest. With the bulk of the agency's employees working day and night on the Copycat Carver case and with reports pouring in from various legal and illegal contacts the world over, the staff at their Knoxville headquarters was suffering from information overload. Add to that the fact that only a handful of agents were privy to the most sensitive information and that meant piles of reports were waiting to be read, studied, and digested. Everyone except Barbara Jean had worked all afternoon and until well past seven. They had taken a long overdue break only when Barbara Jean had summoned all of them to the dining room for dinner. The group had eaten in relative silence, their conversation limited to their compliments to the chef, Barbara Jean, on the delicious meal. She had smiled, said thank you, and had been gracious enough not to point out that no one had eaten very much. Afterward, Sanders had helped with cleanup and then he and Barbara Jean had bid everyone goodnight shortly after nine o'clock. Nic finally persuaded Griff to call it a night around 10:00 P.M., and Maleah had sensed from the way they'd been looking at each other, they wouldn't be going to sleep anytime soon.

Alone in the living room with Derek, she shifted the file folders in her lap into a neat pile and laid them aside on the sofa cushion beside her. She glanced at Derek, who seemed absorbed in a crossword puzzle he had ripped out of today's copy of the *Knoxville News Sentinel*. As if he had sensed her staring at him, he glanced up from the newspaper and smiled at her.

"Alone at last," he said jokingly.

"So it would seem." She returned his smile.

"I could fix us a drink," he suggested. "Or we could raid the kitchen for another piece of BJ's pecan pie."

"I shouldn't have eaten the first piece." Maleah patted her hips. "I think they're an inch wider already."

Derek rose to his feet, dropped the folded newspaper in the chair, and came straight toward her. Before she realized his intention, he leaned over her and placed his open palms on either side of her hips.

"They're wider by a quarter of an inch at most," he told her, barely managing not to laugh.

All the while faking a frown, she swatted at his hands until he lifted them off the cushions and away from her hips. He dropped down on the sofa beside her and rested his head on the back cushion.

"You're tired, aren't you?" she said.

He glanced at her. "Yeah. You are, too. It's been a long day."

"We should probably go upstairs and try to get some sleep," Maleah said. "But I swear I'm so wired I can't imagine being able to sleep right now."

"I know what you mean. It's been a pretty intense day, starting with this morning's top secret meeting. Griff's wound so tight, he's on the verge of snapping. His drinking binge last night didn't solve anything for him and it sure didn't take the edge off."

"I'm worried about Nic. I've never seen her so scared. I honestly think she's afraid she's going to lose Griff, that somehow their marriage is going to implode."

"When a husband and wife keep secrets from each other, it puts a major strain on their marriage."

"I agree," Maleah said. "And the not knowing causes as much damage, if not more, than sharing the secret would. In theory, of course. With what's happening now, a killer targeting the Powell Agency, finding and stopping the killer has to take priority over everything else in Nic and Griff's life."

Derek pivoted his head so that he faced her. "In your life and mine, too."

She nodded. "Finding Anthony Linden has to be our top priority."

"You know, I think I have Anthony Linden figured out, at least as much as I can with the info I have and by gauging his personality by other professional killers I've studied. They all have certain characteristics in common. You'd be surprised at how much a hired assassin has in common with a Special Forces soldier, although society sees one as immoral and the other as a hero."

"Despite any similarities, there is a difference though, isn't there?"

"For some, yes," Derek said. "The fine line that separates the two—villain and hero—is the reason he kills. That and the emotion or lack of emotion involved. Some men enjoy killing. Others hate it, even after it becomes easy to kill."

"The way it did for you?"

"Yeah, the way it did for me." He reached out and twined a tendril of her hair around his finger. "Did I ever tell you that I like blonds?"

"You like brunettes and redheads, too."

"You're right, I do, but I'm partial to one particular blond."

She allowed him to pull her toward him by gently tugging on her hair. When they were face to face, only a few inches separating them, she asked, "Is she anyone I know, this particular blond?"

"All you have to do is look in a mirror."

Her breath caught in her throat.

"Do you have any idea how much I want to kiss you?" he asked.

"Yes." She knew because she wanted that kiss every bit as much as he did. Maybe more. After all, she was in love with him, but she had no reason to believe that he felt the same way. For Derek, this was probably a flirtation that he hoped would lead to sex.

Derek released her hair, leaned forward enough so

that their mouths touched, and whispered against her lips, "I swear to God, I won't ever hurt you. I'd cut off my right arm first."

Excitement and anticipation ignited inside her and spread through her like a wildfire when he kissed her. Aggressive yet gentle, he took her mouth, but otherwise didn't touch her. She returned the kiss eagerly, wanting him and needing so much more.

The urge to touch him became overwhelming. She lifted her arms and draped them around his neck as she deepened the kiss. Taking his cue from her, Derek delved his tongue inside her mouth as he eased his hands beneath her and lifted her up and onto his lap. With their mouths fused together and their bodies straining for closer contact, she clung to him. He roamed his hands over her back and hips while she forked her fingers through the long, thick hair at the nape of his neck.

When they finally came up for air, both breathing hard, their gazes connecting, Derek smiled and then glanced at her throat and the expanse of flesh exposed by the V-shaped neckline of her blouse.

"We have on too many clothes for what I have in mind," he told her.

She nodded. "Your room or mine?"

He chuckled. "Whichever is the closest."

"Mine," she said.

He stood, taking her up with him, still holding her in his arms.

"We'll get there faster if you put me down and let me walk."

He eased her slowly to her feet, her body sliding along his, arousing them both even more. She grabbed his hand and yanked him along with her as she raced out of the living room, down the hall and up the stairs.

*   *   *

Shiloh Whitman often wondered why Dr. Meng had accepted her as a student and wondered if the others saw her as a wannabe psychic. After all, how valuable would she ever be as anything other than a sideshow amusement? She didn't possess the gift of clairvoyance or channeling or precognition or psychometry or telepathy. All she had was the ability to sense psychic energy and entities and to see the aura around a person.

When she was a child, her siblings and cousins had laughed at her when she told them they had different colored lights shining around them. And her parents had scolded her, telling her to stop lying or people would think she was crazy. She had always been a misfit, the one thing she did have in common with the others, especially with Meredith. A sympathetic friend in college had told her she should find someone to help her figure out what was wrong with her. And oddly enough less than a year later, Dr. Meng actually found her, quite by accident, in of all places a bookstore in New York City.

Looking back now, she realized that if Dr. Meng hadn't taken her back to London with her, she wouldn't have survived. She had been on the verge of suicide, her life meaningless.

Shiloh had never been happy and never expected to be. There was an emptiness inside her that couldn't be filled. But she lived a productive life by keeping busy, studying, practicing, and assisting Dr. Meng in any way possible.

Lately, she had begun to feel an inexplicable restlessness and deliberately stayed away from the other students, not wanting anyone to probe inside her mind.

Tonight the peculiar restlessness had grown worse, so much so that she felt as if she were on the verge of

climbing the walls in her room. Feeling trapped, smothered by the confinement, she knew she had to find a
way to go outside, to breathe the night air, to look up at
the stars, to escape from that overpowering sense of imprisonment.

But Dr. Meng had warned them not to go anywhere
outside the sanctuary alone, to go in pairs and always
with one of the guards.

If she slipped out the back way, who would see her?

*What if one of the others realizes you've gone outside
alone?*

That wouldn't happen. One of Dr. Meng's strictest
rules was that none of her students could use their gifts
to invade the privacy of another.

Hurriedly changing from her pajamas and house
slippers into a jogging suit and running shoes, Shiloh
prepared for her escape.

I can't kill her.
I won't do it.
But he's given you no choice.
You must take a life in order to save a life.
*Do what you must do. Do it quickly. She doesn't have to
suffer. Make it as painless as possible.*
*You mustn't let yourself hesitate at the last minute. Once
she sees your face, once she can identity you, you will have
no choice.*
*There she is. See her. She's all alone, as if she's waiting
for you.*

Slipping away had been much easier than Shiloh had
thought it would be. Perhaps because she had been
keeping to herself so much lately, no one really cared

where she was or what she was doing. And although the guards roamed the grounds day and night, she had been able to avoid them without a problem. And even the two agents staying at the sanctuary, Ms. Allen and Mr. Redmond, had no idea she wasn't sound asleep in her bed. After all, they assumed that all of Dr. Meng's protégés would request permission to leave and then be given an escort.

She promised herself that she wouldn't stay outside for very long, only long enough to clear her head and relieve the nagging restlessness keeping her on edge. Even with the bright moonlight, darkness filled the night, and only the security lights around the sanctuary kept the hovering black shadows at bay.

As she followed the clear path along the lake, one used by residents and guests alike for morning and evening jogs and leisurely walks, she paused occasionally to look out over the river. A feeling of calm began growing inside her and ever so gradually the restlessness that had forced her out into the night subsided, leaving her in peace.

She heard footsteps behind her. Had one of the guards seen her? Or had one of the others followed her?

Shiloh turned and stared into the darkness. "Hello. Is anyone there?"

Silence.

It must have been a nocturnal animal scurrying through the underbrush or perhaps it had been nothing more than the wind. She turned around, breathed in the fresh night air and looked at the moonlight dancing on the water.

Odd how bright the moonlight is. Shimmering. Intense. And very white.

Mesmerized by the unnatural radiance of light, she

moved closer to the water's edge. Fixated on the glow, she gasped as she realized what she saw was not moonlight, but the reflection of her own aura. Transcendent. Spiritual. Non-physical.

A white aura often signified a new undesignated energy in a person's aura. Or it was a harbinger of—

There it was again. The same noise she had heard earlier. Footsteps directly behind her.

She turned, sighed heavily, and said, "It's you. I thought I heard someone. Have you been following me?"

"Yes."

Even in the darkness, Shiloh saw the other person's aura, heavy swirls of gray and black smoke, dirty, muddy colors indicating dark thoughts and fear and negative energy. And in that moment, seconds before her life ended, Shiloh understood why her aura had been such an intensely bright white.

A glowing white aura was also a harbinger of death.

Chapter 33

Maleah and Derek barely made it to her room before tearing at each other's clothes. The moment Derek kicked the door shut behind them, his mouth and hands otherwise occupied, Maleah attacked the buttons on his shirt. When she ripped open his shirt, he slid his hands up under her blouse and paused to fondle her breasts through her bra.

"Lift your arms," he told her.

She did. He pulled her buttoned blouse over her head, yanking at the sleeves to free her arms. He threw the blouse on the floor. Repaying him in kind, she shoved his shirt off his shoulders and tossed it on the floor on top of her blouse.

Derek walked her backward toward her bed, all the while unbuttoning her slacks and lowering the zipper as she unbuckled his belt and unsnapped his jeans. When he toppled her over onto the bed, he rose up long enough to yank her slacks down her legs and then divest himself of his jeans.

She reached for him, wanting the feel of him against her, needing to touch him, kiss him, love him. He straddled her, his long, hairy legs brushing her smooth legs as he looked down at her, his gaze moving appreciatively over her from face to thighs.

"If I tell you how absolutely gorgeous you are, will you slap me?" he asked, a playful grin curving the corners of his mouth.

"Not if you don't mind my telling you that you're pretty gorgeous yourself, Mr. Lawrence." She reached up and caressed his chest, loving the feel of the curly hair covering the well-defined muscles.

"I don't mind at all. As a matter of fact, I insist you tell me."

She laughed. "I'll bet you make all your women feed your ego with flattery, don't you?"

Bracing on his elbows, he lowered himself until his lips reached hers. "As far as I'm concerned, there are no other women, and there never have been. There's only you, Blondie, only you."

Emotion caught in her throat. Damn it, she should have known he would know the perfect thing to say. After all, he was a renowned charmer, wasn't he?

"How many women have believed that smooth line?" she asked as she nuzzled his neck.

He kissed her ear.

She shivered.

"You're the first one I've used it on, honey. How do you like it?" He circled her ear with the tip of his tongue, and then took her earlobe between his teeth and nipped playfully.

"I like it just fine," she said. "And just for tonight, I'll pretend you mean it."

Gazing into her eyes, he reached under her to unhook her bra. With their gazes solidly melded, he eased the bra down her shoulders, taking his time, letting the soft material rake over her hard, sensitive nipples.

She gasped.

He smiled.

They didn't break eye contact until he laid the bra aside and looked down at her bare breasts.

"I meant what I said," he told her. "I mean it tonight and I'll mean it tomorrow and—"

She placed her index finger over his lips, silencing him. "No promises, no vows, no declarations."

"Is that what you want or is that what you think I want?"

"You have commitment issues, remember," she told him.

"And you have control issues." He pressed his erection against her. "But tonight we're going to share the control. I'm going to show you that you can trust me to never make you do anything you don't want to do. And you're going to willingly give yourself to me, no strings attached, solely because you want me as much as I want you."

"I guess we both have something to prove, to ourselves and to each other."

"I'm going to start right now by proving to you that I want to make love to you more than I've ever wanted anything in my entire life."

"I like the sound of that."

The moment his mouth covered her breast, her hips bucked involuntarily, lifting her lower body hard against his. He groaned deep and low as he slid his hand inside her silky panties and cupped her mound. When he inched his fingers lower until he found her clitoris, she rubbed his penis through the thin material of his briefs. He caressed her intimately, eliciting a throaty moan.

"I've got some condoms in my pants pocket," he told her as he inserted two fingers inside her.

As her body gushed around his fingers, she writhed beneath him. "You came prepared? You must have been pretty sure of yourself. Or do you always carry around condoms in your pocket?"

"Blondie, I put those condoms in my pocket when I got up this morning because I knew that I couldn't go another day without staking my claim on you." He removed his fingers from inside her, slipped his hand out of her panties and hooked his thumbs beneath the elastic waistband. He kissed her and then lifted his head. "Before you open your pretty little mouth to protest, you should know that before tomorrow morning, I expect you will have laid claim to me, too, lock, stock and barrel."

"You can bet your life on it," she told him.

When he pulled her panties down and off, she cooperated fully. Once he removed his briefs, his penis sprung free. And then he grabbed his jeans off the floor and retrieved a condom from one of the pockets.

She expected him to take her then and there. A part of her wanted him now and she wouldn't have complained if he had rushed through the preliminaries.

But he didn't.

During the next hour, Derek loved her more thoroughly than she had ever been loved. He touched her all over, his mouth and hands familiarizing themselves with every inch of her body. He licked and sucked and caressed her breasts and teased her unmercifully until she ached with wanting. After bringing her to the brink again and again, only to draw back at the last minute each time and make her wait, he finally lifted her hips and thrust into her. Deep and hard.

She gasped for breath when he entered her, filling her completely.

They fucked in a frenzy of ravenous need and hot desire. And when Maleah came, she felt as if she had exploded into a thousand pieces.

Derek grunted and shivered as his orgasm hit.

She clung to him, kissing him, murmuring erotic sweet nothings in his ear as he collapsed on top of her.

Derek woke her sometime between midnight and dawn and they made slow, sweet love again. And then she slept in his arms, her body wrapped around his. When he woke her again, the tender light of dawn peeped through the plantation blinds on her bedroom windows.

He slid his hand between her legs and parted her thighs." Are you sore?" he asked.

"A little," she admitted.

He kissed her mouth, and then ran the tip of his tongue between her breasts, over her belly and dipped into her navel. "It had been a while for you, hadn't it?"

"Uh-huh. There haven't been that many men," she told him honestly.

"God, Blondie, don't you dare tell me anything about any of them." He reached out, jerked her up and rolled her over on top of him. "The thought of another man touching you makes me a little crazy."

She smiled. "I don't exactly like knowing you've had sex with countless other women."

He laughed. "Hardly countless women." He stroked his open palm over her buttocks. "Besides, they were just rehearsals. You, Maleah Perdue, are the main act."

She spread her legs, straddled him, and took him insider her. Then she tossed back her head and shook her hair. He grasped her hips.

She smiled down at him. "Just in case you don't already know it, you, Derek Lawrence, are, as far as I'm concerned, the one and only main act."

This time around, she was in complete control, setting the pace, deciding how far to take him near the edge before withdrawing and prolonging his agony with the promise of ecstasy.

Finally, she put him out of his misery. She climaxed first and half a second later, he grabbed her by the back of her head, tossed her over onto her back and jackhammered into her for a couple of heart-pounding minutes before he came.

Later, damp with sexual perspiration and sleepy with satisfaction, they lay together spoon fashion, his arms holding her securely against his body. He nuzzled her ear. She sighed with pleasure.

"I don't know if you want to hear this or if this is the right time to say it, but . . . I love you, Blondie."

She wrapped her arms around his arm that bound her to him in a possessive gesture. "I love you, too . . . so very much."

"We need to—"

The thunderous pounding on her bedroom door stopped Derek mid-sentence.

"Maleah, wake up. Now," Barbara Jean called to her through the closed door. "Please, come downstairs as quickly as possible. And if you know where Derek is, tell him to do the same. Shiloh Whitman has been murdered."

Meredith had awakened Luke at 6:30 A.M.

"Get dressed immediately. We're leaving," she had told him.

He had stared at her standing there in his bedroom

doorway as he roused from a deep, dreamless sleep. "What's going on? Is something wrong?"

"Anthony Linden is definitely north of London. I keep seeing green fields. He's out in the country some- where. I'm pretty sure that wherever he is, he's not far from here. And he isn't alone."

"He's probably still with the female companion your woo-woo senses picked up on at the airport last night."

Meredith had frowned. "I couldn't sense anything about her last night, but this morning, I'm getting the distinct impression that there isn't anything romantic between them."

"Romantic meaning sexual?"

She hadn't replied to his question, instead she had said, "I'll call down and have them prepare something for breakfast that we can take with us. In the meantime, get ready. I can't explain it, but I feel that we need to start our search immediately."

And that was exactly what they had done. They had left in the midst of Thursday morning London traffic.

Now, more than six hours later, Luke was beginning to think of their trip as nothing more than a wild goose chase. He realized that if Meredith could pinpoint ex- actly where Linden was, she would do it. But as she kept explaining, she had only limited control over her vi- sions. Knowing very little about psychically gifted peo- ple, Luke saw Meredith as a puzzle, one he needed to somehow figure out and then put together. Griff had entrusted him with her care. Babysitting a woman that Dr. Meng believed to have what she referred to as "ex- ceptional abilities" wasn't easy for a guy like him. Meredith needed someone patient and kind, someone who accepted her psychic talents without question, someone who didn't find himself occasionally wanting to shake her until her teeth rattled.

Meredith was certain that Anthony Linden had landed at Heathrow last night and had left London and traveled north with a female companion.

Even if she was right about Linden, north of London covered a lot of territory. He had contacted the head man of Powell's London based headquarters, Thorndike Mitchum, before they left the hotel, given him Meredith's info, and hoped like hell that it would help Mitchum and his team of investigators.

Once out of London that morning, Luke and Meredith had traveled sixteen miles due north to Waltham Abbey, the first stop on their psychic trek to locate Linden.

"No, this isn't the place," Meredith had told him as they drove through the village. "I don't sense him anywhere nearby. Drive west."

And so they had taken M25 to Potters Bar in Hertfordshire.

"This isn't the right place either," she had said after they had fully explored the small town. "Maybe we need to go farther north from here."

Leaving Potters Bar behind, they headed to Abbots Langley and then when that also proved to be the wrong town, they had driven even father north and were now a few miles outside of St. Albans.

Luke could tell that with each subsequent disappointment, Meredith had grown weaker, as if some force she could not control was draining the energy from her body and from her mind.

"When we arrive in St. Albans, we're staying for a while," he told her.

"What if it's not the right place either?"

"It doesn't matter. We need to eat and you need to rest." When she looked at him with gratitude in her eyes, he quickly added, "You're no good to me if you pass out from exhaustion."

The tenderness in her eyes faded and her gaze hardened.

Damn it, Sentell, would it have killed you to be nice to her, to let her believe that you actually give a damn about her as a human being?

"You think I'm some sort of freak, don't you?" she said.

"I don't think you're a freak."

"You do. I can see it in your eyes every time you look at me."

"You're an enigma to me," he admitted. "I don't understand how you do what you do. When I'm around you, half the time, I question my own sanity."

"Thank you for being honest with me." There was a hint of sadness in her voice.

"Look, Merry Berry, I'll make a deal with you," Luke said. "I'll always be honest with you, even if it upsets you or hurts your feelings, if you promise you will trust me to take care of you and you won't question me when I tell you to do something or not to do something."

"I'm a great deal of trouble, aren't I?"

"Yeah, you are. But most things worth a damn are a lot of trouble."

"Oh."

"So, do we have a deal?"

"Yes, I suppose we do."

She remained quiet for several minutes, and then she asked, "Luke, why did you call me Merry Berry?"

"Huh?"

"You called me—"

"It's just something that popped into my head. Your name is Meredith, so the short version is Merry. And you're covered in a million freckles that look like tiny copper berries."

"Oh, I see. I've never had a nickname before. Hmm . . . Merry Berry." She smiled. "I think I like it."

Luke barely stifled a groan.

"The authorities have been notified," Griff explained. "Sheriff Fulton will handle this case personally, as a favor to me. And he'll deal with the TVAP. Fulton has promised to keep his personnel to a minimum and I've promised that we will cooperate fully with his department."

Everyone seated at the conference table remained silent and attentive. Griff had called this meeting of highly trusted personnel to share information about Shiloh Whitman's murder and how the crime would be handled by the Jefferson County Sheriff's Department, the TVA police, and the Powell Agency. Griff issued orders for the agents present to deal with their subordinates.

"I expect Sheriff Fulton's team will arrive within the hour," Griff said. "That gives us precious little time to prepare for their investigation and to secure Griffin's Rest. At no time will any member of our staff interfere with the sheriff's investigation. But that doesn't mean our people can't ask to see everyone's ID, which I fully expect them to do."

Derek watched and listened, his gaze moving from a haggard Griff to his equally fatigued wife. To a person, everyone in the room understood the significance of Shiloh Whitman's death. Someone from the outside being able to break into Griffin's Rest would be the equivalent of someone breaking into Fort Knox. The possibility of that happening seemed highly improbable. How could the Copycat Carver have gotten through security? How could a stranger have penetrated the seemingly foolproof protection surrounding the compound?

"I don't think I have to tell y'all how Nic and I feel about Shiloh's death." Griff reached out to Nic, who immediately stood up and took his hand. "And you've all undoubtedly asked yourselves the same questions we did, and no doubt came to the same conclusions."

"Since the copycat has murdered three Powell Agency employees and three members of employees' families, it would be reasonable to assume the copycat killed Shiloh," Nic told the group. "We are not ruling out that possibility. However, there are two very good reasons to consider an alternate possibility—that the copycat did not kill Shiloh."

As if they were a tag team supporting each other through this ordeal, Griff took over again from Nic. "One: It would have been virtually impossible for a stranger to have gotten inside Griffin's Rest. Two: Whoever killed Shiloh did not slit her throat nor did he mutilate her body in any way."

"How was she killed?" Michelle Allen asked, her voice quivering slightly.

"From what we can tell—and an autopsy will no doubt reveal—Shiloh was attacked, subdued, and her head held under the water at the edge of the lake until she drowned. There is bruising on Shiloh's body and upper arms."

"So you can see that the killer's MO does not match that of the copycat," Nic explained. "But that does not necessarily mean the copycat didn't kill her. If the Copycat Carver is, as we believe he is, a professional assassin, it would have been easy enough for him to alter his method."

"But if the odds of the copycat breaching Powell security are slim to none, then we have to broaden our search and accept the possibility that someone on the Powell staff killed Shiloh," Maleah said aloud what she knew everyone there was thinking.

Luke drove down Chequers Street until he reached St. Peters at the southern end of the main street in St. Albans. Then he headed down Hollywell and turned onto Sopwell Lane.

"There it is," Meredith said. "The Goat Inn. It looks like a nice place."

"There's no point in going back to London tonight," Luke told her. "I'll see if they have a couple of rooms here. If they do, you can rest for a while after we eat lunch and maybe even take a nap."

When she opened her mouth to argue, he held up his hand in a Stop gesture. "Remember our deal. You're going to trust me to take care of you."

She nodded.

After parking the rental car, they got out and walked into the Goat Inn in the old centre of St. Albans. The former coaching inn was now a bed and breakfast that also provided home-cooked meals.

When Luke tried to book two rooms, he was told that only one was available. "It's a nice sunny room," the proprietor told him. "And it has two beds."

Luke booked the room, explained the situation to Meredith, and much to his surprise, she didn't complain.

"I trust you," she told him.

After lunch—hot baguettes, with ale for him and bottled water for her—they went upstairs to the nice sunny room. As it turned out their room was small and neat with white walls, blue curtains at the single window, and two beds with white and blue coverlets and blue throw pillows. One bed was a double and the other a twin.

"Lie down and rest," Luke told her. "I'll run out and see if I can pick up a few necessities like toothbrushes, deodorant and—" he ran his fingers across his jaw "—a razor."

"You won't go far, will you?"

"No, I won't go far. Just lock the door when I leave and don't let anyone in while I'm gone."

When Luke returned with a small bag of toiletries that he had purchased at a local drugstore called Boots on St. Peters Street, he had checked on Meredith. After he found her sleeping soundly, he went back downstairs, drank a bottled lager beer and telephoned Griff.

"Meredith thinks she can find Linden," Luke told Griff. "We've traveled north of London and have been eliminating village after village."

"Linden may not be in the UK after all," Griff said.

"What makes you think he might not be here? Meredith seems pretty certain that she is slowly but surely zeroing in on him."

"Someone killed Shiloh Whitman last night," Griff told him. "One of the guards patrolling the grounds found her body a little after daybreak this morning."

"And you think it was the Copycat Carver. Was her throat slit?"

"No. She was attacked and held down in the lake until she drowned."

"Then it may not have been the copycat."

"Yeah, my gut tells me it wasn't."

"I believe Linden is in England. Between Meredith's weird sixth sense and Mitchum's team of experts, it's only a matter of time until we find him."

"Even if Linden is in England and you can track him down and eliminate him, doing that will solve only one of our problems. If Linden didn't kill Shiloh that means someone inside Griffin's Rest killed her, possibly someone employed by York." Griff paused for a brief moment. "And then there's York himself. Until we find the man masquerading as Malcolm York, no one I care about, no one I employ and no member of their family will be safe."

Chapter 34

He would not depend on underlings to make this very important telephone call, as he had originally planned. No, he had decided that he wanted the pleasure of issuing this specific order himself. As he placed the call, he thought about Griffin Powell, a man he hated with every fiber of his being.

"I assume that Shiloh Whitman is dead, isn't she?" he asked the moment his puppet inside Griffin's Rest answered. "If you lie to me, I will know."

"Yes. I did what you told me to do and I expect you to keep your part of our bargain. Don't hurt her. Please. Let her go."

"No one has hurt her. She is alive and well. And as long as you continue to follow my instructions, no harm will come to her."

"I was told that if I killed—"

"Be very careful what you say. You do not want to be overheard, do you? It would be a shame if anyone found out what you had done, at least not before you are able to give me everything I want in exchange for what you want."

"I am not going to kill anyone else for you!"

"Yes, you are, if you ever want to see her alive again."

"Damn you!"

He laughed, gaining great pleasure from having caused so much anger and pain to someone Griffin Powell trusted. "I've chosen your next target. This time I want you to strike a lethal blow a little closer to Griffin and Nicole. I want this kill to be more personal than all the others. It's time to up the ante before the Grand Finale of Act I."

"Why do you hate Griffin Powell so much?"

"My motives are of no concern to you. Your only purpose is to obey my orders."

"I swear to God if you hurt her, if—"

"You are in no position to make threats. But I have no reason to kill her. She is nothing more than a means to an end. As long as you do what you're told, she stays alive. Tell me that you understand."

"Yes, I understand."

"Good," he said. "Now, while Griffin's Rest is in a state of turmoil today, when no one is expecting another strike so soon, I want you to kill Maleah Perdue as soon as possible. Take her by surprise."

"Maleah? You want me to kill Maleah? I can't. I won't."

"Are you sure you are willing to trade one life for another? Does Maleah Perdue mean more to you than—?"

"How do you expect me to kill her in broad daylight with Powell agents and guards and the sheriff's department covering every inch of Griffin's Rest? It will be impossible to isolate her."

"Find a way. If Maleah Perdue isn't dead by morning, someone else who is very important to you will be."

"No! God, no . . . I—I'll do it. I'll find a way."

"Now, that's what I want to hear. By following my orders, I will get what I want and you will get what you want."

"What I want is for you to rot in hell, you son of a bitch."

Luke had begun to think Meredith would sleep all night. She had certainly slept the day away. But she roused a little before seven and after freshening up, she met him downstairs for a bite of supper. She ordered tiger prawns for a starter, and then honey roasted ham, served with fried eggs, house fries, and baked beans. She ate like a ravenous wolf, as if she hadn't eaten in days. Luke had settled for the homemade lasagna, and when Meredith had suggested dessert, they had both ordered the sticky toffee pudding.

Just as the waitress set their puddings in front of them, Luke's phone rang. "Excuse me." He removed the phone from his jacket's inner pocket.

Meredith nodded. "Yes, of course." She picked up the dessert spoon.

"Sentell here," Luke said.

"We have a couple of possibilities," Mitchum told him, skipping any preliminary pleasantries. "All parties who arrived by private plane in the specific twenty-four-hour period have been accounted for except two. A guy named Horacio Vasquez Luna. He has a Venezuelan passport and he was traveling with a female, supposedly his wife. No one by that name has checked into any hotels in or around London. He hasn't rented a condo, a house or an apartment. And there is no record of a car service picking him up at the airport."

"Any physical description?"

"Late fifties, heavyset, beard and mustache."

"Our guy isn't that old, but then we have reason to

believe he's a master of disguise. Keep looking for Luna," Luke said. "Who's the other possible?"

"A man named Zachary Fairweather. He had a British passport. Our report said early forties, average size. No one at Heathrow remembered much about him, but they all remembered his daughter."

"His daughter?"

"What?" Meredith dropped her spoon in her half-empty pudding dish, the metal clinking against the china.

"Hold on a minute," Luke told Mitchum. He asked Meredith, "Are you okay?"

"Whose daughter are you talking about?" she asked.

Glancing around the noisy pub, Luke realized that no one was paying any attention to them and figured that, over the loud din, it was highly unlikely anyone could hear more than a word or two of their conversation.

"A man who may be our guy got off a private plane at Heathrow last night, along with his daughter," Luke told her. Before he could say more, her eyes widened and she suddenly turned as white as a sheet. "Damn, Meredith, don't you pass out on me."

"Luke . . . Luke . . ." She gasped for air. "His female companion. Not sex. Oh, God, oh God . . ."

"Pull yourself together." He reached across the table and grabbed her hand. Then he said into the mobile phone, "Call me back in five—"

"There's something else you need to know about Fairweather's daughter," Mitchum said. "She's a child of six or seven."

"Then Fairweather wouldn't be our guy, would he?" Luke squeezed Meredith's hand and then released it. "He would hardly be traveling with a kid."

"I don't know," Mitchum said. "Can you think of a better cover?"

"His female companion is a little girl," Meredith said in a strong voice. And when Luke nodded, she told him, "Don't hang up. Find out everything about this man right now." She offered Luke a weak smile. "I'll be all right."

"Anything else?" Luke asked Mitchum, all the while looking directly at Meredith.

"Zachary Fairweather hired a car," Mitchum said. "We've been able to trace the route the car traveled out of London."

"And?" Luke prompted.

"Fairweather rented a black Mercedes C220 Europcar." Mitchum recited the tag number. "He took M10 north out of London."

Well, I'll be damned. North of London, just as Meredith had said.

"Run a detailed check on Fairweather."

"I have people working on that as we speak."

"Contact me again when you have more information on both Luna and Fairweather."

"Fairweather," Meredith whispered the name. "Fairweather."

"What about him?" Luke asked.

"Forget about the man named Luna. Concentrate on Fairweather."

"Are you sure?"

"Yes, I'm sure."

Luke relayed the message to Mitchum, ended the conversation, and stared at Meredith. "You're picking up on something, aren't you? What happened? What got your woo-woo mojo working again?"

"Tell me everything Mitchum told you and don't leave out even the most insignificant detail." She shoved back her chair and stood. "We need to leave now. We have to go farther north as soon as possible."

By late afternoon, the invasion of Griffin's Rest by what seemed to be half the law enforcement personnel in the state of Tennessee had begun to wane. Sheriff Fulmer was still with Griff, the two overseeing every aspect of the investigation, but only a CSI team and a few deputies remained on the property. Shiloh's body had already been taken to the lab in Knoxville for an autopsy. The detectives had questioned everyone there at the compound, beginning with the guard who had found Shiloh's body. And Sanders had followed up with interviews of his own.

Maleah had spent most of the day glued to Nic's side, the two women supporting each other. And Derek had been going over the personal files of everyone living and working there at Griffin's Rest, searching for anything that might alert him to a problem. Every guard employed by the Powell Agency who had undergone a thorough background check before being hired and, to a person, each man and woman now working at Griffin's Rest had been with the agency for years. There was not one single new employee working there at present.

As for the Powell agents on duty at Griffin's Rest . . .

Derek didn't want to consider the possibility that one of them could have killed Shiloh Whitman. He knew these men and women and was on a first name basis with most. In his opinion, both personally and as a professional profiler, they were all good people. Not one of them would kill without just cause.

Or unless they were under duress, forced to act against their will.

"Hey you." Instantly recognizing Maleah's voice,

Derek turned to glance at the open office door where she stood staring at him. "It's about time for a late afternoon break, isn't it?"

"Hi yourself." He closed the file folder in front of him, shoved back his chair and stood. "What do you have in mind?"

She came over to him, lifted her arms up and around his neck and kissed him. As she ended the kiss, she murmured against his lips, "I still love you."

He grinned as he cupped her butt. "I'm glad to hear it since it just so happens that I still love you, too."

Maleah eased her arms downward and spread her hands out across his chest. "I wish we could pretend that everything is all right, that none of these horrible things have happened. I wish we could concentrate on each other and forget everything and everyone else."

He reached up, took her hands in his hand, and held them between their bodies. "Want to get out of the house and leave all this behind for a while?"

"Is that possible? The grounds are crawling with law enforcement and—"

"I think we're down to a few essential crime scene investigators for the most part."

"I guess I'm behind on the latest. Nic and I have been holed up in Griff's study for the past few hours."

"How's Nic doing?"

"She's tough. She'll be okay. She's worried about Griff more than anything else," Maleah said. "He just came back up to the house and found us in the study. So, I thought I'd make myself scarce and give Nic time alone with her man while I went to look for my man."

"Your man, huh? I like the sound of that."

She pressed her cheek against his. "Don't remind me later on that I ever said this, but . . . I need you, Derek. I need for you to hold me and tell me that everything is going to be all right."

"In case you didn't already know it, Blondie, I need you just as much as you need me." He tugged on her hands. "Come on, let's go outside and sit on the patio. We can breathe in a little fresh air and soak up some sunshine while we're holding on to each other."

As they made their way through the house like two kids rushing away from school to play hooky for the day, they crossed paths with Sanders and Barbara Jean, who were walking toward the kitchen. Brendan Richter and Shaughnessy Hood were following them.

"We're all in need of a caffeine pick-me-up. I'm going to put on a couple of pots of coffee," Barbara Jean said. "There will be plenty in the kitchen if y'all want some."

"Thanks," Derek replied.

A few minutes later, Derek and Maleah found the patio deserted. There wasn't another person, not even a Powell Agency employee or a sheriff's deputy, anywhere in sight. Derek guided Maleah to the canopied swing at the edge of the huge brick and stone floored patio that overlooked the lake. He sat down and pulled her onto his lap. She wrapped her arms around his neck and laid her head on his shoulder.

"We should be talking about you and me and being in love and what we're going to do about how we feel," Derek said. "But instead of being able to focus on the two of us, we're embroiled in what would appear to be a never-ending nightmare."

"God, Derek, who could have killed Shiloh Whitman?"

He hugged her to him and nuzzled her cheek, his actions comforting. "I don't believe it's possible that anyone from the outside could have somehow gotten through security and into Griffin's Rest."

"I think you're right, so that means . . ." She paused, obviously reluctant to say aloud what they both knew to be true. "That means whoever killed Shiloh is either working here or lives here."

"I've spent most of the afternoon going over the personal files on every guard and every agent who is here at Griffin's Rest right now."

"I can't believe that it's one of the agents. It couldn't be." Maleah lifted her head and looked at Derek, her eyes wide and round. "What about one of Yvette Meng's protégés?"

"I seriously doubt that one of them killed Shiloh."

"No, I didn't mean I thought one of Shiloh's fellow students killed her. What I was thinking, wondering really, is why didn't Yvette or any of her other students sense that Shiloh was in danger? They're a group of psychics, aren't they? You'd think one of them would have seen it coming."

"I'm not sure I can explain it," Derek told her. "But as far as I know, neither Yvette nor any of her protégés claim to be able to see into the future and predict events that haven't happened."

"I don't understand all that psychic stuff."

"Psychic talents are like any other talents, no one person can do everything. Just as other people are sculptors or painters or writers or musicians, these people have specific gifts, too, and it all falls under one heading."

"I guess that makes sense."

"And it is my understanding that Yvette strictly forbids her students to intrude on the private thoughts of others. She's trained them to control any mind reading or empathic abilities."

Maleah laid her head back on Derek's shoulder. "Do you think the killer could be one of the guards?"

"Possibly."

"I refuse to believe that the killer could be one of the agents," she said adamantly.

"I think at this point, the only people we can rule out completely are you and me, Griff and Nic, and Yvette, Sanders, and BJ."

"It doesn't make sense. What possible reason would anyone have to kill Shiloh? Why her?"

Maleah burrowed closer into Derek, as if she could draw strength from his body. He stroked her silky hair and pressed his cheek against the top of her head.

"I've given it a great deal of thought," Derek told her. "And the only thing that makes sense is that Linden or York or whoever is running this horror show forced one of the guards or one of the agents to kill."

"How could he force them to kill against their will?"

"I'm not sure. He would need some type of leverage."

"A threat, maybe." She lifted her head. Her gaze locked with Derek's. "If he has threatened to harm someone they love, a member of their family, then that type of threat would be some mighty powerful leverage, wouldn't it?"

Luke had gone through three traffic circles and headed due north from St. Albans, straight toward the next village—Harpenden. And that's where they had been for the past few hours, driving up one street and down another.

Hunting.

Up High Street until it turned into Luton Road.

Then they had back-tracked toward town, taking side streets to investigate every psychic twitch Meredith had. Vaughn Road. Leyton Road. Bower's Parade. And all the while, they had both been on the lookout for a black Mercedes.

Searching.

"It's nearly midnight," Luke told her. "I say we call it a night, check into a hotel and get a fresh start in the morning."

"No, Luke, please. I know I'm not wrong about this. I know they're here somewhere. We can't give up."

"We're going around in circles now," he said. "I'm surprised the local police haven't stopped us to ask what the hell we're doing. I saw what looked like a really nice hotel right off High Street, someplace called Eagle Glenn Manor."

"Another thirty minutes," she pleaded. "Take one of the roads leading out of town. I think if they were in town anywhere, I'd have sensed it by now."

"Thirty more minutes isn't going to matter. I'm tired. You're exhausted. I don't think you'll last another thirty minutes."

Disregarding her pleas for them to continue tonight, Luke headed for the hotel. Just as he turned off High Street onto Townsend Lane, his phone rang. He pulled into the hotel car park and stopped.

Meredith stared at him, her eyes suddenly bright with speculation, as if she knew the call was important. Or maybe she just hoped it was.

"Yeah, Sentell here."

"We've got an address," Mitchum said, then gave Luke the information. "It's about a mile outside Harpenden. From the real estate photo, it's a small cottage situated in a wooded area that is fairly secluded."

"You're sure about this?"

"The house was rented by a Zachary Fairweather for an entire month."

"Son of a bitch."

Meredith tugged on Luke's arm. "He's here, isn't he? He's in Harpenden or somewhere close-by."

"Go ahead and put everything into play on your end. I'll take it from here," Luke told Mitchum. "And thanks." He turned to Meredith. "I'll check us into the hotel and get you settled before I leave."

"Damn it, Luke Sentell, you're crazy if you think you're leaving me behind. I'm going with you."

"Like hell you are."

"Like hell I'm not."

"I have a job to do, and your coming along for the ride will only complicate matters. Do you understand?"

"There is a child involved. When you rescue her, she's going to be very, very scared. It will make things easier for her if I'm there, because I'm a woman and she's more likely to trust me than you."

As much as he hated to admit it, her lopsided logic made a weird kind of sense. "No way. You can do your nurturing female thing when I bring the child back here with me."

"No."

"What do you mean no?"

"I mean that I'm going with you and that's that."

"Meredith, I can't do my job and worry about something happening to you."

"I swear that I will stay in the car, with the doors locked. I'll even lie down in the floorboard and hide if you want me to."

"We're wasting time arguing." He held up his index finger and wagged it in her face. "You will stay in the car and out of my way, no matter what you hear or see."

"I swear I will."

"And when I bring the child out to the car, you will not ask me any questions about what happened."

"I won't. I swear." She looked him square in the eye. "You're going to kill him, aren't you?"

Luke didn't answer. He put their vehicle in reverse, drove out of the car park and back onto Townsend.

Chapter 35

Luke parked the Volvo sedan on the side of the road, about a hundred yards down from the driveway leading up to the rental house. When he had driven by, he hadn't seen any sign of a vehicle. More than likely the black Mercedes was parked behind the cottage. He opened the driver's door, got out, leaned over and looked back at Meredith.

"Stay put."

She nodded.

He rounded the side of the car, popped open the trunk, and retrieved his MK23 OWSH, a .45 caliber pistol, a laser aiming module, and a sound and flash suppressor.

Meredith opened the passenger door. Damn it, what part of "stay put" hadn't she understood? He reached the open door before she had a chance to move.

"What do you think you're doing?" he demanded.

"I'm not getting out," she told him. "I just want to tell you . . . to say . . . please be careful."

Shit! Bringing her along had been a huge mistake, a real lapse of judgment on his part. But in his own defense, he had given in to her pleading to avoid having to knock her out and tie her up. He had known some stubborn women in his life, but none as obstinately bullheaded as Meredith Sinclair.

"Close the door and lock it. And whatever you do, don't leave the car while I'm gone."

"Where did you get the gun?" she asked.

"Good God, woman, what a question. I brought it with me. Now close the damn door."

He couldn't worry about Meredith and do his job. If she followed orders, she should be safe.

Creating a path through the wooded area to the left of the cottage, he made his way toward the backyard. Just as he had thought, the black Mercedes was parked at the back of the house and couldn't be seen from the road. The cottage doors and windows would be locked, but with no security system, breaking and entering would be a piece of cake. However, if Linden was expecting him, he could easily be opening a door to his own death. There was a root cellar which could be booby trapped, just as the doors and windows might be.

With weapon drawn, Luke circled the cottage. He peered into the windows, one by one, and found every room as dark as pitch, except what appeared to be a bedroom at the back of the house. A dim light glowed softly on one wall, probably a nightlight plugged into a wall outlet.

Luke swallowed.

This would be the child's bedroom.

If he could get her out of the house first . . .

Not an option. Too risky.

Keeping the child safe was his number one priority.

*   *   *

He woke with a start, his heart pounding and a rush of adrenaline pumping through his body at breakneck speed. Sitting up in bed, the lightweight cover falling to his hips, he listened for any sound that might have caused him to wake so suddenly.

Silence.

The only sound he heard was his own breathing.

He shoved back the covers, got up, slipped his bare feet into his Italian leather loafers, and reached for his SIG on the bedside table. Not taking time to put on his pajama top, he walked quietly out of his bedroom and moved carefully down the narrow hall to the child's room. She lay curled in a fetal ball, the sheet and blanket kicked to the foot of the bed. He scanned the room, from wall to wall and from floor to ceiling. The old house had no closets and the wardrobe in that room was too small to provide a hiding place for an adult.

The room was clear.

Vigilant to any sound or movement, he walked into the room and over to the bed, and then reached down and gently shook the child.

"Wake up," he whispered.

Her eyes flew open. She stared up at him. When she opened her mouth, he knew she was going to scream. He clamped his hand over her face, covering her mouth and chin.

"Be quiet and I won't hurt you," he told her. "I'm going to take you out of bed now and carry you with me. Be good. Don't fight me. If you're not a good girl, you will be very sorry."

He snatched her up and out of the bed. While keeping a tight grip on his pistol, he maneuvered her to his left side and balanced her with one arm.

Pausing for a moment, he heard nothing, saw nothing. And yet he knew someone was in the house. Years of training had honed his senses.

He couldn't understand how someone had managed to find them. An alias had been used at Heathrow. Zachary Fairweather. His employer had rented the Mercedes and the cottage under that name. How had someone connected Anthony Linden to Zachary Fairweather?

It wasn't possible.

And yet someone had tracked him.

Someone had been sent to rescue the child.

Who was the only person who knew where the child was being held?

Malcolm York!

The son of a bitch had set him up. But why?

Regardless of his employer's reasons for betrayal, he had no intention of dying tonight. Survival first He would use the child as a bargaining chip or if necessary a shield. He'd take care of York later.

When he walked toward the open bedroom door, intending to close it, he sensed danger all around him. But he could not pinpoint the presence of another person other than the trembling child he held against his body. He would wait there, in the bedroom, for his attacker to strike. Depending on the other man's skills, he should have a fifty / fifty chance of survival. Just as he reached out to close the bedroom door, a bullet zipped through the darkness and entered the front of his head.

The bullet had severed his brainstem, killing him immediately. Luke came out of the shadowy hallway, grabbed the screaming child as Linden slumped down onto the floor. He hoisted the little girl up and onto his hip.

"It's all right, honey. You're safe. Nobody is going to hurt you. I'm taking you home to your mommy and daddy."

She stopped screaming and stared at Luke with a pair of huge blue eyes.

He carried her out of the bedroom, down the hall and straight through the front door. "There's a very nice lady waiting in my car. I'll take you to her, okay? She will look after you while I make a couple of phone calls, and then you and I and the nice lady are going to leave here and we'll take you home as soon as we can."

As if instinctively believing she could trust Luke, she wrapped her little arm around his neck and held on tightly as he rushed across the front lawn and down the road to the Volvo. The minute Meredith saw him coming, she opened the car door and jumped out.

Damn it. What did I tell her? Stay in the car.

He and Meredith exchanged glances as she held out her arms to the little girl. "Come here, sweetie."

The child went to Meredith somewhat reluctantly.

Luke turned and walked away several feet.

Before Meredith closed the car door, she spoke to the child again. "I'm Meredith Sinclair. Who are you?"

Too far away to hear the child's whispered response, Luke immediately contacted Mitchum, who told him he already had a cleanup crew en route and they would take care of everything there at the cottage. Luke's second phone call would be to Griff. He checked his watch, an MTM Black Patriot, noted it was ten till one and calculated the time difference.

Just as he started to make the call, Meredith opened the car door and called his name. "Luke?"

"What?"

"Please come here. There's something you need to hear."

Luke stomped over to the side of the Volvo. The child sitting in Meredith's lap looked up at him.

"It's okay, sweetie. Luke is one of the good guys. Tell him what you told me. Tell him your name."

"My name is Jaelyn," she said. "Jaelyn Allen."

The name reverberated inside Luke's head. *Allen. Allen. Allen.*

"Good God." Luke knelt down in front of Jaelyn and forced a fake smile. "Do you know someone named Michelle Allen?"

The child's face lit up the moment he mentioned the trusted Powell agent's name. "That's my aunt Chelle."

Derek shared after-dinner drinks with Griff and Sanders in Griff's study. Dinner had been sandwiches and chips served in the kitchen, which had given them all a chance to wind down as much as possible after a grueling day. For the past half hour, ever since the men had left the ladies in the kitchen, their conversation had been limited, as if they didn't know what else there was to say. Sanders had poured their drinks and although he had not told Griff that one drink should be his limit tonight, he had given Griff a stern look as he handed him a second glass of Scotch whisky. Derek had noticed that, like him and Sanders, Griff had leisurely sipped on his first drink.

"Our not talking about the situation won't change it," Griff finally said, breaking the strained silence.

"No, of course not," Sanders agreed. "But perhaps any more discussion should be postponed until tomorrow. It has been a very long and trying day for all of us."

"Before we call it a night, I'd like to run a thought or two by y'all," Derek said.

Griff eyed him, curiosity in his hard gaze. "A thought about what?"

"About who may have killed Shiloh," Derek replied.

Sanders squinted his almond-shaped eyes and focused directly on Derek. "You think you know who the murderer is?"

"No, I can't name the killer, but I believe there is only one reason either a guard here at Griffin's Rest or one of the Powell agents would kill Shiloh Whitman."

"I think we all agree that it had to be someone inside Griffin's Rest, someone we trusted." Griff heaved a heavy, labored groan. "I've tried to fight accepting the truth, but that one thought has been in the back of my mind all day."

"Maleah and I discussed the possibility that the person who calls himself Malcolm York is the mastermind behind all the murders. And this man found a way to force a Powell guard or an agent to kill Shiloh. He's using some type of blackmail to—"

Griff's cell phone rang. He let out a few choice curse words.

"It's probably Sheriff Fulton." Griff got up and walked across the room to where his phone lay atop his desk. He picked up the phone, glanced at it, and said, "It's not Fulton." And then he answered the call. "Luke?"

Derek watched as Griff listened, his face growing darker with each second and his body visibly tensing.

"Charter a jet," Griff said. "You and Meredith bring the child back to the U.S. as soon as possible. I'll call her parents in Paducah to let them know their child is safe. And we'll handle things here at Griffin's Rest."

Griff laid the phone on the desk. He looked at Derek and then at Sanders. "Linden is dead." He paused for a moment. "Linden kidnapped Michelle Allen's niece.

He had the child with him when Luke arrived. She's safe."

"We have to find Michelle," Derek said. "She needs to know that her niece is all right."

"Yes, and after that, we will have to deal with what Michelle has done," Griff told them.

When Nic came out of the bathroom, the test stick in her hand, Maleah rose from where she sat on the edge of Nic's bed.

"Well, are you or aren't you?"

Nic hurried toward Maleah, tears in her eyes, and held out the stick to show her. "It's positive. I'm pregnant." She grabbed Maleah and hugged her. "I'm really pregnant. I had just about given up hope of our having a baby."

Maleah grasped Nic's trembling hands, took the test stick from her and laid it on the nightstand. "Have you been experiencing any symptoms? Didn't you suspect you might be pregnant?"

Nic shook her head. "I guess I've ignored the symptoms and chalked them up to nerves, which is understandable considering the stress we've been under for several months now. But when I missed my period again, I began to wonder."

"Good thing you already had a test kit."

"Yes, it was, wasn't it. Remember I bought several of them about six months ago when I thought I might be pregnant. But it turned out that I wasn't pregnant then."

"But you are now." Maleah grabbed Nic's hands again and squeezed. "You've got to tell Griff as soon as possible. He'll be thrilled."

"We both want a child so very much." Nic swiped the

teardrops from beneath her eyes. "But dear God, what bad timing."

Maleah hugged Nic again. "Maybe it was simply meant to be. We could all use a little good news about now."

"I feel as if I've been given a miracle."

When they pulled apart, Maleah said, "You should take a nice, long bubble bath, put on your sexiest lingerie, and call downstairs to tell your husband that he's needed upstairs immediately."

"I like your suggestion."

"I'll bet Griff will like it, too. And, Nic, just for tonight, forget about everything else and concentrate on you and Griff and your baby."

Maleah kissed Nic's cheek. "I think I'll go back to my room, grab a shower, and see if I can find something sexy to slip into before Derek stops by to say good-night."

Nic laughed. "Can you believe it? In the midst of all this chaos, you fall in love and I find out I'm pregnant."

Maleah waved at Shaughnessy Hood, who stood guard outside Nic's bedroom. The big bear of a man smiled and nodded. She took her time meandering along to the other side of the house where the guest rooms were located. It seemed wrong somehow to be so happy. But Nic was pregnant. Her best friend, who had been trying to get pregnant for several years, was at long last going to have a baby. And Maleah having fallen head over heels in love was as much of a miracle as Nic being pregnant.

She was in love with Derek Lawrence of all people.

Laughing softly to herself, savoring Nic's secret and thinking about the night ahead with Derek, Maleah opened her bedroom door and flipped on the light switch to turn on the bedside lamp. The low-watt bulb gave off a dim radiance, creating a romantic glow similar to candlelight. She took off her jacket, tossed it onto a nearby chair, and then removed her holster and slipped it into the right-side nightstand drawer. She kicked off her shoes and waltzed barefoot across the floor to the bathroom. After turning on the shower, she adjusted the water to a toasty warm. Then she stripped off her clothes, tossed them into the laundry hamper and grabbed a washcloth from the stack on the vanity. After lathering her hair with the floral scented shampoo and following with a silky conditioner, she shaved her legs and under her arms.

If only she had something really sexy to slip into after her shower. Although she owned several nice sets of lacy panties and bras, she didn't have any sexy sleepwear. Considering the fact that her sex life had been pretty much non-existent for a number of years, she hadn't needed anything other than cotton sleep shirts for summer and wintertime flannel pajamas.

After she stepped out of the shower and wrapped a towel around her wet hair, she ran a second towel over her arms and legs.

Suddenly Maleah heard a noise outside in her bedroom. "Derek?"

No response.

"Derek, is that you?"

Silence.

Odd, she could have sworn she heard something that sounded like a door opening and closing.

"Cully says that Michelle has been staying in her room a lot since her stomach virus, which we now know she faked," Griff told them. "Them" being Sanders, BJ, and Derek. "But she's not in her room now and when he checked, Cully found her window wide open."

"She's going to kill someone else tonight," BJ said. "But who? Her target could be any one of the other students or one of the agents or a guard or . . . or even one of us."

Sanders clamped his broad hand down on BJ's shoulder. She glanced up at him and they exchanged looks of care and concern.

"I've filled Cully in on the situation," Griff said. "Sanders, please contact the guards and tell them to be on the lookout for Michelle. Derek, you speak to Brendan and I'll let Shaughnessy know what's happened when I go upstairs to check on Nic. I'll alert Nic. You—" he looked at Derek "—let Maleah know what's going on and ask her to join us. I want an all-out manhunt underway immediately. We have to find Michelle before she kills again."

Maleah yanked her knee-length cotton robe off the hanger on the back of the bathroom door, slipped into it, and took a tentative step over the threshold, one foot in the bedroom and one still in the bathroom.

"Derek?"

Maleah heard only an eerie silence in the semidark bedroom.

She didn't like this one little bit. Her stomach churned with uneasiness. A sense of foreboding spread through her as she took another step into the bedroom. Something was wrong. She felt it in her bones.

Damn it, she had put her holstered pistol inside the nightstand drawer.

"Derek, if you're trying to surprise me, please don't.

I'm warning you that if you grab me, I'm going to clob-
ber you. I'm pretty sure I can adequately kick your
butt."

With her breath caught in her throat, Maleah took
another step before halting and scanning the room.
Her gaze paused on the sitting room, where she noticed
a slender silhouette near the windows.

"Who's there?" Maleah asked.

Not Derek.

The silhouette moved out of the shadows and revealed herself.

"Michelle? What's wrong? Has something happened?"

For a few seconds, Maleah felt a huge sense of relief,
thinking perhaps Griff had sent Michelle. But when
Michelle didn't respond, only stood there staring at Maleah, her eyes wide and glazed as if she were in a trance,
Maleah knew something wasn't right.

"What are you doing in my room? Did Griff send
you?"

As Michelle walked toward Maleah, she brought the
hand she held behind her back to her side. She lifted
the gun she was tightly clutching. And then she pointed
the 9mm at Maleah.

"I'm sorry, Maleah," Michelle said. "I'm so very sorry,
but I have no other choice. I have to kill you."

Derek explained the situation to Brendan Richter
and then headed upstairs only minutes behind Griff.
He hated having to tell Maleah that Michelle Allen was
the one who had killed Shiloh, that she had been
forced to kill in order to save her seven-year-old niece's
life. Apparently Anthony Linden had kidnapped Jaelyn
Allen and held her hostage in order to force Michelle
into killing for his employer. Derek didn't know all the

particulars of course, but he couldn't understand why Michelle hadn't come to Griff and Nic and explained what had happened. He felt certain that Griff could have figured out a way to help her convince Linden that she was following his instructions without her actually having had to kill anyone. But it was impossible to truly put himself in Michelle's shoes. No two people reacted the same way to similar events. He and Michelle were two very different people who had come from vastly different backgrounds and had different life experiences. Not that he thought a man would have handled the situation differently or better than a woman or that a privileged background made him superior in any way. All he meant was that he knew he shouldn't judge another person's reasoning simply because they chose a different solution than he would have chosen.

As Derek approached Maleah's bedroom, he stopped and thought about what he was going to say to her. Maleah and Michelle weren't close friends, but they were friends nevertheless. Michelle had been Maleah's martial arts instructor and had been the one who had encouraged Maleah to work toward perfecting her skills.

He knew his Blondie. She presented a hard-as-nails façade to the world, but inside, she had a marshmallow center. She would take the news about Michelle hard.

If only they could find Michelle quickly—before she killed again.

Maleah stared at Michelle—her friend Michelle—who held a gun on her and obviously intended to kill her.

"Why?" Maleah asked. "I don't understand."

"He has my niece, Jaelyn."

"Who has your niece?" Maleah took a hesitant step

toward Michelle. If she could get close enough, she had a reasonable chance of overpowering her.

"Stop right there. Don't come any closer."

Maleah stopped. "Michelle, we can work this out. Whatever you need—"

"I need for you to shut up." Tears glistened in Michelle's eyes.

Keep her talking. Find a way to move in closer.

"I knew I would have to shoot you," Michelle said. "I knew I wouldn't be able to overpower and subdue you the way I did Shiloh."

"Please, talk to me. Let me help you. I know you don't want to do this."

"Can't you see that I don't have any other choice? If I don't kill you, he will kill Jaelyn."

As Derek reached for the doorknob, he heard voices inside Maleah's room. Two female voices. Maleah and—?

He pressed his ear to the door and listened.

"I'll make it quick and painless, I promise," Michelle Allen said.

Derek's heart stopped.

Michelle was in Maleah's room.

His first instinct was to draw his gun and burst into the room. He had been wearing his holster at Griffin's Rest since Shiloh's murder last night. But if he burst into the room, he might spook Michelle and she might fire her weapon instantly. On the other hand, if he didn't act immediately, she would shoot Maleah anyway.

He reached under his jacket, flipped open the holster, and removed his 45 Colt XSE. Praying with every breath he took, Derek turned the handle and eased open the door, inch by inch. He stepped inside the bedroom, gun in hand, and as soon as he saw both women, he aimed his weapon directly at Michelle.

"Drop your gun," he told Michelle in a deceptively calm voice. He was anything but calm.

In that split second when Derek's command distracted Michelle, Maleah made her move. Before either Derek or Michelle realized what was happening, Maleah sent her arms and legs into deadly motion, ironically enough, using the skilled maneuvers Michelle had taught her. The student against the teacher. Maleah's foot struck Michelle's hand and sent the gun she held flying. Realizing her weapon of choice was no longer an option, Michelle instinctively retaliated.

With his pistol aimed and ready to fire, Derek held back and watched while Maleah and Michelle engaged in hand-to-hand combat. This was Maleah's fight. She wouldn't appreciate him interfering unless it was to save her life.

Back and forth, Michelle attacked and Maleah counterattacked. Both women were skilled warriors, pretty much evenly matched, every move each made a combination of reflex and training. Repeated force-against-force blocks took a toll on both of them. With each kick, each painful blow, each woman weakened, but neither gave an inch. Maleah punched harder and faster, using the front two knuckles of her fist to strike at her opponent, and then successfully blocking each blow Michelle aimed at her.

By the time Maleah pinned Michelle to the floor, both women were bloody and breathless. Sweat glistened on their skin.

"Oh, God, please," Michelle whimpered. "Jaelyn . . ."

Griff, Nic, and Shaughnessy rushed into the room and halted abruptly behind Derek. They looked past him to where Maleah straddled a defeated Michelle.

Derek holstered his weapon and with the others at his back, he rushed over to Maleah, yanked down her robe that had hiked up to the edge of her buttocks, and then pulled her off Michelle and into his arms. Breathing heavily, she put one arm around him as she looked down at her opponent.

Griff and Shaughnessy lifted a bruised and battered Michelle to her feet. Shaughnessy quickly yanked her arms behind her, shoved her in front of him and held her securely.

"She kept saying that Linden had her niece and he would kill her if she didn't do what he told her to do," Maleah explained. "She admitted that she killed Shiloh."

"Luke called. He found Linden," Griff said. "Apparently Linden had been ordered to abduct Jaelyn Allen and hold her captive as a way to control Michelle and force her to kill for him."

"Jaelyn?" Michelle asked pleadingly. "Is she all right?"

"Your niece is fine," Griff told her. "Luke and Meredith are bringing her back to the U.S. as soon as possible. They'll take her home to your brother and his wife."

Moments after hearing the good news about Jaelyn, Michelle fell apart emotionally, weeping, shaking her head, and muttering incoherently. Shaughnessy gently led her from the room.

Nic grabbed Maleah out of Derek's arms and hugged her. Then she stepped back and wiped the tears from her cheeks. "Thank God you're all right."

Griff put his arm around Nic's shoulders.

Maleah looked at Derek. He reached out and swiped away the smear of blood from her mouth. "Blondie, don't you ever scare me like that again. When I saw Michelle holding a gun on you . . . Maleah Perdue, if anything had happened to you . . ."

She offered him a fragile smile. "You're my hero, you know."

"Who, me?" He pointed to his chest.

"Yes, you. If you hadn't startled Michelle, I might not have gotten the opportunity to catch her off guard the way I did." She lifted her arms and wrapped them around his neck. "And you're my hero because once you saw I could handle the situation without your help, you let me fight my own battle."

Chapter 36

Derek had held her in his arms all night Friday night and finally sometime over in the morning, she had fallen asleep.

Maleah awoke to a new day, yet she was haunted by yesterday's events. Physically, she ached like hell from the beating Michelle had given her. Emotionally, she was a wreck. Her thoughts and feelings were all over the place. She was shocked and angry and sad about Michelle's betrayal and equally sympathetic about the intolerable choice Michelle had been forced to make. Maleah wanted to believe that if she had been put in such a horrific position, she would have chosen a better solution. Poor Michelle, her life was all but destroyed.

What was going to happen now that Anthony Linden was dead? Would it be only a matter of time before the pseudo-York sent another gun-for-hire to terrorize Griff?

Most of Saturday passed in a blur. Sanders chauffeured them—Nic and Griff, Shaughnessy, Derek and Maleah—to the sheriff's department to give their statements concerning the attempt on Maleah's life. A distraught Michelle had confessed that she had killed Shiloh Whitman and had been ordered to kill Maleah. Griff had contacted Camden Hendrix, an old friend and head of a law firm the Powell Agency kept on retainer. Despite what Michelle had done, Griff had instructed Cam to provide her with the best legal representation possible. Griffin Powell believed that, no matter what, you took care of your own.

After their trip to the sheriff's office, Maleah and Derek spent most of the day with Nic and Griff and Griff didn't mention anything about Nic being pregnant. When Maleah and Nic were finally alone for a few minutes, Maleah asked Nic why she hadn't told her husband about their baby.

"I'm going to tell him. But not yet. Not for a few more days. Not until we all have a chance to come to terms with what Michelle did and sort of get our bearings."

And so that was what they did the rest of the day Saturday—tried to get their bearings in a sea of mixed emotions.

Saturday night Derek made love to her so slowly and tenderly that she cried. And being the man that he was, he understood that those tears of joy also released a myriad of pent-up emotions. A lifetime of emotions.

Odd that in the midst of all the chaos and upheaval in their lives, she could, on a very personal level, be so happy. Happier than she had ever been in her entire life. She loved Derek Lawrence and he loved her.

That morning, after they made love again, Derek propped up on his elbow, looked down at her, and said, "I think you're going to have to marry me."

Smiling like a lovesick fool, she stared up at him and asked, "Why would you think that?"

He grinned. "Maybe it's because I love you and you love me and I can't imagine spending the rest of my life without you." He swooped down and kissed her. Then he lifted his head and laughed. "I know it sounds corny, but I want your face to be the first thing I see every morning and the last thing I see every night."

When she socked him in the chest, he fell over on his back and laid his hand over his heart.

"You're right. That did sound corny." She leaned down and nuzzled his nose with hers. "But since I happen to feel the same way, I think you're right. You are going to have to marry me."

Griffin Powell stared at the letter in his hand, the letter that had arrived special delivery this morning via an international courier. The return address was a hotel in London, Berkeley Knightsbridge, where Luke and Meredith had stayed.

If that was someone's idea of a joke, that person had a truly warped sense of humor.

Griff had read and reread the letter before he called Yvette.

Once she arrived, Sanders joined them in Griff's private study. Sanders closed and locked the door before Griff gave the letter to Yvette.

After she read the letter, she stared at Griff, a combination of doubt and hope in her eyes. "Could this possibly be true?"

"I don't know."

Yvette handed the letter to Sanders.

He read it quickly.

With concern in his black eyes, he looked from

Yvette to Griff and said, "You cannot believe what this letter says, not without proof."

"I'm well aware of that," Griff replied.

"I want to go to England, to Benenden and see her for myself," Yvette told them. "If there is the slightest chance that she really is . . ." Yvette closed her eyes.

Griff could not bear to see her in such pain. "I don't want you to get your hopes up. This letter proves nothing except that someone wants to hurt us, someone who knows about what happened on Amara."

"Whoever sent the letter signed it Malcolm York and that signature looks authentic," Sanders pointed out to them. "But we know that it is not possible for him to be the real York. This man, whoever he is, is a fraud. And this girl mentioned in the letter, even if such a girl exists, may well be a fraud, also."

"But what if she does exist? What if she's not a fraud?" Yvette opened her tear-misted eyes and looked pleadingly at Griff. "If I can see her . . . touch her . . . I would know. Even without a DNA test."

"It would take a DNA test to convince me," Sanders said. "This man who calls himself Malcolm York has simply found a new means of tormenting us. Apparently killing Powell employees and members of their families was not enough for him."

Griff nodded agreement. "You're right, Sanders, but this letter is not something we can ignore." He walked over, caressed Yvette's damp cheek and said, "I'll make arrangements for us to take the Powell jet to London tomorrow. But before I finalize my plans, I have to show Nic the letter and I have to tell her everything."

"Do you think that is wise?" Sanders asked.

"No, Griffin is right," Yvette said. "He has to tell his wife. She has every right to know." Yvette glanced at Sanders. "Perhaps you should tell Barbara Jean."

"No," Sanders replied. "Not now. Not until we know for sure."

Nic kept rehearsing how she would tell Griff that he was going to be a father. Should she say, "We're pregnant?" Or maybe she should hold his hand over her still flat belly and ask, "Which would you prefer, a son or a daughter?" Then again, she could just put her arms around him, look up into his gorgeous gray eyes and say, "We're going to have a baby."

In the end, it probably didn't matter how she said it. Griff would be thrilled. No, the timing wasn't perfect and Griff, who worried about her way too much as it was, would hover over her night and day. And she had every intention of letting him smother her with attention. After all, why not give him the pleasure of pampering her for the next seven months?

When she arrived outside Griff's study, she found the door open and Griff waiting there alone.

She could tell him about their baby this morning. She could walk right into his study and deliver the good news that he was going to be a father.

But when he looked at her, the expression on his face stopped her cold. Something was wrong. Horribly wrong. What had happened now?

She rushed over to him. "Griff, what is it? What's—?"

He grasped her shoulders. "I love you. If you never believe anything else, believe that."

"You're frightening me. Please, tell me what's wrong."

"First, tell me that you know I love you more than anyone or anything on this earth."

"Yes, I know you love me. And I love you."

He released his tenacious grip on her shoulders. "I

received a special delivery letter from London a little over two hours ago. The signature on the letter was a decent forgery of Malcolm York's signature."

"Then it was a letter from *him*, this man you refer to as the pseudo-York."

"I want you to read the letter." Griff reached behind him and lifted the envelope from the desk. "After you read it, I want you to sit down and let me tell you about what happened on Amara. It's something I should have already told you."

Nic felt sick at her stomach. It could be nothing more than morning sickness, but she suspected it was nerves. Fear-induced nerves.

Griff removed the letter from the envelope and handed the single page to Nic. She took the letter in her unsteady hand. When she first glanced at it, her vision blurred for a few seconds and then instantly cleared.

Dear Griffin,

I hope this letter finds you and your wife well. Give Mrs. Powell my sincerest regards. And please give my regards to our beautiful, delectable Yvette. I think of her so often, of the two of you and dear Sanders, too. Ah, what wonderful times we shared on Amara. How I wish we could all be together again, as we were then.

I have been fortunate not to have spent all these years alone, to have been able to keep a part of Yvette with me. She is almost seventeen now. I gave her a little red Porsche for her sixteenth birthday. She calls me Papa and adores me as I adore her.

I believe I've been selfish far too long by keeping her all to myself. Being a generous man, I have decided to share her with her mother. If Yvette would like to meet her daughter, tell her that she can find Suzette at the Benen-

*den School in Kent. As you can imagine, I've spared no
expense on her education. You will find her to be as
beautiful and brilliant as her mother and as strong of
heart as her father.*

*Sincerely,
Malcolm York*

The letter slipped from Nic's hand and sailed slowly
onto the floor. She lifted her gaze and stared at Griff.

"Yvette has a daughter?"

"She gave birth to the child nearly seventeen years
ago when we were on Amara."

"I don't understand. Where has the girl been all
these years? And how would this pseudo-York know
about her? If what he says is true, this girl thinks of him
as her father. But if the real Malcolm York was her father—?"

"York wasn't her father."

"But Yvette was York's wife."

"In name only."

"What are you saying?" When Griff didn't immediately respond, she demanded, "Exactly what are you trying to tell me?"

"Come over here and sit down." When Griff reached
for her, she jerked away from him.

"I don't want to sit down," she told him. "I want you
to explain. Tell me what happened on Amara. Tell me
about this girl, about Suzette."

"You have to understand what it was like for us, for
me and Sanders and for Yvette, who was as much a prisoner as we were. She was forced to do things she didn't
want to do, just as Sanders was. Just as I was."

"I know that he used you and the other men he captured as prey in his savage hunts, that you were treated
like an animal, that you were forced to kill in order to

stay alive. I know that eventually, you and Sanders and Yvette killed York and . . . But there's more to what happened on Amara, isn't there, a lot more?"

"Yes." Griff watched her closely, a look of agony and supplication in his eyes. "And I will tell you everything. I swear I will. But for now, I have to explain about Yvette's child."

Nic instinctively knew she did not want to hear what her husband was about to tell her. But she had to know the truth. She needed to know.

"Tell me."

"York was involved in numerous illegal activities. That's how he made his billions," Griff said. "His two most lucrative business ventures were drug trafficking and human trafficking."

"Human trafficking?"

"All the captives on Amara were not there just to be used as prey to hunt and kill. Some were there to amuse York and his closest allies . . . his business associates."

"You're talking about selling human beings into slavery. Children and women and—"

"York was a sick son of a bitch. He didn't get any pleasure from sex with his wife or any other woman. He preferred to watch rather than perform."

Bile rose from Nic's stomach, the taste bitter in her mouth.

"Are you all right?" Griff asked.

She swallowed. "Go on. Tell me the rest of it."

"York found Yvette the perfect tool to give him unlimited pleasure. He forced her to use her gifts as an empath to connect with the men's minds, the men he hunted and killed. Everything he could learn about how they thought, how they felt, how they might react in any given situation, gave him an edge over even the most resourceful prey."

Nic felt dizzy. *Don't faint, damn it, don't faint.*

"Are you sure you're all right? You look so pale."
Once again when Griff tried to touch Nic, she avoided
him.

"Please, don't touch me." She couldn't bring herself
to look directly at him. "Don't stop until you've told me
how all of this connects to Yvette's child."

Griff took in and released a deep breath. "York
forced Yvette to have sex with any of his business associates who wanted her. He used her to find out their secrets. When he realized that by her having sex with a
man, Yvette was able to connect with his thoughts and
feelings more intensely than simply by touching them,
he began bringing whatever man he intended to hunt
the next day into his home and forcing him to have sex
with Yvette . . . while he watched them."

Nic swayed. She backed up and braced her hips
against Griff's desk.

"When Yvette became pregnant, York threatened to
abort the child, but being the evil son of a bitch that he
was, he decided to allow her to have the baby. And then
when the infant was only a few hours old, he took it
away from Yvette."

Nic couldn't imagine the agony Yvette must have experienced. "And all these years, what did she think happened to her child?"

"She didn't know," Griff said. "After we left Amara
and managed to claim some of York's fortune for
Yvette, we started searching for the child. We've been
looking for nearly sixteen years."

"What about the child's father?"

"Yvette doesn't know who fathered her child. It
could have been one of several men she was forced to
have sex with during the specific time in which she became pregnant."

And then Nic asked the only question that really mattered to her. "Were you one of those men?"

"Yes."

That single word upended Nicole's entire world, everything she believed in, every emotion, every thought, sending her into a tailspin of confusion and rage.

"Damn you, Griffin Powell. You swore to me that you and Yvette were never lovers!"

"We weren't lovers. Not ever." He grabbed Nic's shoulders and shook her gently. "What Yvette and I did was not making love. God, Nic, it wasn't even having sex, not really. We were forced to perform in front of York."

Nic jerked away from Griff, rushed behind his desk, doubled over and threw up in his wastebasket.

When Griff reached her, she stood up straight and backed away from him. "Please, don't touch me. Not now. I—I can't think straight. You have to give me time to think, time to sort through what I'm feeling . . . about you and me and about Yvette. And . . . and about her child." She looked Griff square in the eye. "She . . . Suzette could be your daughter."

"Yes."

Nic walked across the study, opened the door and without turning back to look at Griff, said, "I'm going upstairs to pack a suitcase and then I'm going to Gatlinburg to our . . . to my cabin." Knowing how she loved the mountains, Griff had given her the cabin as a Christmas present.

Stay strong. You can do this without crying, without screaming, without hysterics, without falling apart.

"I don't want you to follow me or contact me in any way," she told him. "When I've had time to think about everything, I'll come home. I'll come back to Griffin's Rest and—"

"You can't go off by yourself," Griff told her, his voice pleading. "It's too dangerous for you to be alone. If you have to do this, then I'll send Shaughnessy or one of the other agents with you."

"I want to be alone, Griff. I have to be alone. Try to understand."

I need to think. And cry and scream and rant and rave and go slowly out of my mind.

"How about a compromise?" he asked. "Ask Maleah to go with you."

"I won't do that. She and Derek . . ." Nic swallowed her tears. "No, not Maleah. Not now. If you insist on my not going alone, then send someone to follow me on the drive to Gatlinburg. And you can post guards at the cabin twenty-four / seven. But I want to drive there by myself and I do not want a bodyguard in the house with me."

"I don't want you to leave, Nic. Stay here. I'll give you all the time and space you need. Just don't leave me."

"You don't understand. I can't bear to look at you right now." She walked out of the study, her head held high, her shoulders straight, and her heart breaking into a million pieces.

Maleah didn't know all the details, only that Nic had left Griffin's Rest after Griff told her that Yvette had a child, a nearly seventeen-year-old daughter that she hadn't seen since the day of her birth.

"Griff may be the girl's father," Nic had explained. "I can't stay here at Griffin's Rest. I need to get away. I don't want to look at Griff and see the pain in his eyes every time he looks at me."

"I'll go with you," Maleah had told Nic.

"No, no. You and Derek, you two need to be together now. I want you to enjoy being in love. Those first few days and weeks are so incredible. I don't want you to miss them."

When Nic made up her mind, there was no arguing with her.

Maleah stood in the open doorway and watched Nic drive away from Griffin's Rest. When her Escalade was barely out of sight, Griff motioned to the man behind the wheel of the black Hummer. He pulled out and followed Nic.

At that precise moment, Maleah knew what she had to do. She turned to Derek, who stood beside her, his arm draped around her waist, and said, "She shouldn't be alone. Will you understand if I—?"

Derek clasped her hand. "Come on, Blondie, I'll help you pack a bag. But not until after I give you a proper send-off."

"I'm going to miss you terribly."

"Call me every hour on the hour," he teased.

"I'll call you every morning and every night and think about you every hour in between. How's that?"

He pulled her into his arms as they reached the top of the stairs. "When this crisis with Nic and Griff is over, you and I, Ms. Perdue, have a future to plan. A future that includes a wedding and a honeymoon."

"Yes, we do." Maleah stood on tiptoe and kissed him.

Loving and being loved gave her the strength to believe in the possibility of a happily-ever-after.

Epilogue

From time to time, Nic caught a glimpse, in her rear-view mirror, of the black Hummer that had followed her from Griffin's Rest. When she stopped at a gas station just outside Pigeon Forge, Cully Redmond pulled into the parking area and waited for her.

Now, for the past few miles on her drive up the mountain to the beautiful, secluded cabin Griff had given her as a Christmas gift, she hadn't seen Cully's Hummer. Apparently, he had dropped back out of sight to allow her time to arrive at the cabin and get settled in before he parked outside to keep watch over her. No doubt, Griff would send another agent to relieve him in the morning and the two would change shifts every eight hours.

She parked the Escalade in the circular drive, got out, grabbed her suitcase from the back, and walked up to the front door. She drew in a deep breath of crisp, fresh mountain air. She unlocked the door and walked into the foyer. The cabin was so quiet, so peaceful, unlike the daily chaotic noise that had plagued Griffin's Rest recently.

After shoving her suitcase into the master bedroom closet, Nic walked through the living room and opened the door leading out onto the back deck. She went over to the edge of the wooden deck, clasped the top of the carved guardrail, and looked out at the breathtaking view below, the lush green hills and valleys.

Griff lied to me about his relationship with Yvette. He did have sex with her.

But they were never lovers. Griff said that what happened between them wasn't really even sex.

Maybe it wasn't, but I know one thing for sure—Griff loves Yvette.

He loves her because of the hell they shared, because of the torture they endured together.

He loves her because he may be the father of her child.

Nic laid her hand protectively over her belly.

She heard the sound of a car door slamming. Cully Redmond must have arrived. He probably needed to stretch his legs.

With her hand still resting over the tiny life just beginning to grow inside her, Nic jerked around when she heard a noise. Sound echoed in the empty stillness of her mountain retreat, so she wasn't surprised that she could hear footsteps on the front porch.

Damn it, she had told Griff specifically that she wanted to be left alone.

Don't bite Cully's head off. Just tell him you're fine and for him to report to Griff that you arrived here safely.

Nic went back into the cabin and made it halfway across the living room when the front door opened. Great! Cully would be sure to tell Griff that she'd left the door unlocked. How could she have been so careless?

With "get out and leave me alone" on the tip of her tongue, Nic stopped dead still when a man she didn't know walked into her cabin. This was definitely not Cully Redmond. And he wasn't another Powell agent.

"Who are you? What do you want?"

When he simply stared at her, Nic stood her ground. *Show no fear.*

"I'm expecting someone any minute now," she told him. "I didn't travel alone."

"If you're expecting the man driving the black Hummer, then you're going to be disappointed. I'm afraid he's been delayed. Permanently delayed."

Fear clutched Nic's gut. Had this man killed Cully?

"I don't know what you want, Mr.—?"

"Where are my manners," the man said, a bone-chilling smile curving his lips. "Let me introduce myself, Mrs. Powell. I'm Anthony Linden."

"That's not possible. Anthony Linden is dead."

"Yes, I know. And so is Malcolm York. And yet here I am, in the flesh, come to take you to see another dead man. Mr. York is eager to meet you."

Dear Reader,

Dead by Morning was the second book in my *Dead by* trilogy and leads directly into the third and final novel, *Dead by Nightfall*, set for a December 2011 release. The cliffhanger ending I presented in the epilogue of *Dead by Morning* prepares you for what is to come in the next book, which begins where this book leaves off—with Nicole Baxter Powell in grave danger. When Griffin Powell discovers that his wife is missing and soon thereafter learns that she is in the hands of a "ghost" from his past, he moves heaven and earth to rescue her. Griff, Sanders and Yvette, the Amara triad, who suffered unbearable torture during their years as Malcolm York's captives, must come to terms with their past lives. Secrets long buried in the depths of their tortured souls resurface and are revealed in the cold, hard light of their present realities. You will learn more about the elusive and deadly Raphael Byrne, another of York's victims.

For those of you who love the Powell Agency books, you will be pleased to know that I hope to write more novels featuring Powell agents and others associated with the agency. If while reading *Dead by Morning* you found Luke Sentell and Rafe Byrne interesting alpha males, then you will probably agree that both of these hard-edged, dangerous men deserve books of their own.

After I complete *Dead by Nightfall*, I'll be writing the sequel to my September 2010 novel *Don't Cry*, bringing back TBI agent J.D. Cass and mental health therapist Audrey Sherrod. You'll be seeing more of several secondary characters, including J.D.'s daughter Zoe, Audrey's best friend Tamara and Tamara's parents, as well as J.D.'s sister Julia. Many of you contacted me asking if Tamara and Marcus will reunite and if J.D. and Audrey will get married, and wondering if J.D. and Zoe will finally bond as father and daughter. I'll give you all the answers in *Don't Say a Word*, set for release in 2012.

I always love hearing from readers. You may contact me through my Web site at www.beverlybarton.com or by writing to me in care of Kensington Publishing. While visiting my Web site, you can enter contests, sign up for my e-mail newsletter, and check out a list of all my books. You can also find information about my upcoming book signings, speaking engagements, and conferences. And be sure to take a look at the videos about me and my books. Also, go to Facebook and sign up as a friend on my Beverly Barton Official Fan page: http://www.facebook.com/beverlybartonfanpage.

Warmest regards,
Beverly Barton